Skin Deep

Submission

KYLE POWELL

authorHOUSE®

AuthorHouse™ UK
1663 Liberty Drive
Bloomington, IN 47403 USA
www.authorhouse.co.uk
Phone: UK TFN: 0800 0148641 (Toll Free inside the UK)
*   UK Local: (02) 0369 56322 (+44 20 3695 6322 from outside the UK)*

Published by AuthorHouse 06/03/2022

ISBN: 978-1-6655-9900-9 (sc)
ISBN: 978-1-6655-9899-6 (e)

Print information available on the last page.

Contents

Part 2

Part 3

About the Author

Kyle Powell is a born and raised Londoner, whose passion for writing began at a young age. Kyle enjoys writing about philosophy, love, justice and life from both non-fiction and fiction angles. Kyle is keen to write about issues that impact the Black community, particularly from the perspective of the Diaspora.

Kyle has spent time working as a mentor with secondary school students, before becoming project leader. During his time as a mentor, he worked to help increase leadership qualities, lateral thinking for students from disadvantaged backgrounds. He also has worked in and led Diversity and Inclusion (D&I) teams at two large pharmaceutical companies. Kyle's work in the healthcare D&I space included addressing clinical trial underrepresentation, increasing psychological safety and improving knowledge and understanding around racial disparities and experiences.

Kyle has a BSc and MSc in Neuroscience from the University of Bristol and Kings College London. Following his academic years developing his scientific and critical-thinking skill sets Kyle reconnects with his love of writing as part of his career in the healthcare industry as a communications consultant and subsequently a Commercial Director.

Kyle is a life-long Arsenal fan, loves to listen to music, play football and travel, whenever he is not writing.

Acknowledgements

This book has been a long time in the making and I'm really happy to finally have it done! I would like to thank my friends and family for their continued support during my writing process, particularly all those we gave their time to read drafts and share feedback, I am extremely grateful. Your unwavering cheerleading and encouragement have been critical to me reaching this point, this book is for you all as much as it is for me. Without naming names, I would be remiss in not mentioning the muses that helped inspire this piece of work – The romantic history on which so much of this story is based upon.

Preface: Choices of The Heart

It is thought that free will is the ultimate gift provided to humans by the gods. Through that free will we have the opportunity to make many different choices about how we live our lives, but an area of life where we have less choice is in matters of the heart; can we choose the ones we fall in love with and if we can, should we? Love is perhaps one of the most ephemeral, intangible and all-encompassing concepts known to man, it has the power to bring us extreme pleasure and deep pain. For many people falling in love is the *Holy Grail* of life achievement, it permeates almost every aspect of our culture, from the stories we tell, to the music we listen to. Interestingly, when we talk about love we often describe 'falling' in love, suggesting a lack of control ... perhaps a lack of choice. The heart and mind are often in conflict, what is best for us, versus what we desire. Of course, this interplay can become even more complicated, particularly when we consider that outside influences may interfere with what we believe to be our truest desires.

As our world becomes increasingly more connected,

as it becomes easier and easier to interact with people from different places, countries and cultures, we will see love flourish in ways we have not before. This beautiful opportunity can come at a price, a cautionary counterweight based on deep-rooted historical legacy and present-day reality. For those that embark on these romantic adventures, there may be challenges that prior to recent times were not properly considered.

This is a story about the conflict between heart and mind, the duress caused by cultural and societal pressures, and the perceived purity of the heart's desires. This is a tale about two people who choose to follow their hearts ... a choice that is not always easy.

Prologue

CRASH! Went the back door of 41 Fullop Street, as it flew off its hinges. A team of six Special Ops officers entered in formation, weapons drawn close to their chest against their dark blue tactical fatigues. The kitchen was empty, they slowly made their way into the living room, guns still raised, they did not expect to see what awaited them next; an elderly woman tightly hugging her two young grandchildren on the sofa. They trembled in fear facing the officers, while a TV game show played in the background.

The officers kept their guns raised and trained on the old woman and her young ones. "Is the house empty?" The Commanding Officer (CO) yelled... there was no response, the old lady was too scared to talk, one of the children started to cry, quickly followed by the other. "Is this house empty?!" he shouted again, index finger gently moving into position over the trigger. The Grandmother nodded slowly in answer.

"Where are they?!" he followed up, again no answer, fear gripping those on the tired looking sofa. The officer finally acknowledged the state of shock and intimidation in the woman's face, he removed his finger from the trigger, "Where are Richie Morgan and Patrick Reynolds? We know they were residing at this address," He stated clearly. She slowly shook her head in an attempt to say she didn't know, but in a way that could have been read as denial of the accusation. The *slow* progress of the interrogation caused one of the other officers to lose his patience; he pushed past his Commander towards the old woman, yanking her from her young wards and the sofa, proceeding to throw her face down on the dusty carpet. The officer straddled her, placing his full weight on her elderly back, while pushing the barrel of the gun against the base of her skull, "We are not fucking around! Tell us where they are now! Or I swear you'll never see those dirty little kids again!"

The brutal force of the take down and threats sparked a reaction in the pensioner; suddenly her body began to convulse, she was having some sort of fit. The violent shaking caused the officers finger to slip, firing the gun... fewp! Went the 6mm bullet through the silenced barrel on his assault rifle - the last image she had was her grandchildren sobbing on the sofa.

"What the fuck did you do?" the CO asked, pushing his colleague off the woman, "She's fucking dead! What the fuck are we going to do now?!" The perpetrating officer was in a state of shock, he only wanted to scare the woman into giving up the assailants.

"I tell you what, I'm not going down for this, no fucking way!"

He tried to collect his thoughts and think of a solution, "It'll be ok....it'll be fine...we'll just say as we entered we thought she was drawing for a weapon and I fired in response, pre-emptive defence," he claimed, nodding his head convincingly.

"You think people are going to believe that a woman who could barely get down the bingo was ready to draw a gun on Special Ops Officers the CO returned with incredulity.

"Why not? These lot are all fucking animals anyway. She was harbouring huge drug dealers, that's a threat to national security; they could easily have weapons in the house," he defended, looking at the other officers for support.

"Well you're doing the paperwork, that's for fucking sure!" the CO finished.

Meanwhile on the North West side of the estate, a young Jason rushed into the living room, hoping desperately that he hadn't missed the start of the show. He and his friend Lyon were laying on the rug, barely a foot from the TV, eagerly awaiting the start of *Gladiators*. The popular 90s game show that pit everyday people against 'Gladiators', across a range of physical challenges; everything from a race up a climbing wall, to a duel atop two high pedestals using foam combat batons. The duo took great enjoyment from the glitz, glamour and competitive element of the show, they also took a lot of joy from being able to *appreciate* the attractive female gladiators.

"I'm going to marry Lightening when I'm older," Lyon stated confidently, smiling at the curvy gladiator with long Blonde hair.

"I don't care, because I'm going to marry Jet," Jason returned, lovestruck by the curvy brunette gladiator.

"No you're not, why would she marry you?" Lyon returned, elbowing his friend.

"Why would she marry you?" Jason fired back, pushing his friend.

"Nobody is marrying anyone if you guys don't slide back from the TV!" Lyon's mum commanded from the sofa.

The pair calmed down and continued to watch the show. Keeping their playful banter at a lower, more acceptable level.

After the show finished they went to Lyon's room to play on his games console. This was one of Jason's favourite things about being at Lyon's house; not yet allowed to have one of his own, being at Lyon's was the only chance he had to play *Street Fighter*. Jason was a natural with computers; Lyon never understood how he could beat him so easily at a game he didn't even own. The console was not the only thing that he liked about his room, Jason also liked his posters; Lyon's room was filled with brightly photoshopped images of women in bikinis, many from various Baywatch stars like Pamela Anderson. The few times he did lose to Lyon were usually because he was distracted by the scantily clad vixens. Jason selected his favourite character, Ken; the blonde haired

Karate master rocked backed forth in his fighting stance, as he waited for Lyon to pick his fighter. Lyon went for Chung Li, the avatar did an expert spin in response to being chosen, ending with her showing the peace sign. The fight was a fairly close one, compared to normal at least, it typically took Jason a little while to warm up.

Lyon bashed buttons on his controller, while Jason tried to carefully string together combos and special moves. However, Lyon had a trick up his sleeve, "Jase?" he asked innocently.

"Uh huh?" Jason replied, trying to focus on his attacks.

"Who is your favourite Spice Girl?" he said, as he tried desperately to keep Jason at bay, hoping the question would distract him somewhat.

Jason hadn't thought too much about it. His mind began to go through the members "Hmm... maybe Posh Spice," he said with uncertainty, as if this was an exam question and he was unsure whether he'd given the correct answer. "Who's yours?" he fired back, only just winning the first round of the fight.

"Baby," he answered quickly definitely having thought long and hard about this before. "Thought you might like Scary," he said tongue out.

Jason thought about it, "No... she's scary." Not sure if that actually worked as a joke, but happy that it garnered a small laugh from Lyon.

They were barley into their third game when Lyon's

mum shouted from downstairs that Jason's mum wanted him home urgently. Equally deflated that their time had been cut short, although Lyon found consolation in the fact that he didn't have to lose any more games... today at least. Jason got up and headed for the door, "Jase, wait up, I've got a treat for you," he said excitedly, as he rummaged around in one of his draws, before handing Jason a folded sheet of paper. "You'll like this one," Lyon said with a big smile. Jason pocketed the paper and headed home.

It was a short walk back to his place, but he knew when he was called back he better get home quickly, or risk a telling off from his mum and potentially worse from his dad. He slowly turned the key and opened the door, his parents and aunt were gathered in the kitchen.

"Is that you Jason?" his mum called out

"Yes, mum."

"You cyan come and say hello?" she asked rhetorically, flipping into her Jamaican accent.

Jason went into the room to greet his parents and aunty in the kitchen. They were talking loudly, engaged in a heated discussion about what had taken placed earlier that day. News travelled at light speed across the estate, before long everyone was talking about it, but the tragic events were particularly distressing for Jason's family; it had come to light that the police were looking for his Uncle Richie, in connection to drug charges. The drug charges were a fabrication; Uncle Riche belonged to a Pan-African movement, the 'Brit

Panthers', a spin-off of the US Black Panthers that aimed at helping the Black community through education and social activities. Since the group's rise in the past 18 months across different parts of the city and beyond, they had been targeted regularly by the police on bogus charges and claims. Police intel suggested that Richie and one of his associates, miss Johnson's son, were staying at the house. Being a tight knit family, Jason's mum, Richie's sister-in law was worried that her home would be high on the search hitlist.

Her sister, Richie's wife and Jason's aunty came over with her daughter Akira, after hearing the devastating news. Akira was Jason's favourite cousin so he was happy to see her, despite being aware that the grown-ups were stressed about something.

The conversation among the adults was getting louder and louder, not just because of the topic at hand, but also because of the loud music that was playing in the background.

"The fucking Boi-dem, you cyan truss dem ya kno! Any time we try and do something positive they hav fi tek weh," his aunty exclaimed to everyone in the room. All the adults seemed to shake their head in collective agreement.

"She was 83! I can't believe they could be so cold to someone that old."

"Dem Wicked! Pure Evil, me a tell u," his aunty returned.

Jason's dad was quiet, he was locked deep in thought, as he slowly sipped his rum.

"Wicked and Racist!" she continued.

Jason had heard this word, racist, now and again, but had no idea what it was. All he knew was he would only ever hear it when his parents were angry about something; often when they were watching the news.

Jason's mum could sense the tension in the room and was worried about her son and niece being exposed to too much adult language. "What did you guys get up to at Lyon's?" she asked, in an attempt to sway the conversation

"Not much, just watching Gladiators," he replied.

Akira rolled her eyes, thinking Gladiators was a childish show, despite only being a couple of years older than Jason.

"Not on that game for too long were you?" his mum said knowingly,

Jason tipped his head down, aware that he couldn't fool his mum.

"You know we don't want you playing on that thing, and being in his room with all those half-naked women," she said, reflecting on the first time she had witnessed the mosaic of model posters on Lyon's wall, something she did not deem to be appropriate for a 10 year old.

Jason's aunty was only getting louder and more irate, especially as she continued to drink more than her fair share of rum. Jason loved his aunty, especially when she was in a merry mood. Her passion was also being stoked by the music, the DJ playing Bob Marley's 'Crazy Balhead', "Didn't my people before me slave for this country!" she sang loudly, "Fuck dem rahted bal-ed police!" she continued.

"Ok Jase, take Akira up to your room and get ready for bed, brush your teeth and get the sleeping bag out of the wardrobe for her," his mum said, ushering them out of the kitchen and out of earshot of her sister's growing rampage.

Jason knew that some words were naughty, but it always made him feel older when he heard them. When he got to his room he lay on his bed with his cousin and they looked at his ceiling. Sirens were going loudly once again, a sound he was accustomed to by now, but tonight seemed even more intense.

Jason wanted to understand what his family were so upset about, what was going on, he lay in thought, trying to piece together the things he'd heard, *'racist... police... 83 year old.'* His cousin seemed to know most things, so maybe she could explain this. "Why is your mum so angry?" he asked

"The police... I think they want my dad."

"Uncle Richie?!" he replied with shock and horror, "No, Uncle Richie? Why?"

She just shrugged her shoulders, "I don't like them." was all she could muster.

Jason could tell she was sad, he didn't like to see her that way, but didn't know what to do.

At that moment he remembered his gift from Lyon.

"Do you want to see something?" he asked, "Promise not to tell?" he followed.

"Yes," she said, rolling her eyes again impatiently.

He pulled the colourful piece of paper out of his pocket and unfolded it to its full A4 size glory. He held it stretched out in front of him and studied the image of the attractive, brunette, scantily clad woman who was posing on top of a sports car, soapy suds dripping everywhere. His body felt funny, this feeling was happening more and more, each time he would look at these type of photos.

"Yuk, that's disgusting!" she shouted.

"You guys brushed your teeth yet!" his mum called as she climbed the stairs. He dropped the picture in shock, rolling off his bed almost all in one motion. He quickly grabbed the picture and stuck his hand underneath his bed, fishing around for his *special* shoe box. Got it! He exclaimed as he pulled it out. He lifted the lid, folded the latest addition back into 4 and placed it gently on top of the rest of his collection. He quickly returned the box and headed for the bathroom, "Going now, mum."

"Better be or I'm coming back with the belt!" she replied sternly.

At that moment footsteps approached the front door…a few seconds of silence and then… BANG BANG BANG!

Part 1

One

Once Upon A Time In London

Jason slowly lifted the latch on the front door with the delicacy of a burglar making a subtle escape. The small Cavalier King Charles that belonged to his host for the evening was growling as he tried to quietly make his exit. Jason raised his finger to his lips, imploring the dog to be quiet; the dog instead replied by biting one of his trainer laces. Jason shook his foot furiously trying to get free, swearing in the process, and accidentally making noise that could get him caught. He managed to get loose and exit the ground-floor apartment; the guard dog growled at him through the window while he departed. The cool night air hit him. *Freedom*, he thought to himself as he skipped down the street to the idling Uber. He jumped in the back and sped away. He'd had a fun night with Clarissa, but there was a lack of substance, and he hated staying over; it was far too intimate an act for someone he was indifferent about seeing again. *Nobody really wants to share their bed*, he considered, as he pictured the last image he had of her, passed out in a star shape across her sheets. He knew he needed more; single life and casual encounters were starting to wear thin.

A few days later Jason lay sprawled out on his own bed. This time, phone in hand, scrolling aimlessly through his Instagram feed. He quickly checked the time and decided it had been long enough since he last checked his selection of dating apps, enough time to allow some new activity to take place. He may, at this very moment, already be matched with his future wife. Although, history had shown him that it was much more likely to be just another short exchange of pointless messages or a quick affair that wouldn't lead anywhere. He inhaled deeply as he fired up an app. *Gotta stay positive*, he thought to himself.

As he scanned through the app he saw the engaging red notification bubble, blinking incessantly at the top right-hand corner of his screen, demanding his attention—new matches were awaiting! Today was a Tuesday, which obviously meant yesterday was a Monday, a good thing in the world of online dating as it was likely that any swiping performed the night before was not influenced by alcohol—he'd woken up on many a Saturday and Sunday morning to matches that he struggled to understand. After all, he did seem to have a type. He hated the fact he was forming a 'type'.

He clicked on the flashing red speech bubble and saw

his new matches. Three brand new chances for love—or chances for whatever the modern dating approximation of love was. The first two were OK, nothing to get too excited about, generally attractive girls who liked to travel, with the usual selection of *fun* pictures on a night out, at a fancy restaurant, etc. But there was something about the last match that caught his attention, something that made him take a second look and then a third, and actually gave him pause. So rarely in this day and age do we actually stop and take in the moment, but this was it, he was transfixed. This girl had deep bluey-green eyes, an amazing smile, and reams of dark curly hair. He caught himself smiling; he never smiled to himself. The smile quickly gave way to the realisation that coming across someone you actually liked came with pressure, an impactful first message was needed. Start with a joke? Or something clever or abstract? Maybe he was overthinking it. How long since they'd matched? He wondered. He didn't want to message too soon, can't seem too keen.

Jason went back and forth like this for a while, trapped in his own thoughts, a seemingly eternal internal debate. Meanwhile, a few miles away on the other side of London, a tired and overworked nurse was just getting back to her flat share after a long shift. Alice forced open the door that seemed to be sticking more and more these days and turned on the passage light. "Is anyone home?" she called, trying to balance her Sainsbury's local shopping bag, handbag, gym bag, and keys without falling over—quite the feat. "I guess not," she said to herself when she heard no reply.

Alice was approaching her late twenties and lived with a good friend Daisy in what might be described as an up-and-coming part of the city. Up-and-coming being the preferred estate-agent lingo for 'cheap'. Their flat wasn't glamorous, but they had made it cosy, and through lots of care and attention, they'd made it their own. Alice and Daisy had met on a postgraduate nursing course and were lucky enough to also work at the same hospital, although shift patterns meant they rarely saw each other. Alice struggled with her bags into the kitchen, managed to get them all on the kitchen table, and let herself drop on a wooden chair. It was the first time she'd been able to stop all day. Alice exhaled deeply as the moonlight pierced the top of the kitchen window above the sink; she traced its light across the table. *Is this what it's all about?* she thought to herself. Alice allowed herself a couple of minutes rest and then began unpacking her shopping bags. About thirty minutes later she'd had a shower and was eating a premade salad on the sofa in front of the TV. Feeling slightly more human, she decided to take a look at her phone. As she glanced at the phone and it came to life, her home screen was flooded with notifications from various platforms—from WhatsApp to Spotify, it seemed like the world wanted her attention. She scrolled through a few messages, almost opening apps at random until she came to *Timbleinge*.

She opened the app and saw the almost menacing red speech bubble flash in the top right-hand corner of the page. Alice was not a fan of dating apps, unlike the popular consensus among the young who used them en mass—though who were, at the same time, dissatisfied by the outcomes. She wasn't strictly against modern dating in general, but after a couple of failed relationships, she'd been convinced to give the apps a go. Alice received a large amount of pressure from Daisy, who was certain that every girl would meet their Prince Charming through the wondrous bits of code that made up these apps. So far she'd been on a few tragically funny first dates with guys who were so full of themselves they practically forgot she was in the room. She struggled with her generation's dependence on the drug of instant gratification, but was also determined not to become a cynical millennial who failed to see any joy in the world. It was a tight rope to walk.

Alice was a pretty girl, but was something of a late bloomer; so unlike most pretty girls, she had an equally attractive air of modesty. Compared to some others with her stopping power, she didn't let it go to her head, managing to maintain a broader perspective about life. Her dad had always told her that the most important thing was to be a nice person. It didn't matter what you looked like or how much money you had; it was about your character. Alice had fond memories of her father from when she was young, sitting crossed legged on the carpet watching him sing along to Northern Soul and Motown records. As usual, whenever she opened this app, she had a load of messages. The initial excitement of thousands of potential love connections quickly became a chore with little reward. Some of her friends would brag about the number of likes they got or how many followers they had, but that never made much sense to her. To her, these were just bits and bytes, ones and zeroes, not reality or romance, and certainly not meaningful connections to be impressed by.

As a matter of necessity, Alice had become brutally efficient in her vetting process. She had to be, or she'd spend her life glued to her phone. After flicking past a few faces— men hugging drugged-out tigers, topless gym selfies, and posing in convertibles (*probably rentals*)—she came across a face that made her stop. This guy had a kind face, nice eyes, and a smile almost as big as hers. She clicked on his picture and read more. Not too much information, but no red flags either. His favourite song was one she liked, and her dad always said you can tell a lot about someone from their taste in music.

Ooo, she thought to herself. *This could be worth an exchange or two. Maybe even worth shaving my legs for a date.*

Two

Blue Lights

Adrian Adebola was a good kid at heart; he just always seemed to get himself into bad situations — too often at the wrong place at the wrong time. He was walking home late from school, on an unusually cold early summer evening; he'd just left his second detention of the week. Adrian was trying to wrap his head around how he'd already been in detention twice, and it was only Wednesday. This was particularly confusing and disheartening, because he'd been making a conscious effort to talk less in class, and be better behaved in general. He'd made a promise to his mum to improve his behaviour at school, and this time he intended to keep it.

On this occasion it was Adrian's best friend Ryan who had gotten the pair in trouble by constantly talking in their science class. He knew Mr. Owens had it in for them, but they were not helping themselves. Adrian turned up

Charlotte street, the lights from cranes on the construction site cascaded across the pavement. A loud *CRASH!* came from behind him, as two kids in grey tracksuits flew past, knocking him to the ground, wherever they were going they were in a rush.

He picked himself up after being dazed for a few moments and continued to walk home. Rowdy teenagers were common where he grew up. Adrian eased down Harper street and started to think about whether he would have enough time to finish his science homework before *Power* started, when a pair of flashing blue lights sped around the corner and pulled up beside him. Two officers jumped out of the car, "Put your hands against the wall!" one of the officers shouted. Adrian was startled, he froze. "Put your hands against the wall, you little shit!" the officer said again loudly. Adrian was petrified, he couldn't move his legs, everything seemed to be happening in slow motion. A second officer was also shouting, but his cries were muffled. The next thing he knew he was practically lifted off the ground and smashed against the wall by one of the officers, a sharp pain ran through his body as he cried out, "Get off me!"

The commotion had drawn a crowd of shop keepers and passers-by; some younger people were recording on their phones.

"Leave him alone!" yelled a voice from a more senior member of the community, "He's just a boy."

Adrian had his hands yanked up together behind his

back and he was thrown onto the hood of the police car. His hands were tightly secured in place using zip-ties; they were drawn harshly, piercing his skin, he screamed in agony. The second officer, a young Nigerian man petitioned the commanding officer to take it easy, but the commanding officer was not in the mood to be lenient, "You just make sure this crowd is under control, keep them back!"

"Everyone stay back," the younger officer pleaded "It's under control, just stay back."

Adrian was face down on the hood of the car, the officer began interrogating Adrian. "Ok, why did you do it? Answer me!"

"Do what?" Adrian replied as he held back tears.

"You know what you did! You robbed the Paki shop, you and your mate, where is he?!"

The what? he thought to himself, he didn't even know what a Paki shop was, let alone robbed anything. Earlier that evening a few scratch cards, some alcohol and sweets were stolen from a local corner shop. The police were on the lookout for two young IC3 (Africa: Sub-Saharan and the Caribbean - Black) males in tracksuits. Adrian was in his school uniform.

"Ok, so you want to be the 'Big man' do you?! We'll see about that." The officer then picked the boy up by the scruff of his neck and smashed his head against the car bonnet. Adrian's world went dark.

Three

The Information Age

Jason was reading a book on the indigenous tribes of Brazil when his phone lit up, it was a message from his cousin, Akira. She had sent him a link to an Instagram page, "Hey Cuz, a Mz. Afrika debate is about to start. I know she can be a bit much at times, but I think you'll find this one interesting, kinda what we were talking about the other day. Take care."

His cousin was always informed with the latest Afro-centric topics and discussion, she made sure he stayed on point. He'd had enough of the agricultural techniques of the early people of the Amazon, and opened the link. An Instagram live stream took over his screen, it was a virtual panel discussion hosted by the personality behind the page Mz. Afrika. Perhaps unsurprisingly Mz. Afrika was a *conscious* Black woman, who considered herself to be a champion of Afro-centricity and Pan-Africanism. Her parents were Ghanaian, but she was born and raised in London. She promoted content around African history, a narrative of self-love and community upliftment, but would also delve into topics of popular interest to help maintain engagement on her platform.

Once a week she hosted a live debate with like-minded social media influencers, minor celebrities and people she felt had an interesting take on current affairs. Today's topic was about conditioning in love, do we really have any free will in who we are attracted to, or is it actually pre-determined by environmental factors. She had three guests for the discussion, two women; one a University Professor, the other an influencer/blogger who had spent a lot of time around the music industry. They were accompanied by an up-and-coming rapper called Undoubted.

Mz. Afrika opened the discussion by posing the question to one of the women on the panel, the History Professor at a London University, she was slim, attractive and well-dressed; in a pencil skirt, blouse, and fashionable, but comfortable shoes, "So Steffi, what are your thoughts on this topic, can we independently form our own opinions on who we're attracted to?"

"Well, it's an interesting point, we are of course heavily influenced by our day-to-day surroundings. We are facing a constant barrage of information; I think it's naïve to think that the world we live in has no impact on our views, and yes even who we are attracted to. In fact, ..."

"That's noise! Total rubbish," she was interrupted mid-sentence by the influencer Leampha. Leampha had a huge personality, she was about 5'2 with a curvaceous body and bright pink wig. Leampha built up a moderately large online following with a large selection of the usual seductive 'thirst-trap' images that highlighted her voluptuous curves and big personality. She was rumoured to have dated some B-list celebrities from the music world, which she would *accidentally* name drop from time to time on her stories. Stories that were supposed to be aimed at sharing her 'Life-coaching skills'; like so many millennials who were yet to make it through their 20s, they were somehow extremely experienced, (self-certified) life coaches. "I am my own woman," Leampha protested vehemently. "I make my own decisions; nobody can tell me what to do."

The comments on the Insta live chat went into overdrive when Leampha was speaking. 'I love you', 'Boss bitch', 'They can't handle you', were the types of comments that filled the scream from her legions of adoring fans.

The discussion bounced around the panel for a few minutes when Mz. Afrika went off on a tangent. "Undoubted, you are a famous rapper with a growing fan base, and arguable one of the most seminal underground albums of the last decade."

He coolly nodded, agreeing with her assessment. "It's been said that you have a preference for a certain type of woman. Let's say a fairer shade of female, with an hour glass shape and perfectly flat stomach. Do you think this apparent view has been impacted by your environment?"

The panel stared intently at Undoubted. He paused for a few moments as he considered his response. "It's hard to say, I think I like who I like. There is a certain image that is pushed and if I'm honest, I am attracted to it."

His reply was calm and measured, as was his style.

"So, you don't believe you have been *conditioned* to like a certain type of woman? I'm sure all the sisters out there would love to know why they can't get a shot with a star like yourself," Mz. Afrika pressed.

The concept of conditioning piqued Jason's attention. He had an interest in the workings of the mind, occasionally reading Psychology books. The notion of conditioning is a pivotal psychological concept, where repeated environmental stimuli can have a long term effect on a person's behaviour or mind-set. This idea was most famously demonstrated in Pavlov's dog experiment, where Pavlov rang a bell each time his dog was due to receive food. After a certain amount of time the dog associated the bell with food and anytime he heard the bell, began to salivate in expectation of food, whether there was food coming or not.

The debate continued, "Who said they can't?" Undoubted snapped back, with an air of tension in his voice.

"Well, your track record suggests they can't," said Mz. Afrika

"My past does not determine my future, and you

don't know all the women I've dated. A baddie is a baddie, whatever colour she is," responded Undoubted in a cooler tone.

"That may be so. But when I look across the industry you can see a lot of examples of guys like you with women who don't look so much like themselves. Is that an independent and objective choice they're making or is it more sub-conscious?" she said, trying to make the assertion seem less personal.

"You'd have to ask them; I don't speak for the industry," Undoubted said.

Leampha chimed in "All you men are the same, just want some light ting or a White girl with a big back-off," kissing her teeth for emphasis.

The comments section hit another huge spike during the exchange. Seemingly split between gender and race. Girls accusing Black men of being disloyal and a waste, and guys denying that this is actually a real topic. And the odd White girl asking *why can't people love who they want?* The comments were sprinkled by the odd trolling White guy that claimed this whole platform, let alone discussion, was racist.

Mz. Afrika changed the topic, as she could see the tension had built to dangerous levels. She didn't want to burn bridges with the star rapper or any of her other guests, although she was quietly pleased with the level of engagement the spicy exchange had generated. Jason put his phone down and began to float off in thought. His mind cast back to a recent conversation he and his cousin were having by an estray that backed on to the estate they grew up on as kids. From a young age they would escape the intensity of their tower block labyrinth, and chill by the water, where his cousin Akira would always give him useful life advice. As usual, Jason was running late to meet his cousin by their regular spot along *their river*. As kids, they would always describe it as a river, even though as adults they'd had to recognise that it was far too small, but still to them it was their river, their spot.

Jason could see his cousin sitting on a bench, he sped up as he approached her so she could see he was making an effort. "Only 20 minutes late," he said with a laugh. "Not too bad for you I guess, Sprout," Akira replied. Akira's nickname for Jason was Sprout and he hated it. She'd given it to him when they were young after he fell in love with the sprouting green plant, water cress, as part of a Primary school project. The whole class had to grow the water cress plants, and after a few weeks of diligent nurturing, they turned the cress into sandwiches. Jason had eaten one and loved it! He asked Akira what it was and she'd said watercress, they're kind of sprouts. For the next few weeks every time he saw her, he would say Sprout in that inquisitory tone that young people use, which seems to be both an assertion and a request at the same time. It also helped that he had a massive growth spurt at 16 and was now 6'2 towering a full foot taller than his elder cousin. Despite his height advantage, he would always look up to her.

"You know I hate Sprout! ... So, how've you been?" he enquired as he sat down. "You know, same old, same old, paying bills-keeping it real." That was a saying of hers. Akira was a few years older than Jason; they used to spend school holidays together at their Grandmother's, she was always seen as more of a big sister than a cousin. She always had his back and more often than not her head in a book, which meant she was a constant fountain of knowledge, of all things from Astronomy to Zoology. They covered some small talk, and then moved on to more interesting topics, they shared a passion for music, and would spend hours going back and forth with one another on who the greats were or critiquing the latest songs. If it wasn't music it was history or love or politics or philosophy. Hours would quickly disappear when they were together.

"So, what's your love life saying Sprout, still breaking hearts?" Akira asked

"You know me, can't find anyone to hold me down, just yet at least," Jason fired back.

"You've got time on your side, I guess," Akira said. "I was reading an interesting article the other day about the conditioning of Black men in the diaspora. I know you like your *Becky's* and *lighties*," she said, sticking her tongue out in jest.

"Don't start with all of that again, I'm open to dating

anyone, it doesn't matter to me what they look like ... well it does, but you know what I mean," Jason replied defensively.

They had a few discussions on interracial dating in the past. The type of women Jason dated hadn't gone unnoticed by Akira, who felt that Black women were not given a fair chance to shine. In her eyes, they were underappreciated and overlooked. Western beauty standards painted a clear picture of what the ideals of beauty *should* be and sadly the sisters did not seem to fit.

"It was interesting, the author suggested that consistent exposure to Western beauty standards will impact your views, particularly if you are not coming from a strong cultural background that combats these messages," Akira affirmed confidently.

"I haven't come from a strong background? We had a similar upbringing didn't we?" Jason said.

"No, I'm not saying that I'm just saying you see enough pictures and movies with Jennifer Aniston, Scarlett Johansson and Margot Robbie it's going to have an impact," Akira stated as a matter of fact.

"That isn't even my thing, you know Jorja Smith is my wife goal!" He said with a wide smile, picturing her in a wedding dress.

"Sprout, you know that look is just an extension of the same story. Not White, but the next best thing. Black guys always try to play that card as an excuse. At least she has some Black in her; when she's 1/16th and could be from anywhere," Akira said.

"What about looking beyond the skin? Isn't love deeper than that?" Jason said.

It should be, it really should be, but the world won't allow it to be … not in my world at least." She seemed to trail off and look out into the distance.

Jason's phone went into a fit of vibrations as it buzzed with a series of notifications from a group chat that had suddenly come to life. The debate had finished; he really had dozed off.

Four

The Art Of Appyness

A day had passed since Alice and Jason matched, but as yet no messages had been exchanged. Alice was home earlier than usual following a half-day shift, and she was browsing some Pinterest boards as she lay on her bed. Endless pictures of cakes, attractive meals and models in various pieces of high-end Couture made up the majority of her feed; these were interspersed with a sprinkle of Michael B Jordan-esq looking males, every now and again.

Alice considered herself to be a modern and liberal woman. While she didn't enjoy labels or boxes so much, she definitely had a preference - the tall dark and handsome. Her dark and handsome was a deeper hue than the Mediterranean sun-kiss, which was normally associated with the phrase. She came across an image of one of these Adonis type models, and opened the pin for a closer look. A broad smile materialised across her face out of nowhere, and then a sudden thought, this guy reminded her a little of the guy from the app. She closed the page and opened up Timbuleinge, to her disappointment there was nothing yet from Jason. She thumbed through his pictures again. There was something different about him. He was handsome in an understated way, naturally well-built, broad shoulders and with a warm and disarming smile. He didn't have the usual arrogant energy of someone so aesthetically appealing. His pictures seemed more authentic than staged, more candid than scripted. There was a shot of him playing football, one with friends at some sort of celebration and one with an attractive shorter woman, who she hoped wasn't his ex. One thing she could never understand is why anyone would post a picture with their ex?!

Why hasn't he messaged? Maybe he wasn't interested, or he had accidentally swiped her, or he was one of these too good to be true *cat-fishes*. Alice was a self-professed feminist and believed in the empowerment of the gender, but her outlook was also juxtaposed with some more traditional views, including the hope that chivalry was not truly dead! (as is so often claimed nowadays). *I can just message first, what's the big deal?* She thought to herself. If I'm comfortable enough to be on this app, I should be comfortable enough to send a message first; if we are together in 50 years, I won't care who sent the first message. "What to say, what to say," she murmured to herself. Something simple, best to keep it simple.

Meanwhile, across the city Jason was staring at the pictures of Alice, also wracking his brains at what to say. The flat was quieter than normal, with his housemates out and about with various mid-week activities. He liked her and didn't want to mess up the first move. I should say something witty and funny. I want her to know that I'm not a *basic* guy, he thought to himself. He was actually in the notes section of his phone drafting opening lines, not something he'd ever done before, why did he care so much this time? "Did you know there are more synapses in the brain than stars in the Milky way?" ... *too geeky,* he thought.. *too nerdy maybe.*

Maybe I'm overthinking this, I should just say "How are you?" he flipped his phone in his hands, rotating it slowly like a fidget spinner and started to play some music. He hit shuffle and a J Cole tune started to play, the hook ran, "Nobody's perfect, but I'm perfect for you"

He hummed along when his phone lit up, a message from Alice! He dropped his phone in the excitement of seeing the message and it bounced underneath his bed. He fumbled around for it, touching a lot of questionable textures as he did, *I really need to tidy up under there,* he thought. Keen to read the message he rolled off his bed and continued the search, his arm scanning back and forth like a submarine radar, "There you are, got you!" he pulled it out and lifted his head only to catch it on the corner of his bed, thud!

"Fuck!" he shouted. Ok, *calm down*, he thought, relax, be cool, you don't even know what she said. Breathe. He composed himself, sat back on his bed and opened the message.

"Hey, what's up?" it read. Ok, nothing too crazy here, but she did message first, which was a good sign. *Better not go too crazy with the response, try to match her energy*, he thought.

"Hey, not much and you?" he sent. Fuck! too fast, should have left it a bit. Alice's phone lit up, a message from Jason. Quick response! she liked that. Hmm, but pretty simple, not much to go on there.

"What do you do in your spare time? Aside from becoming the next Zaha," she said, referring to the Crystal Palace football shirt he was wearing in one of the pics and highlights her knowledge of the *beautiful game.*

Jason chuckled to himself as he read the message, "Wow, beautiful and you know football [smilie face emoji]. Aside from sports, I'm into psychology, music, reading and a bit of travelling when I can. How about you? What do you do when you're not taking pics with baby animals?" he responded, reefing to the picture she had with a baby lamb from last spring.

Hmm a reader too, he's not just looks. Mental tick. *How can I get deeper*, she thought, as she began to type, "I appreciate a good pair of legs [wink emoji]. I like similar things, I was brought up in a house full of music. What's your favourite book and why?"

They went back and forth with one another for what felt like no time at all when suddenly she heard the front door close, and her flatmate calls upstairs to see if she was still up. It was one in the morning; they'd been texting for four hours. That was a first for her. While she was happy with the natural connection they seemed to have, she also realised that she had to be up in three hours for the early shift at work! She bid her new Boo good night.

Jason had also lost track of time, but was happy to be having a late-night for this type of conversation. As he wished her a good night's sleep, he also suggested they carry on their chat in person some time. She accepted, wishing him good night again *"For real this time,"* she wrote, as he fell asleep with a smile on his face.

Five

Another Statistic

Alice was at lunch with an old friend, Jane. The pair had been brought together in primary school by their mothers who were already close. Jane lived in her own world, and despite their friendship, was quite different to Alice; Jane had fully adopted her mother's values, and was all about money and status. Her Dad had done well in the finance world, and she was his little princess. Whenever they met it always had to be at a ridiculously over-priced place, despite Alice's constant reminders that she was only a mid-tiered NHS Nurse, who was not as comfortable as her friend with the borrowing from the bank of Mum and Dad.

"Don't worry," she'd say, "I'll get it", which was beside the point. Head to toe in designer, Jane was not someone you missed, and she definitely didn't like to miss out on the details of Alice's life, especially when it came to men. Having been in a long-term relationship with what Alice's mother considered to be a very eligible Bachelor, she was forced to live vicariously through her single friends, which worked well with her insatiable love of gossip.

Jane meant well for the most part, but she was just spoiled; spoiled and self-centred, as were so many of the people Alice grew up around. They were having lunch at a trendy café in Primrose Hill. "Tell me, my dear, what is going on in your love life, found *Mr. Right, yet*?" she purred, with extra emphasis on the 'yet' to enforce the fact that she was still single.

"Still on the lookout," Alice replied with a smile to mask any irritation that may have seeped into her face.

"Well, I guess we all can't be as lucky as me and Robert," almost swooning at the dream come true that was her own perfect love story.

"I have met someone actually," she snapped back in a subconscious attempt to wipe the smug look off her face. "Well, we've not actually met yet, but we've connected online and…"

Jane cut Alice off abruptly, "Online!?" with a hint of derision.

"Not on one of those awful apps. My dear, you are so much better than the trash on these apps. Let me set you up with one of Robert's friends, a proper gentleman who can look after you, especially before you hit the big 3-0!" Jane was always trying to play matchmaker, and get Alice even more closely entangled in her life.

"YES! An app, heaven forbid in 2021 actually using

technology for everything in life, including trying to meet someone," she said emphatically.

Jane was taken back by the intensity of Alice's reply, she knew she could be a bit much at times, but was always surprised when Alice finally responded in defiance. Jane looked at her phone as a way to escape the glare Alice had on her face. She saw a BBC news report flash up on her phone "Protestors gather outside of Newham Police station, following brutality claims against local officer." In an attempt to change the topic, and demonstrate she was up with current affairs, she mentioned the story.

"Terrible business this with the policeman and the boy from Newham," she said in the most earnest tone she could muster. Alice paused for a second, knowing how badly past conversations around discrimination had gone.

"It really is," she replied after a moment, regaining her composure. What seemed like an eternity passed without anyone speaking. Before long and as expected, Jane had to continue, "But it's always that way, isn't it?"

"What's the way?" Alice responded tersely.

"Well, it's always them, isn't it? These little ruffians, always seem to get themselves into trouble. I just don't get it. If you behave yourself, you don't need to worry about the police. It's almost as if they want the drama, another excuse to protest and not be at work."

The last point was the final straw for Alice, particularly as Jane was already a lady of leisure who had barely worked a day in her life. She looked at her phone. "I'm sorry Jane, there's an emergency at work, they need me back, I have to go." She dropped a few notes on the table, gathered her things and rushed off. One of the saving graces of being a nurse is having an on-demand get out of jail free card.

"Alice! Alice!" Jane called after her, but she was already heading down the steps of the tube station, relieved she hadn't thrown her drink in Jane's face.

Dr Abefembe Ebowa sat back in her leather desk chair and studied her 32-inch, twin monitors. The profiles of several candidates' key to realising her vision filled the screen. It was nearly time to begin. At that moment an e-mail popped up from a blank address, she clicked through; it was a comprehensive collection of news articles of the Adrian Adebola incident, from more than a dozen news sites. She was expecting information, but not this much, she was starting to feel inundated by the level of *support* being provided by her mystery contact. She spun 180 degrees in her chair and stared out of the window that looked out into the night sky. She slowly examined the city skyline, the twilight seemed to bounce from building to building - she began to think about what was to come.

Jason's first date with Alice was rapidly approaching, he was actually excited, nervous even, this was not like him at all. His eager anticipation for the date also brought up feelings of conflict. Jason was not new to the internal dilemma of trying to reconcile his general *preference* in women, with the wider implications and connotations that came with it as a Black man. Akira had often challenged him on the issue; usually constructively from a place of love, as was her way. This would typically lead to moments of reflection, he would try to dissect his supposed *preference*, even though he was not completely comfortable with the label. Jason saw himself as someone who was attracted to Black women...*some* Black women, many mixed women, and by no means attracted to all White women. *Where do you draw the line of preference*? he thought, *50%/10%/40%, 60%/10%/30%, 25%/35%/40%?*

As much as he hated to admit it, the scales were tipped, even if only slightly, away from Black women of a darker complexion; a reality that was only reinforced by his feelings for Alice. Maybe he needed to analyse things more carefully, not just as an afterthought following a grilling from Akira... He laid back on his bed and began to think about *why* he may have been leaning towards one side of the spectrum. What was he really attracted to? Was it purely physical? What was the psychology behind it?

In opposition of his taste in certain women, Jason was aware of the barriers that came with dating outside of the race; he knew there could be problems of cultural connection, of understanding, but he tried to see past that. Did that make it worse? That he was willing to take on these extra challenges, for what? *For love*, he told himself. His mind went into solution mode, *there must be some studies on this*, he thought; maybe even an algorithm he hoped. He opened the browser on his phone and went to the search engine, he paused for a moment and considered what to search… 'What drives interracial dating?' … No, he thought, 'Why do Black men date White women?', too on the nose, he didn't care about race, he just wanted to meet the right person; 'Can you find love outside of your race?' he typed, hitting search and sending the query out into the trillions of bytes of cyberspace.

There were pages of results in response to the question, Jason wasn't surprised, you could find anything on the net these days. There were links to lots of social media discussions around race and dating, but Jason wanted something analytical, something more methodical. Unfortunately there was not a lot in terms of solid research or empirical evidence, mainly thesis documents from post and under-grad students.

He clicked on one of the few study options, it was titled 'The compensative desire for parity among the races.' Jason scanned the summary abstract; the study was investigating the conscious and subconscious drive for people of colour who tried to gain higher social footing, and acceptance through partnership with White people. The study focused on men of colour and White women. Akira had suggested this theory before, but he never seriously considered it, because he never believed it rang true for him. He looked at the date of the paper, it was published in the mid-90s; he dismissed it as old-school thinking, not relevant for contemporary dating or love.

Jason returned to the results page and continued to scroll through the options. He clicked through another link, this time to a Pro-Black site; the page was focused on the value of the Black family, unity, the need to build a strong community and even Nation. He perused a section that stressed the importance of Black love, *intra-racial* love *(if that's a thing*, he thought).

Jason could see merit in parts of this worldview; being with someone who understood your struggle, someone with a shared cultural heritage, similar foods, music, ways of being, all organically. In addition, and importantly, providing the foundation for growing a strong economic base of the Black community. The page went on to discuss how love and marriage were actually more political than anything else, a demonstration of your commitment to your race. Moreover, if you were to date outside of your race, you were deemed to be a traitor. This rhetoric was on the extreme end of the spectrum, and while he could understand it theoretically, he somewhat romantically still hoped that love could transcend the social construct of race.

Perhaps, something a little lighter, but still analytical, he thought, as he considered the search results one more time. He picked up an interesting link which seemed to be some sort of self-evaluating questionnaire. Jason found these types of exercises intriguing and from past experience knew they could be fun, even if he didn't always trusted the quality of the scoring algorithms used. He opened the page which filled with a header of 'What's your Preference and Why?' and some introductory blurb. He had to create a profile, username, password and provide his e-mail. Jason hoped that sharing his e-mail wouldn't lead to a lot of spam.

The multiple choice form began in simple enough fashion with the standard personal information questions, date of birth, etc. These were supplemented by some more unusual additions, such as location and time of birth, which carried an astrological aura, but Jason decided not to judge and continue regardless. The form was detailed; lots of questions about your personal interests, country of residence, where you were raised and the make-up of your local community/neighbourhood - that was just to begin with. In addition, there were questions around what type of physical and personality traits you gravitated towards most. There were markers around the importance of heritage and also cultural significance. The comprehensiveness of the approach gave Jason some comfort.

He was about half way through when a knock on his door caused him to quickly close his browser and put his phone to one side. He wasn't sure why he was so rattled; he felt like a teenager being caught red handed on a porn site by a parent. 'Come in', he said more nervously than he would have liked.

It was Lyon, "You good?" he began, looking around Jason's room, seemingly noticing that something was off, almost unwittingly assuming the role of a parent looking for a hidden girlfriend in their child's bedroom, 'We're thinking of getting a pizza, interested?' he asked.

'Yeah, sure, I'll be down in a sec,' Jason responded, sub-consciously trying to get him out of his room. Perhaps he needed a bit of a break from his analysis. He slipped his phone in his tracksuit bottom pocket and headed downstairs to join the rest of the guys.

Six

First Dates

The day had finally arrived, the first date. Jason was up early, and felt particularly energised and excited for the day ahead. This was novel for him after having so many dates, he was used to being more ambivalent about meeting a new person. He headed towards his office, practically skipping down a street of cobbled stones. He was emitting a glow that raised the mood of everyone he came across. An almost annoyingly infectious energy that grabbed you against your will. He gave the office receptionist a big hello and a warm wave, which was not so unusual for Jason, but even she could notice the extra zip in his step.

Jason had been working as a data analyst at MI6 for just over three years, but he would still stop and appreciate the magnificent piece of glass architecture that housed his office. From a young age, he'd always been good with puzzles and pattern recognition, it was one of the attributes that had him ear-marked as a grammar school candidate back when he was in primary school. During his childhood years he loved spy movies, especially watching old Bond films with his dad; so much so that he wanted to be a secret agent when he grew up. He was over the moon to get the opportunity to combine his love of spy-dom with his programming and deciphering skills, when he applied to work for MI6, the secret service itself. After making it through the gruelling selection process, his first year on the job was challenging, but his newly appointed manager, Violet Mc Kenzie, had helped him adjust. Before long he was on a path of fast progression. Jason had been impressing Senior Analysts with his work and insights for some time now; innovative thinking around a systems issues that stumped Senior Team members, was just one example of the type of ingenuity that Jason was starting to gain a reputation for. However, it was his ability to build programmes that could penetrate defensive security systems that generated the most interest from Senior observers.

Jason was generally well-liked by his colleagues, despite being the only Black face in the department, and one of the few minorities in the building, his affable nature and polite tone seemed to put most people at ease. He had become adept in the art of seamlessly immersing himself in White spaces. A talent that was only surpassed by his colleague from digital architecture, Whitney Walker. Whitney was an attractive, intelligent, mixed race girl, who grew up in one of the conservative counties surrounding London with her mum and Step-Father. Jason who never forget the first time he saw her, he was awestruck by her statuesque bone structure and bright eyes. Bumping into her in elevators or in coffee areas always brought added sunshine to his day; he saw relationship potential in her.

Unfortunately, as he got to know her better it became apparent that they lacked any genuine chemistry. Despite her dual heritage, half of which matching Jason, they had little to connect on. He wondered if their lack of vibe was anything to do with her Black dad leaving the family when she was only young; he'd seen examples of mixed race people developing sub-conscious feelings of resentment against those that reflected their absentee parent.

In truth, they came from different worlds, while Jason had tasted morsels of middle-class life during his schooling, he never felt at ease with how much Whitney embraced her comfortable upbringing, public school education and conservative outlook. On top of that she was relentlessly ambitious, which meant that engagement with her could come across as calculated and disingenuous. A factor that at times gave Jason a feeling of paranoia; a feeling that was compounded by the fact she had an uncanny ability to message him at positive times: whenever he was being praised for his performance, somehow in the lime light, or just if things were going well in his life. This was particularly strange because they worked in different departments, so she really shouldn't have been aware of his achievements. Her sixth sense for Jason formed a basis for flirtatious interactions, a back and forth that culminated in a drunken kiss at a Christmas party. Despite the mutual intrigue, there seemed to be an unspoken agreement to not pursue things beyond the spontaneous cheeky message and sporadic coffee. Something about their dalliance led Jason to believe she was not genuinely interested or perhaps it was more that he shared the sentiment.

As if by magic, she reached out again in timely fashion; *maybe she's tapped my phone with screen mirroring software and knows I have a date*, he thought with a smile as he read the message. 'Hey stranger, long time, we should grab a coffee soon, would love to update you on some stuff we have going on in Arc.'

On the surface of it, there was nothing inappropriate about the message, she really had flirting down to an art, innocent but suggestive. On occasion, she'd message Jason's personal mobile, it had come up once in a conversation with a male colleague who was immediately filled with an envious pride; envious that it wasn't him, but associatively proud because he knew Jason, like she was some kind of minor celebrity. In a way she kind of was, in the building at least, most work places have their most desirable *assets,* and most of the men in the office loved to be around her, even if she was young enough to be a daughter to many of them. She carried the attention in stride well, as if it was her birth right. Jason hadn't heard from her in a while, but was too excited about his date to get into flirt tennis with Whitney; he'd reply tomorrow.

The day had shot past, before he knew it he was alone on the elevator heading home to get ready for the date, when out of nowhere he began to hum an old RnB song from his school days, as he hummed his mind cast back to his secondary school years.

Jason was bright for his age, a budding intelligence that was encouraged by some teachers, but stifled by more. Despite a mixed level of support in his early educational years, his parents recognised his talents and managed to get him into a grammar school, following the successful completion of his 11+ exams. His secondary school experience at St. James' Grammar school opened up a whole new world for Jason, new facilities, opportunities and most importantly new people.

Jason would always remember his mum fixing his tie and blazer in year 7 when he began at St. James, he never understood the need for ties, he thought they were for adults and it made it hard for him to breathe. Unfortunately, the tie was not the only thing that made Jason uncomfortable at his new learning institution. Jason's primary school was very mixed, kids from seemingly all over the world, a stark contrast to the Lilly White population of St James'. He could feel the stares as he walked the corridors, if he were older he could have dismissed the awkward feeling as paranoia, but that concept was yet to reach him.

Standing out, while normally uncomfortable, can come with its privileges. He started his secondary school journey as an outcast, but that didn't last long, particularly with the girls at the school. Jason came from a part of the city that was diverse, in the sense that it lacked White faces, but was a plentiful mix of different backgrounds from Africa, Southern Asia and the Caribbean, including different religious backgrounds. So being unique based on sheer appearance was a fairly new concept for him. The attention from the opposite sex, during adolescent years when hormones begin to kick in and play havoc with a person's desires and character, occurred whilst Jason was practically living a double life.

Life at home with his family doing things they'd always done from listening to rare grooves and revival in the early hours of the weekend to having traditional Jamaican dishes on a Sunday, from ackee and Salt fish to stew peas and rice. This coupled with hanging with his friends on the estate, riding bikes and playing football, was in stark contrast to what he experienced when he was at school. The duality that he was forced to embrace at a young age became second nature, almost natural code-switching that many in the Diaspora have to learn to master. It didn't feel odd that he was developing an attraction to girls that looked different to those from his estate, or that he had a friendship group at school that had a very different aesthetic.

Alice rushed down the hospital corridor on her way to the changing area, she was keen to be on time for their first date, but was already running late, because of a last-minute emergency on her ward that required all hands on deck. Her flatmate Daisy caught her power walking in the distance and wanted to wish her luck, "Al" she shouted down the corridor, but Alice was too focused on her mission to get changed, and get out of the hospital in record time to register her friend's call.

She was equal parts flustered and excited, as she tried to force her way out of the tube at Camden Town station. She finally made it to her flat, collapsing on her sofa. *Five minutes,* she thought, *five minutes and I'll get moving.* Checking her phone, it was already quarter past six, she had to be at the bar by eight. She dragged herself upstairs into her room and opened her wardrobe. Alice hated when she needed to dress up, because she would end up making a mess. She had many gifts, but could never decide if her borderline OCD tidiness was one of them. She threw piles of clothes on her bedroom floor, and started to wade through different heaps almost at random. Alice was starting to get frustrated by how much trouble she was having with what she considered the simple task of getting dressed. Her anxiety grew with the growing mess she was creating; this was the worst part of dating, in her eyes. *Music*, she thought. *Music will help.* She connected her phone to her blue tooth speaker and started to play some Sza.

Jason was singing to himself in the mirror, topless while brushing his neatly shaped beard. Bryson Tiller set the backdrop to his date prep. They were going for some drinks in Shoreditch so he wanted it to keep it relatively casual, jeans, trainers and some sort of t-shit that complemented his body. He liked dark jeans and bright tops in the summer, but the rest of the year he was more mono-tone.

Alice was on the tube in a longer jacket than the weather called for, but she'd gone for a modest, but a well-fitting skirt. She didn't want any more attention than absolutely necessary on her naturally curvy lower half. A shape that now was the envy of most of her friends and colleagues, was a great source of insecurity when she was a teen, who couldn't find jeans that would get over her hips and were small enough for her waist. Irrespective of all the compliments she received, and the body confidence she had developed as a young woman, there was still some residual angst from time to time, it was surprisingly hard to differentiate from 'complimentary' oogles, and the stares of astonished disgust she received as a teenager.

She teetered down the high street in her heels, thin Mack held across her mid-draft. The agreed drinking spot wasn't far from the station, but she still managed to get two wolf whistles, a car beep, and a 'Hey darlin', where a guy felt the need to invade her personal space and touch her hip. She shook him off, giving him a cold glare. She entered the vibrant bar and looked around. The Friday night after work energy was high, it felt like everyone in the bar had a long week. She scanned a couple more times but couldn't find Jason, so she made her way to the bar and ordered a drink.

Despite getting ready quickly, Jason was still about 10 minutes late to the bar. He really had a talent for lateness. As such he constantly seemed to be between a fast walk, a trot or skip and a light jog. He pushed into the busy bar, surprisingly busy for this time on a Friday, the after-work crowd must still be out. He gazed over the crowd and spotted a shapely figure by the bar. He was pretty sure it was her or at least he hoped it was. He dipped and slid through the crowd, looking for the path of least resistance.

He squeezed in next to Alice and another girl who was ordering. Alice was engaged in a chat with the barman. "Hey, any room for a Zaha wanna be?"

The barman was visibly displeased, hoping that she would have been stood up, so that he'd have some more of her time. She turned, smiled and looked at her watch "I don't know, I don't like to be kept waiting," she laughed and kissed his cheek. They exchanged some pleasantries and moved to the back of the bar, where it was quieter and easier to talk. They were both pleased that the real-life looks matched the digital avatars, and the ease of their online conversations translated to real life. "Ok, so give me your top 3 90s RnB artists and why?" Alice said excitedly and with a keenness to get her answer across.

"What do you know about 90s RnB?" he asked in a playful and rhetorical tone. "Probably more than you, as we're about to find out!" Alice fired back. The energy between the two of them was playfully palpable.

"Ok, for me I would go for Jodeci, Usher and SWV ... not necessarily in that order." Jason said confidently as he drained the remainder of his Moscow mule, now several drinks in, the copper cup no longer felt so cold. "Can we say Usher is 90s? He may have started then, but he's still making music now," Alice queried.

Jason shrugged as he sat back in his chair, "Let's hear yours then?"

Having grown up in a house full of music, she'd become particularly enamoured with 90s RnB, and was always up for a debate. In reality, her confidence and slightly argumentative nature meant she was up for a debate about most things, but the music was high on the list, particularly music she was passionate about. "SWV, Babyface and Boyz II Men!" she declared as if she was reading the winners for Best Picture at an award ceremony.

"Boyz II Men ... Babyface, good calls," he conceded. A bright victory smile beamed across her face. Jason didn't mind losing out, as he got to see her so happy. Time seemed to disappear into nothing, and the cocktails kept coming. The conversation was non-stop bouncing from music to politics to conspiracy theories to reality TV, putting the world to rights. Everything was going well when Alice noticed a mischievous smirk emerge on Jason's face, she wasn't sure what was happening. "Are you ok?" Alice said.

"Yeah… I'm just thinking about something we could do …" he said in a beguiling tone.

Alice's mind began to race, "Go on?"

"Are you up for some music? Maybe some dancing?" he suggested, following up with a challenge "If you think you can handle it?"

Alice had mixed feelings of intrigue and unease; was she brave enough to go dancing with a practical stranger; the fact that she liked the stranger just added more pressure to the situation. She was at risk of potentially embarrassing herself on the dance floor, but she was having so much fun with Jason, she decided to go for it, "…Let's do it!" Alice replied.

They called the barman over to settle up. "I've got this don't worry," Jason said firmly. "No, let me at least pay my share," Alice said earnestly.

"NOT A CHANCE! My mum would never forgive me if she knew I wasn't covering my dates. End of discussion." Alice appreciated the sincerity and conviction in his voice. This wasn't a demonstration of male ego or patriarchy, just a genuine display of care and chivalry. The pair wobbled out of the bar into the bright lights of Shoreditch high street. "I know a place close by. Good music, decent vibe," Jason said.

"Lead the way good Sir," she said as they linked arms and headed to the club.

The club was bustling by the time they got in. Low ceilings, low lights and low bass. This was a pretty classic East London scene, but one they were both comfortable with. They danced close and slow, but when the tunes sped up effortlessly separated while maintaining a connection. The DJ spun from 00s hip-hop, through to Garage, dancehall, afro beats and back to slow jams. They say dancing can say a lot about chemistry... and other forms of intimacy; Jason had always been easy on the dance floor, a natural rhythm that kept him on point without doing too much. Alice too had gained a level of comfort on the floor, from her days at Uni and nights out with her friends. She was more self-conscious than Jason, but with the aid of the preceding cocktails they found their flow quickly enough; a natural rapport was beginning to bloom. Despite the dance floor being crowded and sweaty, they felt like they were the only ones in the room.

They'd danced for what felt like an age (in the most positive sense), but even though she was having an amazing time, nature was calling her to the ladies' room. She excused herself as Joe, 'I wanna know', finished playing. Jason headed to the bar to get them some drinks. Jason returned to their dance spot not long after, and looked out for Alice. The crowd during this night was pretty chilled, but Jason had enough club experience to know that attractive girls would get approached, even if they'd been with the same guy all night, even if they were just going to the bathroom. The tunes continued to play when Jason noticed a guy making some off moves near the door of the girl's bathroom, the guy was moving side to side, as if he were shadowing someone else's movement. Alice still hadn't remerged, so Jason went over to investigate.

Meanwhile, Alice was trying her best to politely evade a persistent suitor. "You're cute you know?" the guy said,

"Thanks, but I'm here with someone," she replied.

"Relax, relax, where you going, your guy can wait a minute or two. You know if I was with you I wouldn't let you out of my sight, ever," he said, licking his lips, in what she guessed was supposed to be sexy, but came across as predatory. The guy suddenly felt a tap on his shoulder, he spun around, almost knocking the drinks out of Jason's hands. "And who are you?" the guy, said to Jason.

"I'm the guy she's with tonight," Jason shot back. Alice could feel the tension rising. The two men sized each other up, eyes locked. Jason really didn't want to make a scene, but the male ego was starting to take over.

"Oh swear, I just wanted a word or two, big man, say nothing," the guy said, backing down. He turned to give Alice a smile and a wave as he disappeared into the crowd.

"Sorry about that," Jason said.

"Ha, no worries, I'm used to dealing with guys like him," she replied, trying to alleviate any concerns Jason had for her well-being.

"Oh, is that so, always around the *man dem*, is it?" Jason asked in jest. Alice knew he was joking, but still blushed.

"No, not like that," She took her drink from his hand and pushed him back towards their spot on the floor. *I need a girl, part two* came on, "That's my tune!" Jason exclaimed. Alice draped her arms across the back of his neck, and they began to move.

A few hours later the lights came up, it was time to go. A collective moan from the crowd as one of the bouncers tried to usher everyone upstairs and out of the door – "it's time to find your bed you can't sleep here!" They left amongst the crowd and headed to Alice's bus stop. The countdown timer said 2 minutes. "Thank you for tonight, I've had a really good time," she said.

"No problem, it was my pleasure," he said back. The bus approached; he gave her a big hug. It was a tight embrace, the kind of hug that neither person wanted to end. He let her go so she wouldn't miss the bus. "Text me when you get home, so I know you're safe," he said. He sat back down and watched the bus lights fade into the distance. Once it had disappeared from sight, he exhaled deeply, "That was *A* night!"

Seven

The Debrief

Jason headed to his parent's house for breakfast as he often did on some weekends, if he wasn't too hungover. This was a perk of being on the same train line as his childhood home. He was still full of excitement from the evening before, a kind of nervous energy that was best used on some activity or else could lead to mischief. His mum was frying some plantain, "What's got you in such a good mood today, son?" she asked.

"You know me, I want to get a head start on the day, life's too short to be wasting it away in bed!" Jason said with a smile on his face.

"A tru, mi know mi son, a deh fi di problem... not exactly a morning person, and I thought you were out last night," she pressed, bouncing between patois and English as she would at times, usually in jest or annoyance.

"What can I say? I feel energized. I'm going to hit the gym after breakfast. "Where are Dad and Titi?" he asked.

Titi was Jason's adopted sister, who Jason's parents brought into the family after his mum convinced his dad that they still had a lot more love and life to give. Jason loved his sister deeply, his only regret being that she didn't come into his life earlier.

"Dad's taken Titi swimming," she said as a news update pinged on her phone. She read the update and then switched on the radio, playing with the frequency until she got to her favourite station, Black-Star radio. A short news briefing had just begun; a community leader was giving an address:

"We call on everyone in the community and beyond to support the Adebola family in their time of need. If we don't stand up against police brutality in our community who will? This needs to stop now! Our young ones can't even be safe coming home from school!" Murmurs of agreement could be heard from the crowd.

"So sad what happened to that boy, he's still unconscious in intensive care, you know?" Jason's mum said. "I thought things were getting better from my day, but at times it feels like nothing's changed."

The incident took the wind out of Jason somewhat, as he devoured his breakfast. He had been raised with a strong sense of justice, and knew all too well how often the Black community suffered under oppressive forces. When incidents like this took place it would often drive Jason into a more radical mode; sharing his frustrations about the system with his friends, family, anyone who would be listening, but today was a day for positivity; he was in a good mood, and wanted to stay that way. "I know mum, I know, we're never really safe, even from those who are supposed to protect us. I've got to go." He stood up, gave his mum a hug and a kiss on the cheek, grabbed his bag and left.

Jason was going through his usual upper body routine; a mix of pull-ups, push-ups and bench presses, when he got a message from the boys' group chat. Anton had sent a meme of a goat stuck up a tree, referencing a show they watched; it had everyone in hysterics.

"Yo, are we still meeting up later?" Anton put to the group.

"Yep, say nothing," Lyon.

"The usual spot?" Jason said.

"No doubt," Anton, Lyon and Marlon agreed. The guy's group chat had a fascinating way of switching from hours of roasting and insults to heated football debates, discussions about women and the future to very pragmatic logistical arrangements. When it came to logistics, it was when, where, how, yes or no. Despite living together, they liked to meet at least once a month in person outside of the flat to have a low-key face to face convo over a few drinks, and maybe some food. Everyone was busy doing their own thing; Lyon was always juggling clients and candidates as a recruitment consultant; Anton was a man of many talents, an entrepreneur with his fingers in many pies; and Marlon had his own plumbing business, so was often on call at unsociable hours. Creating this time meant they would actually all have time to catch up properly, and not be just be ships passing in the night. These evenings also differed by being more civilised than their more usual turn-ups, which tended to descend into an alcohol-fuelled frenzy.

Their spot of choice was a relatively secluded Caribbean restaurant and bar. The majority of the group were there by eight but Jason and Anton, who had a young daughter were usually late, and today was no different. Jason arrived before Aaron and they were a full complement by twenty to nine. They hugged and dapped each other, as they usually would. The group had known each other since they were kids growing up on the estate.

Anton was the most mature group member and self-proclaimed father figure, even though he was the same age as the others. While Marlon was the shy guy or at least quieter than the others. He had a pure soul, and always sought to bring positive vibes to the team, something that was needed fairly regularly with the physics of so many big personalities in such close proximity. A waitress approached the dimly lit corner table where they were sat, "Gentlemen?" she said in a fresh Yard accent. They knew their orders by heart, 3 orders of Jerk Chicken, 1 ackee and Salt Fish, 4 x rice and peas, plantain and festival to share. She must have been new because one of the usual staff wouldn't have had to ask. To wash it down they went for 3 rum punch and 1 x Wray and Nephew and pineapple. Lyon was the ladies' man and had to do things differently, the salt fish and Wray Nephew were for him. He had the gift of the gab, and could talk his way into and out of any situation, the situation usually being a woman's heart and often further. He had one of those magnetic personalities, life and soul of the party, people just wanted to be around him.

"So, what's good, fellas?" Anton said warmly to the group.

"Same old. Life, love!" Jason spurted out unwittingly, he almost put his hand over his mouth, but it was too late. The entire table was staring at him. It felt like the DJ had stopped the background lovers rock and the entire restaurant was looking at him. Including a group of four White girls in the booth opposite, who had definitely been there for a while making the most of the happy hour offers; full of rum fuelled boisterousness, the level of their conversation nearly matched music from the speakers.

Jason's group tried to remain focused on the accidental bomb that he had just dropped, and not on the loud sirens sat across from them. "Excuse me?" Lyon said with a huge smirk across his face, practically salivating at the prospect of the *rinsing* that was about to take place. Jason was having trouble closing his mouth. He was slowly trying to mouth words that could be mistaken for love, but weren't that, his head was spinning *loaaath, loofft, light*, he thought to himself.

"Man said LOVE you know!" Marlon said at a high pitch. "Rah the L-word, the big L, early," Marlon said.

"Tell us more Romeo, who's the lucky lady?" Lyon pressed.

"Shh man it's nothing … it's a minor … just a date. I must have been watching too much Love Island," Jason replied sheepishly.

"Don't be shy now Jase, when should I buy my new hat?!" Lyon teased. The others at the table giggled along. Jason didn't take himself too seriously and could take a joke. This was part of group banter; on any given day you could be the butt of the joke. You just had to *man up* and take it, besides, it was usually in good humour.

One of the girls approached their table in an unstable way, the challenge of walking in heels post rum cocktails made her look more like Bambi on ice. She wasted no time inserting herself into the conversation, "Hi!" she demanded brightly, "I'm Christina, I'm over there with my girls and wanted to say 'Hey'," she continued, as she gestured to her group of friends, most of whom were smiling, except for one who had her head buried in shame. "Sooo, what are you guys doing here tonight? Having fun?" she asked.

Christina was clearly the ring leader of the group. Anton's eyes were rolling, Marlon wasn't sure where to look, while Jason was happy with the distraction. Lyon was also happy with the distraction, but for a completely different reason. He appointed himself as group spokesperson, as he usually was when it came to the ladies. Something the others were happy with in this case, as long as he didn't keep the conversation going too long. "We're just vibin', you know?" he said, "You guys come here often?"

"No, this is our first time, but we love the drinks, the music and food here, so will definitely be coming back," she said suggestively.

Anton shot Lyon a look that said 'wrap it up!' Lyon returned a gesture that asked for patience.

"Yeah, well you know if you like the food here, I'm an excellent cook, I can do ALL of this stuff!" he declared.

She liked his energy. "What about your friends, how are they in the kitchen?" she asked suggestively, with an air of entitlement that almost drove Marlon into a coughing fit. Anton was passing his fingers back and forth across his neck to suggest cutting the conversation. Jason had his head down focused on his phone, not wanting to encourage a scenario that would complicate things for him.

"They do alright, but I'm the main guy, if you know what I mean?" he said with a wink, "You know what, let me get your IG and I'll hit you up?" he offered

She swooned at his use of slang, but was disappointed by the lack of interest from the rest of the group, expecting more excitement from her offer; "Ok" she said with a smile as she typed her information into his phone, before heading back to her table to a chorus of shrill drunken screams from her friends.

"Anywayz!" Anton said, perturbed by the presumptuous nature of the girl, as if they should have been honoured that she approached. He was keen to bring the conversation back to Jason's new love interest.

Jason realised he wasn't going to be able to slide out of this one. "Yeah, you know, it was just a date, a good date, with a nice girl," he said coyly.

"Must have been a special date?" Marlon said. Marlon was a straight shooter; you knew where you were with him at all times. Very genuine, no agendas, but always hungry. "How long is the food gonna take, cha!" he grumbled.

"So, what is she like then?" Anton asked.

"She's nice, you know, she likes music, actually knows a bit about football too," Jason replied.

"Calm, calm, but what is she *like*?" Jason knew where this was going. Anton was all about Black love; he would get on to Jason from time to time for his more liberal approach to dating.

"Well, she's a human girl, she has dark hair, a nice smile, and a good bum. Is that enough detail?" Jason said sarcastically.

Lyon jumped in, "If she's got a good back, I'm bless, that's all I need to know, go tru!... Eh what happened to that baddie from your office? The mixed ting, Meghan Markle wannabe?"

Jason laughed to himself, Lyon did not forget a pretty face, "It was a non-starter, we didn't vibe." he explained casually. "Just one woman on my mind right now."

Lyon gave him a confused look that queried why you

would need to worry about vibe if a girl was hot, while trying to decipher why would anyone just want only one woman on their mind

Anton gave Jason a piercing stare. "Just be careful, you know what these Becky's can be like. You look like some anglicised version of 50 cent to them, but when shit hits the fan they won't be down for you like the sisters will, never forget that. And if she's got family P, don't get me started about how quickly she'll be missing when Mummy and Daddy threaten to pull the trust fund. But seriously, just be careful… A city full of beautiful sisters and man always ends up with Posh Spice." Anton stated, shaking his head in disappointment.

"I know, I know," Jason said.

"As long as she isn't bait, like those girls from earlier. Lord have mercy, Jarring man!" Anton finished.

The waitress brought the drinks over, a great time to change topics … "Who arda the Wray and Nevew?".

Meanwhile, across the city, Alice was sitting in her pyjamas on her flatmate Daisy's bed. Daisy was more than just a flatmate; she had become a close friend since they first met as trainee nurses on the hectic East London wards. Daisy was archly sincere and clumsy in an endearing way, she lacked a filter, which could lead to the occasional uncomfortable moments, but she wouldn't hurt a fly. The pair were eating popcorn and giggling like schoolgirls, as she recounted the evening before. "He's tall... But not too tall, good tall and well built, not skinny. Listen to me, like height is that important. He had such a nice vibe and we just clicked you know." Daisy was nodding along emphatically. "You know when you just like know. It's something good, different, meaningful. There was even a point in the night when a guy tried to approach me, kind of pinned me against the wall, but the way he handled it; strong, but composed at the same time, very assured." Daisy was ecstatic for Alice; the way good friends are for one another; as if Alice's success was also her own.

"We can talk about any and everything. No dead space. I know it's early, but it just feels good. And he has these deep brown eyes, and a lovely smile... He even smells good, can't even describe it, like a rich oak..." she sighed as if she had been blown up with love gas, and needed to release some before she popped.

"He must be special," Daisy said, it's not like you to be so smitten so early. "I'm really happy for you babe. So, when are you going to see him again?" Daisy asked

"I don't know, but hopefully soon," Alice said, no sooner had the words left her mouth did her phone buzz with a message from Jason. A smile immediately materialised across her face without even reading the message, *maybe she was smitten*, she thought to herself. However, her mood quickly changed when she was about to open the message from Jason, only to receive a message from her mum - "Call me when you can, Darling," the message read. Daisy sensed the change in Alice's energy, and decided that she may need some space. "Al, I'm going to make a cuppa, do you want anything?" she asked.

"I'm ok thanks Dais," Alice replied, appreciating her flatmate's intuition. She lay back on the bed and stared at the message, her mind began to wonder. Alice had a strained relationship with her mum, she was always more of a daddy's girl. At times they seemed so different, she often wondered if they were actually related. Her mind danced between opening Jason's message and thoughts of her mum.

As a teen, her mum had not been the most supportive character when it came to Alice's interests, nor her early taste in men, something that had followed her into adulthood. Her mother would constantly question her choices; from becoming a nurse, to moving to London and of course any man that did not match her ideal of a suitable partner she dismissed. Alice was swept up in the excitement of the early stages of courtship, as is often the way with those that give us the feeling of butterflies. Her romantic optimism had her already envisioning Jason as someone she would introduce to her parents, and while that image was very positive on one hand; knowing how her mother is, she would likely dampen her spirits. *Best not to get too ahead of myself,* she thought, *it might never happen.*

Eight

The Wrong Side Of The Law

The *Close* Council of the African Decent (AD for short) organisation sat around the table, as Abefembe, the head of the group began the presentation. "Quiet," she said in her calm but authoritative way, she got the desired response immediately. "We're going to discuss the proposals for the sub-team candidates, starting with the insights team." A selection of pictures and names filled the screen. These are the potential options that ranked highest against our metric analysis, unless there are any objections we will contact these first. Akira was shocked to see Jason's face on the screen, but even more shocked with what she heard next from Godfrey. Godfrey was a tall, strong, Cameroonian; he was educated in England from secondary school, following his family's escape from political turmoil. He was the prototypical Alpha male, Akira often sensed that he didn't like taking orders from Abefembe. "I know this guy," he said

"Excuse me?" Abefembe replied.

"I know Jason Andrews, we were at Uni together, I don't think he's right for the cause," he continued.

"And why is that?" Abefembe asked.

"Let's just say his level of commitment to his people is questionable," he replied.

Abefembe turned to Akira knowing the family connection, with a look that invited her to comment. Akira's defensive instincts kicked in, "Jason is one of the smartest young men we have, and he cares about his community," she said strongly.

"How would you know?" Godfrey challenged.

"Because ... He's my cousin," Akira shot back. The room fell silent. Akira wasn't sure if she'd done the right thing, is this something Jason would want?

The rest of the meeting went smoothly with only a couple of minor contestations on some of the other candidates. Abefembe closed the meeting, and the council filed out of the room.

"Akira, hang on for a minute," Akira was expecting to be pulled aside.

They waited until the room was empty, "What's up?" Akira asked.

"You must have been surprised to see Jason show up today?" Abefembe asked.

"You could say that," Akira replied

"He was on the recommended shortlist, he's got a lot

of potential, I thought you would understand," Abefembe continued.

"Yes, but he's still my cousin, you should have spoken to me first," Akira replied.

"Do I need to remind you that what we are hoping to achieve here is bigger than all of us?" Abefembe asked.

"You don't need to remind me of *anything*," Akira said, more firmly than intended. They both paused. "Just let me speak with him first, ok?" Abefembe nodded in response.

In many ways it was no great surprise that Akira had found her way to the AD or rather that it found her; some things are just meant to be. Akira was raised with a strong sense of history, in fact more than that, she was raised with the heritage of revolution. Her father, Richie's leading role in the Brit Panthers, meant her home growing up was a shrine to revolutionary forefathers of the Black Western struggle, and if she wasn't being schooled directly by her father or mother, she was subconsciously imbibing an environment of resistance.

Her largely inspirational childhood came with its own baggage, she spent many evenings comforting her worried mother, who stressed about whether that night would be the respective night the police finally caught up to him. Sadly, his Fred Hampton lifestyle did catch up with him, the police task force that had been tracking key members of the group for years finally caught up to him and other key members, the operation ending in a fire fight in which he was a fatal casualty. Akira was only a young teen when she had to endure the pain of burying her father, another Black life lost at the hands of the oppressors. Her tutelage and formative life experience galvanised her own anti-establishment journey; while she wasn't quite the revolutionary icon her father was, she did embrace the opportunity to be a part of the AD and continue her father's fight.

Back in Newham, Sargent Trevor Watkins had been dragged into his Chief's small office, along with two other even more senior officers, and a small man in a suit with rimmed glasses. The small man stood quietly in the corner with his back against the wall, holding a collection of files under his arm. The office had never felt so tiny to Sargent Watkins; so many bodies crammed in, a feeling of suffocation began to take hold, as he sat in the chair opposite his Chief.

Watkins had been on the force for nearly 20 years and knew the Chief well; he was sure he would have his back. "Trevor," the Chief began slowly with his hands tented in front of his face, seemingly struggling to find the right words. "Trevor… this is bad. I don't want to sugar coat it; the kid was 13 …"

"Officer Watkins interjected, "But he fit the profile… and looked suspicious…"

The Chief cut him off "Trevor, this isn't a discussion, times have changed, this isn't the good old days anymore. We have to maintain an image ... there'll have to be a trial, but you will be protected."

"I think what Chief Bradberry is trying to say is we need people to believe in the police force and act like there has to be ... accountability." The small man said, still leaning against the wall.

"You see Trevor ..." the Chief continued.

"I understand what he's saying!" Watkins shouted, momentarily forgetting his place. There was a brief pause. Watkins collected himself, "I was told I would be looked after, but what I'm hearing now is I have to get fucked because we've given this country to the Blacks and the Pakis."

"Trevor!" the Chief said feigning surprise and outrage at the remark. Watkins stood up and stormed out of the room.

The two chatted non-stop, and had arranged a dinner date for the middle of the following week. Jason was going to borrow his parent's car for the evening. He had to do a lot of sweet-talking because they were very protective of their chrome silver e-class Mercedes, which they both had worked very hard to afford. In return, Jason had agreed to cook them a special dinner at a later date.

Jason and Alice were both moderately health-conscious, and had spoken about the importance of balancing what you put into your body. Alice had actually spent a few years as a vegan before a stressful period in her life had forced her to quit. Jason planned to take them to a little vegan Chinese restaurant he knew about in the North-side of the city. The vegan substitutes there were really good, the place was authentic, and not in the least bit pretentious, which was something he wanted to reinforce about personality. This was another area where the two bonded, despite her comfortable upper-middle-class upbringing, Alice always managed to remain grounded. A genuine work ethic and respect for people from all walks of life had been instilled by her dad from a young age, who had grown up in a gritty working-class environment in the North of the country. His dad, her grandfather, had spent his life down the mines, before Thatcherism ended the industry. Their humble natures were one of the many areas of synchronicity for the pair.

Jason picked her up at 20:00. He climbed the stairs of the old local authority tower block and buzzed on the door. Daisy rushed to the door, expecting their guest and wanting to ensure she got a chance to give this dream guy an in-person once over before Alice had the chance to whisk him away. The door opened and a short, blonde girl with a full face of make-up, but a comfy tracksuit and slippers greeted Jason with a warm smile. This was not her date, but Daisy was not one to be caught looking sloppy, something she'd learned from her mum.

"Jason!" Almost shouting, but with a warm smile and energy. "Welcome to our humble *abode*," Daisy said waving her arm across her body, as she invited him in. Daisy was not in the least bit posh, she was a classic East London girl, born and raised, but was infatuated with all things regal and *high* society. She had binge-watched The Crown and Downtown Abbey on multiple occasions. The conflicting narratives of a quasi-cockney, and part overtly posh accent, which she stressed for visitors; mixed with the full face of make-up and lounge clothes was striking, but a disarming sight.

"Hi, I guess you're Daisy?" Jason said with a little chuckle. Alice had given him the heads up on Daisy, and her description was down to a T.

"I'll be down in two secs," Alice shouted downstairs.

"So, Jason, I hear you nearly dropped some guy, for stepping to Alice – good lad!" Daisy raised her hand to her mouth immediately, realising that probably wasn't the first thing you say to someone you've just met. Daisy, as sweet as she was, spent a lot of time trying to take her foot out of her mouth.

Despite Jason's briefing, he was still taken aback by her directness. "Umm ... kind of I guess ..." he said with an awkward laugh. In an attempt to redeem the situation, Daisy tried to change gears, "Would you like some water?" I hear you're taking Alice for a Chinky ... I mean to a lovely Asian establishment," she corrected herself in her best Queen's English.

Jason's mouth was wide open. Luckily Alice was finally ready and headed downstairs. "She didn't scare you off, I hope," Alice said with a smile as she hugged Jason and pushed him out the door, all in one motion, knowing the quicker they left the better. "Bye Dais…" Jason managed to say as he was ejected from the building. "Toodles," Daisy shouted sarcastically, while also giving Alice a not-so-subtle thumbs up before closing the door closed.

The pair left the tower block and Jason approached the car opening the passenger door for Alice. Alice unwittingly continued to walk, not expecting Jason to stop at the flash chrome car. "This is us," he said with a chuckle.

"Wow…" she said with genuine surprise. Alice was not new to nice cars, but had not thought Jason would be driving this. "What do you do again?" she asked, jokingly. Jason read the joke, "Very funny, but this isn't *mine*, it's my folks. Thought you deserved a carriage this evening," he said, with a formal wave to the open passenger door.

"Ooohh, my Prince Charming," Alice said sarcastically as she curtseyed, almost slipping on a discarded chocolate wrapper. Her natural, yet endearing clumsiness had Jason in hysterics.

The couple were driving along, lights of the city cast across the car. London was a very special place at night. He was playing Party Next Door in the background. There was an easiness between the pair. Even at this early stage, there was a comfort between them, which enabled them to have that chilled silence that was just tranquil.

"Where are you taking me?" She asked with intrigue and playfulness.

"It's a surprise" he said. She put her hand on his and smiled. About half an hour later they arrived at the restaurant. It really was a surprise, much more modest than she was expecting and dressed for. He really should have given her more clothing guidance. "I thought we were going somewhere more … ummm" she struggled to find the words, and didn't want to seem ungrateful.

"Sorry, I should have said you could dress down," he said calmly, even though he was also over-dressed.

He took her hand and they walked into the restaurant. It was homely, but busy. The Hostess knew Jason well from his previous visits, usually with friends. The welcome was frostier than it should have been considering he was a regular patron. She eyed them closely and shouted something back to the kitchen in Cantonese. Something Jason imagined to be *the Black guy is here… and he's brought a White girl*. The two workers exchanged some phrases and some laughs before she asked them if they wanted a drink.

"It seems … nice," Alice said, starting to seriously question his judgment. "I know they're a little chilly at first, but I promise you the food is great, and it's totally vegan. I thought you'd like it because you were vegan for a bit," she smiled, this was the kind of attention to detail and thoughtfulness that every girl dreamed about. They ate, chatted and laughed. Jason had a question, mouth full of faux crispy chilli beef, "hey, would you say you have a type?" he squeezed out between chews.

"What do you mean by type?" Alice replied.

"You know, a type, like certain things you look for or like in a guy?" Jason clarified. Alice's phone began to buzz in her bag, she decided to let it ring out and not be rude. Jason paused as people do when another person's phone rings during a conversation. "You can get that if you like," Jason said with a smile.

"No no, it will just be my mum or something, nothing to worry about," Alice replied. The phone stopped for a couple of moments and began again, just as Jason was about to open his mouth. "You sure?" He asked.

She started to feel a bit awkward, under the spotlight. "Ok, let me quickly check," She said, her cheeks beginning to flush. She took her bag off the side of the chair and pulled her phone out, 7 texts, 4 WhatsApp's and 3 missed calls, all from the same number. She quickly returned the phone to her bag. "What were we saying?" She squeezed out in a not so composed voice. "Oh yes types, well yeah … I guess a bit … I mean, I don't like the Ken doll look if you know what I mean," she said with a cute snort that Alice would slip out from time to time.

"So, you're more Travis Scott than Justin Bieber?" Jason said with a smirk.

"I'd say I'm more Idris Elba than I am George Clooney," Alice quipped.

Jason laughed; he loved her wit. He followed up, "I'm asking because of a debate I saw the other day on Insta, which suggested that people have an attraction based on their environmental conditioning. So, if you were exposed to a certain type of person a lot during your formative years, this could shape your attraction later in life."

She paused for a moment and considered the hypothesis. "I guess I've never given it much thought, to be honest ... I have been exposed to different cultures growing up and my dad was a big influence on me musically. He was really into Motown and pretty much anything soulful. Jason listened intently. "I guess that shaped my taste earlier on, I was always more into MTV Base, whereas most of my class were into Indie bands." Her eyes flicked up at a 45% angle to the left as she reminisced. "Oh, and I did have a poster of 50, from the Get Rich or Die trying album on my wall in Sixth Form!".

"How about you? What's your *type?*" she followed up, adding air quotes to the word type for effect. "Well, I kind of like what I like, I guess ... I try not to be too prescriptive. If I'm attracted to you I just am, or so I thought. But I've spoken to my cousin about this before, and she's a firm believer that our attractions are shaped by our environment.

The more I think about it, the more I think about what I was exposed to as a kid, movies, magazines, the schools I went to etc. Maybe there is some truth in it," he answered, almost in confession.

"Yeah … well maybe you watched too much Baywatch growing up, which is why you like me, I'm pretty much the spitting image of Pamela Anderson," Alice replied in jest, sticking her tongue out. Her dark hair, small chest and big bum were pretty much the antitheses of the 90s pop culture icon.

Another thing Jason liked about Alice; she had the ability to naturally disarm potentially tense situations with levity. Jason followed her lead and switched to a more light-hearted discussion about who was their favourite *Suits* character. He could not accept that Louis was misunderstood and actually had a heart of gold.

It was another great evening that went by too quickly, the way all the best evenings seem to. They settled up and left the restaurant. Jason felt that the staff were always happier to see him leave than arrive, but he was less sure whether it was because he'd paid, or the fact he was no longer on the premises. The irony of marginalised groups being discriminatory to other marginalised groups always fascinated him – the cycle of the abused becoming the abuser was present in so many walks of life.

Back in the car, Alice had asked to connect to the tunes so she could again demonstrate her great taste. She put on some old Frank Ocean, and once more slipped into an easy silence, each at peace in the presence of the other. Unfortunately, this peace was short-lived. Jason was coming off an A-road not too far from Alice's place when he saw flashing blue lights in his rear-view mirror, followed by the sound of sirens. He didn't often drive his parent's car, but had never been stopped before, so carried on as normal assuming the police car would overtake. However, the lights did not waver and the sirens seemed to be getting louder. "What's up with these guys?" Alice asked rhetorically.

Jason looked more closely in his mirror and could see the policeman was beckoning him to pull over. *Fuck*, he thought to himself. He slowly pulled the car over, the police car pulled in behind him. He shut off the engine, two policemen exited and approached Jason's car, one on each side. The Officer on Jason's side tapped on the window and Jason rolled it down.

"Evening young man. Where have you been tonight?" the lead officer said in an authoritative tone.

"We … I've been, I mean we were out for dinner," Jason said nervously.

The second officer asked Alice to roll her window down. She did. He leered at her in an overly familiar, almost predatory way; Alice squirmed in her seat.

"You guys having fun tonight?" he asked Alice and carefully scanned her up and down lasciviously, while intensely chewing his gum; it was clear that he was imagining her with no clothes on. She tried her best to ignore him.

"I see. Whereabouts?" the first officer asked.

"Archway," Jason forced out.

"Hmm ok, ok. This is a nice car, what is it that you do?" The officer asked in an accusatory fashion.

The question shook Jason; he felt violated and it stirred an aggressive response. "What does my job or my car have to do with you?" he responded sharply.

"Don't take that tone with me boy, or I'll have you in a cell before your girlfriend can say Stormzy."

Alice's unease and frustration began to turn to anger. She'd heard about situations like this, even seen them in films, but had never in her life had to endure this type of treatment. "What is this about? Nothing better to do tonight, *Officer*?" she said with sass.

"Shut your little mouth," the second officer said. Jason put his hand on Alice's to calm her down.

"Actually, we have seen a lot of luxury car robberies in this area, and your *friend* over here … fits the bill," the first officer said slyly.

The second officer chuckled at the assertion.

"So, a Black guy driving a nice car is automatically a criminal?" Alice shot back.

"It's ok," Jason said calmly, trying to defuse the situation.

"Clearly, you weren't raised with any respect," the first officer said to Alice, glancing at Jason with implied derision.

"I'd like to teach her some," the second officer lewdly.

"Let me see your license, *son,*" The first officer asked.

Jason gave over his license. The officer stepped away and mumbled into his radio. The second officer was leaning into the car, musty breath in Alice's face. "What is it with your generation? You can't seem to get enough of 'em. You should think more of yourself. Especially a pretty girl like you."

"Back off!" Jason said, coming to her aid.

"SHUT UP, I wasn't talking to you," the officer commanded.

The first officer came back to the car. "Ok, everything checks out, get off on your way, before I run some more checks and find out your wanted for stabbing some *Yooot,*" he said in his best *urban* voice; a poor attempt to be funny and patronising.

The second officer seemed deflated that they were letting them go so easy. He blew Alice a kiss as they left. Alice shuddered.

The drive home was silent, but not the tranquil silence of earlier in the evening, it was a charged silence; minds racing at 100mph, the car going well under the speed limit. Jason was shaken, with outrage and anger, as much as anything else. Alice put her hand on his as they made their way back to her place.

Jason pulled up near Alice's flat. The glow of a yellow street lamp sprawled across the chrome bonnet. They sat there quietly, waiting for something, but not sure what, neither person sure what to say. It was as if someone hit a pause button. I'm sorry," Alice said at last.

"Sorry for what? You didn't do anything wrong," Jason replied more sharply than he intended.

"I don't know… I just am … sorry you had to go through that," she said.

"This is the world we live in… Could have been worse, I guess," Jason offered.

The sad thing was she knew he was right. She put her hand on his cheek, turning his face towards her own. "I know I can't understand how you're feeling, but I'm here for you, however you need me," she leaned in and kissed him on the cheek, before slowly leaving the car. Jason just sat there for what felt like forever, replaying the incident over and over again. He leaned forward and placed his head on the steering wheel. He didn't shed a tear, yet somehow he felt like he was crying.

Nine

Home Truths

Jason was out of sorts for the next couple of days, even having nightmares about what had taken place a few evenings before. He felt so powerless, so hopeless, he hated it. The stop had affected him so much that dreams were starting to merge with memories. Jason did not have many reoccurring dreams, but there was one that resurfaced in times of stress. Psychologists suggest that most adult problems are connected in some way to childhood traumas. A memory that was forever lodged in his brain, was from when he was in year nine, hanging out with some school friends near a parade of shops close to the campus. This space was typically reserved for the year 11s, who would congregate close to the chip shop when they had free periods. Only the coolest younger kids shared that territory, and if you managed to gain acceptance on this hallowed space you had made it. Jason's charm, uniqueness and footballing ability meant that he was one of the few year nines who was accepted in the cool zone, achieving the status without having to leverage an older sibling, as many other younger students did.

As if in a VIP area of a nightclub years before their time, Jason and a couple of his friends were shooting the breeze near the chippy. The discussion flowed between football, girls and music freely. As they wound away the afternoon before they would have to head home and start their homework, a police car pulled up flashing its lights. The arrival of law enforcement was enough to send some students on their way; especially those who didn't want to answer questions about their smoking. Two officers got out slowly and began to talk to different groups of kids that were standing around the parade, the conversations with each group were pretty quick as they moved closer to Jason and his group.

While Jason was used to police coming around the block, usually messing with the older kids, he'd learned at a young age that they were not to be trusted, and at best to be kept at a distance. Jason's school friends, on the other hand, had a very different view, police were very much trustworthy, and definitely not something to be feared, so Jason was the only one who felt tense as the police approached, and began their questioning.

Jason put his head down as the officers arrived. "Gentleman, how are we doing today?" one of the officers said. The kids murmured in response. "Have you been approached by any kids selling drugs?"

Jason's friend Charlie was quick with a witty response, "We're a bit young for drugs officer." Charlie and Andrew the other gang member laughed away. The unwitting privilege of the pair was astounding to Jason.

An officer stood over Jason and asked him directly, "Do *you* know of anyone who is dealing drugs around here?" Jason kept his head down hoping the officer would move on. "Listen, boy, I'm talking to you! And I don't care what uniform you have on," He continued.

"Leave him alone," Charlie said, stepping in.

The other officer pulled his colleague away, "Let's carry on down the street." The officers returned to their car and pulled away. Even when living one side of his double life, it seemed he was unable to escape the other. Jason was visibly shaken up; there was something about encounters with the uniform that had him on edge in a way that he could not yet comprehend. "You ok, Jay?" Charlie asked, noticing that Jason wasn't himself. Jason barely registered the question, looking into the distance he nodded gently.

Jason's family, friends, and even his colleagues could tell that he was not his usual self. Jason wanted to speak to one person most of all when he needed comfort – his cousin,

Akira. He hoped speaking to her
like it usually did.

Jason slalomed his way throu[
pedestrians as he tried to escape the exit
station, the events of his date with Alice still i
his mind. A young man in a thin Black mac
against the side of the station, waiting patiently for h.
He caught sight of Jason heading out of the station, mak
his way through the crowds, he stood slowly and began his
approach. Jason clipped the elbow of an older lady he was
trying to dodge, she let out a shout in pain, he stopped to
check if she was ok, before spinning back on his path to
Akira. As he turned around he was faced directly by the
young man in the mac; he stared at Jason intensely. "Sorry,
do I know you?" Jason asked meeting the guy's stare.

"No, you don't young King, but we know you, and we
need a moment of your time," he said softly, but clearly.

Jason felt uneasy by the approach, "Sorry, not now, I'm
running late," he said politely, wondering who the "we" the
lone man was referring to, while attempting to sidestep him
to no avail as the man matched his movement, maintaining
his position in front of Jason.

"This will not take long and is of the utmost importance.
Are you for your people?" he asked firmly and somewhat
rhetorically. Jason paused without answering. He repeated
himself, this time a little louder "Jason, are you for your
people?!"

on was stunned to hear this stranger use his name, ..rted to look around to see if there were cameras, to see ..ey were being watched. His anxiety levels were rising ..ickly, paranoia started to kick in, he began noticing ..assing eyes glance at the pair, and then quickly away again; the way people do when they see a couple having a public domestic. Jason nodded in response to the question. "That's good, that's good because your people need you!" he said slowly and emphatically. Jason wished he would get to his point more quickly.

"You will have heard about the incident with our young brother Adrian Adebola, violently assaulted by the police. They have made it clear that it is on us to protect our community, are you down?" Jason motioned in agreement, hoping this would help speed things along and end the awkward engagement. "Well then young King, please join us at an upcoming meeting," the man offered him a shiny Black business card. Jason was losing patience, he grabbed the card from the guy, shimmied one more time, managing to evade him. The young man shouted down the street, "We look forward to you joining our mission!" Jason stuffed the card inside his jacket pocket, as he sped up trying to make up for lost time.

They met at their usual spot by the *river*, but strangely this time Jason was slightly early. Akira immediately knew something was up, this wasn't like him. "What's up Sprout?"

she said as she embraced him. He gave her a look in return to communicate that this wasn't the best time for nicknames.

"Ok that's not good ... are you going to tell me, or am I going to have to put you in a head-lock, like when we were kids," she said, trying to add some levity to the mood, not even sure she could actually reach his head without a foot stall.

He sighed, he didn't know where to start, his head was hung low. "Something happened the other night ... when I was out on a date ... with Alice."

"Wow, the emphasis on Alice, and an exciting event," Akira said, still trying to raise the mood.

"We were out for dinner... I was driving her home. I was in the car, must have been around 11. Then we get pulled over by the Feds ... And you know ... they're harassing us, making inappropriate comments to Alice, taking the piss out of me ... it was embarrassing... I felt small ... vulnerable. I knew the police could be fucked up, but I'd never experienced anything like that. It was peak," Jason recounted.

Akira sat in shock, not because she couldn't believe the story, but because she had never seen her cousin so shaken. Her blood began to boil; her protective instincts kicking in. She was no fan of law enforcement, and knew that harassment was not out of the ordinary, but it is particularly painful when it's someone you love. Akira went into solution mode, as she often did, perhaps this presented an opportunity to test the *waters* with Jason, but was it the right time …

"I'm sorry to hear that Cuz," she said as she gave him a hug, and just held him, the way she used to when he was younger, and was upset. She hated to see him like that. "You know these feds are messed up. Can't let us live in peace. Look at what they did to that kid the other day, he's still in intensive care … they won't hold you back though … they can't," she said softly. They sat and looked out across the river to the other side of the city.

"You know I hate to say it, but being with them … being with her will attract more attention for you. Even in this time, some people just don't want to see it," Akira said. "Do you hate to say it?" Jason replied. "She was there for me; she did well considering …" he continued.

"Considering what Sprout? Considering her people want you back on the plantation, and felt gracious enough to let you slide with a telling off?" she caught herself in mid-rant, remembering that he was still shaken up, and the victim in this situation.

A few seconds passed. "They'll never truly be there for you, not really … but anyway you do your thing, as long as you're happy … Still don't see why you can't find a nice sister, but imma stop," she said with a laugh.

Jason rolled his eyes and smiled. "You know what? It's times like this I wish Uncle Richie was still around," he said wistfully, fondly remembering his heroic uncle.

The comment hit Akira in her chest, any mention of her father was met with the pain of loss and warmth of love, "Me too... every day," she said softly. They both took a moment of personal reflection on their lost loved one.

"Sprout have you ever thought about trying to hit back?" Akira said, her mind cast back to seeing Jason's photo in the AD selection meeting.

"What do you mean, hit back?" he replied.

Akira sat and thought "No ... don't worry, it's nothing," she said. Spending time with Akira always made him feel better, even if the conversations were sometimes cryptic. They stared out across the *river* again as the sun began to set.

Alice was still in shock from the end of her date with Jason. It had felt so surreal, as if she were watching some sort of low budget film, did those things really happen? To real people? She had seen the stories on social media posts, the recounts from those effected but it was so different when it actually happened to you. She had no idea if she handled the situation well, did she say the right things? Was she supportive enough? Was she defiant enough? She just wanted to be there for Jason, but past experiences had taught her that at times it was best to tread carefully around sensitive topics, and part of her was scared she would say the wrong thing, making him feel worse.

The actual date was fun; she was really enjoying getting to know Jason. She felt that they naturally bounced off one another, conversation was easy. In an attempt to get herself to a more positive place she decided to reflect more about their time at dinner and not the horrific ending. Alice remembered Jason asking her about what kind of guy she liked; something she hadn't thought too much about, she just liked what she liked. She couldn't even remember where her feelings began, is it even really possible to pinpoint one moment... her mind began to wonder.

It was a rainy October afternoon, a day that always stuck out in her memory. After another day of obscurity at school, fending off the odd insult, while switching between trying to remain innocuous, or sticking close to Jane for protection, she couldn't wait to get home and barricade herself in her room with the latest Harry Potter book. She intended to slip in and go straight to her room, so as to avoid any conversation with any parent who may have been lurking downstairs. The creaky latch on the door betrayed her with a loud squeal as she pushed it open. "That you Rolly?!" her dad shouted from the living room as he heard a rusty latch screech. "Yes, Dad," Alice replied resignedly, while cursing her Dad's relaxed attitude to odd jobs around the house.

"Come in here, come in, I've got something to show you," he said excitedly. This was somewhat strange for her dad, who wasn't usually this excited unless he was watching the football, listening to music, or had a free Sunday afternoon to himself. Alice trudged into the living room to see her father feet up on his armchair, watching the TV with a big smile on his face. Great, called to watch dad watch TV; *very meta*, she thought to herself.

"Isn't it great," he said "just look at it."

"Look at what Dad?" she replied, slowly starting to think her father was losing it. "The TV! The TV! We have Cable! Over 92 channels, sports, music, documentaries, films, it's amazing! She got an insight into what he would have been like as a kid at Christmas. "And as an extra surprise, I got you one for your room too. Best not to tell your mum that too soon. He said with a wink."

Alice still couldn't tell what the hype was about, she was more into books than TV any day, but decided to indulge her father's happiness. "Ok dad, *Amazing!*" she said with strained enthusiasm. Her Dad was already lost again in the plethora of channels. Alice headed to her room, threw herself on her bed and began to read; *wizards were better than cable*, she thought to herself. After about an hour of reading, she cast an eye at her TV, and the new small black box that was sat underneath it; perched atop was a remote. *Might as well see what the fuss is about*, she thought. She switched it on and flipped through the channels… *boring, boring, lame*, she thought to herself - until she got to the music channels. There were so many, each for a different genre. The rock channel would have been ideal for her Goth phase, but there were other options now, other things to check out. Before she knew it her mum was calling her for dinner, she'd been transfixed watching the hip-hop channel. *This I like,* she thought to herself. In truth, it was more the RnB than the hip-hop that she enjoyed musically. There was an energy that was magnetic about the videos, a coolness and masculinity… and to her surprise, there was something about the guys … *they were not bad to look at,* she thought.

Ten

Sexual Healing

Jason needed some reconciliation following the incident with the police; he couldn't get it off his mind. On top of everything, the conversation with Akira was making him think twice about pursuing things with Alice. Maybe he had it all wrong, could he really be happy with someone from the other side of the table? Would an undercurrent of resentment based on years of oppression be an ever-present barrier between the two of them? He needed to speak to her.

Jason sent her a message inviting her over. The guys were out, Lyon and Marlon at football, and Anton had a church event. He needed the space and privacy to have a candid conversation. Alice had noticed that he was off since everything went down, but she didn't know how to address it. She'd dated Black guys before, and had experienced the odd racially motivated comment, but had never been through something so intense. She tried to cheer him up with some funny memes, but their usual playful dynamic was missing. When he asked her to come over, she was relieved because she wanted to make sure he was ok, that they were ok. She couldn't put her finger on it, but for some reason, she felt anxious about having to talk about the other night.

In truth, Jason didn't really know what he wanted to say, just that they needed to talk. She arrived bang on time, as she typically did, something Jason was learning to expect. She wore a pair of well-fitted grey jeans, a Black blouse, and a pair of Converse; effortlessly communicating a dressy casual vibe. He gestured to her to enter ahead of him, chivalrous, as he was raised to be. She walked down a short corridor to the living room. Music was playing quietly, it seemed to be some sort of Afrobeat track, but she couldn't place the song.

"Have a seat, you want a drink or something?" He asked.

"Water is fine, thanks," she replied. Not knowing what the tone of this night would be, and with work in the morning, she thought it best to keep a clear head. Jason brought the water and sat down on the sofa next to her. Not as close as she would have liked, but not far enough to make it awkward. She suddenly felt like she was struggling for words, her throat felt dry, she took a sip of water. Jason's palms were sweaty, unsure about how best to start the conversation.

"So, how's work going?" he asked.

"Not so bad, trying to save lives and not bite anyone's

head off," she gave a little laugh and let out a little snort, she raised her hand to her mouth, as if she could push it back in after the fact.

Her unintentional comedy put Jason at ease. "I guess decapitated patients aren't high on the NHS list of objectives this year," he said dryly.

"It's good to see you again, I've not been in the best headspace since the whole incident," he continued, "I think I just needed to talk about it."

She listened closely, careful not to interrupt him as he expressed himself; she always hated how certain friends would cut her off when she was speaking about something, especially when it was something important. He paused after every couple of words, struggling to articulate his emotions. "I just needed to try and figure out what I wanted to say, obviously it was a heavy experience. I wanted to thank you for being supportive."

"Stop," she said. "You definitely don't have to thank me. Those officers were Pigs. I was disgusted and ashamed," she followed quickly, inadvertently cutting him off. She realised and apologised.

"I wanted to thank you… but also let you know that it didn't make me feel great. I mean all this stuff… this shit gets to me," he said. He didn't think it would be this hard to say, to get off his chest, *RACISM!* he screamed internally. Perhaps it was because he didn't know her so well, but the words seemed to be stuck in his throat. "I don't know, I guess it can get in the way, make it hard for us... you know?"

She knew what he meant. Astute as ever, Alice could read between the lines. Even though he couldn't craft the right words, she could feel the sentiment. It was obvious to anyone who took the time to think about it; after experiencing something like that, and whatever else he had experienced, it's natural that he would have some reservations about their situation. "It's ok, I understand and if this isn't something you want to continue ... I get it." She said reluctantly.

He exhaled and looked at her, their eyes meeting and locking. Jason's mind was all over the place, he didn't know what was right or wrong, but at that moment he wanted her, he leaned in and kissed her. She was taken by surprise, but as soon as their lips met she realised how much she wanted it, needed it. She dropped her glass as she kissed him back, water spilling all over the sofa. He held her underneath her chin with one hand and kissed her more deeply, back and forth they matched each other, passion for passion. The flood gates were open, auto-pilot had kicked in. They began to undress each other, quickly, as if they were impatient teenagers, worried about being caught by strict parents.

She kicked her trainers off; he pulled her jeans off forcefully, and kissed between her legs. As he kissed, she shuddered gently. Jason wanted to slow down and enjoy the moment, but his heart was racing, imploring him to speed up. Alice pulled his top off, he lifted her blouse and kissed her stomach. She moaned and twitched; spellbound. They kissed again, rolling off the sofa and onto the carpet. An eternity seemed to pass, a time neither wanted to end.

Jason picked up speed and began to drive harder, almost too hard, but Alice just dug her nails deeper into his back, a mix of pain and pleasure they both embraced. When it was over she lay on his chest and listened to his heart; it was beating quickly, but firmly and despite the tempo, its rhythm was relaxing, she felt at peace. Jason was calm, Alice felt like a natural fit on his chest. He hadn't said exactly what he wanted to say, but he felt like a weight was lifted. Jason stared at his bedroom ceiling, as Alice drifted off to the sound of his heartbeat.

Jason lay on his bed, and just stared at the ceiling; the adrenaline was subsiding slowly. He heard some of the boys come back into the flat, he was quickly able to identify Lyon's voice as was typically the case, with him being the loudest, "Does it smell funny in here?" he heard him ask.

Jason rolled onto his side and looked out of the window, it was a clear night, he could even make out a couple of stars, which was always an achievement with the level of light pollution in London. Jason thought about his first time with Alice, he couldn't decide if it was good, great or something else. On one level he was extremely satisfied, her body did not disappoint; it was passionate and intense, but part of it felt wrong as if his head was in the wrong space. He had so much pent up frustration, sex had never been like that for him, it didn't sit quite right.

Alice opened the door quietly, hoping to slip in without Daisy noticing, after an emotional evening she was drained and just wanted to go to sleep. Unfortunately, Daisy had amazing hearing; Alice had always thought she'd be better off as a prison guard or some sort of human security system, "that you Al?" Daisy said, as if anyone else had keys to their apartment.

"Yeah, it's me," she replied.

"Fancy a cuppa?" Daisy followed up.

"No thanks, just going to head to bed, I'm beat," Alice said as she slipped her shoes off, and quickly headed upstairs. Daisy could sense something was up, practically smelling the gossip in the air. She sprang up off the sofa to confront Alice, but Alice was already closing her bedroom door.

"Ok, catch up tomorrow," she said suspiciously, it wasn't like Alice to run off like that without saying hello properly. Alice put her PJs on, she didn't want to shower and lose Jason's smell. She hugged one of her favourite stuffed animals, and let her mind think about their earlier embrace as a smile crossed her face, she was happy. It was as passionate as she hoped it would be, although it was a little rough at times, she decided that was something to fine-tune, she was looking forward to perfecting the process.

Jason lay on his bed waiting for his mind to settle, he studied his ceiling, examining the cracks in the paint work. *I should be tired*, he thought to himself. His mind seemed to be caught in a low buzz, as if it were a TV stuck on static. Then suddenly he realised he hadn't finished the questionnaire! *That might calm my mind*, he thought. He opened his phone browser and scanned back through previous web pages.

The program had saved his previous responses, allowing him to pick up where he left off. He took a moment to check his answers and refresh his memory. He was all set, but the next question caught him off guard; 'What is more important to you, personal compatibility or a person's physical attractiveness?' Compatibility was his gut reaction, but then he considered if it could ever be more than friends if there was no physical attraction. The questionnaire had similar questions, phrased slightly differently in an attempt to ensure people provided consistent responses. Jason wondered if he was sub-consciously editing his answers in an attempt to beat the algorithm and get a certain outcome, he dismissed the thought, deciding that it was a bit too meta, especially considering how late it was.

He went to the next question, he read it carefully, again catching himself trying to decode its underlying objective, reading between the lines - 'Have you ever felt less than or insecure because of your background?', 'Always, most of the time, occasionally, rarely and never', were the multiple choice options. Jason wanted to hit 'never', but caught himself and decided to take some thinking time. *The results will only be as good as the answers I put in*, he thought, reminding himself of an old Technology maxim, *GIGO – Garbage In Garbage Out*. As much as it pained him to admit it, there were times where the world, his environment... White people did make him feel *less than*; the Police stoppage was a clear example. It was not to say that this was his default mind-set, a feeling of inferiority, but it was an admission of the psychological and physical pressure racism can cause, often a burden carried without due consideration paid towards it. His finger hovered over the 'rarely' option, his mind began to race through a montage of microaggressions and instants of swallowed pride, moments of self-minimisation to make *others* feel more comfortable, at the last second he switched to 'occasionally'.

Jason powered through some simpler questions, as he approached the end of what was now feeling more like an interrogation. 'Is it more important for you to be happy with your partner or for your loved ones to be happy with your choice?', the question read. Jason's first reflection was that this must be aimed more at those from strict religious backgrounds. The answer like many seemed initially obvious, but on greater inspection required some thought. Of course he had to be happy about it, but then he considered what it would mean if his parents, Akira and his friends were unhappy with his choice. They'd never shown any strong aversion to the people he dated, although he knew that his mum and Akira would prefer if he was with a Black girl. His mum was much more subtle about it, but he could tell.

Ultimately she would want him to be happy, but ideally everyone would be happy with his choice...could they be happy with Alice? Did Alice make him happy enough to ignore his family? His brain began to throb, time to take a break.

He flicked back to the search page, as he browsed the options, he realised that if he wanted something a bit lighter he would have to settle for a social commentary of some sort, whether it be podcasters on social media platforms or some form of microblog. He opened a link to a video of a social commentator, one who was more afro-centric than mainstream, which for some reason seemed to add credibility. The commentator speculated on the amount of conditioning that takes place in the West, leading to the control of the masses, while socially engineering integration.

"You see, the thing is, when these guys get a bit of cash they flip, it's like it's part of the contract or something, they have to get with a YT (White person)," she said with passion, mixed with distain and humour. "It's not all of them, I guess, but it feels like most, right?" she asked her audience, triggering the chat function to spike with responses. She continued with her monologue "It's not just that these guys tend to pick outside the race when they become financially successful and famous, it's that these couples are amplified more so than those with Black partners are. This is not necessarily their fault, they don't control the media outlets, but we have to ask why the interracial couples are encouraged and amplified as they are?"

She paused for a moment, almost encouraging her listeners to also think about the question.

"You even see it in these stupid 'reality' love shows, they throw a couple of token Black guys in there who are only ever interested in White or mixed girls, the best they can offer the Black girl is *friendship*," her point triggered a huge spike in supportive engagement, hearts and thumbs up all around. "What message does that send to everyone watching? Your own dudes are not interested in you! No wonder some of these White girls try and take liberties when you're out."

As much as he wanted to, Jason could not refute her point.

"But, it gets deeper!" she exclaimed, "If that is the case what might be the objective of communicating the message that your most 'talented' (air quotes employed), most 'successful' men want to be with different women? Psychologically does that impact the masses of young boys and girls who see these images every day on social media?"

Jason could see she was postulating a trickle down type approach, where the few in the spotlight at the top of the pyramid could influence the many lower down.

She continued, stating that "over time, this promoted integration could take hold of the small diaspora population in Western countries leading to the phasing out of people of colour in the West."

It was a lot to think about, definitely not as light as he hoped, but all the exerted brain power did mean he was ready to call it a night. He opened his messages with Alice, clicked on her profile pic, he studied it while trying to also be mindful of what feelings were being evoked…would he pick her on a romantic reality show, in front of the entire nation, his family and friends, the thought made him feel uneasy, but underneath it she still triggered a feeling of warmth and happiness, *so confusing*, he thought. This is 'over-thinking' he told himself, time for bed. He turned his phone off and headed to sleep.

Eleven

A More Innocent Time

The heart rate monitor on the ventilator beeped quietly, as Adrian's mum sat curled up on a chair in the corner of the intensive care room. She had barely left his side since the incident; family members had brought food and fresh clothes at regular intervals. Despite being exhausted, she found it hard to sleep, she would nod off for moments at a time before her motherly intuition would bring her back round, sub-consciously keen to be awake, should her son need anything. Adrian was out cold, the doctors were unsure when or if he would recover, but his vital signs were stable, for now.

The sound of the door closing brought Adrian's mum back to life, she was startled but gathered herself quickly thinking a nurse or doctor had arrived, maybe with an update, instead she was met by a short woman wearing a Black knee-length leather trench coat. "Sorry to disturb you,

Miss Adebola. I'm from an organisation that is desperate to get justice for Adrian and other people from the community that have suffered at the hands of the system."

Adrian's mum was still slightly disorientated; it took her a moment to register what was happening. "Excuse me, who are you? You shouldn't be here; it's after visiting hours." She protested, unhappy with the intrusion.

"I know, I apologise, it's just I wanted to speak to you alone, without any interruptions." She responded earnestly. Adrian's mum studied the girl's face, she was young but sincere, and with the fortitude of someone much older, more experienced.

"Miss Adebola, our organisation can only imagine your pain, but we do share your frustration, we know that Adrian is not the first and won't be the last if things don't change, and that's why we're here," she handed her a business card, it was a shiny Onyx Black, there was a circular logo in the top right-hand corner, which was red with green circles around a Black centre. Below the logo read AD in gold letters, there was a phone number on the other side. "We believe the African Diaspora has suffered enough at the hands of the police and we are here to make a stand, by any means necessary," she continued. Miss Adebola looked blankly at the card, trying to process the information, still somewhat unsure whether she was having a dream, or if this was actually real. The girl could see that this was a lot to process. "Take the card, have a think about it, if you want to know more please call the number," she left almost as quickly as she arrived.

The staff cafeteria felt quieter than normal, but Alice could not tell why. She was on her afternoon break, eating yoghurt, and lazily thumbing through a gossip magazine. A story about a famous American couple had half caught her eye. An upcoming rapper had supposedly proposed to his reality star girlfriend, after less than two months of dating, with a huge diamond engagement ring said to be worth upwards of two million dollars, all of Hollywood was abuzz with excitement. The article contained commentary from members of the public, who were asked to give their thoughts on the legitimacy of the relationship, and early engagement. The feedback was mixed with some people celebrating the upcoming nuptials, while others criticised the intentions of the female reality star, suggesting that she was just in it 'for the money,' noting that it was common for 'these women' to go after high earning Black men; going on to state that it was 'unnatural' for them to be attracted to Black men because they were not raised around them. While part of Alice hated the salacious nature of these articles, with an air of shame, she had to admit she found them compelling at the same time - this particular comment got Alice thinking again about her own preferences; from her perspective there was nothing calculated or mischievous about her feelings, they were organic. When she thought about her younger self she released how unaware she was, if anything it was the music that she was most passionate about, her somewhat serendipitous relationship with *Urban* music. Alice sucked on her spoon finishing the last of her yoghurt, as she reflected; her mind taken back to teenage years.

Her mum burst into her room, determined to unload her frustrations on her only daughter. "Couldn't you hear me shouting you for supper?!" she shouted. Alice was sitting staring at her ceiling posters as she listened to Aaliyah's 'Are you that somebody?' trying to mimic the cool, dulcet tones. Alice slowly raised her head, lowered her headphones from her ears and looked at her quizzically, "Sorry, what Mum?"

"You and your bloody music," she replied as she scanned her eyes around her daughter's room and saw all of the various hip-hop posters. "You're worse than your father with music, I swear," she continued. Alice's mum was concerned about her daughter's *urban* music taste, but decided it would only be a phase, even if it meant that for the time being, her room had a few too many half-naked African American men for her liking; she did on some level find it more appealing than the hardcore rock music from Alice's Goth phase. "It's time to eat," she continued, "You would know that if you didn't have that garbage blasting in your ears. Hurry up and get downstairs before your food gets cold."

"Yes, Margret," Alice replied. She always said "Margret" in a passive-aggressive tone when she was upset with her mum, it had the dual impact of disrespectfully calling her mum by her first name, but also the less preferred version of her first name, as she would ideally be called Margot. She laid on her back and looked around at her posters, ignoring her mum, her mum did not understand her at all, how could she, Alice could barely understand the change she was experiencing herself, but she knew it was more than a growling love of RnB and Hip-Hop. Margot exhaled deeply and walked away, "If you're not down in 5 minutes, I'm giving your food to the dog!".

Margot decided to switch targets as she walked to the dining room and began to berate her husband. "You need to have a word with that daughter of yours," she said.

"Daughter of mine?" he responded quizzically as if he'd manage to magically create her on his own.

"Yes, daughter of yours. She's up there, head in the clouds, listening to that music again," she said.

"What music sweet pea?" he said in a saccharine tone that he knew would annoy his wife.

Margot rolled her eyes in frustration with her husband. She hated to admit it but his boyish mischievousness was something she always loved about him. "I guess this is what

I get for marrying a man who loves music," she returned in concession and with an element of appreciation.

"I don't think it's a good idea, I don't think we can trust him and I don't think we need him," Godfrey declared in the description of Jason.

"I know you two have 'history', but he is talented, and clearly meets the criteria for the support we need. I know you want to do everything yourself, but what we are trying to achieve here is bigger than any macho dick measuring, is that clear?" Abefembe fired back.

"Yes," he replied quietly, pride and ego sore from being batted down by his female boss. Godfrey left the room and decided to do some of his own research on Jason. If he was anything like the guy from Uni, he was not the type of man AD needed or wanted.

Part 2

Twelve

Happy Days Are Yours And Mine

Alice sat on the empty bus on her way to the hospital. The sun was rising slowly, as if it too was begrudgingly starting the day. One of the few good things about the early shift was not getting caught up in the rush-hour mayhem - a big city phenomena she was yet to adjust to. She scrolled through her Instagram feed as she yawned, mouth wide open, despite nobody else being around she still felt like she had committed a major faux pas. Her feed was full of posts about a Black footballer who had been caught cheating on his wife with three other women, somehow simultaneously. Alice shared in the outrage of all the female commentators under the respective posts, but also felt that it was somehow a weird achievement to keep so many women entertained for that long, *where did he find the time?* She thought.

She continued to peruse the comments, they were usually even more interesting than the respective posts, especially if mini arguments broke out between complete strangers, which happened surprisingly often. Alice began to pick up a theme; many Black women were highlighting this as another example of Black men cheating, apparently a common occurrence. Alice sat with the accusation, was that really true? *All men cheat*, she thought; moreover, anyone could cheat, women included, they were just better at hiding it. Her train of thought brought her to Jason, could he? *No, not her Jase.*

Things had been going well for the young lovers, *almost too well*, Alice thought. In an age of endless dating apps and social media platforms, was it actually possible to find romantic happiness without it being spoiled? Jason was a handsome, intelligent, successful man, he could have his pick of women, why was he interested in her? She wondered, in self-deprecation - or if he was actually into her, it couldn't be just her, there were probably other girls he saw, that messaged him – how could you ever really know? She caught herself in her own paranoia and tried to pull herself out… maybe it was her own guilt driving these thoughts.

Inevitable moments of modern day dating anxiety aside, Jason and Alice were closer than ever before; the quintessential Jack and Jill, young lovers embracing the honeymoon phase. The couple had *the talk,* and decided to be exclusive. Things were going so well they wanted to take the next step and meet each other's friends and family. Friends first of course, in many ways co-signage from the friends was more important than approval from the family. First up was Jason to meet some of Alice's friends. Alice decided she wanted to do this in the most efficient way possible, fortunately, Annabell a friend from home had a birthday coming up, which would cover most of her school friends, and a couple of her London friends. Somewhat annoyingly, Jane wouldn't be at the party as she was away on a family trip to the Bahamas. The party approach was a slightly risky strategy, as this crowd in her home town location could create an intense environment, but she hoped for the best.

As they sat on the speeding train heading for the home counties, Alice's mind began to wonder about the evening ahead, hoping her friends would not embarrass her, but also hoping that Jason would enjoy some time in the place she called home.

Alice's phone began vibrating in her bag, aggressively bringing her back to reality. She looked around, and gathered her bearings. Jason was absently flicking through his phone. She reached into her bag, saw the number and quickly hit decline, placing the phone back in her bag. Jason failed to properly notice Alice's smooth action.

"Are you sure you're ready for this?" she asked, deflecting his attention.

"I guess so, hoping I can handle some posh kids from the shires - you talk like we're going to war!" he replied with a smile, initiating their secret handshake that had developed randomly one Sunday afternoon, while taking a break from a Suits marathon - A spud, followed by a high-5, 2 backhand slaps, and ending with a little finger lock, like a 'pinky' promise. They held hands and walked into the fray.

The door was left open, this was the country after all and things were safer here. Jason was a little shocked, stopping to check if the lock was broken. "Come on," she said, pulling him in. The house was large with lots of people milling around everywhere. Alice made her way to the kitchen as she guessed most people would be in there, or be in the Garden. Commercial Indie music played softly in the background as people chatted away to one another. Alice suddenly heard someone call her name in a distinctive high pitch tone that she immediately recognised.

"Alice! Alice! I thought that was you! Come over here, I haven't seen you in aagggeeess!" It was Annabell the hostess for the evening, who in addition to a pixy like voice tended to hang on to certain words. "And who is this strapping fellow", she continued casting her eyes up and down Jason.

"Annabell, so good to see you!" Alice's voice had suddenly risen a few octaves. Jason nearly choked on his drink when he heard her new tone. "This is my boyfriend, Jason," She said with a smile.

"Nice to meet you," Jason said in an attempt to match the formality of the room, as he shook her hand.

"No, kisses darlinnnggg, we're all family here," Annabell said, as she dragged him in for a kiss on each cheek.

"How is life treating you? Are you surviving with the N-H-S," Annabell said, seemingly spelling out the word letter by letter. Annabell, like everyone at the party, had come from a comfortable background; now this did not make them bad people, but it did mean they had a certain perspective on life. Everyday things like public healthcare were quite alien to them, and the fact that someone from their flock would choose to commit their life to, tough, relatively low-paid work in that type of establishment bordered on bizarre.

"Yes, I still very much enjoy being a nurse, thank you," Alice replied through gritted teeth.

"Wonderful, well at least you've finally met someone … oh is that Marie, I must say hello, have a great time, make sure you try the Quiche, will catch up with you both later," Annabell said as she rushed off to her next conversation.

Alice was somewhat relieved; it was one of the more challenging conversations they were likely to have this evening. They made their way to the canapés, made a quick stop for supplies before they headed out to the garden. The garden was beautiful, expansive and well-kept, with at least three different fountains, by Jason's current count. As they walked down the stairs, Alice spotted Colin. Colin was what many considered to be a sweetheart, always trying to fit in, but not quite getting it right, yet harmless all the same. She figured they would go and say hello.

"Hey Colin, how are you doing?" Alice said warmly.

"Alice, how are you doing? It's been so long," Colin said, giving Alice an affectionate hug.

"I'm well, thanks. This is my boyfriend, Jason" Alice said, motioning to Jason, who shook his hand. They walked together over to the fire pit that was starting up.

"So, what's life like in the big city?" Colin asked Jason as if you needed a spaceship to get to London, when in fact it was only 90 minutes on a direct train from their village.

"It's busy I guess, lots to do, great energy and vibe." Jason loved London, and couldn't imagine growing up anywhere else.

"Who do you support?" Colin asked.

"I'm a Palace guy," Jason replied.

"Nice. I'm an Arsenal fan, grew up with Ian Wright, Kevin Campbell... Pat Viera," Colin said wistfully.

Jason was pleasantly surprised, especially by the *consistent theme* of his favourite players, he chuckled to himself. Alice was happy to see Jason comfortably hold his own in the convo, but thought she would change the topic to something she could also contribute to. "Colin is into music too, aren't you Colin?" casting her mind back to when he tried to dye his hair to look like Eminem, but instead it came out more of rusty orange.

"Oh yeah, who do you like?" Jason asked.

"I used to be into hip-hop, but I'm mainly Grime now, you know, *Skeppy and dem man*," Colin said in his best *urban* accent. It was Alice's turn to choke on her drink, she wished she'd never brought it up.

Jason actually liked his passion, continuing as if everything was totally normal. "I like Skepta too, and some of the guys from *The Movement*, have you heard of them?" Jason said.

"No, can you send me some of their stuff? What's your Insta?" Colin said, excited at the prospect of making a new friend.

Alice smiled at Jason's patience and compassion, even for complete strangers. She caught herself staring at him as he conversed away with her friends, a warm feeling glowing from the pit of her stomach, emanating throughout her body; it hit her, she was in love. It had been so long since she had this feeling, she was unsure if she had ever felt it quite like this. As she embraced her new found happiness, she had the daunting realisation that Jason may not feel the same way. Alice decided to keep the revelation to herself, at least until she was sure it was reciprocated.

The party rolled on, the music got louder, and as people drank more the conversations got louder. They'd spoken to a lot of different people; Jason's head was starting to spin from all the names and introductions. They managed to get into a group chat by the conservatory, which was starting to take a political turn. "All I'm saying is we need to be careful about our borders, we don't have an infinite amount of resources, we can't look after the world and his wife," A tall, podgy man with blotted pink skin, named Andy said emphatically in a haughty, soapbox tone. Jason had predicted that this type of conversation may come up, and was fully prepared, he was not going to be baited.

Andy continued, "I mean look at the police force, stretched up and down the country, you guys must see it in London, you can't feel safe," he said gesturing to Alice and maybe Jason, but definitely more Alice.

"I suspect Alice feels VERY safe." A girl said suggestively, glancing seductively at Jason. Her boyfriend gave her a glare that suggested he was less than impressed. Alice felt under the spotlight, obligated to comment. "Well London is a big city, with lots of people, it's impossible to feel safe all of the time," she said, with her best attempt at a bi-partisan response.

Andy did not get the hint. "Exactly, you don't feel safe, how could you," he said rhetorically. "Look at these kids running wild on the street, and when an officer tries to do his job, and keep some order, he gets a wrap on the knuckles," This was the first time Jason had heard someone refer to the Adrian Adebola case in that way; actually on the side of law enforcement. He realised that everyone in his circle had very similar views, and that of course there had to be an opposing view. Even in a situation like this, where a teenage boy was in the hospital hanging on for his life. The entire group seemed to be waiting for Jason's contribution; it was his time to shine. He just wanted to break the awkward silence at this point. "I think all our public sector workers deserve to be looked after better, but it's also important that we hold those who are entrusted with protecting society accountable of that responsibility," he said turning to Alice, and holding her hand. *Can't box me in*, he thought.

"Of course, of course," the group seemed to agree in unison.

A couple more drinks and it was time to go. They said their good-byes, the longest of which of course was with Colin, who made Jason promise to keep in touch, closely followed by Annabell who wanted to have brunch with them both soon. Alice rested her head on Jason's chest, as they sat on the train back to London. "Thanks for coming today, I know it was a bit intense."

"Ha, there were some interesting people for sure, but it was fun," Jason said. She was fast asleep before he could finish his sentence.

An evening or two back in the village was nice, but Alice always yearned for more or at least something different. It was as if at her purest form she felt slightly out of place when she was there, even from a young age. Perhaps that was partly why she enjoyed being in bigger cities so much. When she thought about it, she was most at ease back home when she was with a friend like Jane, and even this evening's party was much more enjoyable because of Jason.

Thirteen

Take It To The Streets

The summer was growing warmer, as seemed to be the way in recent years with the effects of climate change, it was shaping up to be another particularly hot few months. Tensions were also growing in Adrian Adebola's borough and further afield, he was still in intensive care, and the local police and government had failed to provide sufficient reassurances to a threatened, and vulnerable community. Skirmishes had broken out across London, and a march to the local police station was set for the coming Saturday.

Jason was visiting his parents, he was in the midst of helping his mum wash up after dinner, they had the radio on in the background. The song ended and the host began to speak, "That was Jimmy Cliff, 'The harder they come'. I hope you and your loved ones are safe and well. We give a thought to those who are not. This brings me to an important announcement – Don't forget this Saturday, we

114

will be supporting the Adebola family by marching to the Newham police station, in demonstration of the horrible abuse, our young brother Adrian suffered, as well as so many others up and down the country. Be sure to join us at the corner of Brackwell Street at one pm, don't be late."

"Are you going to the march?" Jason's mum asked.

"I'm not sure, maybe," he replied.

"You know these things are important Jason, how many times have I told you about the people who have sacrificed for the liberties you have today?" she said passionately. Jason's mum was an erudite woman, who was well versed in Black British, African, African American and Caribbean history. She'd always made sure that Jason knew his history whilst he was growing up.

"I know mum, I know it's important, I'll probably be there," Jason said earnestly. "You should take your girlfriend. If you're really serious about her, she should be able to be there with you at events like this," his Mum finished. He'd finished drying the dishes, and headed up to his room. He checked his phone and there were some messages from Alice, seeing how he was doing, and also sending some memes from Insta. They had a very similar sense of humour, something he'd struggled to find in a girl, until now. He lay on his bed, and played some music; he was listening to some Issiah Rashad, as he relaxed and began to WhatsApp with Alice. They went back and forth about their day, as Jason thought about whether he should invite Alice to the march on Saturday or not. This was a tricky situation for Jason, it was a sensitive topic, and he didn't want Alice to feel obliged to go somewhere where she may not feel comfortable. After all, he knew she was a kind and caring person, but this wasn't her fight per se, or at least he couldn't assume that she would think it was.

"Hey, I've got a question," He said. "You know the situation with Adrian Adebola?" "Yep, it's so sad what they did to him," Alice said, "It's messed up."

"There's a march this Saturday, going from the Townhall to the local police station. I think I'm going, and wanted to see if you wanted to come?" There was a slight pause as Alice processed the question.

"Of course, I'll come," she blurted out, a bit too enthusiastically as if she'd been invited to a gig. Alice realised that this was quite a big thing for Jason to ask, and signified what he thought about her, in a strange way she felt honoured.

Saturday came around quickly. Alice was up early that morning trying to figure out what to wear, she had emptied the contents of her wardrobe on her bedroom floor, again. She felt more pressure picking her outfit today than she did with their first date. What do you wear to a march? she asked herself. Daisy pushed into the room, hearing all the noise from the kitchen, but the door didn't open very far from all the clothes on the bedroom floor.

"What are you doing up here? Looks like a bomb has gone off," Daisy said.

"I'm trying to figure out what to wear to the march. I don't really know," Alice said. "Just wear something comfortable, and not too bright," Daisy suggested calmly. Daisy had many ditzy moments, but now and again she would come up with a nugget of profound common sense. *She was totally right,* Alice thought. Alice put on her gym leggings, a comfortable top, smart trainers, a light, smart coat and headed for the door.

They met up at the Townhall at about quarter to one. Crowds were starting to gather, voices rumbling, some people had brought portable speakers, music was playing and the spirits were relatively high. Placards were starting to spring up, some people were wearing t-shirts with Adrian's face and the slogan 'No justice, No peace' on the back.

Jason gave Alice a hug, "How are you feeling?" he asked.

"Mhmm, Ok, I guess. I've never been to a march before," she conceded.

"Ha, you don't say. Don't worry, we'll just walk along with the crowd, there isn't anything to it. And you'll get to meet the boys," Jason said as reassuringly as he could. The march was a lot to take in, meeting his friends too felt like it could be sensory overload, 'In for a penny, in for a pound.' Her nan use to say.

They were moving along slowly with the crowd, absorbing the environment as they went. A chant started by someone with a microphone caught Jason's attention, as he turned, something else caught his eye in the crowd, it was hard to tell from his angle, but a girl looked like Akira. Automatically, without any conscious thought, he grabbed Alice's hand and made his way to her. Akira was supposed to be at the march too, but had told Jason she would be with her own friends, and unlikely to be able to meet up. He hoped that wasn't because he was with Alice. Jason tapped the girl on the shoulder, she spun around startled, it was Akira. She was with two of her friends; it took her a second to gather her thoughts. "Sprout! You made it," she said warmly, giving him a hug. "You know Patrice and Tanisha," she said introducing him to her friends, she then realised that someone was standing behind him, she peered around him seeing a short, attractive girl, "Who's this then?" fully aware that this must be the magical girl who had her cousin smitten.

"Right, this is Alice," he said, standing aside and gesturing towards her, she gave a timid wave. The girls studied her intently; she could feel the heat from the assessment.

Akira smiled through slightly gritted teeth, while one of her friends gave a 'Mhmm' sound that meant 'Oh, this is what you're into.'

Jason picked up on the energy, this probably wasn't the best environment for them to meet, he needed Akira to be able to have a conversation with Alice, see that she wasn't just some basic White girl after any Black guy. As if being saved from above, Jason's phone rang, it was Anton letting him know that the guys were up ahead if he wanted to meet. "That was Anton, we're gonna link up with them, see you guys in a bit," he said quickly, giving her a swift hug and departing off in a different direction, almost all in one movement. Akira waved as Jason and Alice disappeared into the crowd.

"The guys aren't too far ahead, ready to meet them?" he asked.

She wanted to seem positive and fit in, "Of course," She said brightly, with perhaps too much enthusiasm to seem credible. Jason knew it would be a lot, but also that the guys were harmless. He caught sight of Anton and the others, and weaved through the crowd dragging Alice behind. "Yes boys!" he said, greeting the group, a selection of hand-shakes ensued.

"And who is this lovely lady?" Lyon said gesturing towards Alice, it didn't surprise anyone that Lyon was the first to break the ice, it was one of the benefits of having him as a friend, he was never phased or nervous in social situations. Alice blushed at the introduction, and waved gently to the group. The wave wasn't going to be enough, for Lyon at least, who followed up with a big friendly hug, almost lifting her off the ground. *That happened*, she thought to herself. Thankfully the other guys were more chilled, giving more relaxed greetings. They began to speak amongst themselves, not leaving Alice out, but not swarming her either, she felt quite comfortable enough with the group considering it was their first meeting.

Naturally, some questions came her way about what she did for a living, how they met, some jokes from Lyon about how troublesome Jason could be. Diverting her attention to the guys was a nice way to make the march less intense.

A local community leader and march organiser stood on a bench with a megaphone, and addressed the crowd, "Thank you all for coming today! It means a lot to Adrian and his family." She gestured to her side where Adrian's parents and siblings were standing, arms around each other's backs forming a wall of solidarity. "We are here to demonstrate against the injustice that has befallen young Adrian, his family and thousands of others up and down the country, and around the world. We say ENOUGH! Today we make a stand and say NO, to the brutalisation of our people, of our children!" The crowd roared in unison; fists went up in support.

Alice felt herself being moved by the energy of the crowd, also throwing her fist up in support. She then caught the eye of a couple of girls looking at her in a judgmental way, causing her to sheepishly pull it down. The organiser spoke for a few minutes more, and ended with the chant 'No justice, no peace, no justice, no peace,' as she lead the crowd on the march to the police station, the crowd singing along.

As they walked, Alice was transfixed by the scenes

around them, so many different types of people, some hipster, some more classically revolutionary, to those that would fit a more stereotypical gang look - all here to show their support for Adrian. It was as if she was being given a glimpse behind the curtain. She was not the only White person there, but she still felt an element of fortune at being able to attend all the same.

Alice's phone began to ring, she ignored it, waiting for it to stop, assuming that the noise of the crowd would drown it. It kept ringing. Jason looked at Alice, "I think that's your phone?"

"Is it? Oh, you're, right," she said, blushing guiltily. She pulled her phone out of her bag, looked at the screen and hit cancel. "Nothing important," she said, linking arms with Jason.

People began singing, a warm rendition of *Buffalo Soldier* had swept over the crowd. Jason hummed along. Before they knew it an hour had passed and they were at the Police station. Blockading had been across the door in anticipation of the march. The Chief organiser had climbed the steps of the station and began to speak again. Jason was more vocal this time in his responses to the chants, Alice could feel the energy intensify and followed suit. The placards waved and the crowd cheered, as Adrian's mum took the steps to give a heartfelt speech.

"Thank you all for coming today, it means so much …" she paused as the emotion passed over her. "Adrian is only

14 years old. He's a good boy, he's my boy … our boy (as she glanced to her family) and he didn't deserve to be treated like this by the very people who are supposed to be protecting him," she began to snivel.

"I came to this country when I was 14… and I remember the injustices I suffered, and what people like me had to go through growing up, things are supposed to be better! They are not … Today we make a stand. Today we say no more. Today is for ADRIAN AND ALL OF OUR CHILDREN!" She shouted. The crowd roared in agreement.

Jason noticed a small group of people in black coats that had gathered to the left of the stage, most were in caps, and various types of black hats, some were wearing hoodies. It was hard to make out the faces through the crowds but he was sure that he recognised a face, it had to be, yes, the guy who approached him outside the tube station. As if by magic, the young man turned, and looked directly at Jason, catching his eye; he gave him a subtle nod of recognition, as if he'd known Jason was there the whole time. Alice could see that he was transfixed on something, "Are you ok?" she asked, unsure if she was intruding on Jason having a moment of reflection, at this emotional time. "Yeah, I'm fine, just thought I saw someone," he replied, taking her hand.

Alice felt the passion of the crowd and the injustice even more so. She had never experienced anything like it. *Why have I never been on a march before?* she thought to herself. She never had a reason to protest before, there had never been anything that challenged her existence in a significant way. The realisation brought on feelings of guilt and embarrassment, but there was a part of her that fought against these negative emotions, after all, it wasn't her fault that things were the way they were. She was a *good* person in her own right, never tried to harm anyone. But she couldn't shake it, she had never been subjected to, or known anyone subjected to this type of injustice based on their skin colour alone ... she looked around and wondered if she would ever be able to truly identify with that reality, while a smaller, yet firm voice in the back of her mind wondered if she should have to.

Godfrey sat at his laptop skimming through Jason's various social media accounts, he was pretty active he mused, unsurprising for someone like Jason, who always enjoyed being the centre of attention. *Likeable*, he thought of the description some people had given him at the African and Caribbean Society (ACS), more like hollow. Godfrey saw lots of pictures with friends, and family having fun, at least he had some Black friends. "Here we go, here we go..." as he came across pictures with Alice, "One minute you're posting about injustice, but you're in bed with the enemy, same old Jason, some people never change.".

Fourteen

Big Little Lies

Alice was exhausted by the time she made it home. The march, meeting Jason's friends, Akira, had really taken it out of her. She lay sprawled out on her bed and stared at the ceiling. The moonlight drifted in through her partially open curtains and cast across her bedroom wall. It was quiet, giving her an opportunity to let all the thoughts from the day wash over her, there was a lot to take in. Despite the importance of the day, the significance of the new perspective, and the experience she had received, she was troubled by the call. *I can't keep ignoring it*, she thought to herself, *I need to sort this out once and for all … but how? He just won't listen.*

About 18 months before, Alice had met a guy on the underground. She remembered being sat on a fairly quiet carriage on a Northern line train heading towards South London. Sat across from her was a tall guy in a cap that tipped 45 degrees, covering part of his face. He was absently thumbing through his phone, while she was reading her book, but was somehow distracted by his presence. She found it hard to focus, and kept catching her eyes drift up from her novel. Almost in sync, his eyes were also slowly transcending the top of his phone, to catch a sneaky look at Alice. In London of course this is a subtle art, if you get caught staring at the wrong person in the wrong way, it could be trouble. They finally caught each other's gaze and smiled at one another. He gestured towards her in a way to ask if he could approach, she read the motion and just blushed and smiled in response; that was enough of a green light for him to approach. Alice was impressed with his confidence, she'd only ever had weird guys approach her in public, but here was a handsome and assured guy. He introduced himself as Damian, was charming, funny and sweet... in the beginning at least.

They seemed to have a good connection and went on a few fun dates. He was easy-going, chilled, and made Alice feel protected; a feeling she didn't know that she liked. When they were intimate it was amazing; like nothing she'd experienced before, he really made her feel weak, despite the intimacy only being physical. Then almost as suddenly as meeting him that night on the tube, things began to get strange, he changed. He became controlling, less complimentary and at times aggressive, Alice didn't know what to do. At first, it was the shock of the change that took her by surprise.

On one occasion they were out for dinner, and she made an innocent comment about one of the waiters, she hadn't even registered what she said at the time, but she soon would. He was silent all the way home. When they arrived at his place he slammed the door, pushed her against the wall, stared at her, and began to shout, don't you ever embarrass me like that again. She was petrified; she didn't know if he would hit her, or what would come next. The fear of what might happen was only matched by the terror generated by her surprise at the outburst.

He began to blow hot and cold with her; she was constantly on edge. Alice found herself changing with him, she wasn't herself, everything she did was to please him. After one of his explosions, he would apologise, and become the sweetest guy ever ... for a time, but then it would happen all over again. She tried to reach out to him and get a better understanding of what was happening, but he would never let her in, at best he would say he was under pressure at work, or that there were financial issues. If she offered to help it would make him angrier as if her trying to be supportive was an affront to his manhood.

The *situationship* began to take its toll on her, she was constantly drained, she looked terrible, and her friends and family began to notice. When she was confronted about her poor health, she would play it off and claim that everything was ok, but Daisy could often hear her crying herself to sleep after her regular arguments with him.

Alice finally gathered the strength to leave, it took so much out of her to do it, but she did. He threatened her, pleaded with her, promised to change, everything under the sun to get her to stay; but it was too late, she'd seen too much. Like an addict going through withdrawal, it wasn't easy, she ended up taking some time off work, but as the days and weeks passed she started to feel like her old self, perhaps even stronger than before.

Now she'd moved on, met someone new, in love and happy – he pops up again, *it's always the way*, she thought to herself.

Jason was chatting with the boys on the group chat after the march. "Nice to meet the special lady" Marlon said. Everyone agreed. "You look very sweet together," Lyon said with a tongue emoji. Lots of crying-laugh faces followed by the other group members. "Keep laughing guys, but I'm happy," Jason replied with the sun-glasses emoji.

"You know it's all jokes bro, we're all really happy for you and she seems like a real one," Anton said sincerely, a response Jason wasn't expecting so soon from him. Unanimous agreement followed from the group.

"One thing, not trying to be funny, but I swear I've seen her somewhere before," Lyon said.

"Bro, you think you've seen every girl in London somewhere before, isn't that usually your opening line? Lol," Marlon said. Everyone laughed in agreement.

"Ha maybe you're right, ignore me," Lyon said.

While Jason was happy with how things went with Alice at the march he was unsettled, and slightly intrigued by seeing his new acquaintance in the Black coat. Did he know he would be there? He crossed his room and found his jacket draped over a chair, he reached in and found the AD card. He studied it closely, spinning it around in his hand slowly. He looked at the number, thinking about calling, *but why?* he thought to himself, *what's the point?*

Jason usually aired on the side of caution, but he was struggling to fight the intrigue. Why not call, he said to himself, what's the worst that can happen? He dialled the number and placed the phone to his ear; it rang three times and then someone answered without saying a word. Jason broke the silence, "Hi, I was given this card and told I should call … " he said.

"Hello Mr. Andrews, we've been expecting your call …"

Fifteen

Friends Of Friends

Jason was happy that Alice seemed to fit in fairly well with the guys; sign off from the boys was important. However, the march environment was not the most social setting; not the best for conversation and getting to know someone, so Jason was happy to take Daisy up on her suggestion to meet some more of Alice's friends, by hanging out together as a group. Jane was having some drinks in town, and was open to Jason and his friends joining them.

Friday came about quickly; Jason and his friends were having some pre-drinks before meeting up with the girls. Jason had provided the bottles as it was kind of his night, one bottle of Wray and Neph, 63% Jamaican White Rum and one bottle of Ciroc Vodka. They would have to take it easy with the Neph as they needed to be on best behaviour for later in the evening. Lyon loved a drink, and his wrists were notoriously loose when pouring up.

"Take it easy! It's a long night, and I know what you're like already Lyon," Jason said.

"What does that mean, you know I'm always calm and in control, look how well behaved I was the other day at the march," Lyon replied with a cheeky smile.

"Well, yeah a protest against racism isn't the best pick up scenario, even for someone with your *expertise*; you can get up to a lot more mischief on a night out, especially if you have too many Nephs, let's not bring up that time you came to visit me at Uni," Jason said with a laugh.

"The night we never speak of?" Anton said.

"The night we never speak of ..." the group replied in harmony as if it was some sort of clubhouse code word before they all broke out into laughter. Anton connected his phone to the wireless speaker, and put on some music. Anton enjoyed different types of music, but he was currently going through a phase of UK Grime, and a bit of Drill. The deep base kicked in from the speaker. "Eh what's the tune called?" Marlon asked.

"Don't watch that," Anton snapped back with a grin as he vibed to the tune in his seat.

Marlon rolled his eyes in response, "You always want to be the DJ!"

"That's because I have the best taste, bro, you know that ha!" Anton declared confidently, as he continued to Jam.

Marlon decided to go with a different approach, "So,

Jase, what's the chat with these girls? Are we your three wingmen, Black-man and three robins or what?"

"Why say it like that? We could at least be the Justice League!" Anton added.

"And I'm superman!" Lyon chimed in. Everyone broke out in laughter. "Why is that so funny, you haven't noticed the gym gains?" he said as he flexed his slim arms. "Actually, I'd rather be Aqua Man, he gets more girls anyway," he continued.

"Well, we just thought it would be cool if the two groups hung out. Alice and I vibe, so why not all of us," Jason said rhetorically.

"In case you haven't noticed, we're not all like you Jase, we didn't all do the Uni thing, and speak the *Queen's English*," Anton replied, pretending to drink an imaginary teacup with his pinkie finger extended towards the sky.

"What's that supposed to mean? I'm very refined... init," Lyon responded sharply now stroking his thin goatee with this thumb and index finger.

"You can't spell 'refined'," Jason snapped, "but it doesn't matter, this isn't some kind of test, it's just some guys and some girls getting a few drinks, it's not that deep."

"Exactly, drink! That's the first sensible thing you've said all evening," Lyon said as he raised his glass and began a toast, "To Jason and his Mrs, may they both be very happy in multi-cultural paradise!" he exclaimed, in a very sarcastic tone. The guys raised their glasses and began to drink.

The drinking session was a short one, as they needed to be in town before the bar got too busy. The girls were halfway through their second bottle of wine when Jason and the team arrived. Jason dropped Alice a text as the queue got closer to the door. Two huge bouncers protected the door like towers at a fortress gate, one had his arms folded, looking solemnly into the distance, while the other was periodically speaking to someone on a Walky-Talky. About half a yard in front of the bouncers stood a tiny woman, with short hair dyed a deep red. She wore a stylish, bright pink coat that fell to her knees, and had a headset and clipboard. Quickly alternating between conversations in her headset and managing the guests in the queue, watching her go back and forth was making Jason dizzy.

Tonight's venue was Che Che's, a trendy bar in Soho that was less than a year old. The nightspot had been frequented by some lower wattage celebrities in recent months, generating some mild buzz that the owners were keen to maintain and capitalise on. As with many places like this in the capital, a key tactic to create intrigue and allure was exclusivity. This was not the type of place Jason and his boys would normally hit, not just because of its pretentious nature, but also because experience had taught them there was a good chance they would be turned away. Jason didn't want to tell Alice when she mentioned the venue, there was something about questioning the option, which almost reinforced the discriminatory rationale these types of establishments used to not let people in; equally, he hated the idea of trying to get into a place that may not want him or his friends. So as not to rock the boat he decided to go with it, and made sure that his friends were well dressed to ensure there was the lowest chance of any trouble on the day.

A couple of guys were being patted down by the bouncers as they approached the door. The clipboard girl took a long look at the group, scanning up and down as if she were analysing every aspect of their attire. A few seconds of silence passed as the assessment continued, which felt like a lifetime to the boys. From previous experience, the guys knew they had to play it cool, and be sure not to speak first. The impression had to be one of confidence, as if they came to places like this all the time, that there was no question that they would be let in. Lyon pulled out his phone in an air of disinterest, he skimmed through the device absent-mindedly, depicting an air of boredom at the wait.

The clipboard girl turned 45 degrees away from the group, and spoke into her headset in a muffled, inaudible tone. She nodded a couple of times and turned back to the guys and said, "Not tonight guys," the declaration made without the question being asked. Jason and the guys were prepared for this, this was not their first rodeo. Jason approached politely, he'd learned that as soon as the shouting starts, it's game over "Excuse me, Miss", he actually heard chords from the Jay-Z song play in his head as he spoke. She attempted to cut him off before he could plead his case. Fake sympathy drawn across her face, "Sorry guys, nothing I can do, it's out of my hands... you need girls tonight," she said, as she gestured with both hands raised up, clipboard tucked under her arm, before turning away from him. The bouncers had been monitoring the situation closely, while Anton had been monitoring them even more so; having been on the wrong side of bouncers a few too many times.

"Yes, but ..." Lyon's cool facade faltered and he protested.

"She said no, Pal!" A boom came from one of the towering bouncers, as he stepped forward. Marlon and Lyon instinctively reacted to the encroachment by closing in behind Jason in a show of support. This demonstration of camaraderie heightened the tension, as the other bouncer also stepped forward to demonstrate an equally united front. This is exactly what Jason did not want to happen.

Meanwhile inside the girls were having a great time easing into the evening, there was a sense of excitement with the anticipation of meeting the boys; particularly the opportunity to dissect Alice's new flame. A group meeting was really out of character for Alice, which added to the interest. "Alice, dear, why the big group function? You've never done this for one of your prior precious, rude boy Romeos," Jane asked in her usual passive-aggressive tone.

Alice decided to ignore her provocative tone, and just answer the question, keen to not give Jane any extra reason to try and derail the evening. "I just thought it would be nice for you to meet Jason, and some of his friends, they seemed like really nice guys at the march and we rarely get together like this," she finished, almost questioning the logic of the evening as she gave her response.

"Ah yes, the march …" Jane said insipidly. "And what are they marching for now? More funding for after school clubs?" She finished with a sarcastic grin.

Daisy jumped in, spotting that Alice needed some help, "Well, I think it's a great idea, Alice. Jason seemed lovely, I'm looking forward to meeting the group." Alice loved Daisy, smiling at her warmly in acknowledgement of the support, which only served to irritate Jane.

Jane had a couple of her own friends in tow that Alice did not know so well. They were very quiet, seeming only to speak to agree with Jane, or compliment her. Alice reflected, hoping she did not share the same dynamic with Jane. Alice had brought another friend, Desree, one of Alice's few Black friends. Desree was in a happy relationship and was a busy lawyer, which usually meant that she didn't have much time to go out, so was happy for a girls' night, even if it did include some guys, a fact she avoided mentioning to her boyfriend. Desree also sensed the growing tension between Alice and Jane, and thought she could help out by changing the topic of the conversation. "Have any of you heard of the new Ella Mae track, it's really good, right?" she said with a smile.

Daisy chimed in before Jane could remark, "Yeah, I liked it, good beat."

Alice was about to pile on when Desree cut her off pointing out of the window towards the door. "Is Jason a tall Black guy, with short hair?" Desree asked.

"Yes, why?" Alice responded.

"Does he have a short Black bomber, with a grey strip?" Desree continued.

"Yes, I think so, why?" Alice said, slowly turning around.

"It looks like he might need some help." She finished. Alice sprang to her feet and rushed to the door, with the girls following behind. Jane and her friends, pulling up the rear.

The gang came bursting out the front door, almost spilling down the awkwardly steep stairs of the bar entrance. "Excuse me, excuse me!" Alice exclaimed loudly towards the group of bouncers, "They're with us."

"And who exactly might you be?" The door lady said in a pointed tone.

"Well… nobody in particular, but I mean they are with our group. If you check the guest list, you will see the names," Alice continued. The guys and the bouncers backed away slightly. Alice shot a reassuring smile towards Jason. Lyon was focused on perusing Alice's friends to see if there was any potential talent in the group.

"And your name is?" The door girl asked, in apparent annoyance that the opportunity to turn people away may be taken from her. Alice froze as it hit her, she hadn't made the booking; it was Jane's recommendation and in her name. She spun to see Jane gliding slowly down the stairs, always moving at her own pace. She assessed the frenzy of the group below, and saw the innocent, helpless look Alice had on her face from time to time, she loved to be the one to save the day, and was revelling at the moment.

"Calm down everyone, there's no problem, we are all one party," Jane declared with grandeur and a whisk of her hand, in a regal way only she would.

The door girl knew Jane as a frequent patron, and immediately adjusted her attitude. "Jane, sweetie, I didn't realise," she claimed, not wanting to get on the wrong side of a preferred customer, and hoping that she would not communicate any ill-feeling to her manager. "Of course, of course, they can come in. Are you happy with the table you have? I will send Alberto over with a round of complimentary drinks," she finished quickly.

Jane shot the door girl a piercing glare, "Thank you, kindly," she said with authority.

The bouncers had fully backed off at this point, reading that this was not a situation they were going to win. Marlon kissed his teeth at the bouncers as they walked in, Jason gave the door lady his best *disappointed* look. Alice embraced Jason with a hug and a kiss on the cheek. "Are you guys ok? Why didn't you call?" she said. "Yeah, we're good. It was all happening pretty quickly, there wasn't much time to call," Jason replied. Alice went on to say hello to his friends, giving all of them hugs as they walked inside back to their seating area. The ladies all sat, apart from Alice who stood along with Jason to make the introductions. She began with Jason and worked her way around the guys, all of the ladies responding with warmth, even Jane to a degree, which was a pleasant surprise for Alice. Jason sat next to Alice, and the other guys pulled up cube looking stools that were quite low, and not particularly comfortable to sit on, but they didn't want to make a fuss. No sooner had they sat, before Alberto arrived with a complimentary bottle of champagne, and several flutes. Their glasses were filled; Jane thought it appropriate to have a toast "to new friends, from different worlds," she said, Desree and Daisy raised their eyebrows, while Alice nearly choked on thin air. The guys were looking at each other slightly confused, but Jason decided to run with it, repeating the toast "to new friends, from different worlds," it somehow sounded less offensive coming out of Jason's mouth. They clinked glasses and drank, a nice way to end the initial awkward encounter.

Jane assumed her usual leadership role and asked the first question. Having had an opportunity to survey the guys, she was now excited by the prospect of an evening with the type of men she would not normally encounter; admitting to herself that up close she could see what was driving Alice's attraction, physically at least - "So, what is it you do Jason?"

"I'm a civil servant," he replied modestly.

"This isn't an interview Jane, let the guys relax, and he's

a bit more than a civil servant," Alice interjected defensively. She caught herself mid-reply, unsure where the moment of pride came from; she wouldn't care if Jason worked in waste management.

"Relax! Missy, I'm just trying to get to know him. You've said so little about him," Jane replied with feigned offence.

Alice rejected the assertion that she'd kept Jason from Jane. If she had been quiet about him around her, it was because she felt that Jane would not appreciate him properly, as he was not a 'good boy, from home.'

Anton sniggered at the suggestion that Jane wanted to get to know anyone; he didn't like the vibe she was giving off – *She has no interest in getting to know anyone like us,* his gut told him.

Lyon decided it was time to get involved. "Ladies, enough of the work talk, what was the name of your first childhood pet, and the street you lived on?"

Jason chimed in to prevent the embarrassing porn star name game from moving forward. "Ah, don't answer that," he said. Marlon giggled.

"Well, I don't want to do the boring, what's your job and favourite colour chat, they wanted a night with some guys from the endz, let's make it interesting!" Lyon said. Anton rolled his eyes. Daisy smiled, and put forward a suggestion that took the guys by surprise. "Have you ever played, *Never have I ever?*"

Alice did choke on her champagne this time.

"Ok, this is interesting," Desree said louder than she

would have liked. Alice shot her a stare, akin to a teacher about to scald a naughty pupil. "What? This is one of my few nights out, let's have fun."

"Great, it'll be like we're back in secondary school … all over again," Jane said sarcastically.

"I don't think you could pass for someone in secondary school", Desree said sharply. Jane was stunned by the comment, mouth left slightly open, for once lost for words.

"Come on, it'll be fun. Live a little. I'll even start," Daisy said warmly, catching eyes with Lyon, not for the first time.

"Let's go!" Lyon said energetically.

"Oh shit." Marlon muttered under his breath, Jason and Alice shared a concerned look, but decided to go with the consensus. Jason was wishing he'd drunk a little bit more Neph.

"Never have I ever, kissed someone I met through a friend," Daisy said, looking squarely at Lyon. Lyon gulped deeply, taken by surprise, and then gathered himself, finding a wink in response, while all the guys drank. To the surprise of Alice, Desree and Daisy; Jane rolled her eyes and drank along with one of her friends, who looked especially bashful. "Jane?!" Alice asked with inquest.

"Come on don't play innocent we all had fun at Uni, at least I did," she said with renewed self-assurance.

I'm next Lyon said, "I have never… dated more than one person at the same time," he chuckled to himself, as he took a long sip, not accepting that the drink part of the game was supposed to be a punishment.

"It's *"never have I ever"*, genius," Anton said sardonically.

"Yeah, whatever, *I have never ever*," Lyon fired back, with alcohol-fuelled inflated confidence. His sheer lack of regard for the rules and focus on fun brought the entire group to laughter.

"You may as well finish that," followed Anton. Jason drank, Alice looked at him with mild judgement, he averted his eyes, and smiled. Daisy and Jane drank too, Desree laughed at the revelation that Miss prim and proper had another side to her. Jane beckoned the waiter with a gesture of her hand, another round please she said without consulting anyone, although everyone was enjoying the game so much that they were happy for more drinks.

The drinks flowed, the music seemed to get louder, and the questions got more and more daring. Lyon prompted a discussion about sex positions, Jason pulled rank, deciding it was time to call it quits on that part of the evening, to Lyons visible disappointment. "You lot are no fun!", he said as he stood up and headed to the toilet, Daisy tracked him the whole way. It was clear to everyone how enamoured she was, Desree tapped her leg, "Try not to look so hard, make him think he has to at least buy you a drink before you give up the goods," Daisy let out a snort-laugh that triggered a collective outbreak of laughter from the group.

Desree was one of many Black girls who was ambivalent about the perceived dating preferences of Black men. She didn't buy into media portrayals of beautiful White girls that were supposed to be the most sought after. She knew she was beautiful in herself. Not that she was someone who ever needed external validation, but she had that too; Black men had always loved her for her, not just Black men, men from all races. Although, she always felt that the gaze she received from White men was tainted with a fetishisation that made her cringe.

During the brief recess, Jason approached Alice, "How are you doing? Going ok?" he asked.

"I think so," she replied with a smile, kissing him on the cheek. Her phone began to buzz on the table, Jason reached to grab it for her, but she instinctively blocked his arm, the kind of automated flight or fight response that suggests that danger is present.

An unknown number showed up on the screen; "Going to take that?" he asked with a feigned suspicion.

"No, it's probably some sales call or something," she replied with an awkward laugh. At that moment Lyon returned. "Alright people, let's go! Who's starting?".

The group had 3 guesses to find the secret crush or they all had to drink, if they got it right the current subject of the game had to drink. "Ok, I'll start," Desree said. The group sat in silence, pondering their options, of course, the guys had no frame of reference, having just met her that night, but that didn't stop Lyon; ever the optimist. "I'm gonna say DMX?" hands tented, with a seriousness that suggested there was a real reward at stake.

"Well, that wasn't exactly who I had in mind, but he's on my list!" she said happily as she drank her drink.

"Maybe you found your calling," Anton said with a laugh.

"You know, I know women," he shot back, glancing quickly at Daisy to make sure she heard. Daisy blushed in response.

"Ok, I'm next," Jane said. Anton rolled his eyes.

Daisy went first, "Hugh Grant." There was a collective chuckle of agreement in the group that the polished, public school charm of Hugh Grant would be a clear and accurate match for Jane.

"No," Jane replied, slightly offended that she was deemed to be so predictable. Jason followed up, "Prince William?" She reluctantly nodded her head, and finished her drink; the group broke out into laughter again.

Lyon was up next, his was Aaliyah, which had Daisy slightly crestfallen. Lyon tried to allay her concerns by stating that he saw the beauty in all women, which prompted Desree and Alice to roll their eyes, seeing straight through his sweet-boy act.

Alice followed. "Well, this is going to be easy."

Jane said, "Surely some rapper man," still upset from being the subject of the group's humour. "60 cent?" Jane continued, the answer spurring more sniggering, as she misnamed the famous New York rapper. The alcohol was definitely catching up with her, "Well, I don't know, they all look the same to me."

The statement shocked everyone; even the DJ seemed to hear it, with an imaginary record scratch and stoppage of the music.

All eyes were on Jane, "Not like that, but you know what I mean?" scanning the circle for an ally, but coming up short; even the friends she brought along had their heads cast down, looking at their feet. "Just that, that's your type, big and strong and … *Dark*," she continued with what in her head was complimentary, but in reality, was just digging herself deeper. Alice and the other girls were speechless. Anton was fuming, "Yeah, we are all the same, just big fucking gorillas!" he made a monkey gesture as he got up and left the group. Jason went after him, Marlon followed. Desree put her head in her hands. Lyon wasn't sure what to do, but decided to take his chance to get closer to Daisy. Jane gave Alice the faux innocent, *what did I do face?* as she put her hands in the air as if totally confused by everyone's reaction. Alice shook her head in disappointment. She looked at her watch, it was approaching one am, and she had work the next day; *probably time to call it a night*, she thought to herself.

In the taxi home, Alice stared out of the window, watching the lights of London pass. Jane was on one of her alcohol-fuelled monologues, which worked best with a silent audience, enabling Alice's mind to drift away.

Alice was always on the rounder side of things, especially as a youngster when she carried most of her puppy fat – this led to her Father's favourite nickname - *Rolly*. Her soft curves and shy nature coalesced in a cocktail of unpopularity, always off the mainstream radar from most of her peers. This is something she came to embrace, enjoying the sense of freedom it gave her. She didn't have to be like the other kids and try to fit in, she could find her own lane. On reflection, she realised that this was what drove her to identities like being a Goth, in her early adolescent years, though while the make-up and rebellious nature of the movement were fun, she was not quite sure what she was rebelling against.

Her school was set in a picturesque country establishment. The type of place surrounded by green fields, and made up of grand old buildings. She was playing Snake on her Nokia 3330 as she walked up the school drive towards the main building; a Ludacris CD playing on her Discman. A group of boys from the local rugby club were staring and giggling at her, when Jane ran up from behind, linking arms with her. "You know they only laugh because they like you, right?" she said. Alice wondered when she'd asked the question. "They're just stupid boys, unable to control their hormones," she replied. "I don't care about them. I just want to finish my exams and get to a Uni far away from this village."

"Look at where we are," Jane replied, waving her arm to take in the landscape around them. "Why would you want to get away from all this? To be in some tiny flat in a dirty city," She continued, imagining a busy urban area that made her shudder, moving Alice's arm at the same time. Alice tried to continue listening to her music without taking in Jane's local propaganda.

"So, what are you listening to?" Jane asked, grabbing one of the earphones without an invitation. Jane was always direct; which Alice had learned to like over time. While others found her insensitive, Alice felt she had an authenticity about her that most of the moderately wealthy teenage drones in their student body lacked.

A few weeks later Alice was at Jane's house getting ready for the dance, which her mother had forced her to go to, even though she didn't have a date. Jane had agreed to bring Alice along as a third wheel to her date. Despite her difficult ways, Jane did care about Alice, and couldn't have her friend miss out just because she didn't have a date. Alice changed the music channel as they were getting ready, an Outcast video was playing, she bobbed along to the track. "What is that?" Jane asked.

"It's Outcast," Alice replied, matter of factly.

"Out-what?" Jane asked, looking at her with a patronising look. Alice knew this wasn't a fight she was going to win, and flicked the channel back to something that would be appreciated by Jane; Avril Lavigne crooned Skater Boy.

Josh came to pick the pair up. Alice tried to keep a safe distance from the couple, so as not to encroach too much on their evening. Alice was ahead of her time, curvy in a day that didn't appreciate that type of shape, at least where she lived. The lack of sincere male attention didn't bother her so much, because she wasn't interested in the guys at her school, but she couldn't deny that it would have been nice to have a date.

Fortunately, she wouldn't have to wait too long for tides to change. Alice went to university in the midlands, and found herself around people from different backgrounds, importantly guys from different backgrounds. As if by magic, Alice became highly sought after, in what felt like a matter of moments.

Sixteen

Welcome To The Revolution

Jason had been given the details for a 'highly-selective' get together, following his conversation with the mysterious voice from AD. He was assured that he would be provided with all the information he needed if he chose to attend. His curiosity was piqued, and when he reflected on recent events, from what happened with Adrian Adebola, his stop and search incident, and even the night out with Alice's friends, there seemed to be an invisible hand steering him to at least hear them out. The meeting was due to begin in a couple of hours, he lay on his bed flicking the Black card around in his hands, almost as if it was a coin going from head to tails; to attend or not. "Fuck it, you only live once," he said to himself, as he hopped off his bed and put his trainers on. He headed for the door, past the living room where Lyon was laid strewn across the sofa playing FIFA, "Where are you off to? Seeing Alice again? She's got you whipped boy!" he laughed to himself before Jason could even respond.

"Got a meeting to go to," Jason replied, as he closed the door behind him.

A small Black sign at the entrance of the ally caught Jason's eye, as he switched back and forth between the GPS on his phone and the surrounding area, trying to find the meeting address. The round blue location icon seemed to move slightly every time he looked at his screen, but something about the small Black sign told him he was in the right place. He walked down the alley that was filled with recycling bins from neighbouring shops until he came across a tall man in a long black coat standing by a door; the coat surprised him as it really wasn't that cold.

"I'm here for the event," he said in hushed tones that seemed to befit the secretive setting. The man studied him closely, eyes sweeping up and down Jason's body, "Ok, follow the stairs down," he said with a basey voice, standing to one side and opening the door. Jason followed the stairs down into darkness, the air felt damp and heavy, he could see a dim light at the bottom of the staircase from an exposed hanging bulb. At the end of the stairs was a short corridor that led to another door, this time sentineled by a woman with a beret and tablet sat at a small desk. A broad man was standing to her left almost watching over her. "How can I help you?" she asked politely, but with strength. The tall man stared at him intently, carefully watching for any sudden moves.

"I'm here for the meeting," Jason said somewhat nervously.

"How did you find out about it?" she asked.

Jason paused, caught off guard by the environment and questions. "A guy told me ... I was called ... well first I was approached ... outside of the tube," he said, as he fished around for the card inside his pocket, unsure where these nerves were coming from.

This movement triggered a reaction from the man, "Hey, hey!" he said, with as much base as the doorman. Jason stopped, and slowly pulled his hands out, not wanting to escalate the situation.

"It's ok," the woman said, in an attempt to relax the doorman, she flipped the tablet to Jason, asked him to sign his name using his finger, and gave him a small card with a number on it.

On entering the room, Jason was surprised by how large and bright the space was, the stark contrast to the dimly lit staircase and corridor caused him to squint. It took a moment for his vision to adjust before he could actually make out who was in the room. There was vibrant energy, almost tangibly static, with groups of people congregated in small huddles engaged in passionate discussion. Jason was struck by the eclectic mix of people: different shapes and sizes, varied dress sense, some formal, and others casual, all seemed quite young and perhaps unsurprisingly all people of colour. As he continued to scan the room a lady took the stage, and began to beckon everyone to their seats.

She wore dark jeans, Black boots with a small heel, and a fitted Black short sleeve shirt; her hair was natural, and kept quite short. She approached the microphone, leant forward, tapped it twice and began to speak, "Welcome everybody! Shhh shhh!" she said in a tone that was a higher pitch than he expected. "Can everyone please take a seat; we are about to begin." People found their way to their seats. "It's amazing to see so many of you here today, in what is an important time for our community, and the AD organisation. We have some great speakers here for you today, none more important than our council chair, the Queen herself, Abefembe!" The audience roared with applause and yelling.

Abefembe was tall and slim, but somehow imposing at the same time. She carried herself with a presence, importance that commanded attention; regal in her own way. The room fell quiet as she approached the mic, an almost palpable anticipation drifted across the entire venue, as silence fell. "My brothers and sisters, my Kings and Queens, so good to see you all. We are here today to discuss what is needed for our community to protect ourselves, from the ongoing subjugation we are facing at the hands of law enforcement and across different societal dimensions," she spoke calmly but firmly, there was a lot of nodding and murmurs of agreement from the seats.

She spoke passionately about the challenges facing the community, and how they could be tackled from within, by utilising the organization. Jason had to admit that she was compelling, he couldn't tell if it was what she was proposing, the way she was delivering her messages or a combination of both, but he was fully engaged. Before he knew it an hour had passed, and the plenary session was closing. Jason felt there was a lot to take in, but almost immediately, they were told to head to doors at the back of the room that coordinated with the numbers they were given on arrival. The room slowly split into their cohorts, and approached their respective rooms, each room was manned by someone who would check their number. Jason found a seat towards the back of the new smaller room. With fewer people in attendance, there were more mutual nods of acknowledgement, before the door was closed and another speaker took the floor.

"Welcome everyone, you have been invited here to support our insights, data and technological division. Each of you has expertise in the area of data analysis, pattern recognition, surveillance, data security systems, and programming, all skills that will be vital to our efforts," Godfrey said, tall and broad-shouldered, hair kept to a low number one all over. Jason had to readjust his vision, he knew this person, but he couldn't place him. At the same time, his brain was trying to process how the organisation knew so much about the candidates in the room; were they being monitored? Godfrey continued, "if we are here to make a difference, we need to be smarter, do things differently, this division is pivotal to that effort. You should be proud that you have been selected for this cause," Jason was in a state of mild shock, this felt more intense than the previous speech, more like a war rally, and he still couldn't place the man speaking.

What was being asked here? he thought, *Espionage? Treason?* Jason recalled the strict training, and compliance programmes he had undergone on taking up his post at MI6. These were underpinned by his respect for and notions of what it meant to be part of the Service. Even with jokes of fictional characters like James Bond aside, he could see jail time for saying the wrong thing to the wrong person. He sat quietly and listened; he couldn't stand up to leave; he'd be singled out. The speaker continued for about twenty minutes more, roughly outlining how intelligence gathering could support the effort, periodically highlighting that this was public data, and for the greater good, without actually speaking about what would happen if they were found out.

The speaker began to close, and it was almost as if his brain had gone into overdrive in the realisation that the meeting was nearly over, Jason figured out the speaker was Godfrey from Uni! ACS Godfrey! the guy that seemed to hate him for no reason. Godfrey finished the presentation; they were told they could leave and that they would be contacted individually for the next steps. Jason was still shocked, as he had been for most of the afternoon, he wanted to be sure so decided to hang back for a closer look. Godfrey picked up on Jason's slower movement, heading over to him, *no point dragging this out*, he thought. "Remember me?" he asked, offering him a spud. "Godfrey?"

Jason replied, "Yeah, how you doing?" he asked.

"Can't complain, found a purpose," Godfrey replied in a self-assured tone that could be read as conceited, as he gestured to the room around him. Jason started to remember why they didn't get along; his confidence became arrogance too easily, what should have been self-assured, felt like veiled insecurity.

"Yeah, this is a lot," Jason said.

"I'm sure we can rely on your commitment," Godfrey said pointedly, almost daring Jason to back out like he truly hoped he would.

"You guys have given me a lot to think about, for sure," Jason replied in concession. The room had practically emptied, with only a couple of people remaining, it was starting to feel awkward, especially as the friendly vibe was never something they genuinely had at Uni; there was only so long they could fake it here. "I should make a move," Jason said backing towards the door.

"We'll be in touch," Godfrey returned in a tone that almost sounded like a threat.

Akira sat quietly in a secure room with two other members of the council, they watched screens that were recording the breakout sessions; there was one room that interested her more than the rest. Abefembe came up behind her, "He decided to come then," she said rhetorically, looking at Jason's room.

"Looks that way," Akira said, with some unease,

"And you're ok with him being here?" Abefembe asked in a loaded fashion, pressure on an affirmative response.

"He's a big boy," Akira responded, while still wishing she had a chance to speak with him first; however, a larger part of her wanted Jason to be able to make his own choices, he was a smart guy, much more than a big boy, he was a man, and if he wanted to get involved that had to be his choice, free from influence from his older cousin.

The crowd bustled toward the main exit, crammed in the narrow corridor, and up the steep staircase into the evening air. Jason sat on a bus headed for home, he reflected on the meeting, still, in a mild state of awe, it made him think even more about the events of recent weeks; even more about his situation with Alice, and now on top of it all, seeing an unfriendly blast from the past in Godfrey.

Jason thought back to when he first met Godfrey at the ACS mixer at University. Godfrey was a year ahead, doing the same computing course and already an established member of the committee; he was pretty much top-dog. Jason found it hard to place the energy between himself and Godfrey, he had never experienced seemingly unwarranted tension. Godfrey often kept his distance from Jason at ACS events, only ever talking with him in group conversations where there was an audience to observe him being faux friendly. Jason saw himself as a fresher that just wanted to meet some people from his community, and enjoy his time at Uni, but from day one it seemed as if Godfrey had it in for him.

Reflecting on things as an older, more experienced person, he knew it was something to do with a perceived threat, potential competition to Godfrey's Alpha status in the organisation, but Jason always found it strange because he never had any interest in his crown. Life is often more complicated than theory, in reality, it can be more than just your intent, and even your actions, it can also be how other people take to you or view you, which could be entirely out of your control. In this instance there was perhaps some envy of Jason's popularity; he was a likeable person, he didn't have to try very hard, with girls or guys, which was likely to have irked Godfrey. But, the icing on the cake of the recipe of incompatibility between these two young Black men, was Jason's perceived willingness, comfort and desire to be around his White peers. Playing both sides as Godfrey saw it, was almost worse than someone who decided to completely turn their back on their people. *Godfrey, Godfrey, Godfrey,* he thought to himself, as if things weren't interesting enough already, another wild card was added to the equation.

Seventeen

Case Closed

Alice arrived early at the meeting spot, she was nervous, she hadn't seen him in so long. Keep it together, she said to herself, say what you have to say and then leave. She started to hum the melody from a chewing gum advert to help calm her down.

They agreed to meet in a park they used to hang out at some time. There was a bench that had a great view over the park, a little more sentimental than she would have liked, but it was public, busy and felt safe enough. "Al?!" a deep voice called from behind; it was him. She turned and tried to force a smile on her face. "Hey, how are you?" she said.

"I'm ok, and you?" he said sweetly, in a way he could, when he chose, as Alice remembered oh so well. He gave her an awkward hug and sat next to her on the bench.

"Yeah you know, just working hard," she said flatly.

"No doubt," he replied. "So, it's been hard to get hold of you recently," he continued.

She paused for a while, "I've been busy."

"Got a new man?" he said. Damian had been monitoring her Instagram from a ghost account, and had seen pictures of her and Jason.

"I'm seeing someone," she said as coolly and collectedly as she could manage. "Cool, I'm happy for you," he said with fake enthusiasm.

"Listen, I agreed to meet you to let you know once and for all that it is over, and to back off. I'm with someone else, we're over," Alice said. She saw his face fall, her compassionate nature started to kick in.

He was silent. "I'm sorry... but you have to stop calling and texting me, it's been over for ages," she finished.

"I just wanted to show you that I've changed... I hoped that I could have one more chance to prove to you ..." he stopped himself. "I know I wasn't the best guy; I know I don't deserve another chance ... I just ... I just couldn't stop thinking about you, you were the best thing that ever happened to me." Tears started to roll down his face, he tried to wipe them away quickly without her noticing. She felt sorry for him, but she had tried her best when they were together. Maybe if he had allowed himself to be this vulnerable with her way back when, maybe they would be in a different place.

It was a warm evening; Akira was going for a power

walk through the park. She was trying to get in a bit more exercise, but wasn't one for the gym; a compromise she could live with was regular long walks. With things starting to heat up at AD, and still unsure about what to do with Jason, she needed some time and space to collect her thoughts. She loved this park, it really had great sights across London, plus it allowed her to indulge in one of her few guilty pleasures, people watching. Akira had her workout tracksuit on, reams of curly hair squeezed under her cap, so she didn't have to put her sweaty face on show for the world.

Akira headed up a curvy path that led to a hilltop, she saw a guy and a girl sitting on a bench engaged in what seemed to be a deep conversation. There was something about this woman; something that made her stand out. She slowed down and sat at a bench a few meters from where the couple was sitting. She didn't want to make it too obvious that she was spying, so pulled out her phone as a distraction.

The girl's face was not clear from her position, but it looked familiar…*but from where?* Then like a lightning bolt it hit her; it looked like Alice. She even had the same coat from the march, same hair, she was almost certain. But who was she with? *Who was this tall, well-built mixed guy,* she thought. Maybe a friend, maybe an associate … a colleague? But why was she chilling with a colleague on a Sunday afternoon? She didn't seem the type to have many Black male friends, unless they were more than friends. She needed more evidence, maybe if she could hear her voice, but she was too far away. She switched between looking at her phone and the active stakeout intermittently, trying her best not to be too obvious. They were close, she was stroking his face and he was holding her hand, it looked like a lot more than friends.

Alice wasn't sure what to do, it was starting to get too awkward. Despite their tough times, she didn't want to see him hurt, but the truth was their chance had gone, she'd moved on, she was happy with Jason. She needed to draw this to a close, the longer they spent, the harder it would be to leave. "I know this is hard, but this is goodbye, I'm sorry, I really am," Alice stood up, leading him to his feet, she shifted her body weight to her tip-toes and kissed him on the cheek, a split second later he'd taken hold of her and was giving her a long, deep kiss.

Alice was stunned by the shift, but it felt familiar, warm. As they kissed she turned, her body more visible to Akira, it was her. Akira was watching it all unfold with her own two eyes, she couldn't watch anymore, she got up and power walked back the way she came.

Alice didn't realise how long they were kissing before she regained control of her sense and pushed him away. "No!" she said firmly, her mind racing, head dizzy with emotion. "No! we are not doing this Damian, it's over, I'm happy," she finished.

Damian hung his head like a badly behaved puppy. "I'm

sorry, I just can't help myself when I'm around you," he said in a supposedly romantic defence.

Alice just shook her head in disappointment and made her exit, leaving Damian to ponder his actions. She was partly relieved to have things over and done with, a huge weight had been lifted off her shoulder, but the kiss had tainted things somewhat. Sub-consciously did she enjoy it? Could she have pulled away sooner? All she knew was she wanted to see Jason.

Akira didn't know what she was going to do, how was she going to break this to Jason, *he'd be heartbroken!* she thought to herself.

Eighteen

Upon Reflection

Jason was over at Alice's to watch a Sunday evening movie as had become their custom. They usually watched something easy going like a comedy, and on the odd occasion a Disney film. Today's choice was Meet the Parents, though they didn't spend much time watching as Alice was keen to know how Jason felt the group night went. To add more trepidation to her mood, she had mixed feelings about her meeting with Damian; on one hand, she felt relieved to achieve some closure, hoping that he would actually stay true to his word, but on the other hand, she felt a bit guilty for not mentioning anything to Jason. *One problem at a time*, she thought to herself, Jane's performance was more pressing at this point, after all, Damian was her past, something she could bury and not bring up again.

"It was nice to get together like that. Everyone seemed

to have fun?" she said in a half question-half statement kind of way.

"Yeah, it was good, after we got in at least," he replied, with an awkward laugh. "Sorry about that, I didn't even think there would be any trouble on the door," she said.

"Well, you don't have to really think about it," he said, the words leaving his mouth before he could even process them. There was an awkward pause. Jason felt pressured to fill the silence. "For guys like me, guys like us … it's kinda par for the course."

Alice felt a bit stupid. Taking a moment to think about it, of course, these things happened, she knew that, but never really reflected on it, because it never impacted her reality. Alice struggled for words, "She was a complete bitch," was the best she could come up with; a response she was immediately unimpressed with. Jason could see her squirm with discomfort and looked to change tact.

"It looked like Daisy and Lyon were getting along well," Jason said with a smile.

"Yes, I was a bit worried about that, she loves a ladies man," Alice replied.

"Oh, he's a ladies man now is he?" Jason said sarcastically.

"You know what I mean, the hyper-confident, loud guy," she said plainly, trying not to fall into his trap.

"Confident too! Here I am just the boring quiet guy," he said with feigned offence. "Come here, crazy, you know there's only one ladies man for me," she said as she brought him closer and kissed him on his forehead. He always liked the way she did that.

Jason was grazing on some sweet and salty popcorn as they watched the film. Alice was struggling to focus because she was stuck thinking about how insensitive she was with the door issue. *I need to do better*, she thought to herself, as she replayed the skirmish with the bouncers, her mind went to Jane; he must think Jane is a total racist, and me an idiot for being friends with her. She wanted to mention it, to show that she had observed it, but didn't know how best to do so …

Jason could sense that something was off with Alice, she seemed restless, squirming, as she lay on top of him, which was not like her at all; she was usually so relaxed when she lay on top of him that she would fall asleep. After she had changed positions a couple of times, he decided to ask her what the problem was.

"Everything ok?" he asked.

"Sure, why wouldn't it be?" she replied evasively.

"Just seems like you're a bit off, you won't settle, you're normally passed out 20 minutes into a Sunday film," he said with an air of faint humour.

She tried to think of an excuse as a way to evade the questioning, but she was never a good liar, or as one of her primary school teachers put it, she was never very *imaginative* - a key precursor to being a good liar. Jason was also annoyingly good at reading her, something she loved about him, but again didn't set her up to lie so well to him.

"Ok, I was just thinking about how Jane was the other night; I know she can be rude, but it's usually just me having to take it. I didn't think it would go so far with you and your friends," she said apologetically. Jason had been waiting for this to come up, he had heard a bit about her before they had met, but was also shocked by some of her comments. He was expecting at least some intimidation, meeting a group of Black guys, but her sense of privilege definitively trumped any media stoked fears of dangerous Black men. He remained quiet, allowing her to continue.

"I apologise for her; she was way out of line," she finished.

"It's not your fault, you don't control her," Jason said in a non-confrontational way. "No, but she is my friend, so what does it say about me," she said sheepishly.

Jason didn't want to go down that road of logic. He felt like a hypocrite because it was something he would usually think about. "It's ok, but I guess it's something to consider. This is a life-long friend of yours, someone you're close to. Alice ... these are not thoughts that Jane has alone, your other friends, family, may think the same, have you ever considered that?" He said calmly, not wanting to turn the incident into an inquest, but also not wanting to miss out on a good learning opportunity.

Alice was beginning to accept that the dynamic between herself and Jane was becoming too unhealthy. She was *protected* in Jane's shadow for so long when they were young that she rarely challenged her the way she should. Alice was unsure whether it was that she felt indebted to her or had just become accustomed to letting her lead.

Jane was one thing, but she hadn't dated anyone who had made her think about her network and their view of the world, she realised she'd taken it for granted, like so many things. Part of her loved what she was learning about herself and the world with Jason, but at the same time also hated it. Hated that it made her feel uninformed, insensitive … inadequate in a way. She knew that was a negative way to look at the experience, but it was hard to shake.

"I guess it's something I need to think more about," she said with acceptance. Despite the relatively inconclusive end to the conversation, Alice felt more at peace for having had the discussion, which was reflected in her subsequent lack of twitching. Her phone began to ring, she was annoyed to have to move from her position of snugness to check it, but *it could be work*, she thought. She reached over to the coffee table to grab it with a groan of dissatisfaction, that comes with the perceived unnecessarily exertion of energy. She flipped her phone and saw her mum's name, she hit decline. *Not now*, she thought.

"Anything important?" Jason asked.

"No, nothing at all," she responded.

They didn't spend the night together as Alice had an early start the next morning and didn't want to force him up that time. When he left she thought more about their discussion and what her friends and family were really like, what view did they have. Her initial reaction was that while some of her close networks may be a bit misinformed or ignorant, they were not inherently bad people. She was almost sure of it or was she trying to convince herself she was sure.

A few days passed and she couldn't shake the thought, was she coming from bad stock? Was she racist? Raised by racists? Surrounded by racist friends? No, surely not. She scrolled through Instagram and saw a post from Mz. Afrika, it was a series of interracial couples, the men were all footballers of varying degrees of fame.

The posts were from the partners who had children, and were not publicly complaining about their absentee baby daddies. Mz. Afrika's short caption highlighted the issue of Black men, particularly those in the entertainment world dating outside of their race, and used these as examples of how White women would ultimately betray them. As usual, her post attracted a lot of comments; analysing the comments was almost more interesting than the post itself. Many people agreed with Mz. Afrika, stated that *these* women were gold diggers, generally condemning the interracial unions as damned from inception. While Alice disliked the narrative, she felt compelled to improve her knowledge base around race, and what it meant to date someone from a different background.

Then she had a spark of inspiration … *A demonstration*

of commitment, that's what was needed now she thought; show Jason how serious I am, that I'm all in. I'll arrange dinner with my parents, and I can show him that not everyone in my network is like Jane. She had been thinking about introducing him to her parents, so what better time. Her mind started spinning with logistical plans and details, how best to make this a success. She started with a message to her Dad, "I've got an exciting idea."

Jason arrived earlier at work than usual; he was reading through some e-mails that came in overnight while having his morning coffee. The office would be quiet for another half an hour or so, so he would use the time to flick through some of the football articles from the games the evening before. Jason's manager, Violet was next in, she had a good relationship with Jason, taking him under her wing like a younger brother.

"Morning Jasey!" Violet said brightly. Violet was one of those fortunate, but annoying people who always seemed to be energised, and never had any need for caffeine. Jason wasn't a fan of the name, but enjoyed the relationship they had, and how she had coached him, that he let it slide. "Morning Violet, how are you?" Jason said in return, unable to match her energy, even with a coffee. There seemed to be even more bounce in her step this morning, Jason was not sure if that was a good thing or not. "Grand, just grand, and it is a grand day I think too. How about you?" she returned happily.

"You know, can't complain, Palace won at the weekend," he said as he typed away, sensing that Violet was keeping something from him.

"Of course, and that's a good thing?" She returned, acknowledging the open joke they had about Violet pretending to have an interest in, and football knowledge. She sat opposite her desk, which formed part of a set of four connected desks or 'pods', with one seat currently vacant, and the other filled by their colleague Susan. Before long, the office filled up with the remaining employees. One of the Directors, Ben, took to the middle of the office floor and loudly proclaimed that there would be an office meeting in the main boardroom in five minutes. These events were not a regular occurrence, and usually meant really good news or bad news. The entire office squeezed into the large boardroom, which struggled to house everyone, leaving half a dozen of the more junior employees standing at the back of the room. Sat on either side of the large oval table nearest Ben were the three other partners. Jason and Violet were sat close to one another, about halfway up the table.

"Quiet now, quiet everyone," Ben proclaimed. Ben, the Head of Strategy for the department was always the consummate professional; he subtly commanded authority. The room settled down to attention. "Right, we have some important news. As you will be aware, a key strategic priority for the department is to broaden our partnerships, and engage with key external entities that have influential control of the digital space. Over the weekend my superiors informed me that we would have the opportunity to pitch an idea for a collaborative approach to data security with Armidex, I don't need to remind you that Armidex is the leading tech outfit in search and online data, so this is a huge opportunity." Murmuring began around the room. "So, for this initiative, we need a star team," Ben said, as Violet smirked towards Jason, giving away the unveiling. Ben went on to announce the team of which Jason was a member. This was a great acknowledgement of the potential the Senior leaders saw in him. This was, after all, the best the agency had to offer. Chris did not make the team and was visibly disgruntled. Jason was pleasantly surprised, though was concerned about how this would add to his current workload. As the meeting closed, the various members of the pitch team were congratulated by the rest of the company, with the Directors throwing some knowing nods at the different team members; nods that said *congratulations*, along with *don't mess this up*. Jason passed Chris in the hall, as he left and resisted the urge to comment. That discipline was not held by Chris; he could not contain his envy. "Congratulations mate," he said disingenuously, "I guess it's important to show the diversity of the organization for this pitch." He finished snidely. Jason didn't sweat the jab, knowing that he regularly demonstrated his value. He pulled out his phone and saw a message from Alice, "I've got an exciting idea to discuss with you …" Somehow, today was a day where other people's excitement resulted in something more complicated for Jason.

Jason arrived back at his desk, mystically on cue, there was a chat message from Whitney; 'Congratulations superstar, know you're going to nail it! Xx', *kisses?* He thought, *since when are we sending kisses.*

Jason was shattered by the time he arrived home, pitch preparation was always intense; all current workload is deprioritised or handed off to other team members; then it's all hands on deck until pitch day. Jason laid out on his bed, unsure if he would be able to get back up to make dinner; it was times like this that he missed the comforts of his family home. He was catching up on messages, most importantly the announcement that he would be meeting Alice's parents. Jason was surprised by how positive he felt about the milestone; time with the in-laws is not usually an attractive proposition, but he had to admit that he was curious to meet the people who created and raised his partner. He wondered if he would be able to spot any quirks or traits that she had inherited. Alice had warned Jason that her mum could be 'tricky', he didn't really know what that meant, but thought she couldn't be as bad as Jane.

Above all, it was a sign that they were going in the right direction, a thought that made him smile. Jason replied to Alice with enthusiasm about the upcoming dinner, as he wracked his brain about what tonight's meal would be. Then another message from Whitney; random small talk, that they didn't need to have, she was never this active with him, *she must be bored and want some male attention,* he thought, *that or she really knows exactly what's happening in my relationship.*

Time flew by with preparation for the pitch, and before Jason knew it, it was time to meet Alice's parents.

Akira was in an unusual space of mental confusion, ever since seeing what she believed she had. It couldn't have been her, but something in her gut was telling herself that it was. When Akira was stressed she would throw herself into her sea moss gel business. A long-term proponent of natural health and well-being, she had decided to open up a side business making natural remedies, largely based on the health properties of sea moss. The process of cleaning the moss, creating the gel and adding the supplementary ingredients was therapeutic, she'd become so good at it that she could almost create her products absentmindedly. As she stirred a large batch with a wooden spoon, her phone flashed with a message from Jason. At first, she ignored it, it buzzed again, her brain felt racked with guilt even though she had done nothing wrong herself. "I told him about these girls," she said to herself, exasperated. As much as Alice would not have been her first choice for Jason, she could see how happy he was, and ultimately that was the most important thing – she did not want to destroy his world.

Nineteen

Meet The Parents

"Alice! Alice! Wake up!" her mum shouted from the kitchen. Alice was not a morning person, and she hated the way her mum would scream at her to begin so many days. While Alice wasn't an early riser, she was rarely late for class. She rushed downstairs, simultaneously fixing her tie, while tucking her shirt into her skit.

"Here she is, finally!" her mum said as she entered the kitchen. Her dad was finishing off some toast, as she sat down. "Morning, how's my girl today?"

"Fine, Dad and you?" she responded with a smile, most definitely a Daddy's girl. They had similar personalities and would often laugh together, while her mum would stress about little things. "How's school going, Rolly?" he said, as he flicked through the newspaper.

"I really wish you wouldn't call me that, Dad I'm 17, it's embarrassing!" she replied. "How can it be embarrassing?

It's just me, you and your mother," he said with a laugh. Over the last 12 months, her weight was naturally being distributed into places that led to her getting more attention than she was used to. Sparks of the spotlight were very new for someone who played a background role her entire life.

"Alice is right, Charlie, we gave her a name, so you should use it," her mum said matter of factly. Alice often wondered how her parents ended up together, they seemed so different. Her Dad grew up in the North of the country, making a career in Corporate law, but was not the typical hard-nosed business lawyer, on the contrary, he was light-hearted and gentle. Her mother on the other hand was the opposite, she was *proper,* and serious all the time, she cared what other people thought far too much for Alice and Charlie's taste. This was a trait that had worsened with time, Charlie would often look at his wife, and long for the carefree girl he met as a kid.

"School is fine Dad, can't wait until my exams are over," Alice said.

"Well as long as you do your best, that's all anyone can ask of you," her Dad replied warmly.

"But that's not all you can do is it. Why do you fill her head with these things, Charlie, like it's not important for her to get good grades? You need more than just looks to attract a husband these days," she said with the aplomb of the wise guru who had just shared a large gem of wisdom. Alice and her dad rolled their eyes in unison. She finished her tea and headed for the door. "So, you're not going to eat anything either, young lady?" her mum asked.

"I'm not so hungry," Alice replied, secretly hoping a stricter diet would help control some of the physical changes she was experiencing. She kissed both of her parents on the cheek and left.

Alice's parents agreed to meet the couple in London for dinner; Alice's mum appreciated an opportunity to get into London and do some shopping, something she would conveniently forget when she was giving Alice her disparaging assessments of the city her daughter chose to live in. The restaurant was a quiet place in a backstreet near Covent Garden; somewhere Alice's dad knew from his time working in the city. Alice's parents arrived first, her mum was keen to have a pre-dinner Apéritif, which she felt was well-deserved following a successful afternoon of shopping on Bond Street. "They're already late," she said, in a clipped tone to her husband, who perused his phone slowly through square reading glasses, which he was having to wear more often recently.

"I'm sure they'll be here soon, Beenie," He said calmly.

"Don't call me Beenie, not in front of the boy," she replied swiftly.

He lifted his head slowly from his phone and looked

his wife squarely in the face. "Beenie …Margot… can you please remember you agreed to be on your best behaviour tonight. We've not met many of Rolly's boyfriends, so don't spoil it … or she may not let us meet another."

"Well, I hope there is another one, from what I've heard this guy is not what I would consider being the one," she said.

"Beenie, you're worse than your father was with me," He shot back. A pointed reminder of the hardships he went through during his own courtship phase with Margot. Alice and Jason rushed in at that moment, dripping wet. A delay on the underground had made them late, and they'd walked out into a downpour, neither had an umbrella. Alice could see her parents over the shoulder of the Mâitre d' and pushed passed him quickly to approach them, dragging Jason behind her.

"Mummy, Daddy, sorry we're late. The tube." For some reason, Jason was surprised to hear her say Mummy and Daddy, but remembered that her voice did seem to go up a couple of octaves when she was with home folk.

"No problem, Rolly," her father replied, as he stood up to embrace her with a hug. Her mother followed, "Alice," she said with sanguine, kissing her daughter gently on both cheeks. Jason stood patiently behind.

Her dad was the first to approach him, "Jason is it?" he asked rhetorically as he extended his hand to shake.

"Yes, Mr. Undsworth," Jason replied.

"Charlie is fine, lad," he replied warmly. Jason turned to Mrs. Undsworth who also had her hand stretched out ready to shake.

"Hello Jason," she said more stiffly than she wanted, earning a look of dissatisfaction from Alice.

"Hello Mrs. Undsworth," he replied with a smile, the chill in her grip causing him to shiver slightly; the coolness presumably caused by her constant contact with her cold glass of white wine. There was no attempt to offer her first name to Jason. The group sat down and the waiter brought over menus and water. They were quiet as they considered the options, but there was almost a palpable ticking of thought as they each pondered what to say. "How were the shops, mummy?" Alice asked, knowing this was always a safe area to go to.

"Good, I got some lovely blouses at Max Mara," she replied.

Noting that this was not the most welcoming topic for Jason, Charlie attempted to change direction. "So, you look like a football lad, who's your team?" he asked.

"I'm a Palace fan and yourself?" Jason responded feeling more disarmed with a topic of conversation he was comfortable with.

"Oh, they're not doing so great, but better than my lot, Newcastle," He said.

Alice's mum rolled her eyes and inhaled deeply. "We are not going to talk about sports all night I hope? We're here to get the know the boy, why don't you ask him about him," she shot at Charlie in a manner that seemed to fail to acknowledge that Jason was still in the room.

"Mummy … this isn't an interrogation," Alice replied in a clipped tone.

"Oh, my mistake, I thought that was why we're here," she quipped dryly.

The waiter arrived in a timely fashion to break the tension, "Are you ready to order?" he asked politely with a forced smile. They weren't ready, but felt that it was probably a good interlude. After they ordered Jason thought he would take the initiative and reset the conversation. If this was an interrogation, it could go both ways, it was equally important that he got to know Alice's parents.

"So Mrs. Undsworth, what line of work are you in?" He asked naively. Mrs. Undsworth had never really had a 'proper' job, she was raised to think a woman should primarily be concerned with being a good wife and mother, not a career woman. She had tried to instil the same values onto Alice, but to her dismay, she had not been successful. "I am involved with a lot of community activities. Charlie was always the main breadwinner," she said assuredly, as if that was the natural order of things.

"That sounds *interesting*," Jason said with as much enthusiasm as he could muster, taking a deep gulp of water.

It was her turn to fire back. "How are things as a public *servant*?" Jason could have sworn she stressed the word *servant,* but didn't want to believe it.

Alice picked up on the vibe and interjected, "Jason is doing really well in his work with the *secret service* and is being recognised," adding her own emphasis.

"I enjoy the work, and things have been going well recently, I was asked to be the junior lead on an important upcoming project," he said proudly.

"Ah, *Junior…* I see," she said in an attempt to undercut his momentum. Jason was trying his best not to bite.

"Great that they've recognised you for such an important project, lad," Charlie quickly followed, hoping to mitigate the impact of Margot's comment.

"Exactly Dad, just what I said." Alice and her father were aligned as always, which seemed to irritate her mother even more. The first course came, and everyone began to eat. Alice was talking about how things were going at work, and her Dad asked about Daisy and Jane. She gave some quick updates, noting that Jane had helped them organise the recent get together for Jason and her friends.

"Jane is a wonderful girl, truly the best friend you have; and with such a nice young man too," Margot said pointedly.

Jason couldn't resist any longer. "Jane seemed nice, but Daisy felt more grounded."

"Well, the ground may be alright for some …" she replied before she was cut short by Charlie.

"Yes, Daisy, so bright, so much energy, lovely lass and quite right, grounded too."

Magot was not painting the picture of progression and

tolerance that Alice had hoped from; at least her dad could be relied upon.

"So, Jason what type of things do you like to do in your free time? I guess you're into sports of some sort," Margot said plainly.

"Not so much sport these days, though I like to spend time in the gym," He replied.

Alice joined in, "Jason also reads a lot, like you mummy, and he's very passionate about combatting social injustice." The last part slipped out and she regretted it as soon as she'd said it.

"Ah yes, these riots," Margot said with disdain.

"Protests, mummy," Alice replied.

"It seems in this generation everyone has something to complain about. It was different when I was growing up, people just got on with things," she said.

"Well, there are lots of social issues that have historical roots that still need to be addressed today," Jason said firmly.

"Issues? Yes, there are always issues, but people are free to leave, if this country has so many issues, why don't they just go back ..." She caught herself before she finished. Alice was glaring at her and Charlie's face was drawn with disappointment. She finished her wine glass and excused herself for the bathroom. Alice's mum was pretty quiet for the remainder of the dinner, allowing the other three to drive and maintain the conversation. They parted ways and

Alice's parents headed towards Waterloo to catch the train home.

Alice gave her Mum a very light hug, in stark contrast to the big kiss she gave her Dad, Margot knew she was in trouble with her daughter. Jason and Charlie shared a firm handshake and they bid each other farewell. Alice and Jason took a cab home, "I'm sorry about her, I really thought she would have been on better behaviour," Jason pattered her knee as he stared out of the taxi window watching the city lights pass by. He wanted to be positive and didn't want to get too far ahead of himself, but couldn't help but think that a mother-in-law like Margot would cause problems.

Twenty

History Repeats

Jason needed to clear his head after the in-law's dinner. Relationships with in-laws were never meant to be smooth he told himself, as he re-tied his running shoes at the top of his street, his trainer perched on a low street sign. It wasn't that bad, he continued as he began to jog ... or was it, maybe it was a sign. After all, family is important, they would have an impact on their relationship one way, or another, and Alice's mum was clearly not a fan. Jason upped the tempo, feet pounding against the pavement as he turned into Curbit Street on his way to the park. His breathing was more shallow than normal, his chest tighter than it should have been. Maybe he was overthinking it, he entered the park, and his mind cast back to his later teen years at St James'.

The first year or so was a challenge for Jason as he sought to adjust to his new surroundings, but after the novelty of a new, different-looking kid had passed, he'd made some friends and had begun to establish himself in the school, particularly with his football ability. Something that on reflection was a bit cliché, had given him serious cache back then, often picked to play for teams at higher age groups, his on-field prowess drew a lot of attention, especially from the girls.

One girl, in particular, caught his attention from the moment he saw her, Vanessa. Vanessa was blonde with a big smile, also sporty in her own right, Jason would always put in an extra 10% when he knew she was watching. She cheered on with her friends when he had the ball, and he always looked for her when he celebrated a goal. The connection of eyes and subsequent smiles left her bright red with bashfulness, and triggered an onslaught of playful teasing from her friends.

When they first began to date it was in secret, subtle rendezvous behind the technology block, kisses behind the library. When the time came for the spring formal they agreed to go together. Their secret was pretty open by this stage; considering the way they were around each other in public places. Jason had agreed to pick Vanessa up so they could go to the dance together. He would never forget that evening, the beginning at least. He arrived at the large home, in an affluent North West suburb of the city. The type of home that did not scream extravagance, but clearly communicated comfortable fortune.

Jason had dressed smartly in his rented suit and bow tie, he had flowers and a gift for Vanessa. He thought that he'd spent enough time in blazers, shirts and ties by now being at St James, but he still felt stuffy in this suit. His napkin was damp with sweat as he continued to wipe his brow, nerves starting to get the better of him. Jason rang the doorbell once, triggering a symphony of chimes, the likes of which he'd never had heard before. The door number was spelt out with letters, which he checked for the third time in quick succession to ensure he was at the right place. He waited for what seemed to be an eternity before the large door was opened by a small, attractive, blonde woman with a big smile, surely Vanessa's mum.

"Hello! Jason!" she said warmly, as she bid him to enter, "Do come in, Vanessa is just finishing off her make-up," she waved him through to a room on the left of the entrance, a room with lots of books and big leather seats, something like an old school library from a red brick University, or a very fancy waiting room. Vanessa's dad was sitting on one of the chairs reading a newspaper and smoking a pipe, he seemed startled as Jason walked in. "Robert! Robert!" Vanessa's mum called loudly, "come and say hello to Jason, Vanessa's date." Jason picked up on the sizeable age difference between the couple.

"Yes, Yes!" he replied somewhat flustered, but still in a formal tone he stood and walked over to Jason. "Yes," he said again as he assessed the boy who would be taking his daughter out for the evening. "A different crop nowadays at St. James," he muttered to himself.

"Be nice." Snapped Vanessa's mum

"Yes, Yes," he muffled again," he stretched his hand out to shake "*Jawan* is it?" he asked with little enthusiasm.

"Jason, Sir", he replied as he shook Robert's hand. *Sir*, he thought to himself, where did that come from? he really had spent too long at St James'. Jason could feel the awkward tension build as the man struggled to think of something to say. Vanessa's mum interjected, "Let me take those flowers, Vanessa will love these, great taste," she said with a wink in Jason's direction. "Offer him a seat Bertie, for Christ's sake!" she said as she left the room.

"Yes, of course," he muffled again seemingly to himself, with his pipe perched at the corner of his mouth, He gestured to a large green leather chair. " Women eh?" he said in reference to his wife, attempting to make some sort of small connection with Jason. "Take a seat young man," Jason followed the instruction, almost convulsing at the softness of the leather. Robert clearly didn't have much interest in Jason, which Jason was surprisingly disappointed with, he was not sure what he was actually expecting, but he felt like the ambivalence was an indication that he'd somehow failed to impress. Perhaps it was because he was wired for positive reinforcement, or perhaps some other reason, but this outcome made his stomach sink. Robert raised his newspaper and began to read again, satisfied that he'd played his part. Before long Vanessa appeared in the doorway, wearing a long blue dress, Jason was in awe. Vanessa's mum popped up behind her, "Isn't she beautiful!" she said rhetorically. Jason could not agree more, nodding almost like a zombie. They had a fun evening, definitely the envy of the rest of their year group, but Jason still felt low after meeting her parents.

A loud bark from a dog that could see Jason steaming towards his owner and her pram brought Jason back to life. "Sorry!" he shouted as he danced past the pram and dog, that had now wrapped itself around the pram in all the excitement.

By the time Jason made it back, Anton was frying eggs and singing along to Ludacris, I got hos. "Bro, what's good?" Anton said.

"Hey man, yeah I'm ok, a bit tired after last night, dinner with Alice's parents," Jason said.

"Ah ok, the big meeting. How did it go?" Anton said with a laugh.

"It went," Jason said.

"That bad?" Anton replied.

"Well, it could have been better. Her mum is a ... *Character*," Jason said.

"Had you up on all charges for being young Black and proud, yeah?" Anton said with a laugh. "Something like that. I had a bit of a warning, but you know when you actually face the person, it's still different," Jason said.

"Hey, you don't need to tell me, I know they are different ... As long as she's worth it," Anton said.

"Yeah ..." Jason said slowly, as he opened the fridge to see if anything was interesting to have for breakfast. "I'm going to head to my parents, see if I can grab something."

When Jason arrived, his mum was stirring a pot of cornmeal porridge. She jumped as he opened the kitchen door "Don't scare me like that Jason!" Jason laughed, as he gave his mum a big hug and a kiss.

"Good to see you, mum," he said.

Jason's mum welcomed the embrace, "What have I done to deserve that?" happy and slightly taken back by the strength of the embrace. "Everything ok? still, happily, married? Didn't think you would have time for your old mum anymore," she continued with a smile.

"Had a tough night with Alice, met her family," he shared candidly, as he sat down at the kitchen table.

"Wow, met the family already? Things really are going well," she said.

"I guess time flies ..." Jason replied.

"What is the rest of that saying?" she said with a laugh.

"I don't know if meeting her mum could really be described as fun, but I guess it was a good thing to do," he said. She sensed the weight in his voice, stopped cooking and turned to face her son, leaning on the cooker as she always used to do when he was younger. "What did this woman say to my boy?"

"I don't know, it wasn't exactly the words she said, but more the way she said things, the energy she gave off. I knew she wouldn't be my biggest fan, but it was almost like it was something personal," Jason finished.

She was not surprised by the cold reception Jason had received from Alice's mum, but wanted to show support. She knew what it could mean to embark on a serious interracial relationship, and if he was serious, he better prepare for some waves. "You know son …" she said. Jason knew things were getting serious or a lesson was coming when he was called "son". "Son … those of us who are most blessed often have the largest burdens." She always had a way of saying things in a way that made sense, just not always in the moment. He sat quietly and pondered what she said. His mum turned back around and continued to cook. "Anyway, the only person you need to impress is Alice. But, if she does overstep her mark again, I will step in - cyan hol mi bak!" she said with sincerity.

Twenty-one

Friends Like Mine

Anton and Lyon were engaged in a debate when Jason arrived back home. Anton was often trying to school the guys on the ways of the world, something that often turned into a lecture, and at worst an argument. "Here's the thing …" Anton began. "You can't expect things to be given to you by your oppressor, that doesn't even make sense," he continued.

"We have to do better at doing for-self," Lyon, ever the integrationist had a more collaborative view on what was needed to achieve real progression. "We need to do for ourselves, but can't do it alone," He stated. "They have all the keys, all the power, it's their game," he said. Lyon of mixed heritage and love of all people, especially all women, would sometimes surprise his friends with his passion on issues of equality.

"Alright boys?" Jason said as he stuck his head in the kitchen, resting against the door frame.

"Yes, Jase," Lyon shot back,

"You good?" followed Anton.

Lyon began to scroll through his phone. "Look at this," Lyon said to nobody in particular. "This is what I mean. The case with Adrian, how can we not work with the police, with the politicians on this issue, can we create our own police force?" Lyon said with a slight laugh.

Jason thought back to his meeting with AD, something Abefembe had said about looking after the community, he chimed in, "Well it may sound unrealistic, but maybe we do need to police our own neighbourhoods better. I'm not saying have our own force necessarily, but better community support to look out for the kids … we could have done with that growing up."

"Thank you, Jase," Anton said, "That's what I mean, doing more for ourselves." "What are you guys up to today? watching the game later?" Jason asked, in reference to the Palace match.

"Might have a sneaky link," Lyon said with a cheeky grin.

"Of course, why did I ask?" Jason said, tapping his forehead to signify his stupidity. Anton laughed along. "And you?" He asked of Anton.

"Gotta take a look at a few things." Anton was vague as ever, always with fingers in many pies.

"Wait, you were with her folks last night, right?" Lyon asked with interest.

"I was. Why can you never remember anything important, but you remember this stuff." Jason replied with mild annoyance and confusion.

"Stuff I don't need to remember, and girls' phone numbers," Lyon replied with a shrug.

"Go on then, how was it? Don't stand on ceremony," Anton had stopped cooking, and had taken a seat to hear the feedback from the evening.

"I was friendly, tried to make a good impression and all that," Jason began. "I don't know... it could have been better."

"Better how? Did you say something out of line?" Anton asked earnestly.

"No, I think I was fine, it was her mum, she had it in for me from the start," Jason said.

"Was she hot?" Lyon asked, seemingly missing the tone of the conversation. Jason and Anton both looked at him as if was crazy. "What?" Lyon said in defence. "It's a fair question ... Alice is going to grow up to look like her, take a look at what you're signing up for is all I'm saying."

Anton exhaled in frustration with Lyon. "Continue Jase," Anton said.

"Like I said, she was just off from the beginning, attacking me almost. I knew I wouldn't be the ideal guy to bring home, but I didn't think it would be quite like that. Questioning my job, commenting on the Adebola protests, you know basically saying you are not good enough for my daughter," Jason finished.

"Wow, she went in!" Lyon said.

Anton shot him another disapproving look. "How are you feeling about it?" Anton asked, trying to be supportive.

"I don't really know to be honest. Mum says don't let it worry you, but after meeting Jane and now her mum, I'm kinda wondering if this has any real future," Jason said with a forced acceptance. The reality that this may not work out dawned on him for the first time. The guys could almost see the real-time acknowledgement live on his face.

Lyon, ever the optimist tapped him on the cheek, "Don't worry bro, we got you, and if it doesn't work out there are loads of ladies who would be happy to have you. I could do with some competition too; I'm cleaning up out here!" Lyon said in jest.

"Thanks, bro," Jason replied passively, still processing his revelation.

Anton being of greater experience and maturity read the concern on Jason's face. "I know this may be hard to accept, but not everyone is going to be as happy for you guys. If you are going to get closer to her, better you know what her people are like, sooner rather than later. Lyon is right about one thing, we're here for you."

"Cheers man," Jason replied with a bit more optimism. Anton took his food into the living room, leaving Jason alone in the kitchen. Jason felt really alone for the first time in a while. The sunlight shone in through the glass door at the opposite end of the kitchen; he stood and watched the light dance across the floor. His mind began to travel when his phone began to buzz on silent. A message from Alice, "Hey, up for doing something fun later? feel like I owe you (embarrassed face emoji)." Then a second message from Akira "Hey Cuz, how's it going? I hear you've been busy! Let's catch up soon. Luv." His mum had already reached out to his cousin. *Damn news travels fast*, he thought.

Daisy was making a coffee for Alice, who was sitting at the kitchen table eating a bit of toast. "She said what?" Daisy said with incredulity.

"I was so embarrassed," Alice said as she played with the piece of toast in her hand. "I gave her strict instructions to be on her best behaviour, she promised me. By the time we arrived, it looked like she was 3 sheets to the wind. Just one time I needed her to do something for me and she couldn't."

"I'm sure it's not as bad as you're thinking, Hun." Daisy said reassuringly as she stirred the coffee gently. "These things always seem worse when you think back. And I bet Jason hasn't even mentioned it?"

"Well no, but that's like him. To think of my feelings. I gave him a heads up that she can be 'difficult'. But she overstepped." Alice said. "All this after the nightmare with Jane, this was supposed to make up for it, show him that I have normal people in my life," she finished in frustration.

"Well, he met me, babe, so you don't need to worry about that," Daisy said with a laugh. And like you said, you gave him fair warning."

"I don't know; it just seems like the more I try the more I mess things up. I'm trying to read up, follow more "Woke" pages (Woke in inverted commas), listen to podcasts, become a better Allie," Alice said with an air of fatigue.

"I think you are overthinking it; you're trying too hard. You and Jason are great together," Daisy said. She put the coffee on the table and rubbed her shoulder for comfort. Alice appreciated the reassurance but wasn't convinced. *Why were things so hard*, she thought, she couldn't decide if this was the reality of dating someone from a different background, or whether it was because she was actually exploring a partner in a way she had never before. Alice wasn't a quitter, more what her mother would call stubborn; what her Dad would say she inherited from her mum. More than that she had genuine feelings for Jason. She didn't want to let something special go without a fight. Her Nan use to say that "anything worth having was worth fighting for," in her broad Yorkshire accent. They could figure it out, she was sure of it, they just needed some fun, sometimes one on one. Then she had a flashback to something she loved as a kid, "Karaoke!" she shouted out loud.

Daisy shouted back from the living room "What?!"

"Nothing, don't worry," Alice said as she began to search for local karaoke places on Google.

Jason needed to clear his head. Shouts from the living room brought him back to reality, Anton and Lyon were playing FIFA and as usual, it was a rowdy affair. Jason headed into the living room, "You want to jump on?" Anton said to Jason thinking that this type of distraction may be just what he needed. *Worth a shot*, he thought, as he took a seat on the sofa and picked up the control pad. He was up against Lyon, who was by far the worst player in the flat, but always the most enthusiastic to play. Lyon picked his favourite team, Liverpool, proceeded to go through all of the team management changes, ensuring that the formation was just right, down to the types of run each player would make. Jason clicked through the screens absent-mindedly, ready to begin way before Lyon. The game preceded in a fashion that matched the intensity of the preparation of each play, and unusually Jason was down by three at halftime.

"Hey, you sure you're good?" Lyon asked. He's never had such an easy game against Jason, who was usually the best player in the group.

"Yeah, I'm just not into it," Jason said, as he looked at the controller, struggling to focus. He looked at the screen, back down at the controller, and then with one motion threw it towards Anton who instinctively caught it. "See if you can come back," Jason headed upstairs to his room.

After opening the door, he flopped onto his bed stared up at the ceiling. Maybe he should speak to her about it? And what was this fun thing she wanted to do? He really wasn't in the mood for anything *fun* right now. Reading would always clear his mind, so decided to pick up a book. Jason always enjoyed philosophy, reading works of the great thinkers was always a great way to escape. He opened his kindle and thumbed through his collection, maybe Marcus Aurelias, some Stoicism was in order, or not, he flicked through and decided to look at Descartes Meditations. The concept of dualism always intrigued him, good and evil, mind and body, Black and White. He felt like he was experiencing a dualistic paradox at the moment, being torn in two different directions, his heart and body saying one thing, but his mind another.

In Descartes first meditation, he ponders doubt as a source of truth. Anything that has shown a flaw, a weakness, a crack should be discounted. Following the questionable experiences with those close to Alice, he was beginning to doubt what he actually had with her. There were flaws in it, Descartes for sure would discount his feelings for her. Then another message from Alice, this time a meme of a cute puppy, felt like a peace offering and a trap, he couldn't tell which, but something told him to go with it. He asked what the plan was and she sent him back an address for the surprise.

Twenty-two

Sing Your Heart Out

Part of Jason wanted to check the address online and figure out where he was going, but he decided instead to go along with the surprise and show up blind. He hopped off the 37 bus, and followed the GPS on his phone down a few winding backstreets. It was early evening and the sun was beginning to set in the East of the city. Hipsters and trendy folk were milling around the streets, popping in and out of various bars, there was a gentle buzz in the area. Jason reached the address, he arrived at a thin set of stairs trailing into a basement. He cautiously walked down the small steps into the subterranean entrance, incandescent neon flashing lights above the door spelt out the name of the establishment - JOEY'S. Jason entered with a mix of trepidation and intrigue, he was greeted by a warm welcome from a small South-East Asian woman; "Welcome to JOEY'S!", she exclaimed over the loud soul music from the reception speakers. It took a second for Jason to adjust to the sensory assault projected by the venue; the lower lighting of the reception room contrasted with the scattered neon lights, musky odour and powerful sound system. "I'm Anna, how can I help you?"

Jason collected himself, remembering the instructions in Alice's message, "Ask for Alice, room 7." Jason replayed the instruction and the lady typed the information into her computer. He gazed around the room, noticing lots of old framed photos of different soul bands from the 60s and 70s, the penny was beginning to drop.

"You can follow me," she said with a broad smile as she led him down another dark corridor. They walked past several rooms which had heavy-set doors, with bright lights protruding from the cracks around the edge of the doors. Muffled tones escaped each of the cell-like rooms, each resembling padded quarters from some sort of psychedelic mental asylum.

They reached a door marked 7, "Here we are," she said gesturing to the door before she opened it and led him inside. The room was much brighter than the corridor, containing a large couch that bordered the space, a big screen mounted on the wall, with a couple of small tables in the middle – and most importantly two microphones sat on the table. *Of course*, he thought to himself as Alice looked up from her phone with a smile. "You made it!" she said happily.

She popped out of her seat to welcome him with a big hug, a kiss and their secret handshake.

"Ok guys, here are your menus, you can just hit this buzzer when you're ready to order, and I think you know how to work the system, right?" Alice nodded in response and as if by magic, the girl disappeared.

"So, I thought we needed a bit of fun, but just us, and I know that you think you have a terrible singing voice, so what better date night than some Karaoke!" Alice said in a sarcastic tone, shaking the microphone in her hand.

"Karaoke!" Jason replied with a laugh "Really?! Well, if you're up for death by earache, bring it on!" he said more enthusiastically than he expected. The establishment's aura had a seducing effect that subtly worked its magic on him. She was right, they needed some fun.

"Ok, so this place has a huge collection of songs, and a load of Motown classics too, but also more modern stuff. Basically, we pick a song, order a drink and get to singing," Alice said picking up the controller.

"Sounds good, but I have a better idea, why don't we pick songs for each other?" Jason replied with the wry smile of a man who had just cracked a mystery.

"Ok, you're on! Ladies first," Alice replied. She scrolled through the menu of song choices, she thought she would start with something easy, knowing from past experience that this was a sport that worked better following some Dutch courage. "What to pick, what to pick ..." she said to herself as Jason squirmed, awaiting his fate. "Aha, got it, this is the onnneee!" she said with a squeal of excitement! She'd clicked on 'Rock Steady' by The Whispers, a song that had come up in one of their music debates, and one she had noted as a favourite of his.

Jason smiled at the selection; he knew this song inside out, lyrically at least. "Ok, your funeral," he said with a resigning smile. She clicked play and the song fired up, lyrics began to trail along the bottom of the screen. Not a natural extrovert, nor introvert, taking to the stage was not the most natural thing for Jason. As the song played and Jason sang "And we begin to Rock! ..." he felt that this was not his best work. Only *the first song*, he thought, *early days*.

"That was good ... for a *first* try," Alice said in a slightly patronising tone.

"Wait until I warm up! Let's see what you can do," he said, as he looked through the catalogue of songs. Jason felt his competitive side kicking in and he didn't want to be upstaged, even this early on, so he was not going to pick something too easy. Anita Baker ... 'Caught in the rapture', "Here we go! Now we're talking."

Alice was sure she couldn't do this justice, and wasn't really comfortable with the words outside of the hook, but she agreed to play along. They ordered some drinks and snacks, sang more songs and laughed a lot, they even managed to squeeze in some duets. The two-hour time slot went by quickly, but they were having so much fun that they decided to pay for another hour.

Several drinks in and any initial shyness long gone, Alice was belting out Tina Turner's, 'What's love got to do with it?' with the passion of a budding singing in their last chance audition. Jason was thoroughly enjoying the show, not just for her commitment, but because of her silly, care-free nature. As she hit the final note with aplomb, Jason began a round of pretend applause, followed by wolf whistles. Alice responded with bows and curtseys to an imaginary audience. "Now where do I sign?" she asked in jest.

"Oh you think you're ready for a deal?" Jason asked.

"I think I've earned it," she replied sticking her tongue out.

"You're so stupid, that's why I love you." The words had left his mouth before he could realise what was going on.

Alice dropped her microphone, she was dumbstruck, she'd dreamt about this moment for so long. "Jase, did you say?..."

Jason was caught in the moment, an out of body experience, as if he were watching the scene play out in a cinema. He nodded slowly, confirming what she had heard. His mental avatar that was watching the scene play out, while snacking on popcorn, wanted to know when she was going to say it back.

She jumped on him, tears flowing, she kissed him and

hugged him tighter than she ever had "You don't know how long I've waited to hear you say that. I love you too!"

Jason was starting to struggle under her powerful embrace, "That's great bub... just need a second..." as she realised that he was finding it hard to breathe. She eased off, allowing him to catch his breath; they both began to laugh, tears were still flowing for Alice through her laughter, nose now running too, a rainbow of emotions being expressed simultaneously.

After pulling themselves together, they sang a few more love songs before completing their session. They settled up with the hostess in reception and made their way to the main road to wait for their Uber. Oxygen-filled night air exacerbating the effect of the alcohol, all while happily humming songs with tipsy smiles. As they waited, two Black girls approached them from a nearby bar, both girls teetered in their heels, giggling at a private joke. The shorter of the two and furthest away, locked eyes on Jason and Alice first. Jason was oblivious, still singing a song from earlier in the night, Alice was busy tracing the pending taxi on her phone. The shorter girl kissed her teeth, nudging her taller friend and gesturing in the direction of Alice and Jason. The taller girl looked over in response, realising what she was being shown 'Stop it T!', she said, in a pre-emptive attempt to prevent any further comments.

"Why should I? You can't go a night without seeing them, I swear!" the shorter girl replied as they walked passed.

Her comment was loud and clear enough to capture their attention. The short girl shot visual daggers directly at Alice, before her taller friend grabbed her arm and yanked her back on their walking path.

It happened quickly, over almost before it began, but the point landed; particularly for Alice. Jason was unsure what to say, his mind still trying to properly register what had happened. The best he could come up with was a comforting arm around her shoulder and a less comforting question about how far the taxi was. Thankfully the Uber was almost there. They bundled in the back of the car; Alice had subconsciously distanced herself from Jason in the back seat. She stared out of her window, away from his face, all on auto-pilot, seemingly no conscious decision made. Jason could tell something was off, he held her hand, she reciprocated, again without thinking. He pulled her close, she turned to face him, nestling her head in his chest and dosed off.

They tried their best to make their way to Alice's room while making the least amount of noise, so as not to disturb Daisy, they were unsuccessful. Alice loudly fumbled with the locks as she tried to secure the door for the night; the drunken pair then clumsily poured glasses of water. Shhhh!" Alice said, as she stumbled over shoes in the hallway, before making it to her room.

"Shhh yourself!" Jason replied, mimicking her finger over her lips.

Moonlight pierced the darkness of her bedroom, instinct kicked in as they adorned one another, they began to undress each other hastily, with a distinct lack of coordination; Jason nearly falling as he wrestled with his jeans, his comedic performance made Alice laugh. Once they'd successfully disrobed, Alice straddled Jason, she admired his athletic body, as her emotions were stoked to new heights by his earlier revelation and the alcohol racing through her system. Jason reciprocated as he studied her curves in the twilight, both in a momentary state of mutual understanding and peace.

Alice began to grind on top of him, igniting his fuse. He flipped her over forcefully, her legs wide open, dragged her towards him, leant in and kissed her deeply.

The AD council had settled on a team of five, head to toe in Black tracksuits, trainers and balaclavas, allowing them to easily blend into the night. They approached the station carefully; despite extensive preparation, nerves persisted amongst the team. The nerves were understandable, but their shared commitment to the larger goal was more than enough to outweigh any cold feet. They had a good idea of where the security cameras were, slinking comfortably between the camera Black-spots to avoid detection. The station wall was relatively low on the South East corner and with a running jump, you could reach the top. All did, except for the fifth operative who needed to be hoisted up by two others.

Once inside the station compound, they spread out diffusely amongst the patrol cars, beginning their night's work. Backpacks were unzipped, spray cans, keys and crowbars were removed. Like a team of mischievous Christmas elves, they *worked* on as many vehicles as they could. All until one of the elves lost control and shattered the windscreen of a patrol car, the alarm went off, the deafening tone set off a cascade of alarms on the other cars and within the compound itself. Bright lights began to flash and the team scattered heading for the wall in escape. All except one, a solitary figure who stood on the bonnet of a car, facing down a security camera that was trained upon him, along with several lights; he held on to flip both of his middle fingers directly at the camera, before joining the rest of the squad in escape. The cameras followed as he hopped over the wall, leaving behind a dozen or so heavily damaged vehicles, all sprayed with the same words – AD and Adebola.

Jason was preparing to leave Alice's around mid-morning the next day, he'd agreed to meet Marlon and Lyon for a gym session. Alice's glow had returned after Jason's declaration of love and their passionate night together; she didn't want to let him out of bed, but she relented after he assured her he would much rather continue their workout, if he could. Jason's phone went into a buzzing fit for the third time this morning, he had been too preoccupied to look, but now could check who was so keen to reach out. He guessed it would be the boys confirming the session, but he knew a simple confirmation of plans would barely light up his mobile. It was Whitney; more suggestions to 'catch up' at the office, queries about how his weekend was going, updates about her life.

"They must be keen to hit the weights," Alice suggested.

"No, it's just Whitney from work," he replied in a relaxed tone.

This name was new to Alice, why hadn't she heard it before? Why was another women messaging her man on the weekend? Was she some kind of work wife, "Oh…" she said, trying to find the right words of investigation that didn't sound too jealous, "So you guys work together a lot? You've not mentioned her."

"We don't actually, she's in a different department, she just messages sometimes to catch up." As soon as he finished he realised that he probably hadn't hit the level of reassurance she was hoping for, "She's like one of the only other people of colour in the building, so think it's kind of like a support thing," he finished with a laugh to deflate the situation, while ironically knowing that Whitney did not need any support being in a White environment.

"Oh you guys have that too... must be nice for you... both," Alice said, with a hint of annoyance at this potential interloper.

Jason realised he had to shut this down, he got back on the bed and lay next to her; "Bub, look at me, it's nothing, just a colleague I have the occasional coffee with... I love you!" He brought her in for a tight embrace, kissed her on the forehead and firmly slapped her ass. "I've gotta go or the guys are gonna give me more shit about being whipped," he said as he kissed her again and headed for the door.

In reality, Lyon was very unreliable with their Sunday sessions, as it depended heavily on how successful his Saturday night was. After a late-night with Alice, Jason was starting to empathise with Lyon's lack of commitment to the training schedule. Fatigue aside they all managed to make it to the workout.

Alice was suitably placated, she lay in bed as the sunshine poured in through the window, bathing her as she lay naked, happily reminiscing about the night before; Jason saying 'I love you' playing on loop in her mind. She didn't really want to move, but her stomach was rumbling, she realised that she had a lot of calories to replace. She bounced up and headed for the kitchen, striding around the flat with a spring in her step. Daisy was in the living room sipping on some tea and hopping through TV channels.

"Morning Babe, how are you doing? Or do I even need to ask with that smile on your face, and the surround sound experience I was given last night and this morning?" She said with a wicked grin.

Alice flushed red with embarrassment "Oh my god, you didn't hear us did you?" she said sheepishly.

"Love, the whole block heard you. Poor Mrs. Wither from flat B downstairs came to check if everything was ok," she said with a cackle. "I was almost ready to knock on the door to see if I could get a sample."

"Stop it Daisy, I'm mortified!" Alice said with an awkward sense of satisfaction.

"Well, if you don't want the whole world and his wife to listen to you guys making beautiful music you're going to need your own place ... and maybe a couple of acres of land," Daisy said, very pleased with her run of jokes.

Own place Alice thought to herself ...

Twenty-three

Your People Need You

At work the following day Jason felt like he was in the zone, he was energised and ploughing through his tasks. Chris walked past and could see the speed that Jason was typing at, "Behind on a deadline are we?" he asked smarmily.

"No, but gotta hit some extra gears now and again to compensate for you, don't I?" Jason replied with a smile, as his eyes tracked up to meet Chris, while simultaneously typing at speed.

The days went faster with Alice, particularly when things were going well. He thumbed through some selfie videos from their time in the karaoke booth, he smiled as he ate his lunch. Violet walked behind him and looked over his shoulder, what are you smiling at? Didn't know we were allowed to be so happy in this office, she said with a laugh.

"No, it's nothing," Jason said, as he flipped his phone over.

"Nothing," she said with a wink. "I know that nothing, who's the lucky lady?"

Jason felt comfortable with his mentor. "Well, there may be someone in my life," he said, wryly.

"Let's have a look then," she said excitedly. Jason reluctantly flipped his phone and began to scroll through his pictures to find something appropriate and accurate. He found a nice selfie she'd taken of them while they were watching one of their Sunday movies. Jason turned his phone so she could see. "Wow! She's a looker, good work Mr. Andrews," Jason felt slightly insecure at the exposure. "So where are you guys at? Early days? Met friends, family?" She pressed.

Suddenly Jason felt like he was in an inquisition. "Well, we're going pretty well I think, we've introduced each other to some of our friends, I've met her parents."

"And she hasn't met yours?" She said with an air of judgement.

"Not yet..." he replied slowly.

"Well, you gotta fix that mate, girls find that stuff important you know," now toying with Jason, enjoying watching him squirm a bit, in a playful sense. After having her fun, Violet decided to balance her chat with some positive feedback she had been meaning to give Jason, for some good work he'd been doing recently. "Love life aside, you've really been delivering across your projects. I was going to wait for our next one to one, but it's important to know all the good work you're doing is being recognised," she declared positively.

Jason appreciated the feedback, sometimes you can think you're doing a good job, but without external confirmation it can be hard to know for sure. The positive affirmations were all the more important to Jason because he was genuinely passionate about the work he was doing.

"Violet? There's a call for you," a colleague shouted from the office floor, saving Jason from any further interrogation.

He continued with his sandwich as he thought about the personal side of what Violet had said; maybe it was time for Alice to meet his parents. Jason carried on eating his lunch while his mind began to concoct imaginary scenarios of Alice and his parent's meeting; his gut told him it would be fine, but his mind was playing tricks. He could envisage awkward exchanges and misplaced words, "no, it'll be ok he reassured himself." Jason cast his mind back to the karaoke night, how much fun they'd had, even after her energy had dropped following the run-in with the two girls, they were still close later that night, maybe it was time. He typed a message to Alice suggesting the idea.

Almost instantly his phone began to buzz, he thought she'd be excited, but wasn't expecting such a fast response. But, it wasn't Alice, it was an unknown number that read, "Meet in 10 minutes, 108 Lombard street." Lombard street was a road away from Jason's office, he remembered this because there was a nice Thai place there that he would occasionally go to, but who would be randomly messaging him in the day for a meeting, and how would he leave his office when he was due back at work, Jason's mind began to race.

Violet popped her head around the corner of the kitchen, "Jase, apparently you've been summoned for a workshop at M branch in the next 10 minutes." Jason thought this was almost as strange as the request for the random meeting, his phone buzzed again, "We've arranged an alibi meeting at M branch". He could not believe what he was reading.

Violet was still looking at him "Chop-chop Jasey, you can check your messages from your sweetheart later, you're needed now." As if on autopilot he began to head for the door and towards the meeting spot.

Jason checked the time on his phone as he approached the destination, he was about a minute early but decided to hit the buzzer on the door. A voice replied, "Hold, please." In a nasal tone, Jason stepped back from the door. A few moments passed, he rocked back and forth on his heels waiting to be let in. The door was opened by a short woman with long hair, she didn't welcome Jason, just turned and asked him to follow her. Jason walked down a short corridor and up a tight staircase, the girl reached a door, knocked three times and heard a call beckoning entry, she stood to the side and opened the door. Jason didn't move, she gave him a look that neared frustration, motioning him to enter. Jason walked into a small room with an old fireplace below a large mirror, there was a desk in front of a big window and sat behind it was Abefembe, on the other side of the desk were two chairs, one with someone sitting on it. "Jason, thanks for joining us, take a seat," Abefembe said, gesturing to the empty seat. Jason sat and turned to look at the person next to him, it was Godfrey from the insights session at the AD meeting a few weeks before; Godfrey from uni. "I believe you know Godfrey." she said matter of factly. Godfrey managed to give him a nod.

"Thanks for the invite," Jason replied slowly, unsure what to say.

"I guess you're wondering why you're here?" she asked rhetorically.

"Well, it would be good to know. How did you get me out of work?" Jason asked. Godfery interjected, "There will be time for that, but that's not why we've asked you here today."

Abefembe nodded, "That's right, today we want to talk to you about how you can support our ... efforts."

Jason listened carefully, "Jason, you have expertise in data analytics and pattern recognition. You also have access to government, local authority and police databases," he didn't like the direction the conversation was taking.

Abefembe paused, Godfrey stepped in, "We would like you to help us cripple... disrupt some of these government systems." The request was direct and plain as if he was asking to borrow a stapler. Jason was speechless, not quite sure he actually heard the ask correctly, he was being asked to break the law.

Abefembe knew it was a big ask, and could see the struggle in his eyes. "I know this is not a simple request."

Jason laughed sarcastically, "That's an understatement, you're asking me to break the law. I could go to prison."

Godfrey rolled his eyes, "I told you he wasn't ready for this. His background and *personal* choices show that he's not committed.".

Abefembe took control again, not wanting to antagonise Jason. "Jason, I know you share our frustration with how our community is treated, I know you share our anger at the treatment of young Adrian and the thousands of others like him, I know you have felt powerless in the face of discrimination yourself … that night you and your girlfriend were stopped by the police, for example," she said emphatically. *How could she know that?* Jason thought to himself, he didn't know whether to be terrified or impressed by their level of intel and capabilities. As ever, Abefembe was compelling, Jason agreed with what she said, he was frustrated, he did want to fight back, but was this the way? He'd worked hard to get to where he was in life, he loved what he did, what would happen if he got caught? To compound his doubt, thoughts of Alice crossed his mind, could he really risk all of that?

"Listen, that is a lot to ask, I want to help, but this …

this is too much, is there anything else I can do?" Jason asked.

Godfrey scoffed gently and shook his head. "I knew you didn't have it in you, from when I first met you at Uni, I could see you for who you really are, some wet integrationist. Everyone gave me shit for saying it how it was." Godfrey ranted, seemingly letting out years of pent up frustration.

The outburst ignited a response from Jason, who was struggling to deal with his decision not to support. "I finally get to hear what you think of me. You never gave me a chance, from day one, I've never done anything to you. You want to be part of organisations to help our community, our people, form brotherhood, but you don't know what it means, not really. You just want control and for people to follow you, but only if they think exactly like you."

Abefembe tried to restore some order, "That's enough!" She interjected loudly, feeling like she was breaking up a tantrum between two toddlers, who were arguing over whose turn it was to play with the toy blocks.

"No. we're done here; we don't have time to waste. Cha!" Godfrey said with disdain. A disappointed look crossed Abefembe's face, "It seems I've misjudged you, Jason. Please see your way out, Emmanuella will escort you to the door,"

Jason felt low, not only by the hammering he took from Godfrey, but for failing to rise to the call. He stood slowly as if he was lifting a large amount of guilt on his shoulders, but also marginally relieved to be leaving the stressful environment.

He was suddenly back outside, strewn back in the cacophony inner-city London, horns, workmen's drills, voices, all-engulfing him. Jason began to make his way back to the office, attempting to process the intense encounter, leaving him with only just enough focus to control his motor skills and walk in a straight line, he was off-kilter in more ways than one, and extremely unsure if he made the right call.

Jason couldn't focus for the rest of the afternoon at work, he left an hour early, which was unlike him. Violet noticed and hoped her teasing earlier hadn't affected him too much.

Alice had sent several excited messages about meeting his parents, asking a lot of questions, what to wear? What to bring? When they would do it? She was very keen to make a good impression. Jason replied as best he could, but he could not think too much about that now. He was stuck on the AD meeting and whether or not he had made the right call. He lay on his bed and reflected on what he was asked, he had never been so conflicted.

He opened his phone and aimlessly scrolled through some social media platforms. Jason stumbled across a story from Colin, Alice's endearingly awkward friend, he had posted a Drill track with numerous flame emojis, illustrating his love for the song. The post brought mixed feelings; on one hand, the thought of this innocent country guy vibing to this aggressive track made him smile, but on the other, he was reminded how certain people had the privilege of enjoying music born from a dangerous environment, while being safely insulated from that environment themselves. He pondered who the music was really for, hypothesising that the labels probably had people just like Colin in mind for their target audience. He tried to shake the thought, realising the rabbit hole he was about to descend into. *Maybe I should finish the questionnaire,* he thought. Instead he opened the earlier search page. Towards the bottom of the screen was a thumbnail of two Black girls discussing interracial dating, he clicked on the video. The girls were reflecting on their view of Black men dating White girls at a seemingly disproportionate rate to Black women dating White men. Jason prepared himself for a tirade of abuse, given his decision not to come through for his community today, the least he could do was watch this. To his surprise, he quickly realised that the two girls were taking a different tact, they were considered, transparent, even vulnerable.

He listened closely. One of the girls was about average height with a willowy frame, she had a naturally pretty face, with some strong bone structure. The other girl was slightly shorter, with a fuller body shape, Jason noticed she was wearing more make-up, which he didn't think she needed. They began by addressing the amount of high profile men of colour in interracial relationships, particularly football players and rappers. They importantly noted that this was not reflective of the broader population, not representative of the average Black man who was still marrying Black women more than any other race. Despite this knowledge they confessed that it didn't necessarily make things any easier for them as Black women, when the narrative that was being communicated, the most (financially) successful of the group, were choosing to opt out. They were shrewd enough to correctly highlight that the people in charge of the platforms pushing the narratives of interracial dating were not Black. Jason took some time to reflect, had he been influenced from seeing famous Black men in interracial relationships? He couldn't put his finger on it, but accepted that influences could vary in terms of impact and ultimately contribute to a collective result.

He was stunned by what came next, one of the hosts shared a personal reflection from her younger days, about how it made her feel to not be appreciated by men that looked like her. She was not bitter, just vulnerable and emotionally naked. She admitted that it made her question her value, her worth, made her want to adjust her look to be more like mixed and white girls, from straightening her hair, to using make up to make her seem more fair. She paused for a moment; beginning to tear up as she shared. She finished by stating that at one point she considered bleaching her skin, although she was thankful that she did not go so far. Her friend put an arm around her as she managed to find some positivity, sharing a small laugh together.

Jason was aware that some Black women felt like this, but he'd never heard such a raw account. Not even Akira had shown him this level of vulnerability, perhaps because she wanted to maintain a presence of strength for him. The girl carried on her positive wave, declaring that she acknowledged the role she had to play in her own self-worth and valuation, and how she had found lots of romantic success with handsome Black men as she got older. 'Yassss' her friend said, in affirmation of her positive growth. They closed out with more candour, both agreeing they genuinely felt sorry for any Black men who decided to deprive themselves from the beauty of Black women, Black love. They stressed the unconditional love and support that could only be provided by them.

Jason found himself smiling. Despite him being someone they could be talking about; he was happy to see his sisters happy and thriving. What could he be missing out on with Alice? As he considered the thought, it occurred to him that he hadn't heard much from the male perspective. He flicked through the results and came across a group podcast with three African American guys, entitled the 'Snow Bunny Season', Jason presumed that was a joke but thought it was worth giving it a chance.

The discussion opened with the guys all admitting that they regularly dated outside of the race, more than that, it was a clear preference for them. Jason was shocked by their level of openness; they seemed to be totally shameless in their view, part of him wondered if he admired them for owning their truth in such a forthright way. There was something off in how they presented themselves, there was an overt air of bravado, not genuine, the type of over-compensation displayed by those who are most insecure. Any potential position of admiration quickly disappeared as the conversation turned toxic and petty.

"You know why I would never date a Black girl?" one of them said.

"Why?" the two others responded in unison, giggling childishly as they asked.

"They are too loud! AND they talk to damn much!" he answered to the amusement of his panellists. *This was about as far from intelligent and analytical as he could get*, Jason thought to himself.

The guy that seemed to be second in command picked up the baton, "Yes, way too loud, too much attitude, all that head shaking, nah not for me bro," he said, shaking his head in dismay.

The lead speaker chimed back in, "And with all that, they're just not good looking. The wigs, the nails; I just can't do the *Tanishas!*" he stated melodramatically.

Jason was feeling more and more uncomfortable as the video continued, there wasn't long left and he was hoping they would somehow salvage their torrent of abuse, though he couldn't envision how.

The third guy on the panel didn't seem to have any ideas of his own, it appeared as if his only role was to laugh along with the other two, like some muted, side-kick pet.

"You can't have someone like that as a partner, it's just stress, they're not submissive or agreeable at all; you would never be allowed to lead," the main panellist finished.

That was Jason's limit, these guys were not worth listening to. He was actually offended; he thought about his mum, Akira, his little sister, hearing Black men speak like that. All that self-hate, wrapped in some skewed *red-pill* version of modern masculinity. The possibility that people would associate him with the likes of them, based on his own dating history made him sick to his stomach.

Twenty-four

But, Why?

Alice and Daisy were sat on the sofa watching a reality show about up and coming models, it was one of their favourite shared past times, every week they would sit together and become vicarious models for an hour. This week was different, Alice was in a strange place, she was excited by the pending dinner with Jason's parents, but also nervous about meeting them. Meeting the parents was huge, she was determined for it to go well. But there was something else, something that had been on her mind since the other night, despite trying her best to shake it. She tried to focus on the show, but her mind continued to wonder.

"Oh no, it's kicking off!" Daisy exclaimed, pointing at the screen at an argument that was erupting between one of the Black models and one of the White participants over who had been given a longer a session with the photographer. The mini cat fight didn't draw much of a reaction from Alice in the moment, but did take her back to the girls she and Jason had seen the other evening.

Daisy could tell that something was off with Alice; she wasn't showing her usual emotional investment or enthusiasm for the strangers they had become so attached to over the past seven weeks. No words of praise for the girls she backed, and no points of critique for those they'd appointed villains. Daisy even performed a litmus test by making a harsh remark about a girl they both disliked, something that would usually spark Alice into a mini rant of her own, but tonight nothing.

"Everything ok Love?" she asked, as she took a sip of her tea. There was no response. "Al, babe, everything ok?" she persisted.

Alice was focused on the TV, but clearly not paying attention to the show. Daisy nudged her with her foot, "What's on your mind?"

The kick brought Alice back to the room, "it's nothing," she replied.

Daisy gave her a knowing look, a look that said I know something's up and you better spill whatever it is. Alice knew that once Daisy was focused on getting information out of Alice she wouldn't let it drop.

She took a second to consider how best to explain what was on her mind. Since the other night with Jason she was having flashbacks of the two girls that had passed them as they waited for their cab, the one who had made the comment and given her that look, that look that pierced straight through her.

"The other night… the other night I was with Jason…" she managed to get out before she was interrupted

"Oh that night, the night heard around the postcode!" Daisy said with a cheeky cackle.

Alice rolled her eyes, "That night… but earlier on. We were waiting for the cab and these girls walked passed. The looked at us, at me and just…"

Daisy could hear the strain in her voice, but didn't understand what the supposed problem was. "What girls? Not sure I'm following love?" she admitted, as she put her hand on Alice's knee for support and paused the show so she could fully focus on her friend.

"They walked passed, looked at us, judged me and made some nasty comment. I don't even know if I heard it properly. I didn't need to; the look was enough. The look was of hatred, like I was some sort of vampire." Alice finished, recounting the story also made her think about how she felt meeting Akira and her friend's at the march, but she tried to tell herself that was more about her being protective of Jason.

Daisy was catching up mentally, joining the dots in her mind. "Al, babe, you can't worry about what other people think of you or your relationship." She put down her tea and gave Alice a hug.

Alice was suddenly overwhelmed; she wasn't sure where this rush of feeling was coming from. "I don't know Dais, I hated the feeling, being under their microscope, but I didn't feel like I could respond. What could I say? Don't mind us, we're just the modern day Romeo and Juliet."

"You don't have to say anything, you just have to enjoy what you guys have," Daisy offered.

Alice knew it wasn't that simple, she knew that on some level there would be things should would have to accept, grin and bear. Things she wouldn't have to worry about if she wasn't with Jason.

Jason followed up on Alice's messages about meeting his parents, trying his best allay any concern she had. "It'll be cool, they'll love you, how could they not?" he typed. "Oh and I think Akira will be there too," he followed. This message triggering a whole new wave of nerves and uncertainty for Alice.

Despite them having a great time at the Karaoke, he knew that she was shaken by the encounter with the girls. Coupled with the nerves around meeting his parents he felt that she would benefit from some face to face reassurance. He proposed spending one of the warm late summer evenings in a park together, a relaxed drink and some time for themselves. Alice was happy with the suggestion and took the opportunity to wear one of her summer dresses that she didn't get to wear as often as she would have liked.

Jason was waiting for her on a blanket when she arrived, there were some beers next to his backpack and he was already playing some music from his wireless speakers. She knelt down to greet him, giving him a kiss.

"How are *we*? Good day at work?" she asked, they exchanged the usual check-ins.

Alice appreciated the thought and effort that had gone into the mini date, it didn't take much, no grand gestures needed, just a little planning, a blanket, some music and a sunset. She lay her head on his stomach and they both stared at the sky as Miguel played in the background.

"Calmed down about meeting my folks?" Jason asked with a grin, that suggested she was making a bigger deal out of it than was needed.

"Stop it, this is important, I just want them to like me," she replied.

"The same way your parents liked me?" he offered with a laugh.

"My dad loved you," she returned.

"Maybe, but your mum certainly didn't," he said with pained acceptance.

Jason decided to change the topic and try to get her mind off the meet.

At the back of his mind he still had the disastrous meeting with Abefembe and Godfrey, he was still trying to process if and why he had any preference. Things were getting serious with Alice, he could see a future with her, this made him call things into question more, was there some kind of sub-conscious programming skewing his view of women? He wanted things to be organic and genuine, not tainted by media programming and narratives. He decided that if it really was Alice, and not some external influence, it would be easier for him to accept the type of person he was being drawn to, irrespective of race.

"Hey, I had a thought the other day, remember when we went for dinner a while back you said you were more into Idris Elba, was that your subtle way of saying you prefer Black guys?" he inquired, as innocuously as he could manage.

Alice was not expecting to hear that; her mind was busy trying to pick out an outfit that respectfully said daughter in-law. In truth despite not having dated many people, only a couple she would consider serious, she knew what she liked. White guys just did not move her in the same way. She could appreciate a handsome white guy objectively, but that was as far as it went in terms of passion, chemistry or stirring in any meaningful way. She didn't consider herself to be crude in her attraction, she felt there was some nuance to what she liked, a guy had to be well put together, handsome, carry himself in a certain way, on top of having a good personality, of course.

"Where has this come from?" she instantly replied, in an attempt to buy herself some more time.

Jason wanted to be transparent, without making her

feel uncomfortable. "I was just curious; you've not said a lot about your past relationships. Kinda wondered if I fit the mould," he said light heartedly.

Alice guessed where he was going, but wondered why he wanted to know now. She felt comfortable with her preference, she didn't see a problem with liking particular things, *we have our preferences in all areas of life*, she thought. "Well... I guess I prefer a darker complexion." she said bashfully, for some reason vocalising it made her feel slightly awkward.

"It's ok, it's not a crime," he replied, trying to make her feel more at ease. 'Has it always been that way for you?" he continued.

She thought for a second, it was hard to say explicitly, but she felt that it had pretty much always been that way for her. "I guess so, as far as I can recall," she confessed.

"Always had jungle fever?! Lots of Black guys in the country?" he said in a silly voice.

She began to blush again, "We're not that isolated us country folk and remember I went to Uni in a Big City!" she said proudly, elbowing him in his leg to show her strength.

"AW!' he shouted in faux pain. Proceeding to rub his leg in jest.

"Have you ever thought about *why* you like what you like?"

This was of course the more important question and hardest to answer. Alice had never given it much thought, if anything it was more 'Why not?'. "I don't really know to be honest, it's just what I like…and I guess those guys have always liked me too," she finished with a slightly nervous laugh.

Jason didn't love the image of all the Black guys who may have found her attractive. He reflected on her answer, she didn't really have 'Why', didn't seem to need one, yet he felt compelled to understand 'why'. He guessed that was another manifestation of her privilege, you don't really need reasons for things when you're at the top, he laughed to himself.

"What's so funny?" she asked, wondering why he was laughing at her answer.

"No, it's nothing, just a funny thought."

He skipped to the next track on shuffle, it was Musiq Soulchild, 'Love'. Alice nestled her head more into his stomach, finding a more comfortable spot, they sat in silence and enjoyed the music.

Abefembe was breaking the news of Jason's rejection to Akira. Her initial reaction was one of relief that Jason would not have to expose himself to anything dangerous or illegal. However, her relief was countered by concern that Alice, an unfaithful intruder, had somehow influenced his decision.

"And you're sure you couldn't talk him around?" Akira said in an attempt to show disappointment at his decision.

"No, we tried and this is not something we want to force people to be a part of, you either believe in it and commit or you don't." Abefembe said. "He and Godfrey were also at each other, that would probably have led to issues down the road."

"I understand. Is there anything I can do? speak with him?" Akira offered.

"No, it's fine, I wouldn't want you to jeopardise your family ties, we will find someone else. That will be all for now," she finished, ending the call.

Abefembe turned her chair away from her desk to face the window out onto the city. She rarely had moments of doubt, but the meeting with Jason had given her some pause for thought, were they taking things too far with this plan? Had she become too radicalised? Was there a way to get genuine results going through the system? She had tried for so long to do things the right way, to no avail. She fortified herself, *this is the only way*, she thought, they had to see it through.

Twenty-five

The Other Side Of The Coin

The time had come for Alice to meet Jason's parents. As the naturally warm and welcoming people they were, well Andrea at least, they were happy to have her over. Jason was happy that Akira was open to joining, giving Akira the chance to meet Alice under more social circumstances, killing two birds with one stone. Akira in truth had mixed views on the dinner, but felt it would be a good opportunity to assess Alice up close.

Jason was placing plates and cutlery, while his dad sat at the head of the table reading a newspaper. Who still reads newspapers Jason thought to himself, but that was kind of like his Dad; mild-mannered, understated, traditional. He had spent his career on and off the buses, along with some managerial positions in the transport sector. His mum was heroic in his eyes, there was nothing she could not do. Tonight was no different, having rushed back from her job as not only a loved History teacher, but also head of department, she was finishing off the food while complaining that her husband wasn't doing anything to help, which was nothing new, but she would complain, all the same, "Is there nothing you can do to help, David? Cha!" She continued, "She'll be here soon and I do not want our first impression to be people who run late." Akira was busying herself, drying some of the spare glasses.

"Are we trying to impress the girl, or does the girl need to impress us?" David said with a scoff. Akira laughed at the comment.

Jason's younger sister was running around the kitchen, happy to be involved with the drama. "Titi please go and play in another room," Jason's mum said, beginning to lose her patience, "Gweh!!" she followed up with a wave of her hand, Titi knew she was on thin ice when her parents switched languages. The places were set and Titi was content on the iPad in the living room. Alice was due at 20:00, it was about five to when the doorbell rang. Titi ran to open the door, Jason chased after, "Come back, you know you're not supposed to open the door," he called. She stopped just short of the door, with her hands behind her back in a show of innocence.

Jason opened the door, "Hey Bub, how are you?" Alice said, as she leaned in for a kiss.

Jason blushed a little, "I'm good and you? maybe we can cool it on the nicknames tonight."

"Ah, yes, ok", she responded. Titi was hiding behind her big brother's leg, peering around.

Alice stooped down, "And who do we have here?" she said to Titi.

"I'm Christina she said sweetly, swaying gently with her hands behind her back, but everyone calls me Titi...She's pretty," Titi said to her Brother.

"She's not too bad," he joked, "Should we invite her in?". She nodded in agreement. Jason took her coat and walked behind Alice towards the kitchen. David put his paper to one side, and began speaking with Akira who was sitting halfway up the table. Jason's mum had just put the last plate down in the middle of the table, a warm dish of fried plantain.

"Everyone this is Alice," Jason said over her shoulder as he presented her to the family. Akira moved first, standing to greet her, as Alice timidly waved to the room "Hi everyone," her voice cracking slightly as she spoke. Titi was trying to peer in behind Jason. Akira gave Alice an awkward hug, followed by a handshake from David, and a kiss and hug from Andrea. Akira was uneasy, what she had seen in the park running through her mind, *was it her? Could she really have the cheek to cheat on her cousin and then come to his family home for dinner? These White girls could be brazen*, she thought.

"Come in, come in. Sit down sit down," Andrea said warmly. Alice obliged and sat in the seat Jason had pointed out next to him. "So, we have lots to eat, just help yourself,"

Andrea said. There seemed to be endless amounts of food, all different colours and smells, from okra to dumplings (festival), rice and peas, brown stew chicken, saltfish, plantain and callaloo; Andrea had really outdone herself.

"It all looks so good," Alice said, "I don't know where to start." She was overwhelmed by the selection, but didn't want to seem cliché or too hesitant. Jason spotted that she was struggling and decided to put some dishes on her plate. Alice wanted to start eating quickly to show how good the food was, while also erasing any pressure there might be around starting a conversation. She filled her folk with rice, when David cleared his throat loudly, Alice looked up, mouth wide open. Andrea stepped in, "we usually start by saying say grace," she said in a disarming tone.

"I'm so sorry," Alice replied, blushing with embarrassment.

"Jason, perhaps you can lead us," David said, turning to his son.

"Sure." Jason replied, having done it enough in the past to deliver, but without any real conviction, as he no longer considered himself a practising Christian. Alice was ill-prepared unsure how to place her hands, she opened one eye and looked around the table for guidance. Jason began, "Dear Father, we thank you for the food you have provided us today. We thank you for bringing us together at this table." He paused. "We thank you for the new people in our lives." The message drove Akira into a dry coughing fit, interrupting Jason. He opened his eyes and stared at his cousin, she drank some water and raised a hand in apology, Jason continued. "We look forward to getting to know each other better over the nourishing blessing you have provided. Amen," he finished to a chorus of Amens.

Despite her uncertainty regarding Alice, Akira thought she should kick off the conversation, having met her before, "I hear you guys had a fun time the other night at Karaoke," she said with a smile, "I didn't think Sprout here had much of a voice." Jason began to heat up with embarrassment.

"Singing?! My Boy?" Andrea said with surprise, "I didn't hear about this, tell me more." David had a look of faint shock mixed with dismay at the revelation.

Jason tried to provide some covering context "It wasn't really singing, not a show, just karaoke."

"Don't look like that David, you used to love to sing around the house when you were younger, all those Marvin Gaye songs," she said with a cheeky smile. David was unimpressed at what he considered the sharing of sensitive information with a stranger.

"Oh, you might like it then; Joey's has all of those Motown hits." Alice said warmly.

"How are you finding the food?" Andrea asked, noticing that Alice was making slow progress.

"It's lovely, thank you," Alice said in response, reading the intent behind the comment.

"It doesn't look like you're enjoying it," Akira stated flatly.

Jason thought he could lend some support, "Alice has been to the Caribbean a couple of times on holiday, so she's had similar food before." He said with an air of pride.

"I bet she has," Akira jabbed, with a hint of condescension.

"Is that so?" David said, "Whereabouts have you been exactly?" He said with mild interest.

"Yes, we've been to Barbados a couple of times as a family," she replied.

"Hmm Barbados, expensive," he countered.

"David!" Andrea shot with a stern look that showed how unimpressed she was. "Yes?" he replied pretending to not know what the objection was about. This triggered a laugh from Akira.

"Ignore them, darling." Andrea said to her with a warm smile, "He's not used to having company around."

Andrea decided to pick up the baton, "Jason tells me you're a Nurse, that's a wonderful job, what made you get into that line of work?" she said with interest.

"I've always wanted to help people, and it's very rewarding work, but can be hard at times," she said openly.

"I'm surprised someone of your background would be happy to do a job like that," Akira said.

"Well, it wasn't my mum's preferred choice, if she had her way I wouldn't work at all," Alice responded.

"Yes, your Mum," David said tenting his hands. "Your

mum seems to have clear ideas about what is right and wrong for you."

"As a mother should," Andrea added, trying to ease the tension and show some empathy for *mums union*. Meanwhile, Jason was distracted by the great food, the food he didn't eat as much as he would like since moving out.

"So, what does the future look like for you, is motherhood involved? A child with Jason?" David asked.

Jason nearly choked on his food. Alice was shocked by the question, it's something the two of them had never really discussed, although she did see herself being a mum one day if she met the right guy. "I'm not sure Mr. Andrews, I've not given it a lot of consideration," she said.

"Well, it's something to think about, raising a mixed child is no joke, and no grandchild of mine is being raised without knowing who he is?" David added with conviction.

"David, enough!" Andrea said. At that moment Titi walked in asking for a glass of water.

Akira took the opportunity to maintain the pressure, she wasn't sure if it was because the jury was still out on Alice's loyalty, her race, or a natural protective instinct for Jason, but she decided that Alice deserved a bit of a grilling. "I think Unc is right, too many mixed parents raising kids without any cultural knowledge. You've got these poor kids, becoming confused adults," Alice felt backed against a wall, *I should have prepared better for this*, she thought to herself. She guessed Akira would test her, she knew Jason's dad was a traditional guy and that his mum was an academic; but, in honesty, she hadn't thought about kids, not to any significant degree. What did it mean to have parents from different racial backgrounds? Facing the challenges that were present in today's world.

Akira continued, "I know there are a lot of people out here trying to have mixed-race designer babies, like some kind of weird accessory. I'm hoping my cousin is smart enough to avoid that type of girl," she said looking directly at Jason, who returned an unimpressed look back in her direction. Akira was on a roll, "How would you feel if your son was treated the way Adrian Adebola was? How would you react and deal with it? Your boy beaten by police officers, just because he was born the wrong colour," she continued almost in accusation.

"Akira is now really the best time for that conversation?" Jason said in defence.

"And why not? It's a direct question," Akira responded.

Alice wanted to show that she could hold her own. "I would be outraged, of course." She said with apparent conviction.

"Outraged and what?" Akira continued. "No action."

"No, I would be down to the police station, speaking to the most senior officer, demanding an immediate arrest." Alice felt her voice climb a couple of octaves, which took the power away from the delivery.

The response was the final straw for Akira, Alice's

optimistic view of engagement with the police sparked painful memories of her dad's struggle with law enforcement, "You don't think people have tried that before you? You've seen the protests, seen the hurt of the family and communities, you think that made a difference? You're going to be in for a BIG surprise when your privilege doesn't get you the win you've been used to receiving your entire life." Akira said with venom as she stood up, "Sorry Aunty, Uncle, I've lost my appetite," as she stormed out of the kitchen. "Akira!" Jason shouted. Shock fell across the table; passions had raised quickly. David continued to eat quietly. Jason wasn't sure what to do, did he console Alice, go after Akira. He caught his mum's eye in a plea for help. His mum offered him an unhelpful shrug in return.

Alice looked at Jason as if she'd failed the family test.

"You know Alice loves to bake, a bit like you, mum. She does amazing banana bread, as good as yours." Jason wished he could retract the last part of the statement, realising it was never a good idea to challenge your mother's cooking. *This could be going better*, he acknowledged internally.

"Not as good as yours, I'm sure," Alice said to Andrea with a smile, managing to maintain her sense of positivity through the evening's challenges.

Andrea could read the tension at the table, and while she wanted her family to be free to engage with Alice how they chose, she also was sensitive to the feelings of their guest, who ultimately was Jason's partner. "Maybe you can show me your recipe some time and we can have a go together," she said offering an olive branch. The rest of the meal passed much more smoothly with less confrontational conversation about Netflix shows, nature documentaries and less than flattering stories of Jason dressing up in random clothes as a kid.

Alice said her goodbyes to the family after the meal, receiving a hug from everyone, even Akira, who had calmed down and apologised for her outburst, offering Alice a light embrace. This was compensated by little Titi, who gave her a huge squeeze that made her feel good. Jason walked her to the waiting Uber, she gave him an anxious look that hoped she'd made a good impression.

"So … how was it?" she asked nervously.

Jason could see the eagerness to impress, mixed with the worry of not hitting the mark, on her face, he remembered how he felt after meeting her parents and others in the past. He kissed her forehead and brought her in close for an embrace, "You were great," he said.

Alice could tell he was being somewhat generous, but the warmth and security of the hug were all that she could think about at the moment. The Uber driver looked at the pair through his rear-view window, beeping his horn to hurry them along. They did their patented handshake and Jason watched as the Prius sped away.

Back at Jason's parent's things were beginning to settle down, following the evening's entertainment. Andrea was putting Titi to bed, she was a bit shaken up from all the commotion at dinner, she could tell something wasn't quite right as children often can, but was too young to recognise the exact problem; what she did know is her cousin was upset. "Mummy, is Aki ok?" she asked innocently, Aki being her nickname for Akira.

"Yes, she's fine sweetheart," Andrea replied, kissing her on the forehead, while feeling proud about the level of compassion her daughter was showing at such a young age.

"But, the noise?" Titi enquired, in reference to the drama at the table.

"Sometimes adults speak loudly, baby, that's all," she returned, in an attempt to put her at ease. Andrea could see that she wasn't convinced, she had already demonstrated an intelligence beyond her fledgling years, and this was another example. She had an idea to help ease the concerns of her little one, "do you want to say night to Aki yourself?" The little girl nodded and smiled eagerly, she pushed her cover to one side and tried to leave the bed in an attempt to see her cousin. "Uh uh, no, you wait here, I'll go and get her." Titi was visibly deflated by missing the opportunity to be up out of bed so late, but was happy none-the-less that she would get to see her cousin again.

Before long there was a crack in Titi's bedroom door, "I hear a little monster wanted to see me?' Akira said sweetly, Titi giggled, she loved when Akira called her a monster, it made her feel big and strong. Akira walked in and sat on the edge of Titi's bed, "It's wayyyyy past your bed time,

241

what are you still doing up?" She asked, with a mock frown on her face.

"I heard some noise and saw you," she replied, in her best attempt at a rendition of the evenings excitement.

"Did you now?" Akira asked.

Titi nodded her head slowly, almost as if she was double-checking that her memory was valid. "Did you not like Al-ly?" She asked innocently, giving Alice a whole new nickname in the process.

This girl really is too bright for her own good, Akira thought to herself. "No sweetheart," she paused, considering the best response, she wouldn't be able to fob Titi off with anything too simple, not with her mind. "So…" Akira scanned the dimly lit bedroom looking for inspiration. "So…you have your teddy bears and dinosaurs, right?"

Titi nodded happily in response, uncertain as to wear her cousin was going, but pleased with the inclusion of her teddys and dinosaurs.

"Well, imagine if your dinosaurs had been mean to your teddys for a long time?" she said.

Titi thought about her dinosaurs, they could be scary she considered, but had never seen them be mean to the teddys, "But, why would they be mean to teddys?" she asked, earnestly.

"Because they were jealous of the teddys and wanted what they had," Akira returned.

Titi pondered the scenario, she had to concede that the

Teddys had nice picnics, which the dinosaurs weren't always invited to.

Akira registered Titi's acceptance and continued, "so, the dinosaurs are very mean to the teddys for a very long time, so the teddys decide they don't want to play with the dinosaurs anymore." Titi's facial expression turned to slight disappointment at the idea of them not playing together, but could understand what it was like to not want to play with someone who was being mean, thinking about disagreements she'd had in school.

"Well, despite the teddys being upset with the dinosaurs, sometimes one of your teddys might want to marry a dinosaur," Akira continued.

Titi was confused and conflicted, but she was happy that marriage was on the cards. "Why would some teddys want to marry the mean dinosaurs?"

Akira paused again, this was tough even to reconcile as an adult, let alone a child. "Some dinosaurs aren't so mean," she conceded painfully, "and…sometimes they fall in love." The words seemed to stick on her tongue.

Titi's face lit up at the word *love*. All the kids TV shows and films had told her love was good, she could picture all the happy princes and princesses.

Akira could see her younger cousin's response to the romance she'd introduced. "But, remember most of the dinosaurs are mean and have been for a long time. So some of the Teddys are not happy when one wants to marry a mean dinosaur!" she finished with some scary hand gestures for added impact. "And sometimes teddys need to protect other teddys."

Titi wasn't so easily swayed, "but you said they weren't all mean?"

Akira rolled her eyes in frustration, realising she'd bitten off more than she could chew with her fantasy analogy. "Yes, yes, I did. Now it's time for you to go to bed, or I'm going to take away your monster's license."

Titi did not want to risk that; *how could she be a monster without her license?* she thought. She laid back on her bed and wrapped herself in her duvet. "Aki?"

"Yes, sweetheart?"

Titi yawned deeply, "Is Al-ly a dinosaur?" she asked carefully.

"… Yes baby, yes she is." Akira replied slowly, she felt some discomfort in her revelation, but knew she would have to know sooner or later.

"…Oh…she's prettier than my dinosaurs," Titi replied, as she turned over to sleep.

Akira laughed to herself as she kissed her cousin on the forehead and left the room.

Jason was distracted from work by the dinner with his parents, and he was struggling to concentrate on the imminent pitch. Lunchtime was approaching and he was having difficulty finding words of inspiration for the introduction that he was charged with scripting. That along with the background research into the digital search landscape, and Armidex as a company. The more interesting and impactful work of strategy and tactical execution had been divided up amongst more senior team members.

He went into the kitchen to make a coffee, where two of his colleagues were sitting at the main table, crouched over a newspaper reading an article about the police car depot break-in. An opinion piece from a right-wing commentator called for the swift and aggressive response to the disruptive minority element of inner cities. "I just don't get why they do this stuff? Just wait for the court case, if the officer has done something wrong he will be punished accordingly," Chris put forward to Fran.

"Yeah, exactly, they don't help themselves, do they? It's always a violent reaction, you would think no other group of people in society ever has any problems," Fran replied.

"Tell me about it, if I see another march I'm going to lose it," he returned.

At that moment Jason trod on an empty Twix wrapper that someone had dropped on the floor, the crackle alerted them to his presence, they spun around to face him in unison.

"Jason, buddy, how are you doing?" They said with an awkward strain, faces flushed red with embarrassment; like two school kids caught with their hands in the proverbial cookie jar.

"How's the pitch prep going?" she followed up with.

"Not too bad," he said as if he hadn't heard the prior discussion.

The mask of faux sincerity was something Jason always struggled with. He wanted to make his coffee as quickly as possible, when Violet popped her head around the corner, "Jason, we're going to have a quick run-through before lunch, can you join us in meeting room B?"

"Sure, on my way." Jason said. *Great, even more reason not to make small talk with these two*, he thought to himself.

The team had gathered in the meeting room ... "Great thanks for joining Jason, I think that's everyone," Ben said. "The pitch is nearly here, and I don't need to remind you all how important this is for us, we need to demonstrate that we can keep pace and engage with these tech giants. The government can't have a perception of being out of touch, this is particularly important in our space, as we all know the world is only becoming more digital, and as it does the line between the state and public becomes increasingly blurred, other government departments are relying on us to lead the way."

"So, who has some bright ideas about how we can secure this partnership?"

The room was quiet, and the uneasy dance of not wanting to say the wrong thing, but also contribute something meaningful began. Jason was confident after doing his research, he was keen to demonstrate what he could offer, especially for those who were more sceptical of his talents; attributing his placement more down to quota filling, instead of any inherent aptitude or drive he personally had. Eyes darted around the room; everyone had their thinking caps firmly on. "I had a thought," Jason said, Ben nodded his way, giving him the floor, "I've been looking through their different service websites, and it's clear to see that everything they do is for the consumer, a big difference to what we do here as a government body, I think what we need to be doing is demonstrating that we can bridge that gap, that we can also be consumer-focused, usable, on the same page … less bureaucracy, more user experience." There were lots of encouraging murmurers from the room.

"I love it. That's exactly the innovative thinking we need." Ben replied with gusto. Recognising that Jason had struck oil, a few others tried to pile on to his idea, safe in the knowledge that solid ground had been found. Violet gave him a knowing look of pride, almost paternal.

Alice was not convinced that she had made a good impression with Jason's parents, or that Jason was pleased with how things went, even though he had made efforts to reassure that things were fine. He was a nice guy after all, too nice to hurt her feelings with the truth. She decided to surprise him with a banana cake and a game of connect four that she'd randomly found under her bed. She rang his buzzer, Lyon opened the door for Alice, "Well what do we have here, I wasn't expecting any surprise female guests tonight." He said with a cheeky grin

"Well, wouldn't be much of a surprise if you knew I was coming." She shot back; Lyon was impressed with her wit.

"Where is Jason?" she asked.

"Who might that be?" he replied.

"The MAN of the house!" She fired back.

"Ok, Ok, damn. Didn't have to do me like that. The captain is up in his room." Lyon stood to one side allowing her passed.

She made her way up to his room, saying hi to Anton and Marlon, who were watching television in the living room.

Jason was laying on his bed browsing through different social media platforms. He liked some pictures of friends and former colleagues who were sharing their life milestones; engagements and moving in, *lots of people seemed to be romantically active recently*, he thought to himself, *or perhaps it was a modern era mirage created by everyone's tacit agreement to only post carefully curated positive moments of their life.* Between work being busy, the various parental meetups and being solicited by AD, Jason had a lot of things to think about, but with the parent stuff out of the way, and things beginning to calm down at work Jason began to think more about the situation with AD, and whether or not he had made the right decision turning down their approach. He wanted to help, he wanted to be a part of the cause, do his bit, but did it have to be like that? Jason reflected on the acts of past revolutionaries, so many men who had given their lives for causes that were bigger than themselves. He wondered if you could even consider yourself truly committed if you don't give your life for something bigger.

A knock on his door brought him back to reality, he hadn't even heard the front door, *who's knocking*? he thought to himself, none of the guys would ever knock unless they thought a girl was over. "Delivery for Mr. Andrews. Can I come in," A soft voice said.

"Come in," he replied with a laugh.

She embraced him and presented him with the cake, "with all that's been going on for you at work, and the parent meetings I thought you earned some banana cake … and I've got something else for you tah dah!" she exclaimed pulling the box of mini connect 4 from behind her back, "fancy a beating?" she said, sticking her tongue out.

This was the type of thing he loved about Alice, she was caring and thoughtful, "I mean if you're ready to lose, let's go."

The pair lay on their sides on his bedroom floor, as they

ate cake and played the game, it was almost as if they were transported back to their teenage years.

After all that went down with the dinner at the Andrews' household, while desperately hoping the two still had a future, Alice was keen to demonstrate how in-tune she could be with Jason. She had seen a poster on her way over for a new film about slavery; this time focusing on the role of Quaker abolitionists.

"Have you heard about the film 'Religious Antebellum'?" she asked innocently.

Jason checked his memory banks, "I'm not sure, I don't think so."

"You must have seen the posters, it's starring Mike Marlon," she returned, hoping that mentioning of one of Hollywood's brightest stars would trigger his memory.

"Ah the slave one," he said in realisation, having dumped the film to the back of his mind, not wanting to see another story focused on Black trauma and White saviours.

"Maybe we can go and see it?" she offered.

Jason could see that she was trying to bridge a cultural connection, he appreciated her considerate nature. He knew that Alice had a soft heart, but guessed that some of the scenes from that type of film would spark some tears; selfishly he didn't want to be placed in a situation where he had to be re-exposed to historical trauma, only to end up trying to make her feel better, when she inevitably ended up crying. *Complicated*, he thought to himself. He decided to defer, "We could…we could... But for now you have to pay more attention to the game," he replied with a laugh, as he completed a line of four to win.

"I wanted to ask you something," Jason said,

"Have you ever felt like you're supposed to do more?"

Alice wasn't expecting the question, "What do you mean, like charity work or something?" she responded.

"No, no, like, do more to contribute to something bigger," he finished by putting a yellow disc in a slot.

Alice began to think, "well, I guess I always had *the call* to help people, which is why I got into nursing, but I'm not sure if that's bigger," she said.

"I guess I mean more when you look back through history and you see these amazing people who have done really big things, sacrificed so much," he said.

Alice loved their deep and meaningful talks, but this was a challenging one. "Well, I think you're amazing and I think you can do anything you put your mind to," she said. It was hard for Jason to explain, but he did feel supported and that was important, something told him that if he had got into something with AD that Alice would try to understand, even if she didn't get it fully, that counted for something.

"Now I have a question for you, well kind of two questions really," she said.

"How did I know this Banana bread was going to come at a price." he replied jokingly.

"I wanted to know if you really felt things were ok with your parents and Akira," she asked with an air of vulnerability.

"Well, I think it went better with my parents than it did with yours, and Titi liked you," he said with a laugh.

"I'm serious Jase, it's important that they like me," she continued.

"I know and I honestly think they did," he said.

"Ok, that brings me to my second question, now we've met friends and parents and we're having a great time together, like the other night after the karaoke, I thought how about we did that with some more privacy," she looked at him with a wry smile. It took a second for the penny to drop. "Oh, privacy, really?" he said. She nodded. "Wait to be clear, you're talking about ..." he said.

"Moving in together," she finished his sentence. "All the banana cake, connect four and privacy you can handle." she said.

Jason liked the idea of that, especially the last part. "Your mum is going to love this," he said with a laugh.

"So is your dad," she replied. They laughed together, he leant in to kiss her, and then they did their secret handshake. Deal.

Privacy had been on Alice's mind for a few reasons, she wanted to connect with Jason as much as she could on all levels, including sexually. Their sex life had been great, but she consistently came across articles and social media posts stressing the importance of a well-maintained sex life for those in relationships and how men these days were being desensitised to 'normal' women, because of a combination of unrealistic images they were regularly consuming through social media and porn. Alice also knew that despite Jason's modesty, he was a sought after man, she wondered how many Whitney-type individuals there were waiting in the wings. *They could wait*, she thought, Alice was determined to ensure her man was fully satisfied.

Alice and Jason had spoken about their preference in adult entertainment, with Jason being more versed in using the tool to stimulate self-satisfaction. They had shared what they liked to watch, and while there was some cross-over, Alice felt that some research may lead to some inspiration to help ensure the fire between them stayed hot. "Speaking of privacy" she began, hoping to try something that incorporated the aspect of danger, which she heard could add spice to sexual encounters, "How about we celebrate properly?" she suggested leaning in to kiss the side of his neck, just on the spot he liked. They rarely slept together when the guys were in the house, especially if they were all awake.

"Really? Now?" he replied, trying to maintain composure as her soft lips continued to make his spine tingle.

"Mmmhmm" she replied, slowly moving her hand up his trouser leg.

Before he knew it, he had her on his bed, ripping off her

jeans. They were passionate as ever, the element of danger adding to the experience. Then something new for Jason, Alice began to talk, dirtier than normal, saying things she hadn't before. "Fuck me harder Daddy! Harder!" Jason didn't register at first, but she continued. "Yes Daddy!"

Jason was thrown off by the new dynamic at play, but also that at this volume they would attract attention from downstairs. Alice could tell that Jason was losing focus, but she was determined to make him climax, enjoying their session much more than she expected. She wrapped her legs around him tighter trapping him in place, she shifted her weight on top of him and rocked back and forth, increasing her speed slowly until she felt him shudder and spasm inside her. She rolled to one side, giving him a chance to recover, she felt a sense of pride and empowerment with her bedroom conquest.

She tapped him on the shoulder like a friend after an intense sparring session in the ring, "All good there, big guy? Need some water?" she said in patronising jest.

Jason didn't love the joke, but had to admit that she did her thing. "What was all that?" he asked, once he'd gotten his breath back.

"All what?" she said with faux innocence.

"All of that!" he replied, laughing and gesturing at her.

"Well, I heard it was important to keep things spicy, I did some research and got some inspiration," she replied, reflecting on the black hole of porn she had slipped down during her research. Alice was still struggling with some of the images she had seen, it was amazing and concerning what some people were clearly enjoying. Something she had picked up on during the interracial portion of her journey was the consistent theme of domination and subordination. She couldn't work out which party desired this dynamic more. As an occasional patron of the genre herself, she had to reflect on some level that she enjoyed it too, unsure herself which part of it she liked most.

"It was hot, you're free to drive any time... but you don't have to do all that Daddy stuff" he said with an awkward laugh. He had to admit that part of him enjoyed the rhetoric, but another side of him felt like it was a small step away from race-based fetish play, and that was a line he didn't want to cross.

The feedback surprised Alice, who was still riding high off her performance. All the social media pages and magazine outlets stressed the importance of keeping things exciting, how it was imperative to keep up with the intoxicating world of adult entertainment, this was what she had seen time after time in the videos, how could it be wrong. "Ok, Dad-... baby," she said, as they both burst into laughter.

Twenty-six

Conversations With Parents

Jason and Alice were going strong, Alice seemed to be even more positive than usual if that was even possible. Jason was going with the flow, despite all the craziness of the world around them, their world seemed to be perfect. They had found a nice one-bed place in the north of the city that worked with their budget. It was time for Jason to break the news to his parents. Now, he'd moved out a couple of times already; to go to Uni and live with the boys, so they'd said goodbye to their son before, but this was somehow different, particularly for his mum; this was her son moving on, moving in with another woman.

Jason had cooked that evening, finally repaying his parents for borrowing their car, while also doing his best to create a positive environment to break the news. He'd cooked stew peas and rice, his mum's favourite. She came in from work fairly flustered. "Ooo that smells good, son," she said as she opened the door, realising what was on the stove. Jason's Dad was sat at the table with his reading glasses, attempting to read an article on his phone, but having to hold the phone at a distance to compensate for his impaired vision, *this is why I prefer newspapers*, he thought to himself. "And what did I do to deserve this?" she asked, knowing it was not like her son to be cooking, and cooking her favourite dish at that.

"Nothing mum, you always deserve special treatment, you know that," Jason said.

"I know that's right," she replied with a laugh.

"And I deserve nothing I suppose," his Dad said sarcastically, giving up on the article.

"You deserve some love too, but ladies first, that's how you raised me, right?" Jason said.

"I guess so," His dad replied, in concession. Jason dished out the food and they sat down to eat. Jason was about to tuck in when his mum reminded him that they need to say grace. Calling on him to take the lead, as he prepared the food.

"Mum, you know I'm not great at this," Jason said.

"And how are you going to get better if you don't practice," his mum said, wise as ever.

His Dad followed up with a look that suggested he better get on with it. "Dear father ..." he began and then paused in thought. Maybe this was an opportunity to seed the ground for the conversation at hand. "Dear father," he repeated. "Thank you for keeping us safe and for providing us with everything we have today. This food for example." Jason was normally better with words, but prayers were something he struggled to get right, probably because of his conflicted relationship with god. "And thank you for giving us patience and understanding," he said, pausing for emphasis. "Thanks for the love between our family and other loved ones in our lives. Amen." Jason finished. "Amen," they said.

"How was work Mum?", he asked. "All good, the kids keep me on my toes, as always. It's coursework time for the GCSE students," she said.

"Ah, coursework! Good times," Jason said sarcastically. The look on his mum's face said she didn't find the joke funny. "So … Mum … Dad, there's something I wanted to talk to you about," Jason began. *Oh, here we go*, she thought, but just nodded in response, as she ate. His Dad was looking at his phone again, only half paying attention. "So, you know Alice and I are getting along really well… well we were thinking that we might move in together," Jason said. 'Might' was an interesting choice of word, considering they had practically signed the contract already.

Silence swept the table. "David, did you hear what your Son just said?" Andrea said. "Yes, he's getting along well with Alice, great news," he replied.

"No David, the other thing."

"What other thing?" he said.

"He's moving in with Alice!" She let out with frustration.

The outburst caught David's attention, he put down his phone and took off his glasses.

Andrea took a moment to compose herself, Jason was unsure what to say next. "Son, you think you're ready for this? It's different being with a woman 24/7, no downtime," David gave a playful look to his wife. She gave him a stern look in return, letting him know she was not in the mood for his humour.

"Yeah, I know Dad, but you and mum did it, and I'll have to do it at some point," he said.

Andrea replied, "Your father and I had to do it because it was cheaper than living alone," showing that her husband wasn't the only one who could make a joke. David kissed his teeth.

"Ok." She said, very calmly. Jason was surprised, something was not right, he was expecting a bigger fight. "Ok?" he asked.

"What do you want me to say, Jason, you're a big boy, a man," she said. He smiled. "As long as you're sure…" she said.

Here we go, he thought. "What do you mean?"

"Just be sure, you know I want you to be happy, but it's harder with … with them, but you know that," she said. Jason rolled his eyes.

Andrea looked at David for some input, "If your mum is happy, I'm happy … Learn that son and you won't have to worry about anything else." Jason laughed, he looked at his parents and thought he'd be happy if he could emulate even half of their relationship.

Meanwhile, across the city, Alice was having dinner with her parents. She knew her mum would make this painful, so she wanted to get right to it. "So good to see you, darling, really must do this more often. Me, you, a nice restaurant, wine … your father," Margot finished pointedly.

Alice's father rolled his eyes, "How are you Rolly?" he said with a warm smile. "There is a real reason why I wanted to see you both," Alice said.

"Of course, Darling, I wanted to see you too," Margot replied.

"No mum, you're not listening," Alice protested "I need to tell you something …"

"Let the girl speak," her father insisted.

"I am going to move in with Jason," Alice said.

"You're going to what?!! I didn't even realise this Jason *thing* was still going on," Margot exclaimed.

"Of course you didn't, because you don't care what's happening in my life," Alice stated.

Margot was hit by the comment. Alice's father could see that his wife was temporarily stunned, not sure how long this would last for, he took the opportunity to step in. "Are you sure you're not moving too fast, sweetheart?" he asked sincerely.

"No dad, we both want this and think it's the right thing to do," she replied passionately.

He could see the feeling in her eyes, "well if you think this is right for you then your old man is right behind you." Alice expected no different, but was happy to hear it all the same.

Margot had recovered and was now back in the game, "I'm not in favour of this at all, I didn't want you moving to London in the first place and now you're moving in with a boy … a boy like him. I'm sorry, I just can't support it," she said.

"Do you think he's some kind of alien, he's just a normal person, a person who loves me?" Alice replied.

"But sweetie, what do you really know about him, what food does he eat, what habits do they keep? We just don't know." She said, as if she were describing a new species identified on some sort of safari.

Alice felt a headache coming on, "He eats food and his habits include taking care of me," she replied defiantly.

At that moment the waiter arrived, "Any drinks for the table?" Alice's father gave Margot a look that said you are not going to win this one, so don't try.

Back in the kitchen, Jason wanted to get more clarity from his mum, knowing this wouldn't have been her preferred scenario. "I just want you to be with someone who is truly there for you, someone who really understands you … I know Alice is a lovely girl, but it's just harder … When you have to deal with some racial bullshit at work and you want to come home and have someone to lean on, is she going to get you? Really get you?" she said.

Jason listened, he understood where his mum was coming from, but he was in love and knew Alice loved him too. "We're in love, mum," he said.

"I know, but sometimes love isn't enough." she said.

The mood had become sombre. Andrea didn't want to rain on his parade. She just wanted the best for her son, she understood that at some point you need to have faith in your children and let them live their life. "Jason, son, if you're happy, I'm happy," she said warmly as she reached out to touch his hand. "So, when are you guys moving into the *love-shack* then?" she said with a laugh.

"Ok, but have you thought it through? … being serious with him? Is that what you really want?" she asked.

"Yes mum, I love him," Alice said.

"Oh love, what do you know about love? You're still a baby. You watch your reality shows and your Hollywood romcoms, and think it's all so easy, that it magically falls out of the sky, but it doesn't. You have to work for love, it's earned, it's hard,"

For you maybe, Alice said quietly under her breath.

"How long do you really think these *feelings* are going to last? What happens down the road? If you have children? What will you do when random people are gossiping about you or worse, spitting at you as walk with your child? I've seen it." Margot finished passionately. Alice remained steadfast, believing her mum to be out of touch with how much society had progressed; unduly fearful again about what others may think.

Margot could tell her damning portent of a future with Jason was not having the desired effect, she decided to switch tact; "It's just things can be difficult, you know, when you're different ... it's just harder", she said with a knowing look.

"Well, it doesn't matter how hard it is, we're in love, we'll make it work!" Alice said. Margot fully aware of her daughter's strong mindset decided to drop the topic. She was already on her third glass of wine, so thought her attention was best focused on the Sancerre.

Jason knocked on Alice's door the following evening, the Thai food was warm in the carrier bags. Alice opened the door with a look of happy surprise, "Jase, what are you doing here?"

"I thought you might not have eaten … and thought we could strategise a bit about the move," he said.

"Come in, come in, you know I'll never say no to food, you're just a nice bonus." Alice said with a laugh. Jason headed into the kitchen and Alice began to get some plates and cutlery out. Before long there was a shout from upstairs.

"Did you order something Al?" Daisy shouted as she made her way to the kitchen to investigate.

Alice rolled her eyes, "Jason brought some food over… for us," she replied, but Daisy was in the kitchen before she could finish her sentence.

"Hello, Jase!" Daisy said warmly giving him a hug. "You've brought *US* some food, have you?" she said with a cheeky grin.

"I guess so," Jason replied, hoping what he'd ordered would stretch for three.

"No actually, he brought this for *US* and *WE* really need to talk about the move, so if we could have the kitchen that would be great," Alice replied politely, but firmly.

"Ok, ok, I hear you, just let me grab a handful of crackers and I'll be on my way … I know when I'm not wanted." Daisy replied all in one motion as she grasped a handful of the fried snacks and headed for the door. "Oh, and Jase, I've still not heard from your mate Lyon, he got the right number, right?" Daisy said with a smile.

Alice used her bum to nudge Daisy out of the kitchen, closing the door behind, "Bye" she said. "Sorry about her, you know how ... spirited she can be."

"No worries, Dais cracks me up." he replied.

They sat down to eat, "Right, so how did it go down with your parents?" Alice asked, Jason had a mouthful of noodles, and a slightly surprised look on his face, already distracted from the matter at hand. "They were ... supportive I guess," he said slowly while swallowing.

"But?" Alice said pre-empting something conditional.

"But, they questioned whether it was too soon." Jason did his best to recount the most positive possible version of events, something Alice had also planned to do. "Right, my mum was the same," she said.

"What are you thinking?" Jason asked, buying himself some more time to eat.

"I don't know, I guess if we think it's right we should do it, right?" she replied.

Jason swallowed, "Mhmm. Yep, this is about us, we're adults if we want to do it, we should." He continued.

Alice took his hand across the table and looked him in the eyes, watching him eat made her happy; *that must be a sign*, she thought to herself. "Let's do it," she said. She triggered their secret handshake and then got up to kiss him on the forehead. Jason wasn't sure if it was the satisfaction from the food, but things felt right.

Jason's bond with his cousin meant she was the next person he wanted to share the news with. This was a big moment for him and something he would usually share in person, but he knew there was a good chance of a negative reaction from Akira. She had been quiet since the dinner with Alice, and this probably wasn't what she wanted to hear as a subsequent update. He decided that he didn't want to see a look of disappointment on his cousin's face, so opted to go with the safer text approach.

He opened his messenger and could see his cousin was online, which was slightly surprising because she would usually make a point of not spending too much time on her phone. He took it as a sign that he had chosen the right form of communication. "Cuz, what's good? I've got some news," he typed.

Akira's phone buzzed with Jason's message, she immediately felt anxious; something she was not used to feeling in relation to her Sprout. She read the message, hmm news, maybe he's saved her some stress and decided to split up with Alice. "Hey, sprout, what's up?" she replied. Three dots appeared to signify typing, they disappeared and reappeared again ... this happened a few more times;

he was clearly struggling to find the right words. Eventually, the message came through, "I'm moving in with Alice!!" followed by smiley face emoji, a heart and the awkward face emoji.

FUCK! She screamed internally, this was not what she was expecting or wanting to hear. She could feel his excitement through the phone. Akira felt trapped, compelled to tell Jason, but not wanting to shatter his reality. Then she had a mini revelation, it didn't have to come from her, Alice should be the one to tell Jason. Why should she be the bad guy? she thought. Akira typed the most positive message she could manage, knowing that's what Jason would really want to hear, while still feeling bad about her behaviour at the dinner. "Congrats Cuz, great news, I hope she doesn't put you on a diet of beans on toast." She finished with a winky face emoji. Jason sat back and laughed at the message, it was much more positive than he was expecting, gotta take that as a win he decided.

Akira browsed through some of Jason's pictures online and found one with Alice tagged in, she clicked through to her page. Despite only wanting to send a message she could not resist a quick stalk. *Who was this Alice?* she thought to herself, aside from being a cheat? Her page was littered with bright, colourful snaps of flowers and food, from various gardens and markets. There were pictures of friends and family, nothing too alluring or suggestive, all painting a very wholesome picture; *it's the ones you least expect ... like butter wouldn't melt*, she thought to herself. Akira clicked onto Alice's current story and saw pics of the upcoming new apartment, she was triggered. She hit the direct message icon and began to type, then deleted and began again, repeating the cycle a few times, she settled on, "We need to talk, I saw you and the guy in the park," she hit send and then flipped her phone face down not wanting to think of the mess that was coming her way.

Twenty-seven

All Change

Jason was not a fan of moving, but then again *who was?* he thought to himself as he unloaded the final few boxes from the rental van. A light summer shower was starting to fall, and Alice was calling him to get the stuff inside before the rain got any heavier. Alice managed to escape the lifting by putting herself in charge of the unpacking, apparently a fair and efficient division of labour. "So, tell me again how I got stuck with all of the heavy lifting?" Jason said short of breath, as he dropped a box that felt like it was full of bricks on the floor.

"Because I'm the brains and you're the brawn," she said with a laugh, as she unpacked some pots onto the kitchen table. "Anyway, I thought all those years of football would make light work of the stairs," she continued.

"Do you appreciate how many stairs we have?" he said, "Probably not as you only came up them once," he muttered under his breath.

"What was that *darling*?" She said sarcastically, in the way she would defuse a situation.

"Nothing *precious one*," he replied, equally asinine in tone, with a slightly sycophantic smile.

They had managed to find a nice flat that was part of an old townhouse, which had been split by the Land Lady Mrs. Chamberlin, an eccentric old woman who resided in the downstairs apartment. She had taken a shine to the couple, remarking that they reminded her of herself and her late husband. The comment had surprised both Jason and Alice, neither of who could see the resemblance between Jason and her RAF pilot late husband.

The shower passed, and the sun began to burn a deep orange as it set in the sky. Alice drank some tea as she stared at its glow, caught in a trance. Jason approached from behind, wrapping his arms around her. "I think that's the last of it," he said, breath warm against the back of her neck. Living with a partner was a new experience for both Jason and Alice. It's a reality that is hard to fully appreciate until you're in it; the nuances and details of a shared life can be a wonderful thing, but it can also come with challenges.

Alice was not an early riser, not naturally, years of working varying shift patterns, often having to do over-time usually meant that when she had the opportunity to sleep she would gladly take it, but her warped body clock also meant that at times she would find it difficult to nod off at more conventional hours. On occasion this would work well with Jason, who enjoyed staying up, even when he knew it was more sensible to be asleep; but could equally lead to them enabling each other's bad sleeping habits.

Alice's early shifts would disturb Jason's slumber, who was a much lighter sleeper than Daisy, and in much closer proximity of their shared bed. It was taking Alice a while to learn to be light on her feet when getting ready, especially when she was still half asleep; doors and cabinets slammed, items were knocked off the table as she fumbled around in the dark. All noises that were not appreciated by a tired Jason, who had likely gone to bed later than he should have. There were however some upsides, for example, when Jason would come home from work and find Alice napping ahead of a night shift, it was a great opportunity to take cute pictures that Alice considered to be less than flattering, particularly when she would dribble.

Cooking was another area of learning for the pair, compromising an ever-present pillar in a shared living space. Jason had learned to cook a few dishes from his mum, and was often responsible for any group cooking sessions with the boys, so he was comfortable in the kitchen. In truth, Alice had never been much of a cook because her shift patterns rarely encouraged it, she always seemed to be on the go and would often steal left-overs from a sympathetic Daisy, who typically overcooked having come from a large family with several hungry brothers. Capabilities and work schedules meant that Jason would usually cook, ensuring there was enough for her, and when they could they would eat together. Alice appreciated the caring and generous side of Jason, the type of thing he would just do without expecting anything in return.

An area of Alice's appreciation Jason definitely embraced was her influence on the housework. In comparison to his time with the boys, and some questionable cleaning rotas, Alice found the majority of housekeeping therapeutic, almost enjoyable. Jason found it enjoyable watching her from behind, while she hoovered with her headphones on, humming along to a song in a state of tranquillity. Jason also recognised that he had the easy end of the deal, which consisted mainly of him taking out the rubbish, and trying to manage any handy jobs; which on occasion Alice would help with or he would outsource to a more competent member of his network.

The pair shared the occasional fallout over TV privileges. Alice had positioned herself as aware, even sympathetic to Jason's love of football, but that was in the courtship stage, that was her trying to put her best foot forward, in reality she had little interest in the game. From her perspective it seemed to be on all the time. She tried to be patient, but at times it was just too much, she would rather sit in silence or have some music playing than hear the inane drone of football crowds and commentators.

Alice could not understand how he could be genuinely interested in so many different matches; he supposedly supported one team, but was often watching games that involved completely different teams, because apparently it would be a 'good game', whatever the hell that meant. She tried not to even think about his Fantasy Football league or football management games; she would often catch herself just staring at him, totally engrossed in his laptop or phone, desperately threating about imagining players and pretend points. She had to remind herself that this was a full grown, educated and talented man, yet caught at the right moment could relatively easily pass for a child. There was something sweet about it she conceded, an innocence, and her mum had always warned her, "They never really grow up. Just make sure you don't become his replacement mum." That thought would always make her smile on reflection.

Of course Alice had her predilections too, but it's often easier to observe others than it is yourself. She had her favourite shows that were obligatory from her perspective, now if Jason wanted to join her he could, but if he was also watching he'd better be quiet. At times Jason would try to pick up some of her shows, he didn't vibe with most of them, it seemed to him that she always had some sort of reality show or modelling competition on. He would sometimes catch himself watching her from the door way, totally engrossed in some faux reality show about people she would never meet, living a clearly orchestrated life. It would surprise him to see this intelligent, thoughtful and relatively cultured person, so infatuated with what he considered to be trash TV. But, he too also saw a sweet side to it, a youthfulness, the need to escape from a stressful world, if only for an hour or so. Once in a blue moon, he would also find himself caught up in one of her shows, somehow invested in the story arc of some fictional or semi-fictional person; at these times Alice would give him a warm smile to acknowledge the moment.

Despite some mini hiccups they were very much in the nesting phase, a time of novelty, enjoyment and relative bliss ... all except for thoughts that lingered in the back of their respective minds; Alice was yet to reply to Akira, while Jason was still uneasy about his decision not to help AD, and some annoyingly persistent doubts about whether Alice and all she brought with her, were right for him.

"Are you sure things are under control; can they be trusted?" The mysterious voice asked.

"Yes, one site has already been executed and the other target locations have been confirmed," The Home Secretary replied.

"I don't think I need to explain to you how important it is that things run smoothly, this is extremely delicate. We need to generate the right response with these attacks, it has to be executed carefully. Impactful without being too excessive, we still have to maintain the perception of control," the voice said.

"Of course, Sir, I understand the sensitivity," he replied. "I will be in contact soon," the voice said before ending the call. The Home Secretary sat back and wondered if they were not overplaying their hand; he was beginning to doubt how much control they actually had over the situation. *Time for a check-in*, he thought.

Abefembe had fallen asleep at her desk again, when the call came in, it took her a moment to get her bearings. She had a sense that the unknown number was going to be from her contact. She tried to sound alert when she answered "Hello". "It's me," the voice replied. "I wanted to check on our progress, are we on track?" She paused, trying to gain some control of the conversation, "Yes, everything is on track."

"Remember, this is a big opportunity, don't let me down," she put the phone down. The agreement was to target certain select police stations, only at specific times, to generate public unrest, nothing more. Abefembe could not agree more that this was a big opportunity, bigger than her handler realised.

Following the completion of her Doctorate in Sociology, Abefembe spent much of her adult life switching between youth community work and working in schools, usually with 'disruptive' pupils. Her passion was always to give back, and find ways to positively uplift the community, she truly believed the majority of problems that her people faced could be transcended from within, given the right amount of organisation and commitment. However, after years of working on different programmes and initiatives, she became frustrated with the speed of progress; something that was often impeded by budget cuts, usually at the hands of the right-wing administration. Abefembe would typically dispense her frustration on her blog page that would cast light on the systemic, and funding challenges that prevented community workers from making a significant difference. After the latest community programme termination, which led to dozens of community workers losing their job and hundreds of vulnerable teens without a safe space to work and socialise after school, Abefembe was at a breaking point. A breaking point that was clearly communicated on her blog page and readily picked up by her future handler, who had an opportunity for her to lead a new kind of project, a project that would supposedly give her a chance to make a *real* difference.

Part 3

Twenty-eight

Growing Pains

Around the bubble of happiness created by the nesting young lovers, an air of tension continued to grow in the city. Following the vandalisation of the Newham police station, several other *anti-social* acts of protest had taken place across London, and in other parts of the country. The London acts of vandalism were being publicly claimed by AD, with videos posted by the group on social media outlets, and streaming platforms. As the Adebola court case approached, more and more clips of acts of vandalism, and demands for justice were showing up online, adding fuel to the rising tension.

When Jason arrived home Alice was sat at the kitchen table, transfixed on her laptop. She was on an early shift, which usually meant she would be having an afternoon nap now, but something had captured her attention.

"What are you watching?" Jason said, hearing the muffled audio through the laptop speakers.

Alice was so engrossed that she missed his question. "Bub?", he said a bit louder. "Sorry, didn't hear you come in, good day?" she asked, without looking up from the screen.

"Yeah, not too bad. So, what are you watching, must be good?" he said.

"It's just one of these AD videos, they've posted another one," she said. Jason grabbed a chair and pulled up next to her to watch, "What's in this one?" he asked. "As far as I can tell just more threats of vandalism if someone isn't held accountable for the Adebola incident," she replied.

Jason was irritated when he heard acts of brutalisation minimised to an "incident"; the incident was so vague and amorphous that it could be anything, from a misdemeanour to a natural disaster. "You mean the assault! The assault of an unarmed child by an adult officer of the law?" he said testily.

Alice mumbled in agreement, too engrossed in the video to pay much attention to Jason's annoyance. Alice let out an exasperated sigh as the video finished and she closed her laptop.

"What was that for?" He asked.

She paused, "It doesn't matter." Deciding she wasn't up for a lengthy discussion about UK race relations.

Jason could tell she had something on her mind, "Go on, just say it," he prodded. She moved to the sink and started to clear some dishes. He didn't want to let up, "What are you thinking?" he asked in the least judgmental tone he could muster. Alice decided to bite, if he wanted to know so badly, she'd tell him, "I just think it's a bit silly to use vandalism as a means of protest if *they* really want to get justice; it's just going to turn *people* against them," she said sheepishly.

"And what do THEY want?... Which PEOPLE are we talking about?" Jason replied sharply, realising he was about to lose self-control.

"Don't get like that Jason," she said calmly, seeing where things were headed.

"Like what?", he asked rhetorically, "Just say what you have to say," he said aggressively.

"Ok, breaking the law isn't the best way to get what you want; how does that make any sense? There's been a protest, and the court case is coming up, so why do all of this. Surely, it's better to play by the rules?" she said in honesty.

"The rules? The rules? And which rules are these, the rules that allow officers to profile Black people, or the rules that lead to more exclusions for Black kids, or the rules that result in more Black women dying in childbirth, please explain which rules?! The problem is Alice the protests aren't ever enough; we wouldn't have to protest in the first place if the 'rules' were working. So, yeah some people get frustrated, and feel like they need to do something else, anything else," Jason flashed back to the clandestine meeting with Abefembe and Godfrey, on Lombard street. He was still trying to process his decision, guilt and frustration hanging over him, still unsure if he made the right call.

Alice could see the frustration on Jason's face, she didn't want to fight, she never wanted *this* fight, but it seemed so hard to avoid. "You're right, I'm sorry," she said, in concession, not a genuine acceptance that she was in the wrong, but rather the quickest way to move past the confrontation.

Jason read the tone quickly, having heard it from her before. He immediately felt bad, she wasn't his enemy … she wasn't *the enemy*. Alice left the room and headed upstairs to fold some clothes. He called after her, "Alice! Alice! I'm sorry," he heard nothing back. "Fuck" he said as he slammed the counter with his fist.

He was annoyed at himself; he should have had more control. He followed Alice upstairs into the bedroom, and leaned on the wall by the door. "Bub?" he asked as she continued to fold the clothes in silence. "Can we talk? I'm sorry," he repeated. Nothing. He approached her from behind and put his nose in the small of her neck, one of her favourite spots.

"Don't Jason," she whispered as she wiped a tear from her eye.

He didn't realise she was so upset. He kissed the back of her neck softly, "I'm sorry … can you just stop for a second?" he said. He spun her around and saw the tears flowing from her red eyes, he embraced her with a big hug, squeezing tightly.

She pushed away from him, "I'm not your punching bag Jason! I'm not." she let out in frustration, as more tears began to flow. It hurt him to see her like this, even more so knowing that he was the cause. He took her hand and brought her close for a kiss, it was one way at first, but he kissed more deeply until she reciprocated.

He stopped, looked at her in the eye, "I know, I'm sorry." The pair lay on the bed, Alice's head on his chest, his arms around her, warm and safe, for a moment everything was right again.

Twenty-nine

Hidden Pasts

Mr. Stevens walked down a particularly clean corridor, several floors below the streets of Whitehall. He was running a few minutes late, but he was not rushed, knowing that this was a meeting that would not start without him. He opened the door to a large room with a long thin table, sat around it were two men and two women; the faces in the room included the Minister of Communications, Justice Secretary, Head of the London Metropolitan Police Force, and Minister for Culture. The Home Secretary closed the door slowly and took his seat at the head of the table, "Evening all, let's get to it shall we." The attendees nodded slowly. "This has come from the PM (Prime Minister), so it's our job just to make sure it gets done, am I clear?" More silent nods from the room. "In accordance with preserving and protecting our Officers of the law, we are to send a clear message in the upcoming court case that civil unrest will not deter our system from delivering a Just verdict." Silence filled the room, as the Home Secretary looked each person in the room in the eye to ensure they understood the message.

The air was lightly charged, the Culture Secretary, a middle-aged portly Black woman with short natural greying hair, cleared her throat, she hesitated to speak but felt obliged to share her perspective in fear of potential backlash down the line. "Home Secretary," she began, "Have we properly considered the ... response ... from the public if the outcome is not what may be ... expected," she had learned to position comments like this as 'We' including herself, when she very much meant have 'You', and by extension 'the PM' considered the *shit show* that will take place if this officer is let off.

The Communications Minister, a portly middle-aged woman, took the opportunity to pile on and provide her counsel, "I think it's worth mentioning the unrest that has been building within certain *communities* up and down the country around this, incident," she said.

The MET Chief continued, "Bloody right, our buildings and vehicles keep getting ruined, my officers are getting abused by members of the public. These damn protests are taking away vital resources, which could be used elsewhere," the Home Secretary looked at the Justice secretary who remained silent, but was clearly listening intently, this wasn't his first rodeo.

"I understand your concerns, but it doesn't change the directive we've been given. Our job is to manage the task as efficiently and cleanly as possible. Is that clear?" The Home Secretary was met with passive, yet obedient nods.

Just as the Home Secretary was about to bring the meeting to a close, the Justice Secretary provided his first and only contribution, "We all need to remember that there is more at stake here than an officer and a boy, this is about preserving Order, without which we are no better than animals." The attendees slowly filed out of the room behind the Home Secretary, the Culture Secretary was the last out, closing the door. She couldn't help but think about what type of *order* the Justice Secretary was referring to.

Jason and Alice were cuddled on the sofa watching a nature documentary as they often would. A group of wild Beavers were vigorously building a dam in a remote part of Canada, they were both amazed by the level of teamwork and coordination. Jason's phone buzzed, he stretched over Alice to retrieve it from the arm of the sofa, it was Akira, "Hey, hope ur good? We need to talk soon?" he read the message preview without opening it, it didn't sound much like Akira; usually when she messaged there was some sort of joke, or asking to hang out or catch up... needing to talk was different.

Alice could see the consternation on Jason's face, "Everything ok? Who is it?" she asked, suddenly feeling uneasy herself.

"It's nothing, just Akira, asking to talk about something ... I was actually thinking I would invite her over here, and we could have dinner together ... the three of us," Jason replied, as he settled back against the cushion.

Alice went cold, she still hadn't responded to Akira, she had to get back to her, get ahead of this before she spoke to Jason. Her mind was racing, constructing scenarios about how things would play out. On one level she had nothing to feel guilty about, but Akira terrified her, and she knew full well that she was not her fan. What had she seen? There was little chance of her believing Alice's version of events, little chance of Jason believing her if he found out.

"Bub?" Jason asked again.

"Huh?" she responded, having completely zoned out.

"I was suggesting that we invite Akira over for dinner, what do you think? ... I know she was a bit tough on you at dinner, but I think if you guys spend a bit more time together you'll get tight ... two of my favourite ladies, don't tell my mum," he said with a laugh.

"Sure, that would be nice," she said softly.

Jason could sense that something was not quite right, he guessed Akira had made a bigger impact on Alice than he realised. "I know you like nature docs, but are these beavers that interesting?" he said, trying to lighten the mood. Alice forced a laugh out in return, but all she could think about was the pending showdown.

The AD council were congregated in a dimly lit room in the Northeast of the city. Akira was quieter than usual at the meeting. She reflected on Jason's decision to turn down the organisation; part of her was relieved, just in case things ended up going south, she would never forgive herself. However, another part of her also wondered if it was completely his own choice, or if his newfound love had influenced him in any way; his love, who was probably cheating, and had still not responded to her request to meet. She tried to refocus on the meeting, it was likely that Godfrey and Abefembe had already written off the Andrews family name following Jason's rejection, the least she could do was be engaged with the rest of the plan.

"So, what happens if we don't get the outcome we want?" said Eve, a curvy girl in a blonde wig.

"Well, that's part of the problem, do we even know what we want?" asked Devaughn.

"If we don't get what we deserve, we take it to the streets!" Godfrey said.

"And what does that achieve? We've protested, we hit the police stations, and they can't even issue a statement of apology. They don't respect us," Devaughn replied.

"Quiet!" Ademola said, her voice carried authority without having to raise it, the room fell silent. "We've made our position clear and if the powers that be decide not to do the right thing then let it burn, let it all burn." They were used to being moved by her words but this felt different, colder.

Alice knew she would have to see Akira sooner rather than later. If she didn't bite the bullet soon enough, Jason would engineer a meeting for them, and there wouldn't be anything worse than Akira spilling everything to Jason while she was present. Knowing that the meeting would be difficult, she wanted to prepare as best she could. She wanted some insight into how Akira viewed her relationship with Jason, she didn't need to be Sherlock Holmes to understand that she had reservations based on her race. Alice only really had one person in her network that could help with this - Desree.

Alice hadn't seen Desree since they were all together for the group drink, which now felt like an age ago, but they had exchanged some messages about that fallout of the evening; primarily Desree trying to reassure Alice that the night was not a complete disaster and that Jason, his friends and Daisy were all good people. Alice knew her omission of Jane was deliberate.

Alice wished that she spent more time with Desree, but in honesty her blossoming Law career meant that she was usually too busy for Alice. However, fate seemed to be smiling on Alice today, Desree had just finished up on a big case, and had a few days off. Not wanting to ambush her friend on of her few days off, Alice decided to flag ahead of time that she would need some advice on something. Despite Desree's lack of free time, Alice still had a pang of guilt knowing that her motivation to reach out was somewhat self-serving; a harsh critic could even go as far as manipulative.

Alice suggested they have a walk around the British Museum. Considering they didn't get to spend so much time together, Alice thought they should do something a bit more interesting than the typical drink in a bar. They hugged each other at the top of the grand steps that led to the museum entrance, Alice thanked her for making time on short notice. They casually walked around, mingling with the light evening crowd, the good weather in the city meant that most people still wanted to spend their time outside, instead of a sheltered museum.

"Good to see you Al, how are you doing?" Desree said.

"I'm pretty good, all things considered. How are you?" she replied.

"I'm great thanks, you know me, thriving over surviving!" she returned with her usual commanding positivity, "So, how's he treating you then? How are loves young dream doing?" Desree asked with tongue in cheek.

Alice felt slightly embarrassed that Desree had predicted that she needed help with something Jason related. "He's fine, he's fine…".

"But?" she replied knowingly.

Alice was unsure how to position her request, "But… he is very close to his cousin, Akira, she's practically an older sister… very protective… and she wants to meet with me one on one… I just want to make a good impression," she finished, not disclosing the full details of why she was really meeting with Akira; Alice felt the objective of making a good impression was enough. "We've actually met a couple of times before, mainly at dinner with his parents, and it didn't go so well. I don't think she thinks I'm *good enough* for him… or that I'm *right* for him." Her mind suddenly created a fictitious image of Whitney: beautiful face, smooth caramel complexion, tight body and able to connect with Jason on issues that were important to him in a way she never could; surely Akira would be happier with someone like her as a partner for Jason, she agonised.

They walked through a large hall dedicated to European monarchs from the middle ages. Desree listened carefully, as if she were being briefed on an important case, trying her best not to get too distracted by the various exhibits. She could see what Alice was really worried about, but like a good psychologist, wanted her to be the first to verbalise it. Desree knew how tough protective female family members could be, surprising herself when she would slip into that same role when meeting partners of her younger brothers; the race element was just an added complexity. "What do you know about her? Do you guys have anything in common that you could use as a foundation?"

The question stumped Alice, it was basic, but she'd been so worried about being judged, not measuring up, she hadn't thought about actually getting to know her. "I'm not sure," she admitted somewhat ashamedly. "Jason talks about her a lot, but what I generally take on is just that they're close… they meet to have one on ones by a stream near where they grew up…I think she has a small business doing something …she's very smart." Alice struggled to think of things, she clearly wasn't paying close attention when Jason spoke about her. There was a pause in conversation as they studied some regal clothing from an old Spanish Dynasty.

"Alice, you're a sweetheart, I don't see why she would have a problem with you, just be yourself," Desree stated, opening the door for Alice to counter with the real issue at hand. Desree kept silent, allowing Alice time to fill the conversational gap.

Alice could feel the pressure building, it was time to come clean, "Well, she does have reason… I don't think she likes me because I'm White." she said sheepishly, but also in relief.

"We got there in the end!" she replied with an exaggerated laugh, nudging Alice with her elbow.

Alice felt silly for skirting the issue, even more so

for thinking Desree wouldn't catch on, her insight and intelligence was the main reason she came to her for advice in the first place. "I know, I know, I still find it hard saying some of this out loud, you know?" Alice caught herself in her minor error, "I mean, not that you have to ever worry about it like me, but…" she tried to clarify that she understood Desree would not view issues of race how she would.

Desree saved her from digging any deeper, "Al, it's ok, I know what you mean and I get the situation," she said reassuringly, acknowledging just how much her friend was squirming. "You know this stuff isn't such a big deal for me, that's partly why we're friends," she said jokingly. Alice appreciated the humour, making her feel less awkward about everything. "I think people should be with whoever they want to be with, but I also get why some of my sisters… some of my community have a problem with it…or are at least wary," she continued.

Alice listened carefully, taking mental notes. Her frustration with having to live up to what the world thought about her relationship with Jason was boiling again. Deep down she knew it was part of the deal, but even after all this time the burdensome extra baggage felt no lighter; *why can't everyone leave us alone?!* she lamented to herself.

Desree could see that Alice was lost in thought, she was unsure if her message was landing. "Am I making any sense?" she asked.

Alice believed she understood what her friend was

saying, but it sounded conflicting. "So, what you're saying is you can be happy for people and unhappy for them at the same time?"

"Not quite," Desree responded, as they entered the West African exhibit. "What I'm trying to say is you can have one view of the world, but understand why others think another way."

Alice nodded intently.

"I may not be the best person to ask, I don't represent the entire Black community, I guess I'm just less hung up on the whole race thing. I get that we've been oppressed, that we are still facing challenges, but I would rather focus on my own reality and those close to me. It doesn't mean I don't care about other people; it's just I have not been personally impacted in the same way," she expressed. "I've never struggled with men; I have a handsome Black man that loves me and I love him. On the odd occasion I've even considered a *Swirl*, and I don't judge those that do, but that's never really been my thing. I've worked hard and managed to make a life for myself, that's my reality. But, as I said, I get that's not everyone's story and I can see why others are not as cool with things as I am."

Alice felt like the message was landing, she always loved how logical Desree was, but was aware that it helped that her view made Alice's life easier. The pair stopped at an interesting artefact from the West African kingdom of

Benin; a miniature statue of a priest in a seated position, carved from wood.

"Look at all this stuff for example, this should not be here right? It belongs to other countries; we know its looted. There will be lots of Black people aware of this or people from other parts of the world who come to see things from their home nations that have been stolen. Now if people were to come and protest the theft outside of the museum, I would understand it fully, but in honesty, I doubt I would be out there protesting with them, it's just not that important to me. So, despite race not being a huge problem for me, it doesn't mean it won't be for his cousin or that she's wrong for thinking that way. But Alice, you can only be you, just be the open, caring understanding person you are and I'm sure everything will be fine," she finished, and rubbed Alice's arm.

Desree had given her fair and objective advice as always. It didn't provide the easy fix she was hoping for, but in truth she knew that was not possible. "I know we're doing the whole cultural thing, but how about we grab a quick drink? I've been dry for the last 3 months because of this stupid case and I could really go for a Chianti"

Alice's head was starting to hurt with all the information, so was more than happy with Desree's proposal.

Jason was sat on the sofa with his laptop ready to start a session on his football management game, he had the place to himself for a few hours for a while Alice was out. He was beginning to learn the importance of alone time when living with someone, something that can be hard to come by and something with increased value when your shared apartment is small.

While he was looking forward to some 'me time', he had his favourite crisps and a one litre bottle of his favourite tropical dink, but he was still feeling bad about lashing out at Alice. It was bad enough being harsh on her, but what scared him most was how quickly his emotions seemed to escalate. He loaded up his latest game, his first task was to go through his managerial e-mails, before he began to tinker with his team selection and tactics for the upcoming cup-tie. He tried his best to focus on the game, but his mind kept drifting; would things always be this way with Alice? Would he always hold her accountable for the actions of others? It wasn't him, he told himself. He was a fair, logical person; he knew that she only meant well, that she loved him, but was that really enough? He knew what Akira would say.

His phone began to light up with messages from the boy group chat, there must be something going down. Maybe, he needed a different perspective, or maybe even a few. *I'm overdue a visit to the boys anyway*, he thought.

Thirty

Woman To Woman

The sun was starting to set when Akira arrived at the café, she was 15 minutes early but Alice was already there. She'd already had two lattes to help her focus and deal with the nerves, but in hindsight they had just made her jittery. Alice caught Akira's eye as she walked in the door, she turned away timidly looking down at her coffee between her hands.

Akira slid into the booth of the busy greasy spoon. Alice chose this venue knowing it would be hectic, and more importantly loud, so any indiscretions would be difficult to overhear. It also had the added benefit of being far away from Jason's office; who was due to work late tonight, so very little chance of him accidentally stumbling across them; as big as London was, happenstance meetings tended to occur all too often.

"Hi, Akira," Alice said with a forced smile, which felt as awkward as it looked "thank you for meeting me."

"Yes, well, I didn't have much choice did I?" she replied sharply.

Alice sheepishly took a sip of her coffee. "This … This isn't easy, but it's not what you think," Alice had rehearsed this in her head dozens of times, but under the heat of Akira's glare, she began to lose her words.

"I'm listening," Akira said.

Alice felt like the entire café was staring at her. She took another deep sip and wondered if the coffee was helping at all.

"Go on. You've delayed this for long enough," Akira said.

"I'm sorry, it's just complicated … What you saw … it was history, I mean he's my history," Alice now stumbling over her words.

"It looked pretty present to me," Akira said.

Alice opted for a different strategy, trying to placate Akira over by appealing to her feminine side; "You know when something isn't good for you, but it's still hard to let go?"

"Aw, isn't that sweet, the girl next door can't let go of the guy who had her dick drunk? Somehow that doesn't break my heart while you're playing house with my cousin!" Akira said with vim.

"No, no, it's not like that," Alice began to blush. "He's my ex and just really messed up, I tried to ignore him… but he wouldn't leave me alone … he kept calling, texting … I wanted to tell Jason, but things were up and down; either going really well, or we were dealing with other stuff, I didn't want to bring my past into things," she said.

"You know how much he loves you? How much he stresses over you, defends you against his friends and family?" Akira said.

"I LOVE HIM TOO!", Alice snapped back, surprising herself, *I really have had too much coffee*, she thought. Akira gave her a stern look that strongly suggested she should calm down. "I love him too … I love him more than any man I've ever loved before, and we don't need any outside influence trying to spoil what we have." Alice knew she wasn't a push over, but the fire that had been sparked in defence of her relationship surprised her a little.

"So, why were you kissing another man?" Akira asked, watching the strain contort her usually attractive face, reading it as genuine.

"I was just saying goodbye. You have to believe me, there's nothing between us," Alice pleaded.

Akira wasn't convinced. She looked out the window, "I've got a question, why Jason?" she asked.

"What do you mean?" Alice replied.

Akira let out a cynical laugh, she turned back to Alice, making eye contact. "I mean why Jason? You're an attractive girl, sweet, a bit of ass for a White girl, I know you get your fair share of attention from the brothers, so why did you have to choose him?" Akira finished, looking piercingly at Alice.

Alice was taken aback by the question; she didn't know how to answer. "I didn't choose him ... we chose each other," she said.

Akira laughed again, she couldn't decide if she was ingeniously manipulative or dangerously ignorant, "Of course, the fairy tale right? Except it's a bit less magical when he's with your parents or your friends, or when you're driving past a police officer."

"That's not fair," Alice replied.

"That's the thing, life isn't fair! Especially for us!" Akira shot back.

Alice looked down at her coffee. It was finished. They sat in silence. "Can I ask you a question?" Alice said.

"Sure, why not," Akira replied, wondering what she would come up with.

"Why do you hate me?" Alice said.

"Hate?! I don't hate you, sweetheart, you're not that special," she replied.

"Well, what is it then? Why can't you just be happy for us?!" Alice said with frustration, a tear rolled down her cheek.

"Oh, here we go, the *White girl waterworks*, I wondered when they would start. I don't hate you; I love my cousin and I will protect him, even from himself. So, you need to tell him or I will," Akira finished.

"Akira, he doesn't need to know, it would cause problems that we don't need," Alice said as the tears began to flow.

"He deserves to know, if you really love him you'll know that. Like I said if you can't do it, I will," Akira said, as she got up to leave. Alice wiped some snot from her nose and tears from her eyes as she looked up at Akira. For a brief moment Akira felt sorry for her, and then she thought about Jason, she turned and headed for the door, leaving Alice to ponder her next move. Alice then put her face in her hands, the waitress approached gently "Another coffee, darling?".

Thirty-one

A Problem Shared

Anton popped his head around the door and then turned back to Jason, "Yeah they didn't hear anything," he said. Lyon and Marlon were fully engrossed in a game of FIFA; Lyon was trying to claw back some dignity from a third straight defeat. "Boys! We have a special guest!" Anton said, entering the room just as Marlon scored another goal."

"Fuck Anton, you made him score again," Lyon said.

"Yep, *I* made him score," Anton replied, rolling his eyes, before opening the door wider to present Jason.

"Jase!" Lyon shouted, dropping the controller, and getting up to greet his friend with a big hug, "It's been a minute bro, I didn't think she'd let you leave the house anymore."

"Mmhhmm," they all agreed.

"Yeah yeah, I missed you guys too. FIFA is it, who wants a beating," Jason said as he took a seat and picked up a controller. The guys played a few games, quickly slipping back into old ways.

Marlon and Jason were locked in a close one when Lyon entered the room with a half-finished bottle of Whisky "who's up for a little drink?" he said with a cheeky grin.

Lyon poured four very generous glasses. "Easy, got work in the morning," Jason said as he was handed his glass.

"Man's change up!" Anton said with a laugh. "How about a toast?" he continued "The boys back together!" They all cheers-ed and had a sip.

Lyon coughed loudly, they all laughed.

"I don't know why you pretend to like this stuff," Marlon said. "How's married life treating you, Big Man?" he continued. They all subconsciously leaned in waiting for Jason to respond.

"It's good … it's great," Jason said, with less enthusiasm than intended.

"Come on, give us the details, what's it like? Blowjobs for breakfast?" Lyon asked, rubbing his hands together eagerly.

"Chill!" Anton said to Lyon. Lyon shrugged in response as if he didn't see a problem with the question.

"Yeah, it's not quite like that, I'm not living with a porn star" Jason said, with a snort of derision. "I don't know, it's good, but we're still figuring stuff out, it's different when you're living together, good and bad," he replied honestly.

"But more good than bad, right?" Marlon asked.

"Yeah, course. Just some stuff on my mind … this Adebola stuff and AD too," Jason shared.

Anton let out an exasperated puff of air. "Eh this wasn't going to be easy ya know?" he said, as he stood up and did a little walk around the room.

"Life's hard enough without letting all this political stuff get involved," Lyon said, "You've got a good woman there, just focus on that man, it's not worth it."

"I've got Lyon's back on this one," Marlon said to everyone's surprise. "What? She's a nice girl."

Anton chimed in, "Don't listen to these man; it's not straightforward when you're mixing … this interracial ting. If it doesn't feel right, then it might not be. Some people think with their big head first and little head second."

"Don't listen to Mr. Pessimistic over here, you love the girl right? You've moved in, focus on that, focus on her," Lyon said.

"When did you become the romantic?" Anton asked.

"I'm not, but when you're in the streets as long as me, you recognise a real one when it comes along. Shit if you don't want her, I'll take her off your hands," Lyon said a bit too eagerly. Jason rolled his eyes. "I'm just saying, it's not easy to find a YT with a bunda like that." Lyon finished, taking a second to happily reflect on his memory bank.

"Is that so!" Anton replied, "Like I said, some things are bigger than us. Some things are bigger than love and bunda, even a big bunda. What does Akira think?" he said, knowing full well what she would think.

"Come on man, that's not fair," Jason replied.

"I don't know bro, she's a smart girl," Anton said.

"Surprised to hear you say that after she shot you down," Lyon fired back.

"I think that whisky has touched you," Anton countered defensively.

"Everyone calm down, things are good, and as much as I hate to admit it, Lyon is probably right. Even though I have a lot on at the moment (he thought about the upcoming pitch), I need to focus on her, get the spark going again," Jason said. "Mmhmm," Anton murmured, as he drank some more whisky.

"Who wants another whooping then?!" Lyon said picking up the controller, sparking laughter amongst the group.

Alice decided to walk back home from the café, despite it being by far the longest option, in fact that's why she chose it. She needed to clear her head after the encounter and definitely didn't want to see Jason too soon, considering Akira's ultimatum. She knew what the right thing to do was, but for some reason it was so difficult to do. Alice had never been good at delivering bad news, perhaps because she was a bit of a people pleaser at heart and generally wanted to make people happy, to take care of them, a desire that guided her choice of career. As she slowly made the long walk home; she thought about one of the first times she struggled to give bad news.

Alice had to admit, *a pattern was emerging*, she thought to herself as she walked back to the halls with a couple of her dorm mates. Some of the activity from fresher's week could have been put down to chance, but here they were, deep into the first term and things were pretty consistent. Alice had never considered herself to be particularly pretty or attractive, her Dad always said she was beautiful, while her mum would normally comment on how beautiful Jane or some of her other friends were. Things were different here, was it being in a city environment? Different types of guys? Raging unsupervised hormones and alcohol? Whatever it was, she got a lot of attention, particularly from a certain type of guy. While she wasn't mad at getting it, she really wasn't sure how to deal with it.

The first few nights out she would get cat-called, walking down the high street to the student bars in her skirt and trainers. In the clubs it went up a level, the guys wanted to dance with her, talk to her, and buy her drinks, well the Black guys at least. Alice's reserved country upbringing, and teenage years had left her woefully unprepared for this type of spotlight. Admiring rappers on TV is one thing, dealing with hot-blooded young men was another. This usually resulted in her going bright red, and giggling embarrassedly. Her awkwardness did not deter her confident suitors, who were usually sporting some sort of oversized, hip-hop inspired T, and flat cap, as was the style at the time. Alice's provincial innocence in this dynamic did little to assuage the envy from certain girls, who preferred to paint her as an attention-seeking 'Ho', and not a sweet, naïve country girl. Her introverted approach did not last forever, she became more accustomed to the attention, better at handling the conversation, and much more comfortable on the dance floor. While it all remained fun for her, she was also coming of age, and very happy that she was finely being seen.

As her first year wore on, there was one guy who caught her attention more than the others, Mark. He oozed confidence and commanded a room when he entered. Mark was tall, mixed race, handsome and played on the basketball team, not that basketball was particularly well recognized at her University. He was the type of guy that all girls could appreciate, even if he wasn't their type. He had his eyes on her from pretty early on, but also had his pick of the ladies. While Alice was only recently getting used to being pursued, she'd been raised well enough to know that she should value herself, and ensure that any guy who was interested in her would do the same. Her father would always say when she was younger that one day she'll meet a boy who loves her as much as he did, something she struggled to believe in her teenage years. Alice was determined not to be just another of *Mark's girls*; she wanted to be more than that to him.

Their dance of power and flirtation went on for months before he finally caved and said that she was the only one he wanted. She was so happy when he finally stepped up that she didn't make him work as hard as she originally wanted to. They were good together, well at least they looked good together, definitely the envy of the fresher community. This was the first relationship Alice had been in, the novelty of being the focus of someone she was into, plus the adulation of strangers was an intoxicating cocktail.

Mark was very easy on the eye, but in time Alice realised they were lacking a deeper connection. A deeper connection that the praise of her peer group could not compensate for. Alice had always been a people pleaser, it was in her nature to make others happy, coupled with her shyness, which could lead to difficult situations. This was exemplified by the difficulty she had telling Mark that things were not working out. The relationship petered out over a year; a year longer than it should have. In the end, she caught Mark with another girl, but she wasn't hurt, it was just the excuse she needed to end things. Alice's fear of upsetting others was something that stuck with her to this day.

Thirty-two

Put That Woman First

The wind blew heavily the following day, as Alice struggled through the door with her gym bag. Alice had found herself going to the gym a lot more recently in an attempt to burn off her tension, yet her frustrations remained. She called up the stairs unsure if Jason was home, "Jase, are you home?" there was no response, the apartment seemed darker than usual, and there was some sort of strange smell. She lugged her bags up the stairs; *extra exercise I didn't need today*, she thought as she climbed. Alice heard soft music playing from the kitchen, she called out again "Bub?", she was mixed with feelings of intrigue and unease, as she approached the kitchen and slowly pushed the door open.

Jason was dancing to Jah Cure, as he lay out plates on the table.

"Jase, what is all of this?", she said with a smile on her face. He spun around to face her, as he dished out some spaghetti, a vase with fresh flowers sat in the middle of the table.

"Hey bub, I didn't hear you there ... take a seat, just give me a minute," he replied. Alice was overwhelmed with the effort, trying to take everything in, "Let me jump in the shower, put on some makeup; I can't eat like this."

"No, no, you're fine, just sit down and relax," Jason said, as he gently pushed down on Alice's shoulders encouraging her to sit.

"Ok, ok, I'm sitting," She said with a giggle.

Jason poured some wine and joined her to eat. "So, what did I do to deserve all of this?" she asked, as she sipped on her drink.

"Nothing, just being you," he replied.

"Ha stop, I can't handle all this wooing, feels like when we first started dating.", She said wistfully, but with an element of rue.

"Exactly, felt like you deserved a bit of special attention," Jason countered. His phone buzzed, "Sorry, gotta check that, could be work." Jason hopped up and looked at his phone, it was Akira. He closed his phone and sat back at the table. "Everything ok with work?" Alice asked.

"No, I mean yeah, it wasn't work, it was Akira. She's been really cryptic lately." Jason said with a puzzled look. Akira's name made Alice's blood run cold, a sledgehammer of reality had hit her in the stomach, temporarily winding her, as she remembered Akira's words, 'you tell him or I will.'

"Is the food ok?" Jason asked, noticing that Alice had stopped eating.

"Of course, it's lovely," she replied. Alice never had much of a poker face, so her feigned contentment, and inability to focus on the conversation was easy for Jason to detect. Jason continued to push ahead with the conversation, but Alice's responses were short and seemingly uninterested.

"Are you sure everything is Ok?" he asked again as he dropped the plates in the sink.

"I'm fine, I promise," she replied with a strained smile. Jason wasn't convinced, but he was committed to making this a memorable evening. "Should we carry on watching Ocean Odyssey?" Alice asked, proposing the next stage of the evening. "Oh no, I have something else prepared for us," he said with a mischievous grin. "Give me one second," he left the kitchen, Alice was alone with her thoughts again, feelings of anxiety rushing back.

Jason was suddenly back, almost taking Alice by surprise in her distracted state. "Ok, I'm ready, I need you to close your eyes and follow me." Alice stood up slowly, closing her eyes, Jason put his hands over her eyes to make sure, guiding her out of the door and to the bedroom. Jason kicked the bedroom door open, and removed his hands from her face, "ok you can look now," spiced incense and small candles burned around the bedroom, old school Mary J Blige played on the portable speaker. Alice was stunned, she knew Jason loved her, but he was never the most romantic guy in the world.

"This is amazing, Bub", she said as a tear fell from her cheek, emotions begin to race, she turned to kiss him.

"We're not done, I need you to undress and lay on the bed," he said

"What do you mean?" she replied,

"I mean get naked; I mean I'm tryna see that ass," he continued with a laugh, firmly slapping her on the bum.

"Yes, Sir!" she shot back ironically, she hated to admit it, but she enjoyed it when he took control.

"One more thing", he pulled out a bright pink eye mask, "put that on," he said.

Alice laughed at how bright and girly it was, "where did you get that from?" she said, "It was the only one they had, and I tell you what, those shops have way too many toys! It's a wonder women still have any interest in men at all," he said, shaking his head while putting the eye mask on her.

Alice was finding it hard to relax, she was unsure if it was the nervous excitement of being blindfolded, not knowing what was next, or something else. Jason straddled her, sitting over her bum, she let out a big groan "Aahhhhh" as if she were being crushed.

"Shhhh I'm not that heavy, although I have been lifting more recently," he joked to himself. He adjusted himself slightly, "Does that help?" he asked

"Kind of ..." she responded gasping slightly for air.

"Just relax, I got you," he said, as he slowly dripped the massage oil down her back. She squirmed at the shock of the temperature, "That's cold!", she yelped.

Jason tried to stifle his laugh in response to her discomfort. "Relax, relax, it'll warm up," he began to rub the oil deeply into her skin, she was tense.

"You definitely needed this," he said almost to himself, as he worked his hands deep into her tissue. She really did need it; she purred quietly with pleasure. "Is it good?" he asked

"Mmmhmm," she responded.

He began working on her legs, staring at her hamstrings and working his way down to her calves and feet. He took his top off, "If people could see me now, they would not believe it, especially Akira," The name caused Alice to stiffen, "Are you ok? Are you not into this?" he asked, slightly frustrated.

"No bub, it's great, please carry on," she said as she tried to relax and keep her mind on the massage and nothing else.

Time to go up a gear, he thought to himself. He began to massage her cheeks, slowly and deeply "A lot of tissue here," he said jokingly.

"Hey, be nice," she replied, still holding some elements of self-consciousness from her teenage years.

"I'm sorry," he said playfully, as he kissed each one of her ass cheeks.

"That's better," she said.

He slipped his fingers slowly between her cheeks and continued to massage, she groaned. He slowly built-up speed, getting deeper. "I know you've not had it like this before," he said, the sexy comment inflamed the wrong buttons for a distracted Alice, she suddenly flashed back to her ex, the park, and then Akira's face; she was out of the zone again. She squirmed and wriggled underneath him, the bed creaked loudly, as it would if too much pressure was placed on certain areas.

The creaks would sometimes disturb Ms. Chamberlin, whose living room was directly underneath their bedroom; depending on if she was there, or how loud she had the TV on, it would sometimes result in her hitting the ceiling with a broom handle.

"I need to go to the toilet." Alice said, in a stressed tone. Tap tap tap went Ms. Chamberlin's broom, almost on cue. Jason exhaled in frustration; this was not going to plan.

Alice looked in the mirror, she looked tired, eyes drawn. She splashed water on her face. Get it together she said to herself, focus! By the time she returned Jason was on his phone and the music was off. He'd given up on the evening, feeling frustrated with the outcome, particularly as he had put in a lot of effort, even though the big pitch meeting was right around the corner. As he scrolled through his messages, he spotted one from Whitney wishing him good luck for the pitch, reaffirming again that he'd do a great job, so he should just relax; she'd also sent a selfie pulling a silly face – she was annoyingly photogenic. For the first time since being with Alice, the thought crossed his mind that maybe he should have given Whitney more of a chance.

"Hey, sorry about this, I'm just feeling a bit stressed, work has been really busy lately, you know?"

"Yeah, sure," he replied, disappointedly.

"Can we pick this up another night? … when I'm a bit less stressed," she asked. "Sure, whatever," he answered quietly. She tried to kiss him, but he turned his lips away, a cheek was the best she could get today.

Thirty-three

What Have I Done?

The team were finishing up their presentation on the 19th floor of the ultra-modern, brand new global headquarters of Armidex. The Rhomboid shaped structure was covered from top to bottom in reflective glass panels. It was unusual for one of the Directors not to close the presentation, but the team had been so impressed with Jason's work that they felt he deserved the opportunity. "In closing, that's why we believe we would make the perfect partner for this incredibly important project. Thank you for giving us the opportunity to present to you today." Jason finished with aplomb. The team answered a few tricky questions, before leaving the conference room and heading to the elevator.

There were congratulations all around from the two Directors present, "great work today guys, and a special shout out to Jason for stepping up and bringing us home."

Ben said. Violet knew Jason better than anyone in the office. She could tell something was up; he'd just delivered a great performance at a major pitch, but his feigned smiles weren't fooling her. When they got back to the office 'Eye of the Tiger' was played for them, as was customary for when a big piece of work had been completed, the whole office stood to give them a round of applause. This was as close as it got to feeling like an athlete for those in the public sector.

There was cake in the kitchen for everyone, another ritual the office conducted on pitch day. Word of their success had travelled quickly around the building and of course Whitney had shared prompt words of congratulations, suggesting that she would treat him in celebration, he noted that she didn't specify the usual coffee meet up, leaving the door open for something more. He didn't want to entertain the thought; he could barely enjoy the big win.

Violet pulled Jason to one side as people milled around the cake and made teas. "What's going on?" She asked.

"What do you mean, I'm fine?" he answered.

"I know somethings up, I've known you since you were a wide-eyed post-grad, you can't fool me. You've just delivered a great piece of work, we have a real chance of winning this account, that would be huge for us – you should be over the moon!" she surmised.

"Just a bit worn out from all the preparation, I guess," he said, trying to deflect her interrogation. She studied him closely, analysing his body language, and micro-expressions; par for the course for those in the Service. Jason felt distinctly uncomfortable, she really did know him too well.

"Come on, you can tell me ... what if I guess?", she said. Jason sighed in frustration. "Is it really work-related? Because if it is, I have to step in as your manager," she scanned him again, "Hmm ok, not work ... not work ... is it family?" she watched for a response, nothing. "Ah, of course, it's woman trouble," she said in a surprisingly objective tone, as if she weren't a woman herself. "Gonna tell me about it?" she continued.

Jason tried to remain stoic, under the battery of questions. She continued to stare at him until he folded. "Fine, fine. Things are just a bit off at the moment. I don't know... maybe we moved a bit too fast," Jason conceded.

Violet recognising the strain in his face, could tell things were serious. "I'm sorry to hear it's not going so great at the moment, but you know that's just relationships, right? ups and downs, it's normal. I've been with Jack for 7 years, I love the guy to pieces, but at times I want to kill him, maybe it's not love if you don't want to kill them sometimes," she said with a laugh. "Try not to worry too much about it, things will work out," she said, reassuringly rubbing his arm. Jason wanted to say that it wasn't that straightforward, that they didn't have a typical relationship. She was right about one thing; things would work out one way or another; he just wasn't sure exactly what that looked like.

"Damian!" Daisy said loudly with surprise

"Be quiet Daisy," Alice replied, placing her index finger to her lips.

"What rock did he crawl back from under?" she said with disgust. Daisy didn't really do quiet, but she tried her best to lower her voice, despite this earth-shattering piece of news, "Ok ok, I don't think we're at risk in this old man's boozer, the only person in here young enough to not have a hearing problem is that guy transfixed with the fruity. Why didn't you tell me?" she continued, not much quieter than before.

"I don't know, I thought I could handle him," Alice responded placing her face in her hands. "The timing was terrible, I was getting to know Jason, I didn't even want to acknowledge that he even still existed, but he wouldn't leave me alone, so I agreed to meet him ... to end things for good," Alice said with as much conviction as she could muster.

"Alice, this boy had you crying so many nights I lost count, it was so hard for you to walk away when you eventually did. You're a strong woman but this guy does something to you ... you weren't you. Why the hell did you meet him?" Daisy asked. "I had to, he said he would leave me alone if I did," Alice responded.

"And you believed him?! That boy would say anything to get what he wants out of you," Daisy said with concern.

"It gets worse …" Alice said, as she took a sip of her G&T.

Jason had just gotten out of the tube when his phone started to ring, it was Akira. "Hey, Cuz, how are you doing?" he said, happy to hear from her.

"Not too bad Sprout," she replied.

He rolled his eyes. "Sorry, I've been meaning to get back to you, what's up? Not like you to push so hard for a meet up," he said.

"How are things with Alice?" she responded. Strange he thought, she was never so keen to talk and rarely showed any genuine interest in Alice.

"She's good I guess," he replied. "So, no major changes recently," she asked.

"What do you mean?" he asked, confused by her line of questioning.

"No, nothing major, why? What's up?" he said, as he thought about their recent failed romantic evening.

"It's better if we meet Jason." Something was definitely wrong, she rarely called him Jason; Jase, sprout, Cuz, but Jason … Jason meant there was a problem.

Alice was on her third large G&T, she needed Dutch courage to even talk about this to one of her best friends.

"You kissed him! Are you Fucking insane!" Daisy was back at full volume.

"No, I mean kind of, I kissed him goodbye and he kissed me more. He looked so sad, I hugged him and he just pulled me in, you know he's like twice my size before I knew it his lips were on me, I pulled back," Alice finished.

"And the cousin saw you," Daisy continued.

"Apparently," Alice replied.

"Well fuck me! What are you going to do? You have to tell him," Daisy said having lost any and all decorum at this point.

"I know, I know, I just don't know how," Alice responded. "Things are up and down with us at the moment, we don't need this."

"It's better coming from you." Daisy said softly, placing her hand on Alice's. "He'll understand. He's a smart guy," she said positively.

"I will, I just need to find the right time," replied Alice.

Abefembe went through the plans, for what felt like the 100th time, she was still unsure if this was the right thing to do, would this be going too far? The agreement that had been made with the mysterious figure was to only cause some mild unrest through the targeted damage of certain police stations, all in supposed response to the Adrian

Adebola attack. In exchange for this, AD would be granted a steady stream of funding for community programmes, and the officer would be held accountable in a court of law, that was the deal, but something told her that her mysterious handler could not be trusted. *When could they ever be trusted?* she thought to herself, history repeats because people never learn. If we are crossed this time, history would remember the consequences.

Thirty-four

Hard To Say

They met at their usual spot by their *river*. Jason was strangely timely. "Hey Cuz, you alright?" he said with low energy. "I'm fine Jase and you?" she said coolly, not relishing the conversation ahead.

"How's life living with the girl" she began ... Are you sure she's the one?" she asked directly, hoping to rip the plaster off quickly. Jason was taken back by the question; he knew she wasn't Alice's number one fan, but had hoped that by now she would have come to terms with the fact that they were together. "Does she have to be the one, can't she just be the one who makes me happy at this moment?" he asked. Akira was silent, she thought she had her conversation points planned out, but things were much harder in person. She could detect some unrest within him; he was less jubilant in his description of things with Alice than he had been in the past, maybe the revelation won't be so hard on him.

Jason filled the silence, "We're trying to make the best of it. But, it's not always easy, I guess that's life, that's living with someone," he continued, more confidently.

"But is it?" Akira replied, sensing an opening, "maybe you don't know her as well as you thought? maybe you moved a bit too fast?" she suggested, with an air of subjective objectivity. Despite the challenges he and Alice were facing, he didn't want to have to defend his relationship with his cousin; if she wasn't going to be supportive, he'd rather she said nothing at all.

"Not now, cuz," he said, almost pleading, "Can't you just be happy for me, try and get behind us? I know she's not your *ideal* girl, but just try and get on the same page as me, please!" he petitioned.

She knew she had to say something now or she wouldn't be able to, as much as it pained her to do so, "Jase, there's something you need to know," she said.

"What is it now?" he replied, starting to lose patience while thinking about an exit. "Alice ... she's not who you think she is ... I saw her." Akira struggled to get it out. "What are you on about?" he said.

"I saw her with a guy, kissing a guy, a while ago". Jason felt like he had been hit in the chest with a wrecking ball; he stared straight ahead blankly, white noise in his ears. Akira looked at Jason for a response, it was as if he had mentally checked out; the lights were on, but nobody was home. "Sprout ... did you hear what I said?" she asked gently, as if she had just shared a terminal diagnosis.

"Why are you saying this?" he asked coldly, she had never seen him like this, she was slightly scared, as much for him as anything else.

"Because I saw it and you had to know and she …"

Jason interrupted, "Shut up! You're Jealous! You're Sick! you really hate her that much that you'd make up a lie like this, it's pathetic!" Jason was fuming, he'd hit 100 in record time.

Akira was taken back, "It's not that Sprout," she said.

"Stop the Sprout shit! Just because you're alone and unhappy, you want the same for me!" he replied.

"She's cheating on you!!!" She screamed back.

"Bullshit!" He said, not prepared to entertain the accusation.

"I wish it was; I really do. but I saw her. She was with another guy, she kissed him," she explained.

"I don't believe it. You never liked her, look at how you were at dinner with my parents. How could I trust you?" he said.

"It's true, I'd never lie about something like this, not to you, you know that," she replied.

"No, you're lying, you want me to be miserable … miserable like you, you hate that I'm progressing and not being your little Sprout anymore," he argued.

"No, of course not. Yes, she wouldn't be my first choice, but I'm happy for you. I don't know what to say, I saw them, I didn't want to tell you, but I couldn't let you stay with a cheat," she said.

"Shut up! Don't call her that! You don't know anything. You're a bitter woman approaching middle age, alone!" he said angrily, he stood up and stormed off.

"Jase! Jase! Come back," she yelled, but he wouldn't look back. Jason wiped the tears from his eyes, his world was spinning.

Mz. Afrika's weekly live stream debate had been growing in viewership, as tensions in the city increased around the ongoing acts of vandalism and pending Adebola court case. On her show this week was a neo-soul singer, Jay Blue, and a budding entrepreneur Chris Arnold. There had been much discussion about the pending court case and whether or not the Black community could trust the justice system. Mz. welcomed them both on, Jay Blue set the tone replying, "Power to the people and the people shall retain the power," while raising his right fist.

Chris gave a mild snort of derision in response. Mz. Afrika turned to Chris, "Chris, I believe these rumours of a public backlash are concerning to you, particularly as a businessman?"

"That's right, not only will it not achieve anything, apart from mindless destruction and arrests, we risk putting Black businesses in danger. The unrest won't be taking place in White suburbs. Better to keep that riot stuff across the pond," he finished smugly.

Blue rolled his eyes, Mz. Afrika nodded his way, giving him the floor. "I don't want to see any unnecessary violence, I don't want to see my people harmed, but there comes a time when you have to send a message and words aren't enough," he said pointedly.

"And you believe that, especially as a musician yourself," she asked.

"I do, generations before us had to sacrifice to make progress, sometimes that's the only way to make them listen," he replied.

Chris jumped in, "This type of fear-mongering is exactly what we don't need, we are part of a shared society, we need to show faith in the system. All we're doing is giving the police more reason to target us," he finished.

"And what good reason do they have now? Adrian Adebola was just walking home from school; the officers didn't need any extra encouragement that day?" Blue countered.

Jane heard the front door open; she quickly closed the debate screen and her laptop. "Tulip?!", called Jane's partner, "Are you home, dear?"

"Coming, darling", Jane said, as she took a sip of wine and made her way downstairs.

Jason was a mess. He couldn't sleep properly, his head was swimming with questions, he didn't know what to do. He wanted to keep things as normal as possible until he figured out a plan.

Akira tried to call every day, she sent streams of messages trying to explain herself more fully, but he didn't want to hear it. It didn't make any sense to him, and he knew speaking to her before he came to terms with what was going on wouldn't help things. He kept spinning it over and over in his brain, Alice a cheat? Her with another guy, kissing another man, laying with another man, laughing with someone else. It made him sick to his stomach. He didn't want to believe it, but why would Akira lie about that? Something didn't add up …

Jason decided to try and put it all to the back of his mind, but it was difficult. He started to reflect on his time with Alice, was any of it real? All the laughs, the supposed connection, the love. As he scanned through their romantic highlight reel, a reoccurring thought began to emerge, like a detective uncovering a pivotal clue that brings the whole mystery together … the unanswered calls, ignored messages on a vibrating phone. Jason had never paid much attention to that stuff, being equal parts oblivious and trusting, but it was starting to fall into place, could it be? Was this guy reaching out to her all that time they were together? The idea made him queasy again. No, he was wrong, he told himself;

he had no proof, and the truth was he didn't want to believe it, he was happier living a potential lie.

The first few days following the revelation trying to forget about things were tough, Alice could tell something was not quite right, something more than their usual rollercoaster of emotions. Her gut told her it was to do with what Akira, after all, it was only a matter of time before she acted on her promise to say something to Jason, but she didn't want to accept it and make it real. It was better to pretend, if nothing was said, maybe they could get past it. Jason was less tactile, less affectionate than normal, and this not long after moving in, when they should still be in the honeymoon phase.

As the days wore on it became easier, slightly easier to ignore the bombshell Akira had delivered, yet he remained in a perpetual state of low level of paranoia; overtly alert to any text messages she received, wary whenever she left the room to speak to someone, inquisitive whenever she was late home, or had a change of plans. In reality their current dynamic hadn't changed so much, she was pretty normal; if anything she was even more loving, seemingly making up for any lack of affection from his side. *Is that what people do when they cheat? Try to overcompensate*, he pondered to himself. Or maybe it was all in his head, he just couldn't shake it.

Thirty-five

Justice Or Just-us

The summer had been long, hot and filled with tension. Following months of discussion and debate around the Adrian Adebola case; online movements, petitions and marches, the trial had finally arrived. The Black community up and down the country were keenly awaiting the outcome, support had even come in from their empathetic American brothers and sisters. The case had run for a fortnight; classmates of Adrian had given virtual testimonies, school teachers, football coaches, family, friends, and fellow officers. The family had managed to get good legal counsel with financial support from charities. Officer Watkins had been charged with aggravated assault, following intense pressure from campaigners, as the initial charges proposed were much less severe. The softness of the initial charges gave the already sceptical Black community an indication that as usual, things were not set up to end with the justice they deeply desired – even with extensive video footage of the assault against the young boy. Today was the day of the verdict.

Jason's mum was tuned into a radio station covering the trial, there were crowds outside of the courthouse, everybody waiting patiently. A young Black woman opened the door, seemingly exasperated as if they'd run all the way from the courtroom, she had the verdict… "NOT GUILTY," she shouted. Boos rang in from the crowd. "Fuck!" Jason's mum shouted, "they always get away with it, always! It doesn't matter how much evidence you have, it's always the same!" Andrea said to herself. She messaged Jason, to see if he had also heard the verdict. Jason was sitting on the sofa following the news on his iPad when the text came in. "Just saw it, there's no hope with these lot," Jason replied.

He put his phone down and switched off his iPad, he started to think. He dropped into a reflective mind state, as he often would following traumatic community events - it was a coping mechanism as much as anything else. He was raised to know his history; Malcolm, Garvey, Bobby Seale to name a few. He understood the struggles his people had endured, all the sacrifices that had been made by so many to allow him to have the privileges he enjoyed today, which is why it always hurt so much when the hand of racism was thrown back in his face again. No matter how much you think you're progressing, an *incident* happens; pulled-over for being Black, macroaggressions at work for being Black, or as Adrian experienced, assault by a grown man that had been entrusted to protect you, just for being Black. *AD were right to take things into their own hands*, he thought; *the system could not be trusted*, he felt stupid for not helping the organisation.

His mind continued to travel, how do you reconcile that level of injustice? How do you continue being a happy, smiling, a contributing member of society, when this is going on? He was taught to give people the benefit of the doubt, not to pre-judge, he knew not everyone was bad. But, where do you draw the line, you're integrated, you want to be, you don't have much choice. The lack of public outcry from the allies when things went wrong always made him think, where do *they* truly stand? Surely if it was a real issue, like plastic in the ocean, or a missing child, *people* would be up in arms, but when its racism, there is a tacit agreement that something is wrong, followed by nothing … let's go back to normal. So, do they really care at all? Really?

He knew progress was never going to lay with the perpetrators, he knew the answer lay within his community, to a degree at least. While the Diaspora were away from home, only so much could be done, effectively on enemy territory, or at least vulnerable. Security, prosperity is surely *back home*, he always wanted that life, a life in the sun, in the Caribbean or Africa, but also had some internal turmoil, dual cultural heritage and a love of the UK, or at least London, even with its drawbacks. And, of course, Alice.

Even with all the doubt and confusion, he still loved her. His mind continued to run until he nodded off.

The sun began to set and the street lights started to sprinkle one by one on the road near the courthouse. A group of half a dozen people dressed in Black approached from one end of the street, towards the front of the courthouse, and a slightly smaller size group approached from the rear. Each group leader checked their mobiles, as the clocks crept closer to 20:00. Abefembe looked at her watch, it was nearly time. She had hoped that it wouldn't come to this, had hoped her mysterious *Allie* could be trusted, but deep down she already knew, she knew that they would never change.

At the top of the magic hour, the coordinated message came through to the various teams scattered around the city, it read one word – 'Begin.' In unison, the carnage commenced, not just at the courthouse, but at civil services and police buildings all over the city, up and down the country. Adebola was sprayed, glass was smashed, and petrol bombs were thrown; small fires in the building grew bigger, and as if by magic, the two groups fled into the darkness to their next locations.

The attacks did not only target physical buildings, but also government computer systems, the various viruses and trojan horses began to cripple key public sector networks.

The systems began to fall like a series of precariously placed dominoes.

Across the city in Whitehall, the Home secretary was bunkered down in his office, every line on his phone had been blinking incessantly, and both his mobiles vibrated non-stop. The PM wanted immediate answers, for the first time in his career he did not have any. He had sent dozens of messages and made numerous calls to Akira, but got no response. It was not supposed to happen like this, the incidents were supposed to be controlled; only to happen at select locations up until the trial, and then stop. Stop under the promise that Adrian would receive justice, The Home Secretary thought he had the AD organization under control, but the plan to double-cross them had backfired massively. He had drastically underestimated the lengths they would go to for retribution; the reality was beginning to set in, he had overplayed his hand.

The Gorilla attacks spread like wildfire across the strategic locations. The squads moved in and out of each pre-planned location quickly. The interconnected nature of London's topography made it fairly easy for the different squads to slip from neighbourhood to neighbourhood, with estates practically adjacent to affluent areas in many places. As news spread of the acts of protest, the domino effect commenced; random individuals seized the opportunity to get involved in the action, some just for the sake of it, some to vent some frustration, and some for their own selfish gains. Before long, small pockets of the city were growing into turbulent trouble centres and flash zones. The emergency services were stretched thinly; every news channel was providing live coverage from the various hot spots of unrest. People were encouraged to stay at home, almost all were glued to some sort of screen, watching the turmoil unfold, whether it be phone, iPad, laptop or TV, traditional media or social, you could not look away.

Jason was feeling tense, as he waited in the apartment for Alice to get home, she left work about 40 minutes earlier and should have been back, but all the drama from the riots was playing havoc with the underground, and she had no reception. Thoughts of her potential betrayal were drowned out by fears of her safety and a deep desire to protect the one he loved; he had to make sure she was ok. Jason had left her text messages, WhatsApp and voice notes to call him as soon as she arrived at the tube, so he could meet her and make sure she got back safely. Jason had already spoken to Margot twice in the past hour, she was very concerned about the reprobates who had taken over the city, having it made very clear to him that she wasn't happy with her daughter living in London; somehow inferring Jason was partly to blame, despite the fact she was living in London long before she ever met him.

He was getting worried; things were out of hand; he knew by now this was a free for all for anyone who was looking for a bit of carnage. He could understand, his pent-up frustration following the verdict was also driving a personal desire to see some carnage. Daisy had messaged him checking on both of them; he wondered if Jane would have been in contact, had she had his number. At that moment his phone sprang to life … it was Alice. In his haste to pick up, he dropped the phone, it skidded across the floor. He slid after it and grabbed it, "Are you ok?" he asked "Jase! They've blocked the station and are only letting a few people out at a time."

"Ok, ok, I'm coming down," he said.

"No, it could be dangerous, I'll be fine, just stay indoors," she pleaded.

"No, I'm coming!" he put the phone down and headed for the door.

Alice was penned in with dozens of other commuters, most of whom were scared by all the unrest and wailing sirens; each of them eager to make it home as quickly and safely as possible. People were pushing and pulling trying to get to the exit. A few community support officers were doing their best to keep everyone calm, in truth, it was clear to all in attendance that they were in over their heads. One support officer was petitioning the crowd to calm down, saying that they would be letting people out in a slow and staggered fashion, for their own safety.

When Jason hit the main road, he could see some of the melee first-hand. In what seemed like no time at all, there was already damage to random cars, even more litter on the street. Jason thought it said something interesting about society, that it could so quickly tip into chaos. It made him think that things were precariously perched on edge; a pile of tinder ready to catch fire at the slightest instigation.

The atmosphere was strange; a post-apocalyptic vibe was created by the absence of bodies from the usually busy high street. A few kebab shop owners were *open,* ready to protect their businesses with freshly sharpened, long shiny blades. Groups of kids were roaming around, many on pushbikes enjoying the excitement the air of lawlessness brought. There was a backdrop of perpetual siren sounds that only added to Jason's unease, as he broke into a jog towards the station.

When he arrived, he struggled to see Alice through the bodies. A small counter group of people trying to meet loved ones had formed across the street, but they were being kept away from the station and told to wait until people were let out. Jason attempted to push past one Officer, who pushed him back, telling him to stay back. The officer's hand motioned dangerously towards his baton. Jason stepped back and took his phone out to call Alice, still, no signal, seems like everyone in the area was trying to call someone. Jason was wracking his brains, unsure what to do, he dropped to the back of the crowd when he heard one of the officers shout that a group were being released. He ran back to the group to see if Alice was in the batch to be released, she wasn't. He didn't know what to do. He thought about other ways to get into the station, but there didn't seem to be any good options. At that moment his phone rang, it was Alice. "They've let me out, where are you?", she said exasperated.

"Where? How? I checked," he asked.

"I snuck out after the last group were let out, I couldn't take it anymore in there. I'm just on the corner of Armon Street. Jason ran towards her, he could see her with her phone in her hand, he made it to her and they hugged and kissed.

"Let's go," he said.

Their flat was less than a 10-minute walk from the station, but they had decided to avoid the main roads as that's where groups were gathering to attack the shops. The streets were eerily quiet with the odd shout, siren and occasional scream, they felt like they were in a horror movie. They'd made it down two streets and were nearly home when they came across a group of kids sitting on the corner, two were on BMXs. Jason thought they weren't spotted at first, Alice automatically picked up speed when they heard a shout "Eh Eh, My man, where you going?" They continued walking, ignoring the call. "Eh, u deaf, I'm talkin to you," the voice called out. Before they knew it the two BMXs had caught up to them and cut off their route, while the other boys were walking up from behind. "You can't answer man, no?" the leader asked.

Jason, turned to face him, pulling his arm across Alice as protection. "We're just going home," he said calmly.

"Yeh, U from round ere?" the lead kid asked. Jason

knew this game from growing up, but thought he was long passed it.

"We're local yeah," he replied.

"Man says he's local!" the boys laughed, "Who do you know from the endz, if you're so local?" he asked, looking him dead in the eye.

Jason was thinking, this wasn't his *area*, even if it was, he was out of touch with what was going on in the endz.

The boys eyed them like hungry jackals, awaiting their response. Jason began to speak when a phone rang. He prayed it wasn't his or Alice's, the last thing they needed to do was pull out a mobile, unsolicited. It was one of the boys, he began speaking in hushed tones, all Jason could make out was "is it?", "swear down!", "mums", "mmm", and "yeh". The boy put down the phone, "Eh Damon and dem man are up on the high street, der about to buss the phone shop, come we roll."

The lead boy begrudgingly agreed to move on, "You caught a bly slyly big man, brave to have the White missus with every ting dats gwarnin," he kissed his teeth and turned towards the high street, "Come we roll den." Alice felt like she hadn't breathed for the last three minutes. Jason grabbed her hand and they walked quickly back to the flat.

Alice was on the phone with her mum for what seemed like forever, Jason could hear her saying the same things over and over again "Yes mum, I'm ok. I know you said London is dangerous. No this doesn't happen every day. Can I speak to

Dad please?" Jason just stared out of the window watching streams of smoke and a dim glaze encapsulate the city. The dull echo of sirens continued. Despite the madness, part of him felt like he should be out there with the others, out there demonstrating his frustrations in a way that could not be ignored. As Alice continued to speak with her parents, "Yeah Jason is fine, he was my hero." As she spoke, Jason got a sudden reminder about Alice's supposed infidelity, it didn't make him feel much like a hero.

Thirty-six

Bullet Biting

Jason hadn't slept well since the verdict, between the subsequent riot and what Akira accused Alice of. It was all getting to him; he was tired and irritable. He woke one morning having dreamed about a version of events, where he was the victim of police brutality and the officer managed to get off scot-free, worst yet, Alice didn't support him, in fact, she was on the opposing side of the courtroom. *It's funny how some dreams can feel so real, that even when you wake up, you still think it's real*, he thought to himself. His subconscious seemed to be coalescing his fears and worries into macabre nightmares, he couldn't get out of his own head. Alice had noticed the difference in him since they'd moved in, and it seemed to be getting worse. She was doing all she could, but he was distant, snappy and restless. She hoped it was just a phase that would pass.

Jason got into work early that day, as he couldn't sleep

341

well, he was avoiding morning cuddles with Alice in favour of early departures to the office. His colleagues had even picked up on Jason's mood, usually so positive, with a smile that lit up the office, he hadn't been his usual effervescent self in recent weeks. Of course, Chris was loving it, and would use any opportunity to wind Jason up. "In early are we ... for once, what's up? Jay-Z tickets go on sale this morning or something?" Chris said dryly.

Jason looked at him coldly "Not today Chris, today is not the day," he said sternly, trying not to raise his voice. Chris got the message and kept his distance for the rest of the morning.

Jason was even off with the colleagues he actually liked; he was short with everyone. In the afternoon, he took himself to the roof of the building where the smokers usually congregated to get some air. His mind continued to bounce between Alice and Akira, back and forth. How could he be with her in a world like this, what did it say about him and what he stood for? He felt powerless. Jason kept his head down for the rest of the day, to decrease the chance of him being curt with anyone else. He was happy to reach the sanctity of his home, able to unbutton his shirt and try to decompress; but then it hit him, living with Alice meant that his home wasn't the place of peace it should be, not while everything was so unresolved - he realised he had to confront Alice; It was weighing too heavily on his mind. He poured himself a drink and tried to plan what he would say.

Alice was struggling with Jason's changed behaviour; the coldness, the lack of intimacy and the distance. He seemed to be spending more time on his phone, that had never been a problem for her before; she wondered who he was speaking to? leaning on his work wife? Confiding in her, her comforting him... Alice wanted to put it down to paranoia, but it was like he wanted a distraction, as if he didn't want to touch her; in fact he hadn't in a while. The disrupted physical connection was particularly strange for them; even when they were at odds, intimacy was something they never seriously struggled with. The changes were starting to effect Alice; for the first time since meeting Jason she felt compelled to spend some time self-satisfying. Of course there's nothing wrong with this, even in a relationship, but Alice rebuked the notion of having to please herself while sharing a roof with the man she loved. Delving deeper Alice knew the issue was more than practical, it was what it represented – them growing apart.

Alice still had some links from her research foray into the world of adult entertainment. She wished Jason would touch her again how he used to, taking a moment to bask in memories of their passionate moments. If he was angry with her, just express it, take it out on her, making up could be very fun according to some of these videos. It wasn't just her *secret sessions* that concerned her, she was noticing behaviour changes in her day to day life; specifically, how she was beginning to interact with other men. Alice was typically so besotted with Jason, she couldn't remember the last time she even acknowledged another man, but suddenly they were visible again. She caught herself smiling back at the cute doctors that would flirtatiously glance her way, she was taking longer to move away from the gym guys who were checking her out as she exercised, she was even starting to read the unsolicited DMs that came in; messages that once upon a time would have been deleted without even opening. In her heart she hoped that she would never cross a line, but she knew something had to change with Jason.

The flat was dark when Alice entered, just a dim light coming from the living room. She called out to see if Jason was in, "Jase, you home?" she said. No response. She walked into the living room and saw him sitting there swirling his glass. "Everything ok?" she said sweetly.

"Yeah fine, just a long day," he replied.

"Well, I'll sort us some food and we can talk about it, or we can get a take-away?" she said brightly trying to lift his mood.

"I'm not very hungry," he said flatly.

Alice left the room to take her jacket off, she was exasperated. Work was intense as ever; she was tired, maybe she just wanted to sulk. She went into the bathroom and splashed some water on her face. She stared in the mirror, she didn't like the face that looked back at her, she wasn't happy. It wasn't supposed to be this way. She'd had a bad relationship, with the unstable guy; Jason was supposed to be different, but he was so out of sorts recently. Did she really know him, maybe her mum was right, maybe they had moved in together too soon?...

She was overthinking it, she decided. One of her key strengths was her positivity, she just needed to get them through this. *A shower will help*, she thought; *a shower and some food*. After a long hot shower, she made some pasta for the two of them. They were watching a debate show, the panellists were talking about the recent Adrian Adebola court case verdict. The show followed the classic pro and against format. Alice wasn't really engaged; she was worried about Jason, trying to get some cuddling going, but he wasn't reciprocating. She gave up and tried to focus on the TV.

A politician was pleading the case for the need to protect the police, who put their life on the line to protect us, he stated. It was time the public cut them some slack and respected what they were doing, to keep us safe. On the other side of the panel, we had an activist supporting young Adrian, who wanted clarity on who exactly he was referring to when he said "us". They shot jabs back and forth, while the host tried her best to moderate the heated discussion. The conversation was frustrating Jason, another old, pompous, middle class; *White man with no regard for Black life*, he thought to himself.

"Look at this guy, typical," Jason said.

"Well, he's just trying to say that the police are people

too, who are doing a really difficult job," Alice said more quickly than she meant to.

It wasn't the response Jason was hoping to hear. "So, because they're doing a tough job, they're allowed to harass people and discriminate," Jason replied.

"No, I didn't say that. It's just they can't all be bad, can't all be bad, can they?" Alice claimed.

"Well, how many are allowed to be bad? How many people should be harassed or worse?" Jason said sternly.

"You were there in the car with me, you saw how they were, or have you forgotten?" "No, I have not forgotten, I still have nightmares about it. It's just … it's just… it doesn't matter," Alice pleaded.

"It's just you don't get it, and you never will. The country girl spends a few years in the city and she thinks she's *down* with the community," Jason said with a venom that he'd never used with Alice before, "You girls are all the same."

Alice was stunned. She was so shaken that it took her a few moments to find words to respond. "What do you mean you girls?" she asked. The frustration of the past weeks had been building up, and she was finally ready to vent what she'd been carrying. "Girls like me? Girls who love and support you, no matter how you're feeling, how low you are, how distant you are, fucking march with you!" she shouted.

"Yeah, girls like you, White girls who just go for any Black guy, even when they're in a relationship. SKETS!"

Jason spat out. *SMACK!* She slapped him instinctively across his cheek, she'd never hit anyone before. He held her arm firmly after taking the blow.

Jason looked her dead in the eye, "Akira saw you! She saw you with him, kissing him."

"I don't know what you mean," Alice said, for a split second she actually didn't know what he meant, she'd tried so hard to block the whole incident out of her head.

"You have so many guys on the go you don't remember the one you were kissing in the park?" he said petulantly.

It hit her, she had told him, it all started to make sense, why he was so off, he must have known. Her world began to crash.

"All those messages, having to step out for phone calls, it's all clear now," Jason said. "And I was the fool that didn't listen to my cousin when she tried to protect me." "No, you've got it wrong. It's not what you think," Alice protested.

"So, what was it then? Bored of me? Needing some extra excitement, a roadman?" Jason said.

"Of course not, I love you," she said.

"Don't, don't say that to me. You don't know what the words mean," Jason said. Jason was full of rage; his eyes were beginning to water. Alice didn't know what to say or do. As much as she knew this conversation was coming, she was still unprepared; like younger versions of herself, she still could not deal with difficult conversations.

"Jason, he was my ex, I was just saying goodbye. I was

moving on with you, for us! I promise," she said, tears rolling down her face.

"Well, why didn't you tell me then?" he said, "Why lie? keep it to yourself?"

"I just didn't know how to tell you. There was always something happening with us, something we were having to deal with, I didn't want to add another thing, that's all I promise," Alice begged.

"How can I believe you? How can I trust you now? I nearly lost my cousin over this!" Jason said, almost spitting with anger. He was furious, the story didn't add up, he didn't care if it did. He needed space; he couldn't breathe. He grabbed his coat and left the flat, slamming the door behind him.

Thirty-seven

Paler Grass

Jason was disoriented when he woke up, after a few seconds he realised where he was; he was back in his childhood bedroom. It was strange to wake up without Alice, despite being on a smaller bed, he still only took up half the space as if she were there. He was dreading the conversation with his parents; he knew his mum would be able to see through any facade he put on. He hoped his parents would presume no more than a lover's tiff and not want to pry, just be happy to have their son home.

Jason felt stupid for not believing Akira. He knew he had to make amends with her first, someone who had looked out for him his entire life. He lay on his bed trying to figure out how things could have gone so wrong with Alice so quickly, the whole world felt wrong. He reached out to Akira to reconcile things, they of course agreed to meet at their usual spot.

Humility was not a struggle for Jason, especially when it came to those who he truly believed had his back. She arrived before him as usual. To his gratitude, she was in a forgiving and gracious mood. The evening air was cool; the sun was low in the distance casting light down the *river*.

"Hey," he said gingerly.

"Hey," she replied reservedly, still slightly hurt at the thing Jason had said the last time they were face to face. Jason had his hands in his pockets, almost doubled over, eyes on his trainers, rocking slowly. Typically, Akira portrayed a steadier visage, sat crossed legged, back against the bench looking across the river.

"It's funny how easy it is to believe something when you want to believe it," Jason said with a sniffle. Akira was silent. Jason inhaled deeply, brought his head up and looked out across the river to the opposite bank, "I'm sorry I didn't believe you from the beginning ... I was stupid," he said.

Akira remained silent. "You gonna say something?" Jason asked.

"I'm not sure what to say," she replied, "I know that it would have been hard for you to hear that ... about someone your care for ... someone you love," she paused. "But I'm your cuz, I've loved you from when you were in pampers, I've always got your back, I'd never do anything to hurt you," she ruffled the top of his head. "I'm going to be here when these girls come and go, remember that. Anyway, I'm sure I would have reacted badly if I found out the love of my life stepped out on me," she said with a gentle laugh.

"I really didn't see it coming," he said with an ironic laugh, as he continued to rock, "Guess I was blinded by love, never thought I'd hear myself say that," he said.

"Don't worry cuz, it will be ok. Maybe you guys can work things out," Akira said sincerely. Jason sighed and looked skyward, "I don't know … things haven't been right for a while. Seems like there's always something getting in the way; if it's not her family or friends, it's the AD protests or Adebola situation. She's from a different world in so many ways, I can't force her to see things the way I do," he stated.

Akira turned and looked at him, she put her hand on his, "Listen, there will always be shit going on in the world, especially for us, but you can't let it stop you from being happy,".

"Yeah, but this has been closer to home, this was our neighbourhood, that could have been me. Then I had the police stop. I don't know if our… love… can transcend the world we live in," Jason said.

"I know, I've given you a hard time about this stuff, but you should follow your heart. There's always going to be complications in this world, but you can't let it stop you find your happiness," she said.

"This is going to keep happening, I hate to say it, but you know it is, and each time do I turn to her, and expect her to support me? Expect her to understand and to *get* what I'm feeling? Is that even fair on her?" Jason said.

"I don't think you can expect anything of her, it's her choice in the end, but if she chooses to love you, with everything that makes you; all of your passions and failings, then you should accept that," she responded.

"I guess … I thought she was different, I thought she could understand more of the nuance, the subjectivity of an individual … and not be one of these basic chicks who just saw me for my skin colour and all the other superficial traits. Her being with another guy when she was with me, hiding everything all that time, she's just any girl," Jason said painfully, it still didn't seem real.

"Sometimes people surprise us cuz, and not always in the ways we'd want. Don't worry; it'll work out the way it's supposed to, things always do," she said.

Thirty-eight

A Shoulder To Cry On

Jason decided to move back home for a while, he needed space, time to think and clear his thoughts. Things had happened so quickly with Alice, and they were both still reeling. He ignored her attempts to meet and talk, how could he meet with her, he couldn't stand to look at her. Maybe this wasn't the right path for him, maybe he had to find a different way. Jason packed up Anton's car with boxes of his stuff, as he was going up and down the stairs he caught glimpses of Ms. Chamberlin, peeking her head around the side of her curtain. He sensed the disappointment in her face, not in a judgmental way, but rather that she genuinely wanted to see them succeed.

Alice couldn't accept what had happened. How did her world turn upside down so quickly, they were so happy, they'd been through so much, and now he wouldn't even talk to her? Alice's mum was keen to be there for her daughter in her time of need, also recognising an opportunity to influence her daughter's next steps. They agreed to meet for lunch, Alice's Dad was busy on an important business trip, so they were alone.

They met at a small, chic French restaurant in the centre of town. Alice's mum greeted her with a warm hug and a kiss, which even given the circumstances took Alice by surprise. "How are you doing, Sweetie?", she asked sincerely, as she held her embrace closely. "What happened? What has that *boy* done to my girl?", She continued.

Alice was surprisingly overcome with emotion by her mum's hug. "Mum, don't start," she said, as she wiped a tear from her cheek. "It's complicated,"

"Well, please '*uncomplicate*' it for me." She responded. She realised that she was perhaps moving a bit too quickly. "Ok, just take a seat, let's get you a drink and we can talk about it," she said calmly. They sat and ordered. Alice didn't really know where to start, she just sat, passing her index finger around the rim of her prosecco glass. Her mum was tempted to break the silence, but knew it was better if Alice opened up in her own time. Alice took a deep breath and began to recount the past few days.

"I messed up ... he found out... he found out about him," Alice said. "Wait, slow down. Who messed up? He found out about whom?" Margot responded, already struggling to follow the story that had only just begun. Alice began to sob a little, her head tipped down toward the table.

"Him, this guy I used to see. And then I said some stupid things about the Adebola case. He just blew up at me. It's a mess."

"Darling, I'm sorry, I'm not quite following. I'm going to need some more detail," she responded.

"I was seeing a guy for a while, it was stupid. It started off well, but he changed, he was aggressive with me, manipulative. I thought I could handle it, make it better, but I couldn't," Alice said.

Margot was shocked "Why didn't you tell me?" her mum responded.

"I don't know, these things happen gradually, one day everything is great and the next you feel trapped," Alice said.

"This godforsaken city; I knew we shouldn't have let you move here," she said, "Don't do that mum," Alice replied in annoyance.

"Do what? Dear" she replied with feigned innocence. "You know how I feel about this place; I've made no secret of that. I don't blame you, Dear, it's this place and these boys who prey on you," she continued.

"It's not about blame, mother," Alice said in frustration.

"Anyway, I finally got out of that situation, at least I thought I did … but he wouldn't let it be. I would block him on social media, block his mobile number, but he'd always find a way to contact me, dummy accounts, new phone numbers, I even contemplated going to the police. He would contact me at the worst times; I'd be with Jason and see a number I didn't recognise or see comments, and you know me, I can't lie, so I'm sure my face lit up like it usually does and he thought something was wrong," Alice said.

"That is illegal harassment, you really should have told us, I would have spoken with John down the road and had him arrested immediately."

Alice subtly rolled her eyes at her mother's 'fix-it' attitude, which while well-meaning on one hand, lacked sensitivity and usually missed the point. "Well, he agreed to leave me alone if I met him once, just to say goodbye. So, I met him, and I don't know, somehow Jason's cousin must have seen us together and got the wrong idea," Alice said.

"Well, can't you just speak to him and explain. He seems like a vaguely rational boy," she replied, the most complimentary thing she'd ever said about Jason.

"I've tried and he won't listen to me. How do I explain not telling him sooner? And then on top of it, we had a bust-up about all these protests," Alice said.

"Well, if you ask me he's lucky to have you let alone worry about you sharing your entire history with him. And you know how sensitive *they* can be about *that* stuff; you can't say anything to them at times. You know what I think, you'd be happier in a *different* relationship, someone more your … speed," she replied, trying to catch herself before she went too far.

"Yes mother, I know what you think very well," Alice paused, "I hate to say it …" She stopped again "… at times ... at times it can be hard," she said. Her mother was trying to hold the smug grin back from her face. Alice continued "it can be hard having to be supportive the whole time, sometimes you feel like you are constantly walking on eggshells. I know it's hard for him, but I can't really understand his world. I try, I really try ... I guess not hard enough," she said.

"Nonsense. You do way too much for that boy if you ask me," she countered. At that moment Alice got a message, it was Jason, just four words "we need to talk." Alice's stomach turned, there was no way she was eating today.

Jason's boys were all there for him in his time of need, but he was not yet ready to spend time with them. They inundated him with supportive messages, memes and jokes in an attempt to lift his spirits. Lyon made it abundantly clear how happy he was to have his wing man back, and how much fun there was awaiting him once he was ready to re-join the *game*. Jason appreciated that they were sensitive enough to not be disparaging towards Alice, recognising his feelings for her and respecting their relationship; even Anton refrained from any comments about being better off without a Becky in his life. He was grateful to have them as part of his support network in his time of need, but all the brotherhood in the world could not make the pain go away.

Thirty-nine

The Toughest Talk

They decided to meet at a neutral venue; no home team advantage for either person. The location of choice was a quiet restaurant near Alice's work, she'd been on an early shift, Jason had taken a half-day. Alice was surprised to see Jason waiting for her as she was about 10 minutes early herself. This only added to her nerves, something she didn't think was possible, given how worried she already was about their meeting.

They greeted each other with an awkward hug, the type of awkward where something was once so natural, suddenly becomes much less so. Alice didn't know what she wanted to say, other than to apologise and try to find a path forward, she hoped Jason was planning on the same.

"How have you been?" Jason asked.

"Ok, not great I guess, and you?" She replied

"Yeah, similar," he said. There was a brief silence.

"So, you wanted to talk? Got a new theory on Suits?" she said with a small laugh, hoping to ease some of the tension.

"Ha," he chuckled a little, he was so preoccupied with what he wanted to say that he was caught off guard by the joke. "Yes, I did. I don't really know how to say this … but … I think we need a break," finally managing to force the words out of his mouth.

Alice was stunned, she had briefly considered that this could happen, but her heart would not let her dwell on the thought for too long, she didn't believe it could actually happen. "What do you mean a break? Why?" she said.

"I just think it would be best for us," he continued.

"I'm not right with everything going on … And everything with you … I don't even know if I can trust you," he said. It pained him to say those words.

"Of course, you can trust me Jase, you can always trust me," she said "Listen, I'm so so sorry about that situation, I should have told you. If I'd known there was even the slightest chance of this happening, I would have told you right away. I didn't want to interrupt things with us, we were going so well … and you know … we always have *stuff* to deal with, I didn't want to add to that … It was part of my past that I wanted to bury, that I thought was gone forever," Alice replied.

The word stuff triggered Jason, "What stuff?" he asked, knowing exactly what she meant, "This is a big part of our problem, the *stuff* that keeps coming up isn't just going to disappear, and if the *stuff* is so much of an issue for you why were you with me in the first place?" he said emphatically.

"Jase, that's not fair, that's not what I meant, you're worth it all." She reached out to hold his hand, but he recoiled at her touch, she rescinded knowing she was not articulating herself in the best possible way, there was too much pressure. She tried to simplify things, "Jason, bub, this is us, come on."

"This isn't easy for me, you know I haven't been right for a while, I don't want to continue like that, it's not fair on either of us," he said,

"We can figure it out, we can do anything together, I know we can," she said, her voice started to break a little, she tried to keep her eyes from watering.

Jason couldn't look at her, he knew he'd break down and he had to stay strong and see this through. It was the right thing to do, wasn't it? He asked himself, for a split second. No, of course it was, he hadn't been his normal self, he was detached from her, she didn't understand him, it wasn't meant to be, the voices in his head shouted. Have to stay strong. "I'm sorry Alice, it has to be this way."

He knew staying wouldn't help, he had nothing more to say. It felt harsh to leave so abruptly, but he just wanted to be out of there. He got up to leave, walking past Alice, he put one hand on her shoulder, she turned away so he couldn't see her tears, but he could hear her crying as he left. "JASON!!!" she screamed in agony as he walked through the door.

The next few months were strange, to say the least, how else could you describe a time when you are isolated from your supposed other half. Jason tried to embrace the time alone, he tried to focus on his family, friends and career, but realised there would come a time when he would have to get back out there.

He didn't know where to begin, the truth was Alice was a stroke of luck, *a winning lottery ticket in a digital sea of unappealing fish*, he thought to himself, in melodramatic fashion. His online dating experience had been a total gamble, he wasn't particularly keen to get back into it, but these days it was the easiest way to meet people.

One evening, he decided to log back into a couple of apps and get swiping. It didn't feel the same, it felt hollow… he felt hollow. He tried to find some enthusiasm, tried to be optimistic about what may lay ahead, but it wasn't easy. He aimlessly swiped while stretched out across his bed, only somewhat engaged in what he was actually doing. Pretty girl, nice smile, good bum, swipe, swipe, swipe. It seemed like he'd been at it for hours, but only 10 minutes had passed. His mind drifted to Alice and he began to wonder what she was up to.

Alice was low. She took some time off work and moved back to her parent's home in the village. Her mum was loving the opportunity to look after her again, or rather have oversight of her life again, complete with smothering privileges. She prided herself on her independence, so on the rare occasions she could be a protective mum, she leapt at the chance. Alice spent what seemed to be weeks in her pyjamas, eating her favourite comfort foods. She was so sure that Jason was the one. She ate her Ben & Jerry's Phish Food ice cream, and thought about what Jason was doing.

"Ok, here we go, time to get back on the saddle, it's time to try this thing again. It's better to have loved and lost than nothing … nothing," he said to himself, "I can do this," Jason was splashing water on his face in the bathroom of a bar. He was in the process of a pep talk, psyching himself up for his first date since his split with Alice. Having decided to bite the bullet, he arranged a date with an attractive girl he'd met online. She was shapely with a cute face, but in all honesty, they didn't seem to have much chemistry over text. His friends and family had been encouraging him to get back out there, pressure to which he ultimately caved.

He left the bathroom and walked to the table where his date was sat. "Everything ok?" she asked, slightly concerned by his early departure to the bathroom.

"Yep, everything is fine," he replied. But everything wasn't fine, he wasn't fine and she wasn't Alice. Jason was an amiable guy; he could hold a conversation well enough, without being fully engaged. This should have been more of a privilege than a challenge, considering how beautiful this girl was. She had thick long dark hair and deep brown eyes that seemed to have no end. To cap it off, she had a mischievous smile, while actually having interesting opinions on various topics; most guys would pray to be in the company of a person like this, but for Jason the experience was bland.

He allowed the date to continue for a couple of hours, had a couple of drinks, but behind his eyes, his mind was elsewhere. Around 10pm he called time on the date, citing an early start the next morning, he walked her to the tube station and kissed her on the cheek, knowing he'd never see her again. He span on his heels and began to walk somewhat aimlessly. He happened to pass the bus stop he and Alice had sat at, at the end of their first date. He laughed to himself; it was as if the universe wouldn't let him escape her.

Jason went straight to his room when he got back, making sure there was no opportunity for any small talk along the way. He was restless, he missed Alice, but having made the call, how could he go back. He needed to take his mind off things. He flipped through different apps on his phone looking for a distraction, and checked his e-mails, in his inbox he saw another reminder to finish the quiz. *Why not?* He thought to himself. After all it wasn't like it worked out with his supposed preference anyway, and the girl he just dated was Greek mixed with Vietnamese; *so I can't be that lost*, he thought to himself reassuringly.

There were only a few questions to go and they seemed to be becoming more direct. The next big question asked how he viewed women of his own race and if he had ever dated any. This was one he wasn't looking forward to answering because he knew his record was shaky, as much as he believed he was attracted to some Black women (he could happily reel off attractive celebrities), however his own dating track record did not support it strongly. He cast his mind back to one of the few Black girls he actually had anything significant with, it was when he was at uni.

The designated meeting room was on the top floor of the student union. Jason was out of breath by the time he reached the room and the meeting was already in session. He entered quietly, picking up a pamphlet from a table at the backroom before finding a seat, an organizer gave him a judgmental look for arriving late. An attractive, mixed-race girl with long braided hair was welcoming the group to the ACS, briefly outlining what the group aimed to do and which activities were provided. Jason felt like the room was big for the number of people in attendance, then again not so surprising given that there were not many Afro-Caribbean students at the university. A key goal of this event was to give the fresher intake from the Diaspora an opportunity to meet one another, and hopefully build some lasting bonds. Before long the group was allowed to mix. Soft drinks, biscuits and what looked to be rum cake and plantain crisps were provided as snacks; Fela Kuti was playing in the background.

Jason didn't have much experience in instigating conversation, friendships seemed to develop organically without much effort for him; this scenario was different, people were gravitating towards one another as if they were destined to meet. Jason scanned the room, there were one or two who appeared to be isolated like him, unsure how to make the move. He reached for his phone which was always a good distraction. He fumbled for his phone with his left hand while taking a drink with his right when he heard a voice from behind him "Hi there!"

Jason span to see a cute face and warm smile, he gulped the squash, forcing it down his throat, so he could quickly reply, "Hi" he said while gasping for air.

She giggled melodically in reply, finding his nerves endearing. "Where are you from?" she asked earnestly.

Jason had a temporary mind block ... "London," he managed to force out.

"Ha no, I mean what's your background?" wondering if there may be some shared heritage between them.

"Oh" he replied, pretending to hit his forehead with his hand, "My parents are Jamaican."

"Yardie yeah, cool, my parents are Ugandan, ever been?" she followed up.

"No, I haven't," wondering if he'd ever met any Ugandans before.

It's a beautiful place," she followed. Her smile was huge, not only did it draw you in, it fully disarmed you, before he knew it, Jason was opening up to Cherry, not long after that they were spending a lot of their free time together between lectures, after football training and often on weekends.

Jason enjoyed his time with Cherry but conflicts came, as he tried to balance his time with other commitments and friendship groups. One of the beautiful things about the University experience was having the opportunity to meet different types of people, and do different kinds of things. Football being Jason's first love meant that he was keen to play for the Uni team, his abilities meant he was highly sought after for First XI duties, this however meant he was unable to play for the ACS team that played their games on a Wednesday afternoon, the same time as the University teams, Jason's choice to play at the most competitive level was not well received by many of the ACS members, especially Godfrey who was also enamoured by Cherry.

Godfrey found Cherry's interest in Jason infuriating, almost as infuriating as the fact she was not particularly impressed that he was the first-ever second year to be appointed to the ACS Council. Cherry tried to fight his corner amongst the other society members, but struggled to get them to see how Jason could so freely straddle different demographics.

As Jason's time became more divided between different activities and groups of friends, he had less time for Cherry and the ACS. Initially, this was not a problem for Cherry, but over time she succumbed to Godfrey's propaganda narratives against Jason and others who were labelled as not committed enough to the cause – denounced as supporters of integration. From Jason's perspective this was tough, as he could see that Cherry was defending him, but could also see the toll it was taking on her; negatively impacting her experience in the organisation; being potentially Black-listed because of her proximity to Jason. Additionally, Jason didn't like the ransom tactics employed by some of the leading members of the group, the kind of all or nothing binary approach that never sat well with him. In response to the growing pressure placed on Cherry, he decided to back off further, driving her into the arms of the ACS.

"Not seen you at many of our meetings recently," she typed to Jason through MSN chat. She could see he was online, but didn't respond immediately, the time between his responses was increasing, she could feel him slipping away.

"Just been busy, they've added an extra training session, and we have mid-terms coming up," he finally replied.

"Still made it to the party at Cronies," she sent with a winky face, as a passive-aggressive joke to highlight that he definitely had some free time, enough to get drunk at the city's legendary student night "Cronies".

"Just a night with some chill people," he replied, inferring that the ACS group were not chill."

Cherry wasn't sure what to respond with "well it would be good to see you sometime," she finally sent. Jason didn't reply with a message, just like the message she sent.

Jason often reflected on his first year at Uni, and whether he should have made more effort with Cherry, with the ACS in general, but a bigger part of him was content that following his gut the way he did was the right approach. *Can't please them all, should at least try to please yourself,* he thought, reflecting on his re-introduction to solo life.

He completed the final few questions and was done. The results summary looked like something from an ancestry or genealogy website, a surprisingly detailed breakdown of personality preferences, compatibility types and of course suggested racial preferences. The document had some commentary around what groups were more dominant in his city, which actually ended up feeling more like a cop-out than anything meaningful. The report didn't specifically state the ethnic background of the person that would fit him best, but rather outlined the characteristics of the person, along with some physical attributes. He scanned through the findings looking for some major revelation that would recontextualise or illuminate his romantic outlook, but he didn't find it. He thought back to when he was in the park with Alice and asked her why she liked what she liked, just as it had hit him then, it wasn't so much so that she didn't have a clear why, but that she didn't feel the need to have one. Maybe he didn't either, maybe it was enough to just have an open heart in the face of everything the world may throw at you.

Forty

Recriminations

Jason worked slower than usual, as he waited for the last remaining stragglers to vacate the office. Despite the majority of his colleagues being passionate about their work, the government pay checks meant that few would work late unless a project deadline was approaching. He double-checked that he was alone, out of sight of the cameras, and then inserted his flash drive into the docking station. His tailor-made programme connected to the core system and then flashed up a password request prompt, Jason hit a few keystrokes and was in. Jason was sure he was alone, but he couldn't shake the paranoia that he was being watched, or that the cleaning team might show up unannounced.

This was new territory for Jason, dangerous and uncertain ground, but he felt compelled to do something to help. The program buzzed away giving him access to things he had never seen before. He worked quickly and carefully wanting to get out as soon as he could. Before long he was done, and hastily heading for the door. As he exited the main office, he bumped into Eddie one of the regular cleaners, and an older gentleman who Jason really felt should have retired already, but Eddie was a widower, who always said he loved having something to get him out of the house, especially in the most lonely evenings. "Working late, Mr. Andrews?" he asked, with deference from a by-gone era.

"No, no, heading home now, mate," Jason replied.

"You sure? I can do one of the other floors first, give you some more time?" he offered kindly.

"No need Eddie, I'm done. Take Care," Jason said, as he jumped in the lift, heart racing.

"Nice lad," Eddie thought to himself, as he entered the office to continue his work.

The Home Secretary sat quietly and patiently, as the PM stood, back facing the Home Secretary and looking out onto the city. "Justin this was always going to be a risky initiative, but this was not the outcome we expected, someone Senior has to take the fall." The Home Secretary knew exactly what was going to happen before the meeting had even begun. The fact that the PM had asked to see him in person was nothing more than a formality, and to help ensure the paper trail was as short as possible. The PM turned to face him, "It's an election year, critical for the administration, particularly as we have lost so much ground to the opposition in the polls. You promised that this *initiative* would be a *controlled* way to create a strong public distraction that would enable us to build a tough on crime manifesto, yet you lost control completely of your asset, and worse yet, facilitated a nationwide riot. Not only do we not look tough on crime, but it also looks like we've lost control of the fucking country."

This was not a discussion or an opportunity for debate or recriminations, this was a dressing down; he knew exactly what was expected of him. "I'll have my resignation on your desk in the morning Prime Minister, it's been an honour to be part of your cabinet, Sir," he said with a slight whimper.

The Prime Minister nodded, and sat down to fire up his laptop, "That'll be all, Justin," Home Secretary, Stevens, stood up quietly and left the office.

The lead tactical force expert glanced down to check his digital watch one last time; it was 05:00 am on the dot. "On my command," he whispered. He stooped down on one knee and held up his hand; the countdown began using his fingers, 3-2-1 BOOM! Went the hand-held battering ram, smashing a door off its hinges in a Hackney council estate building. Coordinated dawn raids across the city went off in synchronized fashion in search of members of the AD organization, but all the apartments were empty. The tactical officers exchanged bamboozled looks with one another. Captains radioed into head office, "that's right, it's empty, no sign of them."

Jason read the news report on his phone, as he ate his breakfast. The article stated that many of the leading members of the AD group had fled following a botched police operation. Lead members were wanted and at large, but key information about the suspects had gone missing, in what was described as a systems breakdown. Jason chuckled to himself. The article went on to speculate that some Government officials, including Home Secretary, Justin Stevens was also implicated in the series of events that led up to the riots. The public outcry at the ruling that led to the riots had triggered an independent inquiry into policing in the city and other parts of the country. In addition, community groups had been launched to help educate youngsters on their rights as citizens, while also providing a safe space after school.

Jason's phone buzzed with a message from an unsaved number. It just read, "Thanks for coming through … in the end," with a smiley face emoji. Jason continued to eat his cereal with a smile on his face, happy that he eventually found his own way to help. Jason had used a combination of his hacking skills, and new clearance privileges from the Armidex project to wipe all the files on AD, and its members. In addition, he also came across the plans for the upcoming dawn raids, vital information he was able to share with AD. He always wanted to do his part for the cause, respecting what Abefembe and the other AD members were trying to do to make a difference. It's funny how some things work out.

Forty-one

Moving On

Alice was starting to come to terms with life without Jason. It didn't feel natural, but she was managing to get through the days, primarily by burying herself in work – something that was easily afforded in an underfunded NHS, where there was always plenty of work to do.

Daisy was happy to have her flatmate back, but she was starting to worry about her current lifestyle. All she seemed to do was work and sleep and anytime she tried to ask how she was doing, or suggest that she was not at her best, she shut the conversation down or changed the topic. She knew Alice was strong, but this felt more like denial than strength. She was determined to get some real answers out of her. She decided on a ploy to get to the bottom of it by confronting her at a girl's night.

"Hey Alice, you know what I was thinking the other day?" Daisy asked.

"No, what?" Alice replied.

"That we haven't had a girl's night in forever! You know, chocolate, films, mani-pedis," Daisy said.

Alice was a little surprised at the level of enthusiasm from her flatmate. This was something they did for fun from time to time, but in all honesty, the regular girls night thing wasn't something she wanted to do on a regular basis. *Nonetheless*, she thought, *it would be a bit of fun,* and if she was being honest with herself she needed it. "Sure, sounds good, let's do it," Alice agreed.

The days continued to pass slowly for Jason. He kept going on dates in the hope it would get Alice off his mind, but it didn't work. He would attend the dates physically, but his mind and heart were elsewhere. Despite the fact he missed her deeply he was still conflicted as to whether she was the one for him. His heart told him, yes, but his mind was still unsure. Could he really trust her? Would she ever really understand him the way he needed to be understood?

In a world where there was so much pressure to identify and be affiliated, he felt compelled to make the right decision. He strolled around the back streets of central London, hoping to find one of the small green spots that were hidden from those who were not in the know, but were everywhere for those who did. After about 15 minutes of winding back streets, he managed to find one. He took a seat on the bench, opened his salmon sandwich, hit shuffle in his music library and let his mind drift.

Jason was brought back to reality by pings from his phone, more messages from Whitney, who was again demonstrating her sixth sense for changes in his life. She was determined for them to meet up and celebrate. While Jason was in no mood to celebrate, he realised that her driven nature meant she wasn't going to let up until she got her way. He agreed to grab some food with her after work, nothing fancy, just simple, to her disappointment.

He suggested they go to small burrito stand near their office, one of his favourite lunch time haunts that also ran into the early evening. Whitney was punctual, affording her a few minutes to peruse the simple menu before Jason arrived. She tried her best to find something that she would enjoy, but came up short, just as she was ready to give up Jason arrived.

"So, you've finally found some time for me, Mr. Andrews," she said jokingly

Jason was determined not to melt to her charms, even if he was moving on, it still didn't feel right, "Things have been busy, you know how it goes?" he shot back

"I do, I do, these promotions won't achieve themselves, especially for people like us, right?"

He'd never heard her refer to them as being different to others at the company, she really was trying to pull out all the stops, but she was unable to temper her ambition. Jason felt slightly bad for thinking she should, what was wrong with ambition? But her seemingly win at all cost mentality didn't sit right with him. "I bet you have another promotion coming soon?" he suggested

"I've earned another one, but you know what it's like, you have to pay your dues, wait your turn," she reflected with pride, but also astute insight into the division's politics.

Her pride and ambition just made him think of Alice, these were not things she cared for, those were things he loved about her. Perhaps he was being too harsh, he was supposed to be giving her a chance.

"What puts a smile on your face when you're not in the office, aside from the designer bags and shoes?" he asked jokingly, making reference to her taste for high end fashion, a taste that wasn't easy to facilitate on a public sector salary.

The question stumped Whitney, she didn't see a whole lot of point in doing much that didn't contribute to her future or her wardrobe, "Dining at good quality establishments, I was at Garbondi's in Mayfair last week... we should go some time," she suggested looking down at the messy burrito, which was beginning to drip all over her carefully manicured hands.

"I've never really been one for those fancy places, I just enjoy good food, the more homely the better, comfort food you know?" he replied earnestly.

Whitney tried her best to match his excitement, but the prospect of greasy, fatty home cooked food did nothing for her.

Jason could see her struggling, he tried again, "What

have you been listening to recently? Have you heard the knew Undoubted tune?"

Whitney looked blankly, "I have Spotify, but I don't really have the time to listen to much." She could tell that she was not winning him over; she was not used to a man not bending to her will, an air of panic kicked in.

"Jason, I want to be straight with you, I know we've done our dance for a little while now, but I think maybe it's time to give us a real shot. Look at us! Intelligent, beautiful, successful people, we're power couple material! ...And I hear you have an opening now..." she said empathically and rhetorically, as if she were proposing an irresistibly compelling business case.

For a split second Jason wondered how she knew, but then realised she always knew what was happening with him. He reflected on the proposition for a moment, she wasn't wrong; they looked great together, she ticked so many boxes, but yet something was still not quite right. He didn't care about being a power couple, he didn't want to care about what the world thought about him, he just wanted to be happy. "Ha, you and me?!" he returned with faux surprise, as if he didn't initially have that thought from the first moment he saw her. "I don't know, you think you're ready for a guy from the estate?" he followed jokingly, trying to deflect from the serious question at hand.

Whitney rolled her eyes, knowing that while he came from a tough place he'd long since transitioned, and while he might like to think of himself as being from the block, his future looked very different. "I'm serious Jase, I know we have some differences and that I can be a bit of a Princess at times, but I think we could be good... winter holidays with my family either skiing or in the Caribbean," she finished semi-jokingly.

Her use of 'Jase' threw him, it made him think of Alice, of how natural things were between them, she never needed to try and 'close' him with incentives. He felt an emotional pang in his gut. "I'm flattered, honestly, what guy wouldn't be attracted to you... it's just...things with Alice." Saying her name out loud rocked him again, "it's just all a bit fresh."

Whitney understood, but was also perturbed, she couldn't tell if it was because she wasn't getting her way or because she really wanted Jason. *Either way I've eaten this horrible burrito for nothing*, she thought. "I get it, it's not been long, I guess I jumped the gun a bit," she said, trying to take the knock back as graciously as her ego would allow.

The two carried on talking, still subtly in search for a point of magnetic resonance that was hard to find. However, Jason did enjoy how much she was struggling with her burrito; by this point Black Bean sauce had dripped all over her designer pant suit. "Need a hand?" Jason said while laughing, as he offered her a napkin. Whitney was trying her best not to freak out; she wanted to show that she could be a chill girl, one of the cool kids too. Jason knew this was out of her comfort zone and appreciated the effort. He tried his best to be upbeat and engaged, but he knew this rendezvous was just more evidence of what he was missing.

After a while Jason called time on the evening, they made tentative plans to meet up again, Whitney adamant that the next time would have to be at a place with cutlery, at least. An ephemeral plan neither party felt obliged to honour – for some things, the idea is better than the reality.

Friday was here before Alice knew it, in reality, every day felt like the same to her. She arrived home to a very excited flatmate. "Tonight is going to be so much fun! really just what you need … annnddd I have a surprise for you!" she squealed with excitement. Alice didn't like the sound of the 'surprise', but thought the least she could do was play along. Before long they were sat on Alice's bed watching the Notebook on her laptop and eating chocolate; lots of tears ensued as the romantic film played. "Why aren't guys like this in real life?!" she demanded, as she grazed on her snacks; "I mean I'm not expecting a house or anything but maybe a poem or something," Daisy complained.

Alice nodded along in agreement, all this really did was make her think of Jason and what their life could have been like together; maybe they could have had their own house by the water. Daisy could see that Alice was trailing off, tonight was not just about watching a gushy film; she didn't want to lose her. "Al, hun, I know you've not been right recently … since Jason and everything. It's only natural, but I thought it might help to talk about it a bit, and maybe think about moving on … you know, life goes on," she said gently.

"I don't know what you mean, I'm fine," Alice replied flatly.

"Well, you don't speak very much, all you seem to do is work, even longer hours than before; I don't even know how that's possible," she said in a non-confrontational tone.

"I'm ok, I promise, things are just busy at work," Alice claimed.

"That's not true, I know you, Alice. I know you're just hiding behind work. Well, you've done that for long enough, and I have just what you need to help you move on," she declared excitedly as she reached for Alice's phone. "You know how they say the best way to get over someone, is to get under someone else? How about getting under this!" she squealed, as she thrust the phone with the picture of Dr Luke Johnson under Alice's nose.

Alice was not a fan of that phrase and didn't believe in the theory. She glanced at the photo, feeling very uncomfortable with the whole situation. "It's too soon, I appreciate the thought, but I'm not ready."

"I thought you might say that, so I already reached out to him and said you'd have a coffee," Daisy replied emphatically.

"You did what! Why?!" Alice shouted in outrage.

"Because I know you'd need a push. It will be fine, he's a Dr, he's got a splash of caramel in him," she said, with a wink, "and he's my cousin's close friend. He's charming, kind and loved your pictures, and it's only coffee! Nobody is saying you need to marry the man."

Alice paused for a second. I guess she was right, what would one coffee hurt, she guessed she would need to try and get over Jason at some point. As much as she didn't want to, she had to admit that he was very attractive.

Forty-two

Man-Made Mistakes

Akira was keen to catch up with Jason, he'd been avoiding her, but she'd managed to get him to agree to meet with her, with the promise of free food; always a good way to a man's heart, actually to the heart of most people. They met at his favourite burger joint in Covent Garden. "So, what's been going on Sprout, you've been a hard man to get hold of?" Akira said warmly.

"You know how it is, work and stuff," Jason replied.

"Really?! That's all you have for me? "Work and stuff?" I'm gonna need more than that?" Akira fired back.

"What do you want me to say? I haven't been at my best, I think you can understand that given everything," Jason said passively, without the energy to argue.

Akira read his tone and eased off. "I get it, times are tough, everyone goes through heartbreak at some point ... I just wanted to check on my Cuz, if that's ok?" She said sarcastically.

Jason paused briefly acknowledging his cousin's efforts to try and cheer him up. "I guess that's ok," he said with a smile.

"So, what are you getting? The New Orleans Burger is a lot!". They chatted away about the usual stuff, work, family, music, Netflix. But despite Jason's efforts, his cousin knew him too well, and could see through the mask of bravery he had on; this wasn't the happy Jason she knew so well. After milkshake desserts, there was a lull in the conversation. It may have been the food coma setting in, but Akira knew something wasn't right.

"You miss her don't you?" Akira said.

"Miss who?" he replied.

"Her! Who do you think I mean, stupid!" she said with a hint of frustration at his wallowing.

"I'm fine, I told you," he stated, again.

"I know what you told me and I know you. I know you better than you know yourself, and you miss her, look at you, you're miserable, even after one of your favourite burgers!" she said. He tried to present an expression of disbelief, but he knew it was a waste of time. She did know him; she was right, probably better than he knew himself.

"I've tried. Ok. I've tried… I know there are things about me that she can't fully appreciate, but she saw me in her own way, and I saw her. I loved her … and yeah I miss her… I've tried to not miss her, but I do. I've tried to date other people, but it's not the same, I still think about her," he said, almost liberated to get it off his chest. Akira could see the pain in his eyes; the mix of anguish and love pulled on her heartstrings. She had hoped that she had given Jason the right advice, but she wasn't sure, even reflecting on how certain she was about AD, only to find out what was going on behind the scenes, maybe she was wrong about Jason and Alice. "Listen, I know what I said before, but if you really love her this much, you need to try and work it out."

Jason couldn't believe he was hearing this from Akira. His cousin was really in support of Alice, after everything that had happened, after everything she'd seen and said. Akira could see how stunned he was. "I mean it, don't listen to me, well listen to me now obviously. Just go after her if you love her, idiot!" Jason looked away, Akira felt the pressure building, she had to say something, but how?

"Jase, when I was little, you would have been a baby in those days, my dad used to sit me on his lap and we'd look out of the window onto the estate, the sun always seemed to be shining, that's how I remember it anyway. I would point at random people as they walked by. There was something he used to say that stuck with me, 'at their core people wanted to be good, sometimes they just needed a bit of help'. What I think he meant was that even though there are mean, vindictive, evil, bad people in the world, there are more that are good, if given the chance. Dad fought for us, our family, our people because he felt he had to, but in honesty, I think he didn't want to fight at all."

Jason listened carefully, falling into a state of tranquil focus, as he usually did when he thought about his uncle.

"Sprout, I need to tell you something," she spurted out. Jason was still in thought, "Jase," she said again, almost shouting now.

"Yeah I get it, I should go after her, suddenly you're her fan. Wish you would have said that earlier," Jason replied.

"No, Jase, listen, the AD stuff, I knew they approached you … I should have said something," Akira said.

"What do you mean you knew? Wait? You knew they made contact? Invited me to meetings? Asked me to break the law," Jason said.

"I was a part of the organisation, your name came up, I didn't want you involved," Akira said.

"Why didn't you say something? How much did you know?" he asked.

"I knew they were interested in you; I wasn't sure exactly what they would ask of you. Things moved quickly; I was conflicted. I wanted you to make your own decision. I don't know if any of this affected you and Alice … but … but," she said.

"But what, Akira? Like we didn't have enough to deal with, without all this?" Jason said angrily.

"I also know you helped some of the guys by giving them a heads up, thank you," she said proudly.

"Thank you?! After all that, thank you? You're wild

sometimes Akira. I know you love me but, It's too late now, I've messed it all up."

"It's never too late. Never too late for love! Ok, that's a bit cringe, but you know what I mean," she said with more excitement than she anticipated. Despite the weird rom-com style scenario, she was right, he had to try, but he didn't know how.

The more he thought about her, about their relationship, the more he missed it. He missed her thoughtful nature; just making him a cake for the sake of it, her endearing clumsiness and how she never got too embarrassed when she did something stupid, because she didn't take herself too seriously, the way she cared for others and how she would put in extra hours just to make sure her patients were ok, or be the first one to cover a colleagues shift. He missed her wit and the banter they had between each other. He missed her smile and her smell, the way she would nuzzle into his neck when they were chilling on the sofa, he even missed some of her ridiculous TV shows. He missed how much she tried to show that she cared about things that were important to him, even when it made her feel awkward or inadequate. Most of all he missed how she made him feel when they were together, the peace and happiness that she evoked in him. He was so focused on what she didn't have or may not be able to bring or what he may be missing out on, that he missed all she brought and the great thing he actually had.

As he sat and pondered what had transpired, contemplated how long this feeling of loss would last, his phone buzzed to life with a notification. It was a news alert, Adrian had regained consciousness; his vitals were looking stable and doctors were confident he would fully recover. *A silver lining of sorts through this current cloud of despair*, he thought to himself.

Alice agreed to meet Luke for a coffee on a Sunday afternoon. She hoped that this would correctly signal her level of interest; she was willing to meet on a weekend, but not on a prime weekend day, and not in the evening ... and not with any alcohol - So he had no reason to get his hopes up too high.

They met at a café in the East of the city, known for its famous espressos. Luke was early and welcomed Alice with a warm smile and a big hug. He was taller than she expected, she was taken by surprise by the length of his arms and the warmth of his embrace. "Great to meet you Alice!" he said energetically. "I understand you were a bit unsure about this, so thanks for taking a chance," he continued sweetly.

She was slightly shocked by the brightness of his demeanour and his candour; he was definitely full of life. "Great ... to meet you too," she said slowly

"Take a seat. Take a seat. What would you like? The

espressos are amazing here! You do drink coffee right?!" he said almost all at once, words tripping over one another.

"Uh… I do, do they have a menu," she replied.

"Yes, of course, I'm sorry, I'm just a bit nervous, and I've actually had a couple this morning. I'm a huge fan, I have my own machine, a Biaggio, do you know it?" he continued with the same high energy.

Alice was starting to worry about what she'd let herself in for. But she was here now, so decided to go with it. "No, I don't. I like coffee, but try not to drink too much, gives me the jitters," Alice replied.

"Yeah, smart, smart, too much caffeine isn't good for you, ha," he said, as he finished his espresso. "Waiter! Waiter! Can we get a menu?" Luke called across the restaurant. "Are you hungry? The paninis here are brilliant!"

"No, I'm good thanks," Alice felt the need to take control of the conversation, or this could turn into an hour of coffee talk.

"Luke, tell me a bit about yourself? I understand you're a consultant at the Royal Free?" Alice was surprised that her mind went straight to work chat, she knew that was bad form, but she put it down to them both working in healthcare, rather than a subconscious barrier to getting to know him properly.

"That's right, I've been there a couple of years, I'm on the Urology ward, we have a great team *down* there, no pun intended," he laughed away to himself innocently, very satisfied with his joke. Alice gave out a pity laugh, so as not to be rude.

"And when you're not at work, and not drinking coffee?" she asked with as much intent as she could muster.

"HAHAHA, of course, I love other things outside of coffee too; I love sports, I play a lot of tennis, I love to travel, I try to go on a few holidays a year. Do you like tennis? Are you sporty?" Luke asked.

"Yeah, I'm a bit sporty I guess, try to make my weekly Zumba classes. Tennis is fun, but can't say I'm Serena Williams. I played a bit when I was growing up, I haven't played in a few years."

"We should play sometime!" Luke fired back enthusiastically.

"Ha ... I guess we could," she answered softly, doubting that would ever happen.

The waiter appeared with the menus. Alice and Luke ordered some more drinks, and they got back to getting to know each other. Alice thought she would see if he had a deeper, more cerebral side. "So, Luke, this might seem like a strange question, but what do you think about the whole Adebola situation?" Alice asked.

"What do you mean, the situation?"

"Well, what's your take on it? Obviously, it's horrible and something that happens way too often, but what do you think about it?" she pressed.

"Yeah it's terrible, of course," he repeated and then paused, not sure what to say next."

"Do you not think there is a huge problem of systemic oppression, especially at the hands of the police?" Alice asked emphatically.

He was taken aback by the line of questioning. Expecting to spend more of a first date talking about hobbies and Netflix, than a political discourse on race relations.

"Yeah, I guess so … I've never really thought about it in depth," Luke said defensively.

"Never really thought about it?" she shot back a bit too quickly. She realised that she was coming on a bit strong for a first encounter and decided to ease off. "I'm sorry, it's just something I am … I've become passionate about … So, what's the best place you've travelled to?" she asked in a more relaxed tone.

Luke happily received the change in topic and continued with his previous high energy chatter; Alice tried to match his enthusiasm. She wanted to warm to his positivity, after all, he was a very handsome doctor, what more could she want? but for some reason the spark wasn't there … not like it was with Jason.

Jason stood on the walkaway outside his front door, and looked up into the night sky, the diminished starlight from the city's light pollution was compensated for by the brightness of the skyline lights. His thoughts danced back and forth as his eyes did from the skyline of the city to the sky and back again. Across the city, Alice was also stood outside her front door looking up into the night sky. Not something she found herself doing often, but tonight it felt like it was somewhere she needed to be to clear her thoughts.

Forty-three

Turning Back Time

In the following days, Jason found himself in a mental fog, on auto-pilot, just going through the motions. Work, gym, home, eat, work, gym, home, eat, repeat; it was hard to know where one day began and another ended. Friends and family could do little more than watch and wait for him to pull himself out of his funk. The boys tried to get him to go out, or even come round to play FIFA, but he would always decline, he just wanted to be alone. The weekend arrived, and instead of spending another evening looking at the stars, he decided to go for a walk. He hadn't been sleeping well and hoped that maybe a stroll might help clear his mind.

He walked and walked; mellow neo-soul playing songs of heartbreak through his buds at a modest level as he wandered. Did it matter who he was with if he wasn't happy? Alice made him happy, ok it wasn't perfect, but would it ever be? He missed her deeply. As he walked trapped in his thoughts he blindly stepped out into the street, a car screeched to a stop in front of him blaring its horn. The shock brought Jason around. He pattered the bonnet of the car in apology to the driver. As he gathered his bearings he realised he was close to the bar where he'd had his first date with Alice. He decided to walk over and grab a drink. He sat and watched all the happy people, drink, dance and talk. His mind wandered back to the night, how easy it was, the rapport they shared. He smiled as he drank and reminisced. One drink magically turned into five as he enjoyed the combination of people watching and reliving that first night. He looked at the table that they once sat at and pictured himself being there with Alice. He wanted to order another drink but it was closing time, something he wasn't ready for. Closing the bar felt like he would lose the moment, the subtle reconnection he'd formed with Alice. "Sorry buddy, we're closing up, going to have to ask you to leave," the barman said as he collected glasses.

Jason staggered out of the bar and continued to walk, before he knew it he was at the bus stop where he and Alice had ended their first date. A couple of girls were sat talking to one another about something on one of their phones. He perched himself at the end of the bench so as not to encroach. He sat back rested against the plastic glass of the bus stop, put his hands in his jean pockets and imbibed his surroundings. He felt his mind drift off again as the music continued gently.

"Hey, wake up you idiot?" a voice said quietly. Jason was disoriented, but recognised the voice.

He opened his eyes and there she was, Alice. "What are you doing here?! Asleep at a bloody bus stop!" she continued.

"I don't know; I went for a walk … I've been trying to clear my head…I had a drink and ended up here," he replied, still not totally sure if he was dreaming or not. "What are you doing here?" he asked.

"Trying to clear my head too I guess … something like that," Alice replied innocently, as she sat herself down next to him.

"How've you been?" she asked, appreciating that if he's falling asleep at bus stops that he probably wasn't in the best shape.

"I'm ok, I don't know, I guess I'm trying to figure things out," Jason responded. "Figure what out?" she asked in a hopeful tone.

"I don't know … life?! Everything," he offered.

She understood what he meant. "Maybe we're not supposed to figure it all out, maybe that's a part of life," she said.

She sat next to him and placed her hand on top of his. They sat quietly for a few moments, hand in hand. A bus arrived, a clamber of people got off and a few got on. The touch of her hand seemed to dull his environment, the lights began to blur and the noise from the traffic and people were muffled. He was at peace. "I missed you," he said quietly.

"I missed you too."

"Can I ask you something?" Jason asked,

"Of course," Alice said.

"Did you think we could have made it?" he asked.

"I never doubted it," she replied.

"But with everything that is going on. With how involved I get; can we really handle it?" Jason pressed.

"I can't predict the future Jason, I wish I could, I know that I'll be there for you through whatever, that's what I can promise you."

"I know a lot happened, we moved quickly, but deep down it felt right. Can I be honest?" she asked. Jason looked back as if to say it was a stupid question, she continued. "I grew a lot with you …" she paused trying to find the right words. "I mean, I learned a lot about myself, I had an opportunity to reflect." Jason listened intently. "I never questioned things before I met you, I kinda just glided through life, you know me, ever the optimist," she said. Jason tried to interrupt, but Alice was in full flow. "Please, let me finish. I never really thought about where I came from, who I am and what that might mean for the person I meet. I just thought about love, which is idealistic, but perhaps a little unrealistic. I can see how that is part of my *privilege…*" she stopped on the word feeling slight unease with the concept, even though she acknowledged the advantages that had been afforded to her. "… Even when I was dealing with my mum or Jane, it didn't feel like a big problem for me, and I know that was insensitive. I've never had to think further than that. But Jase, it wasn't always easy for me either; being scared to say the wrong thing, feeling uninformed, feeling like you can't fully be there the person you love." She took a break to catch her breath, she felt a weight lift from her chest.

Jason looked at her "Are you ok?". She nodded and gave a small smile in response. "Thanks for sharing," he said with a sarcastic laugh. "It's nice to hear you say these things. For the record, I don't think you're insensitive. I know it was hard for you, I loved that you tried and I felt supported. I guess I could have shared more, but you're right, it's different for me, and I don't even know if it should be that different; maybe love should be enough, whatever that means … There are just things I want; things I think I want … or ways I think things should be."

Alice could see his mind searching for words, something Jason rarely had a problem with. "With everything going on in the world, I have to be focused, I feel like I have to be involved. I have to be with someone who is aligned to how I see the world, who can relate to what I'm going through." He gave her a pained look.

"With us, I never knew if it was that. We had so much fun, it felt great, but at times … at times it didn't feel right. I wasn't sure if our connection was enough to endure everything that is going on. I wanted you to get it, not just have sympathy," he expressed as openly as he could.

"I know this is stupid, but even optically, how can I say I care about this stuff and be with you, is that even right? And yeah, you mentioned your mum, your friends, what happens when we fall out? I become another Black guy right. Alice tried to be patient and hold her tongue. Jason was exasperated and could see she wanted to talk. "Go on ..." he said, giving her the floor.

"You're right," she said. "On this how could you be wrong, but what about you? At the end of the day, what about what you want? what about what makes you happy? Don't you deserve to be happy?" she asked sincerely.

"I don't care about what my mum thinks, what Jane thinks, I LOVE you, and that means I'm willing to do whatever you think is right, even if it means walking away."

"Jason, I don't want to walk away."

They sat and spoke for hours, more honestly than they ever had before. London passed by in the background, before they knew it, the sun was coming up; her hand never left his.

Forty-four

Newer Beginnings

They'd spent the whole day moving back in. The new apartment, which was strangely on the same street as their previous one, was still full of boxes. Jason was sat on the sofa staring at a blank television screen.

"What are you thinking about?" Alice asked as she watched him in his trance.

He didn't hear her at first, his mind replaying the fight that led to them splitting. "Nothing," he replied, snapping out of the daze.

Did you see this, she said to Jason, holding a small brown box with a tag that read "Jason and Alice."

"What's that?" he asked, "I don't know, some kind of package," she said.

Jason recognized the handwriting on the label but couldn't place it. "Open it," he said, too late, as Alice had already begun the unboxing. It was a jar filled with a gooey liquid with a label attached that read 'To new beginnings.' The box was filled with straw, with a folded note inside. Jason knew what it was and guessed where it had come from, "read the note," he said. Alice unfolded the light blue lined sheet and began to read …

"First off, congratulations, you weathered the storm! While I know I had a role to play in some of the gusts, I am pleased to see you make it to calmer waters. Sprout, Jase, you will always be my little cuz and I will never stop looking out for you, but it seems you have found another good female influence in your life; continue to look after her like I know you will. Alice, Alice, Alice, I'll hold my hands up and admit I could have been fairer to you in the beginning, but as I'm sure you can appreciate, family is very important and Jason has a very special place in my heart. That said, I now recognise that he has a special place in yours too. The joy that you can bring one another should be your focus, even when your world gets tough, remember that. I hope you both enjoy the gift; should give you guys a nice health boost when you need it, maybe Alice can work it into the Sheppard's Pie or something Ha!

Love and blessings, Akira xxx."

Alice held the jar of sea moss and studied it closely, "What is this, and why on earth would I put it in a Sheppard's Pie?" she asked earnestly.

Jason laughed at the innocence of the comment, kissing

her on the forehead "I'll tell you all about it," he said with a smile.

This was their new start, all the cards on the table, no secrets, no regrets and no omissions. Just openness and honesty.

"Have you got my back?" Jason asked. "Always," Alice replied.

Epilogue

Jason was working in his home office when he heard the familiar pitta-patter of furious steps approach him from the hallway, he checked his watch, he couldn't believe it was 16:00 already. The door slowly opened as two little hands and a head peered in ever so carefully. Once in, it was time to pounce... just as she leaped towards her father's chair, he spun around to catch her in his lap 'raahhhh' they both said harmoniously, in their best Lion voices.

Little Sade was back from school, and as she did every day her dad was working from home, she went through their daily ritual of trying to scare one another, she was yet to catch him off guard.

"How was your day butterfly? What did Miss Collins teach you today?" Jason asked eagerly, one of the many surprises of fatherhood was how interested he was in the daily developments of his little one.

"It was ok, Daddy..." Sade answered in her high pitch tone, that Jason was looking forward to lowering. He could tell something was off with his daughter, even her roar was less fierce than normal. "We learned about dinosooarss, they were big! Big as houses! But gone now."

"Where have they gone?" he asked, enthusiastically, "Surely they can't hide, if they're so big?"

"They're txtinct." She replied, trying her best to say the word.

"Oh, well that's good, because I heard they like to eat little girls!" He said in a silly voice. He could tell she wasn't quite right, the parental instinct kicking in. "Are you sure you're ok, princess? Anything else happen today?" He enquired gently.

She shook her body in denial, hands innocently placed behind her back. At that moment she had decided that she'd had enough of the afternoon interrogation and shot off towards the kitchen. *Probably time for a break anyway*, he thought to himself as he slowly followed after his swift girl.

Alice was getting dinner ready in the kitchen when Jason entered. "Hey bub, everything ok with Sade?"

"Not now Jason, don't start please, I need to get dinner ready before her piano lessons, we can talk about it later."

Jason wasn't sure what was going on, but he could see that she was stressed.

"Talk about what? I don't know what you mean." He said as he leant on the edge of the kitchen table eating an apple.

"Oh it's nothing, one of the girls said something to Sade and she got a bit upset. I spoke to Miss Collins and it will be fine," Alice returned, as she furiously chopped some onions.

"Said what?" he asked calmly, but with growing interest.

"She called her mud face, and said no matter how much she tried she would always be dirty. Sade was upset, but we had a chat in the car and she's fine now," she relayed, wiping tears from her eyes, unsure if they were being caused by the onions or something else.

"She said what?!" Jason shouted "and what did you say to her?"

"Jase, I said not now, we can talk about it later, it's under control. And I don't want you to bring it back up with her now, she needs to be able to focus on her piano lessons, ok," Alice dictated.

Jason was infuriated, but decided to be a team player and wait until later for the details.

Before long Sade was all washed up and asleep in bed, Alice was having a well-earned glass of wine, legs laid across Jason's lap. They were watching the 10' clock news, a sub-section of the evening report focused on the rising number of Police stop and searches that were targeting Black teenagers in the capital.

Jason was not focused, he wanted to discuss what had happened to Sade, "So, can we talk about it now?"

"About what?" she said absent-mindedly, as she flicked through the channels, totally exhausted from another long day; she knew being a working mum was hard, but people didn't say it was quite this hard.

Jason gave her a look to suggest she knew full well what he wanted to talk about.

"Oh it's fine, and better I was the one to handle it. The girl said something stupid and I told Sade that sometimes people say silly things, but we can't let them get to us. I told her that she was the most beautiful, intelligent girl in the world and that if anything Clarissa was the one who was probably dirty, and not nice for saying what she did – is that ok?" she answered slightly petulantly, as if she were preempting a pending deconstruction of her approach.

"You didn't tell her that she needs to speak to a teacher if anyone says anything racist to her?" he asked

"We don't even know if she was being racist, they're just kids and I don't want… I don't want Sade to have to worry about things before she needs to, can't she just be young?" Alice offered.

Jason accepted the point, but also knew that the race conversation would have to happen one day, it wasn't a question of if, just when. "Al she is young, but we spoke about this, she isn't like the rest of the kids at that school, she's always going to be different, I just want her to be proud of who she is and to be able to defend herself."

"And I don't?! I know who my daughter is Jason, I was the one we carried her for nine months, I was the one who pushed her out!" she retuned passionately.

Jason realised it was time to de-escalate. They had many discussions about what it would mean to have mixed-race children, Alice was not ignorant, but even with all the sharing, education and conversation in the world, there were still differences in how they saw certain things. "I think I'll have a word with Miss Collins, just to make sure she's looking out for any potential troublemakers."

"Jase, don't go down to that school causing trouble for our daughter. Like you said, she stands out as she is, as do you, the last thing we need is for the one of the two Black men in the town causing a scene at the primary school," she said in earnest, trying to protect her family.

"I'll just drop her off in the morning, I won't make a scene…"

"Promise?" she said offering her hand

"…Promise," he eventually replied, taking her hand and executing their secret handshake.

Sade was playing with the radio stations as they drove to school, unable to find a song she was happy with. "I heard someone said something mean to you yesterday, butterfly?"

Sade stared out of the window; she nodded her head slowly.

"You know you can tell Daddy when these things happen? I won't let anything happen to my princess, right?"

She nodded again.

"And if it's at school, and me and your mum aren't around you go and tell a teacher first and then you tell me and mum, ok?"

She nodded again, as they pulled up to the school gates.

"Do you remember the story of the of the magic caterpillar?"

She thought about it for a second and then nodded her head.

"Remember how he was special, but being special meant that he was different to some of his friends. Well that's a bit like you because you're the most special person to me in the world," Jason said lovingly.

"You know Daddy loves you, right?" he asked, looking at his daughter.

"Yes Daddy." she replied, hoping to get out of the car quickly.

"How much does Daddy love you?" he asked, triggering one of their jokes.

She opened her arms as wide as she could "You love me this much" she said with a smile.

"Even more, but your arms are too short!" he leant in and gave her a kiss on her cheek. She bounced out of the car with her book bag and ran through the gates.

Jason sat in silence for a moment, it hit him how quickly time was passing, she'd be in secondary school before he knew it and then Uni and then gone. He was brought back to reality by a parent who tapped the hood of his car to highlight he was blocking the drive, he pulled away and changed the radio station, 'just the two of us' was playing, a smile came to his face, he began to sing along.

He drove back in a better mood for seeing that his daughter was ok, and because of the selection of songs coming through on the radio. He continued to drive, hoping he might be able to catch Alice before she left for work, when a message came through on his phone. The message appeared on his car's dashboard as the phone was connected to the car's computer system; it was an unknown number. He rolled to gentle stop at a traffic light. Jason tapped the screen and opened the message, it read: 'Jason, I hope you're enjoying country life, but we need you. AD.'

Afterword

In life we can make many choices, but when it comes to those we truly love, we usually have very little influence. Most of the time we just end up falling, I think that powerlessness is a beautiful part of the experience. The heart wants what it wants of its own volition; that freedom and autonomy is probably a good thing. While the mind would like to control everything, some things are not meant to be controlled.

The desire to control our heart is not something we typically want to impose, but rather something that we usually choose to do as a form of protection, for example not letting people in, for fear of getting hurt, or perhaps it is something forced upon us by cultural and societal pressures. These external pressures should not be dismissed without consideration; with regards to Black and White interracial couples, there are important aspects to reflect on, which if given the appropriate amount of time and attention should make connections stronger. Too often people either underplay the importance of history and present-day barriers, or choose to ignore them entirely. When this happens the likelihood is that you either end up further apart because you do not understand each other well enough, or the issues that were ignored end up manifesting in an unhealthy way.

While at risk of contradiction, I would not be being true to myself if I didn't also stress the importance of having an open heart and being truly brave enough to follow it, irrespective of where it may lead you. Love in its purest form is free from outside influence, it just is. So for those who are fortunate enough to find the real thing, I hope they honour it, even in the face of a challenging world. Ultimately, it's up to us to decide how important these pressures are, and how much they guide our journeys.

In a world where things are being increasingly quantified, dissected and measured, perhaps it's better to keep some things sacred, beyond the scope of rational thought, protected on a higher, more emotive plane. Lead with your heart and enjoy the freedom of having the choice taken out of your hands.